Born in Sussex — 'The Poets' County' — Charlotte Bingham, the daughter of two authors, was a keen writer from the age of ten. After leaving school, she resided for a while on Paris' Left Bank, working on poetry and revelling in the literary atmosphere. Discovered and published at the age of nineteen, she is now a full-time author.

Charlotte is married to the actor playwright Terence Brady.

Visit the author's website at:
www.charlottebingham.com

OUT OF THE BLUE

Florence Fontaine is recovering from a family tragedy when she discovers a young man asleep in her guest cottage at the Old Rectory. She offers him breakfast, only to rue the day as she finds herself caught up in the resulting drama of his life. Florence's young and beautiful daughter, Amadea, is suspicious of Edward, fearing that he might be a fraud. Florence enlists friends and neighbours to help discover who he might be. United in their quest, their dedication to help the young man takes Florence and Amadea on an adventure that takes them into many pasts. In doing so they are finally able to put tragedy behind them, repair their once disjointed lives, and embrace a new and happy future.

Books by Charlotte Bingham
Published by The House of Ulverscroft:

GRAND AFFAIR
LOVE SONG
THE KISSING GARDEN
THE BLUE NOTE
THE LOVE KNOT
THE SEASON
DISTANT MUSIC
FRIDAY'S GIRL

CHARLOTTE BINGHAM

OUT OF
THE BLUE

Complete and Unabridged

CHARNWOOD
Leicester

First published in Great Britain in 2006 by
Bantam Press, a division of
Transworld Publishers
London

First Charnwood Edition
published 2007
by arrangement with
Transworld Publishers, a division of
The Random House Group Limited
London

British Library CIP Data

Bingham, Charlotte, 1942 –
    Out of the blue.—Large print ed.—
Charnwood library series
1. Amnesia—Fiction
2. Large type books
I. Title
823.9′14 [F]

ISBN 978–1–84617–916–7

Published by
F. A. Thorpe (Publishing)
Anstey, Leicestershire

Set by Words & Graphics Ltd.
Anstey, Leicestershire
Printed and bound in Great Britain by
T. J. International Ltd., Padstow, Cornwall

This book is printed on acid-free paper

Prologue

There are times when people's lives seem to have been put on hold, and they appear, even to themselves, to be set about their world as so many pieces of chess abandoned in mid-game — some left lying to the side, others standing in useless positions, unable to move one way or another. They know that two players are needed to bring them back to life, and they are nowhere to be seen.

Of a sudden two sets of distant footsteps are heard. Two figures enter the room. Two shadows are thrown across the board. The competitors write their names in the book of life. The first one writes *Past* in an old-fashioned sloping hand, the second, pen grasped in a modern manner, writes **Present** — following which they both move towards the table to sit down, their hands placed ready to reach out to the pieces.

After a long brooding silence, during which they stare down at the beautifully carved but hapless figures, they start to move them, slowly sometimes, with great pauses; at other moments as swift as a darting dragonfly — there, there, there!

Once he has made a move, *Past* will look up with haunting, hooded gaze at **Present**, the look in his opaque eyes always challenging. For a moment **Present** is stumped. He can't think of a way to win, and it may well be that he never will

1

think of a way. He raises his gaze to heaven, looking for inspiration, but the sky is dark: no light to be had from there. His eyes return to the board, and as they do, a beam of sunlight hits the Queen, illuminating her, and at once dissolving all his doubt. It seems suddenly that **Present** can, after all, see a way through, slowly at first, then more swiftly, moving against the *Past*'s pieces, until finally the Queen reigns triumphant, and with her the **Present** too.

1

It seemed it had been raining for weeks. Not the slow relentless rain that is so much part of West Country life, but driven by a fierce wind, whipped up to a frenzy by outside forces, howling round the rectory. At times it could be heard knocking at every window pane, as if it was seeking shelter from itself; or as if, like the sole occupant of the small country house, it would prefer to be staring into the lazy flames of a log fire, not driving the last flurry of small autumn leaves about the lawn, or bending the trees to its fierce will. In short, it was not an afternoon to be out; so when the old bell in the cupboard under the stairs rang out faintly, it was not surprising that, at first, it was only Punch the sheepdog who heard it, and in response sprang up and ran, barking excitedly, to the double front doors.

Florence, her face flushed from the fire, her back cold from the lowered temperature of the old house, followed her dog to the half-glassed front doors. A man stood in the stone porch, his figure bent against the elements, one hand holding on to a weathered trilby hat.

Florence frowned, reluctant to open to someone whom she did not immediately recognise, and Punch continued to bark incessantly.

'Ah, it's Colonel Willoughby,' she told Punch,

and she started to undo the lock at the top of the door. 'Colonel Willoughby. How are you?'

The colonel, upright once more, but still holding onto his hat, smiled. 'My dear lady, my dear, dear lady, how is you indeed?'

He held out a tray of charity ribbons towards Florence as if she might be too short-sighted to see them.

'I am collecting, as you can see, my dear Mrs Fontaine, collecting for the — ' but his words were lost as the ribbons housed neatly in the cardboard tray were thrown into the air, dancing off up the front lawn to join the already frenzied ballet being performed by the leaves.

'Oh dear, oh dear . . . '

The old white-moustached gentleman turned to follow his recalcitrant collection, as did Florence and Punch, Florence darting about the lawn and snatching at the small ribbons, followed closely by a now joyously barking Punch.

'Come in, come in, and have a cup of tea, do,' Florence insisted as they finally retrieved the last little tie of ribbon, and retreated once more to the comparative shelter of the porch, and from there into her small hall.

'I don't think I may, dear lady.' The colonel looked momentarily embarrassed, as if he had already been asked this many times that afternoon. 'The memsahib is waiting for me at home with tea and a Victoria sponge, more than my life's worth to slake the thirst before I pitch up at her tea table. More than my life's worth indeed. And to be truthful, if I take tea at every house, I end up with what they used to call 'a curate's flush'!'

They both laughed, after which there was a pause as Colonel Willoughby glanced down at his collecting box in rather the same manner that Punch would look from Florence to his empty food bowl and back to Florence again, hinting that it needed filling.

'Oh, I am sorry, wait a moment.'

Florence pushed a pound coin into the box, then she pinned one of the mud-bespattered ribbons onto her cardigan.

'I'm afraid that's all I have in the house at the moment,' she told him in a matter-of-fact voice. 'I am flat to the boards until Monday morning.'

'Most kind of you, Mrs Fontaine, very much appreciated, I do assure you.'

'The widow's mite . . . ' Florence told him and shrugged her shoulders, because she knew he must know of her impecunious situation.

'How are you going along, Mrs Fontaine?'

'Oh, you know.' She smiled, avoiding the colonel's kindly eyes, looking away, not wanting to see the sympathy in them. Sympathy was always so weakening. Besides, she had grown used to the embarrassment that her recent tragedy brought to people's faces, their eyes looking everywhere except into her own. 'I am going along all right, you know. Quite used to being on my own, since my husband Henry was always away so much, being a concert pianist. You know how it is? Quite used to it, really.'

Florence cleared her throat.

Of course Colonel Willoughby didn't know at

all — he had no children and his wife was still alive, waiting for him to come home and take tea with her.

Colonel Willoughby nodded. He had always found Florence Fontaine a very appealing woman. Brown-haired, grey-eyed, with a rounded feminine figure and a pale Dresden-china complexion, offset nowadays by a haunting look of permanent, if unsurprising, sadness. After all, to lose both your husband and your son within a short space of time — as the present Mrs Willoughby always said so sadly, and so often, as soon as Mrs Fontaine's name was mentioned, 'That poor Florence Fontaine, her plight is somehow unimaginable.'

'Thank you for your donation, Mrs Fontaine. It is most appreciated.'

Colonel Willoughby raised his old battered hat and backed out into the weather once more, struggling up the front lawn, his head bent determinedly against the force of the wind, before finally reaching his car.

Florence watched him until his car disappeared from sight, when she shot the bolt up on the door and returned to the fire, to the sound of the howling wind — and dear heavens, it did howl — to her library book, and to her thoughts. Punch settled down beside her, and as he did so, she started to stroke the top of his head.

In her mind's eye Florence followed Colonel Willoughby back to his small Georgian village house. She imagined 'the memsahib', Mrs Willoughby, greeting him at the door, tut-tutting around him as she removed his wet coat and hat and hurried them off to the drying rail in the kitchen. She even thought she could hear him recounting his collecting failures and successes, giving his wife an account of his rounds, telling Mrs Willoughby who had put what sum of money into the collecting tin, before he finally confided to her.

'*Oh, and I called on poor little Mrs Fontaine. She put in a pound. A widow's mite, poor soul, that's what she called it herself, a widow's mite. I think she has been left quite badly off, really I do.*'

Florence continued to stroke the top of Punch's head, slowly and rhythmically. She would give anything to be sitting drinking tea in front of the fire with someone else, to be laughing about some funny incident in the village, or reading out an amusing item from the newspaper. Well, not *anything* perhaps, but it would be nice.

Still, she must not feel sorry for herself. She clenched her fingers, making one hand into a small fist. As her mother used often to remind her, feeling sorry for yourself was the worst way to be in life. No, she was much more fortunate than some; besides, tomorrow was Amadea's birthday, and she would be coming home for the weekend. She must begin icing her cake. She was lucky. She kept telling herself that. She was very, very lucky.

★　★　★

Amadea lay as still as she could, for as long as she could, listening to the distant sounds of the town going about its business below her bedroom window, hoping that by some miracle her head would clear. Then she fell back into a half-sleep, a fitful and uncomfortable doze from which she was finally awaked by a noise somewhere in her flat. She was sure of it. There was a noise, not just in her head — but *in her flat*!

Sitting up a little too quickly, she listened, but whatever, or whoever, she might have heard had now lapsed into silence, a silence so intense all she could hear was the thumping of her own vastly over-stimulated heart. Unable to prevent herself giving a long, soft but heartfelt moan, she slowly swivelled her body to the edge of the bed, putting her feet on the stripped wooden floor and standing up to reach for her dressing gown as she went in search of something that might relieve what now seemed like a truly life-threatening headache.

Before making her way to the kitchen, one hand on her head, one on the corridor wall, she stopped for a few seconds, still half listening for the noise, until she realised it must have been Fred Chopin, her cat. She pushed open the sitting-room door.

Oh dear heavens, of course!

There had been a party, although why the party should have been at her flat she could not quite remember. Parties meant people and people spelt chaos, a room full of people shouting at each other, drinking and dropping finger food everywhere; some of them even forgetting to go out on to the landing to smoke.

Oh please God, it had been fun, hadn't it?

With growing despair, her pained gaze took in the dirty glasses, all of which appeared to have gone forth and multiplied before falling over or acting as ashtrays. Large and greasy pizza boxes lay naked and abandoned; small cheese muffins, sausages and vol-au-vents sat about in deadly groups, their insides removed, a culinary holocaust. It seemed that, unlike the finger food, the guests had all decided to go home together.

'So who was here exactly, Fred?' Amadea wondered out loud to her Blue Point Siamese cat as he followed her back into the kitchen, where she slowly and very, very quietly placed a half-dozen glasses at the correct angle in the dishwasher. 'We really must be able to remember that.'

Happy birthday, Amy! The room was full of cards from everyone at Psemisis. Oh God, of course — it had been her pre-*birthday* bash. Of course today was her birthday — what could she have been thinking? Holding her head in one hand and her coffee in the other, Amadea screwed up her eyes and went full on for total recall just as the telephone rang, far, far too loudly. It was her mother.

'Amadea? Happy birthday, darling. How are you? I've been waiting for over an hour now — you said you would be here about midday, didn't you?'

'Mum?' Amadea chewed her lip, agonised, and not just because of her headache. 'Mum, I'm afraid I'm not feeling terribly well. I can't come over until tomorrow. There was a bit of a party

9

last night, a birthday surprise from everyone at the office, you know, and it's . . . well — it has left me wiped out.'

Amadea thought she could see the pain of rejection crossing her poor mother's face, feel her hurt, and understand her disappointment. But what could she do? In her present state driving was out of the question, birthday or no birthday.

'It's all right, Amadea — I haven't started cooking the lunch yet, love.'

Amadea could hear her mother clearing her throat, and there was a short pause before she continued.

'Did you open my present, by the way? And, and — the cards?'

'Yes, yes, of course, it's lovely, they're lovely.' Anguished, Amadea could not remember where she'd put either the parcel or the cards. They must be under all the stuff that everyone at the office had given her.

'Did you like the card from Punch? I thought it was so like him.'

'Yes, yes, it's brilliant.'

'And the present?'

'The present's lovely . . . ' Where *was* the present? Worse, *what* was the present?

'But did it fit? I was worried, in case it didn't fit. Sometimes Dottie's alpaca knits come out a little smaller than they should, I always think.'

God, of course, it *would* be one of Dottie Stuart's knits. Dottie was her mum's country neighbour. Although reassured, Amadea now knew for certain that she had to proceed with extreme caution.

'I wasn't too sure of her choice of buttons, but they are hand-painted by a hippy in the village, and I believe they are quite fashionable again — hand-painted buttons, quite fashionable.'

Ah, it was a *cardigan*. Thank God, anyway, it wasn't one of Dottie's hot-water-bottle covers, although it would probably look like one when she put it on. God, that woman's taste was bizarre.

'I will wear it when I come tomorrow. You will see how good it looks.' Amadea's hand was still on her lowered forehead as the hangover hammer continued to hit out with deadly, rhythmical accuracy. 'I will wear it tomorrow, with that nice skirt you gave me at Christmas, Mum.'

Amadea closed her eyes as she tried not to remember that the skirt her mother had given her for Christmas was still hanging unworn in the back of the cupboard.

'Yes, well. Pity about today, Amy, but there you are, if it's not to be, it's not to be. Let me know how you're placed tomorrow, won't you? You know, what time you can get across and so on. I'll put the lunch on hold until then. Only hope the Russian salad will last. Fingers crossed you can make it by tomorrow, love. 'Bye.'

Her mother cleared her throat once more and replaced the receiver.

Amadea stared at her own telephone before replacing it on the table. Oh *God*, she had hurt her mother — *yet again* — and nothing to be done. *God*.

Amadea turned away and sighed as heavily as her pounding head would allow. It really wasn't her fault that the office had decided to throw a surprise party for her in her flat. Jamie, her boss, said she had planned it all ages and ages ago. It really wasn't her fault. She had just been so surprised. God, she had been so surprised, the door of the flat being thrown open and suddenly the whole of Psemisis was pouring through the door, waving bottles, carrying trays of food and embracing her with their good wishes.

No, it certainly had not been her fault that she couldn't schlep across and see her mother today, as arranged. But it would be now. It would be *so* her fault.

'Why oh why can I never do anything *right*?' she murmured to Fred Chopin. 'Because I can't, is the answer.'

She stared at herself in the mirror. She was fairly sure that she did not normally look so dreadful first thing in the morning; fairly dreadful, but not *that* dreadful. She tilted her head sideways. Mind you, the dark patches of eye make-up gave her an interesting panda-like look.

'Ouch. No, it's no good fighting this,' she informed her entirely uninterested cat. 'I'm going to go back to bed and surrender to pain and lassitude, not to mention a four-hourly dose of paracetamol.'

★　★　★

Florence stared at her beautifully laid kitchen table, in the centre of which was placed the birthday cake she had baked and decorated for Amadea. *Happy Birthday Amadea*, it proclaimed. She bent down to look a little closer at the writing. She should really redo it now so that it read *Happy Late Birthday Amadea*.

For some reason she could not make out, the white cloth that she had ironed and starched now looked positively limp, as did the Russian salad — despite the magazine recipe being 'a new exciting variation on an old theme'. From the perfectly prepared salad her eyes travelled to the herby chicken breasts wrapped in foil, the scrupulously scraped very early new potatoes from the garden, and the tray of ready-to-be-roasted tiny vegetables. She had thought Amy's birthday lunch was all going to be so nice.

'Ah well, teach me to look forward to something,' she murmured to Punch. 'I'll put it all back in the fridge until tomorrow. Only thing to do, really.'

Amadea worked twenty miles away in the newly emergent, ever-expanding town of Swinton. Florence knew that she was personal assistant to a woman called — for some reason best known to either her parents or herself — *Jamie* Charlbury, and that they both worked for a company called Psemisis. Despite working so near to where Florence lived deep in country seclusion, Amadea hardly ever came home, except for bank holidays and the odd weekend.

Florence accepted this. It was only understandable. Amy had to have a life, after all, and now there was only Florence and Punch, well, in truth, there was nothing much for poor Amy to come home *for*.

Florence finished putting away what now looked such a forlorn feast. Her celebration lunch for Amy had turned into a right Eeyore of a birthday: all it lacked was an empty honey pot and a burst balloon.

'My fault, Punch,' she told the dog, before they both settled back in front of the fire. 'Never look forward to anything. If you look forward to anything it means you've enjoyed it before you get there, and are therefore bound for disappointment.'

Later, for want of something better to do, she went to bed early, and lay awake for hours listening to the howling wind still hammering to get in, still insisting on trying to knock the glass out of her windows. Would it never stop? Would anything ever stop? And if it didn't, what could she do?

★ ★ ★

The following morning she awoke early, and because it was not yet light, the morning only just starting to creep towards dawn, she made a cup of tea and went back to bed, where she and Punch lay listening to her Roberts radio. She dozed fitfully until the room lightened considerably, and the wind dropped to nothing, after which she realised, guiltily, that she must let poor

Punch out and busy herself.

She pushed open the doors to the garden and walked out into the still grey light of dawn, but as she did so she was greeted by an overwhelming sound — a sound so original, so exquisite, as to make both her and Punch pause for a moment, before continuing across the lawn. Songs of every kind of bird from blackbird to willow warbler seemed to be welcoming them on this late spring morning. Henry had always said that the miracle of a bird's singing was that it came from such a tiny creature.

'The first compositions came from birds,' he would joke, 'long before Mozart or anyone else. And what do they get in return for their creations? The destruction of their habitats, poisonous sprays, people shooting them. We don't deserve our world, we truly don't.'

How Henry had loved nature. Florence sighed with sudden nostalgia as she remembered the early days with Henry at the house, the wonderful first evening when they took charge of the keys, and Henry had quite literally galloped, like a young horse, all over the front lawn. It had rained constantly in those first weeks too. The hill that led up to the local estate had run with twin rivers of water that gushed down the road, leaving only the narrowest of spaces for cars; but they had loved those early weeks and months when there was nothing ahead of them but a bright future. Not that they had ever had much money to spend on the house, but what they had they had spent wisely, and all too well, until there was nothing left in the bank, only enough to last them until Henry had reluctantly gone on tour again.

Punch was now moving quietly among the shrubs and trees that made up the back garden, putting up an indignant wild duck, leaving the robin sitting on the old apple tree to hop undeterred among the tiny, pale green leaves.

And still there was no sound of anything but birdsong, and the gentle movement of the dog, until Florence, a fraction of a second before Punch started to bark, heard a low, insistent groaning. She froze for an instant, her heart starting to beat at twice its normal rate. She knew she was not physically brave, but nonetheless she found herself seizing a large, heavy-handled spade that was propped up against a nearby wall, and starting to walk behind Punch towards the one-bedroom guest cottage at the bottom of the lawn, from where the sound was emerging.

There was no light on in the little thatched cottage, just the steady sound of low, rhythmic groaning which was now competing with Punch's indignant bark.

Who on earth? she began to wonder, only to be interrupted by an outburst of even louder moaning. With Punch beside her, still barking furiously, Florence reached out to the dark green door, above which Henry, who was a fan of Winnie the Pooh stories, had long ago painted the name of *Saunders*.

'Who's there?' she called out in a firm voice, still clutching her spade, while at the same time preparing to run back to the house. 'Who's

16

there?' she called again, but now there was no answer.

She stood still, thinking quickly. The groaning could be coming from someone violent, someone with a knife, or someone drugged. On the other hand, it could be coming from someone who had hurt themselves and somehow stumbled into the unlocked guest room, perhaps from the fields beyond, or from the neighbouring estate.

'Dear Lord,' a tragic voice called out. 'Where am I?'

'Hallo?' Florence shouted, pressing one ear to the green-painted door before knocking on it. 'Hallo — are you all right in there? Is something the matter?'

'What *is* this place?' the voice continued to wonder, even more emotionally. 'Will somebody please tell me where I *am*?'

'Excuse me?' Florence called through the door. 'Excuse me, but who are you? And why are you here? I think you will find you are a bit off course when you come to, really I do, because — because this is my guest cottage.'

'Who am I?' the man echoed. 'Who am *I*? What is this *place*? Someone must tell me. What is this place?'

'This place is my place. You are in my guest cottage,' Florence replied slowly, still speaking through the door. 'You have somehow found yourself in my guest cottage.'

Florence thought guiltily of how many times first Henry, then David and now Amadea had warned her to put a proper lock, or any old lock, *something*, on the door of the little place, but

17

Florence, following the habit of years, had merely shrugged, made a note of it, and promptly forgotten.

'This is my cottage, my guest cottage,' she repeated, taking a deep breath. 'I don't know what your name is, but my name is Florence Fontaine,' she went on determinedly above the sound of Punch's insistent barking which she was reluctant to hush, feeling, as she always did, that with a barking dog she presented less of a 'lonely woman' impression. 'As I say, you are in my guest cottage. And it's Sunday,' she added. 'Just in case you've forgotten.'

'*Sunday?*'

The inmate, the present incumbent of her guest cottage, made that particular day of the week sound as if it was a swear word, something shocking, something repellent to him.

'Yes, Sunday.'

'Sunday? Sunday? Sunday when, for pity's sake? Sunday where and Sunday when?'

Florence felt immediately emboldened by the despair in the voice, so still holding the spade she pushed open the cottage door, and stared into the pale yellow, chintz-decorated bedroom with flower prints on the walls. On the bed lay a man, a tall, dark young man, sporting light designer stubble, and dressed in what looked like white jodhpurs, a white lace-trimmed shirt, and a pink and gold brocade coat.

He sat up as soon as he saw her, and as he did so Florence found herself staring at him, as anyone would, for he was stunningly handsome

18

— no, he was actually beautiful.

'Who *are* you?' he demanded.

'Who are *you*?' she heard herself retorting.

* * *

Amadea glanced at the telephone which had been ringing for some time in her still-darkened room, and then she picked up her small, leather alarm clock and stared first at the time and then, with mounting indignation, at the number calling her. Dear God! What was *wrong* with her mother? Six o'clock in the morning? Had she totally lost it? Or worse, was she about to ask her to drive across for breakfast?

'Amadea — '

'Ma — '

'Amadea — '

'Ma, I don't wish to be rude, but do you realise what time it is, lovey? I mean it is practically dawn on a Sunday morning. I mean, please, please tell me? Who are you working for — the Triads?'

'The — the — no, love, no. I'm not working for anyone, no. No, it's just that I er . . . '

Florence stopped. For no reason she knew, she could not say what she had been going to say, not exactly. And anyway, Amadea sounded so put out she couldn't tell her anything. In fact she must have had a brainstorm to ring her at all. She never rang Amadea before at least ten in the morning.

'Oh sorry, Amy. Really, I am so sorry. I've lost my glasses, rung the wrong number. I was *meant* to be ringing Dottie, you know she likes me to give her an alarm call in case she sleeps in — the goats, you know, she has to get up for the goats, and she worries, because she has to wear earplugs because her pugs do snore so,' she improvised, rather too quickly. 'I am sorry, lovey. Really. Speak later.'

Florence had no idea why she had found herself phoning Amadea, when really it was the police she should have phoned straight away, and the truth was she had been just about to, when something had stopped her. She pushed the button on the handset to divert all further calls to her voicemail, then hurried back across the lawn.

The young man was still lying on the bed, although the groaning had stopped. He looked up as she came in.

'Ah, my lady returns,' he said in his woebegone voice. 'My lady returns to this poor shadow of a man.'

Florence stood at the bottom of the bed. She wanted to tell him off for lying on her good coverlet in his long riding boots, but somehow could not bring herself to do so. For some reason she did not feel afraid of him, rather the reverse, she felt sorry for him. There was something about him that reached out to her, perhaps because, despite his beauty, the expression in his eyes was so pitiful.

'Look,' she said. 'It's probably none of my business — but are you *on* something? What I mean is are you *taking* anything? Have you taken any — any . . . ' She paused, reaching for a word that was always being used in the newspapers. 'Are you on any *substances?*'

The young man shook his head almost violently.

'I have not taken anything, I swear to you, madam. I am not in the habit of taking things that are not mine. I believe I may have been taken *from*, but I have never taken anything from anyone on God's earth.'

'Yet, if you don't mind me saying so, something is obviously wrong,' Florence persisted. 'Seriously, you are acting in a most peculiar way.'

'I am lost — I do not know who I am, or why I am here.'

'That is what I said, I thought you must have got lost,' Florence prompted him helpfully. 'That is what I imagined. You were at some party — and you got lost, and wandered in off the fields, or from the nearby estate, from Harlington Hall, which is just across the fields over there. And — and then, finding this bed, fell asleep on it. That is what I imagine.'

'Madam.' He sat up, placing his feet on the old stripped and polished pine floor. 'You may imagine what you will, if only you could imagine what I may be called. What is my name?'

'I would not know — I mean, I wouldn't know,' Florence quickly corrected herself, realising that she was beginning to sound like him. 'You must remember your own name, surely?' she added, in a lightly scolding tone.

'And what is your name, madam? If you tell me your name, it may prompt me to remember mine.'

21

'My name is Florence Fontaine, and I was out there in the garden when I heard you groaning. I thought you might be ill. Perhaps you are ill, and if so you really ought to go to hospital, except you can't go like that. Do you know where your real clothes might be?'

But the stranger didn't seem to be listening to her any more. Instead he had begun to stare into the distance, shaking his head slowly as he seemed to be examining his thoughts.

'You are perhaps some sort of maidservant then?' the young man continued, staring at Florence.

'No, I am Florence Fontaine, I own this house and I keep telling you, this is my guest cottage. Back there is my house. House — guest cottage.' She pointed out through the door and back again into the chintz-decorated bedroom.

'But what would a guest cottage be?'

'It would be just that — *a cottage for guests*,' Florence spelt out.

'Yes, but what in God's name am I doing here?'

'Are you quite sure you're not on something, perhaps some medication, which has made you a little woozy?'

Florence stared at him, her head on one side, a tolerant, kind look in her eyes. He stared back at her briefly and then closed his huge eyes, his startlingly long eyelashes seeming suddenly to cast shadows across his pale face.

'I must be dreaming,' he decided. 'This is a phantasmagoria, a dream, a strange fantasy — an odd and deeply disturbing reverie.'

'I know how you feel but it isn't, I assure you.

What it is, is time for you to get up and go to your own home. Don't worry, I won't complain to anyone about you landing up here, just so long as you get on your way, pronto.'

'But which way should I be getting on, may I ask? Which?'

Florence looked round the room to see where her uninvited guest had discarded his clothing.

'I don't see any of your ordinary clothes. Where are your ordinary clothes?'

Instead of answering her questions, he put his head in his hands.

'I do not understand. What has become of me, why am I here?'

'As I said, I think you must have been to a fancy dress party and somehow — what do they say now? — perhaps done your head in.'

Florence couldn't help feeling mildly proud that she had remembered a modern phrase like 'done your head in', and at the same time she felt a little impatient, because the truth was that she was not prepared to deal with someone who had done his head in. She didn't mind being polite and kind to him, but really he ought to be on his way, as soon as possible. She herself hadn't even eaten breakfast yet.

'What has happened to me? You must tell me.'

He reached out and clutched at Florence's arm, which Florence gently removed from his grasp.

'Look, young man, I am sure you have been to a very wild party, but I'm equally sure that I'm beginning not to care very much what has befallen you.' She paused. 'What I do know is that it's time you went *home*. I have a hundred and one things to do, so if you wouldn't mind telling me where you put your clothes last night, or whenever it was . . . ?'

'My clothes?' The stranger frowned again, before repeating the question as a statement. 'My clothes.'

'Clothes. Yes, your clothes. As in what you wear normally. If you find your clothes, you will find your wallet, and if you find your wallet you will find your credit cards and suchlike; and if you find your credit cards, you will know who you are, won't you?' Florence finished helpfully.

The stranger shook his head.

'These are my clothes.' He looked down at his brocade coat. 'This is my coat. Those are my breeches. But who am I, madam?' He looked round the room. 'This is not my home, nor my lodgings, of that I am quite sure.'

'Don't tell me you have nowhere to go, because I simply won't believe it. Who did you come here with? You must remember how you got here, even vaguely. You don't remember?'

She stared at him, and seeing how hard her unwanted guest was shaking his head, she sighed and shook her own head.

He started to walk about the small room, the expression on his face one of increasing distress.

'I have no idea as to how I came here, madam. None whatsoever. All I remember — all I remember is being *somewhere* — and then — then not being there, but not being here. Here

24

is not where I was, and you are a stranger, that I do know.'

Florence stood for a moment by the cottage door, regarding the stranger as steadily as she could, trying to solve the mystery of his appearance in her guest cottage, wondering what on earth to do next. She could not call the police, would not call the police, for a very simple reason — there were no police to call, unless you'd been murdered, and by that time you couldn't call them anyway. So that really was that.

'This has to be some sort of a joke,' she decided, speaking slowly as the realisation came to her. 'OK. So, if that's the case — fine. Joke over. Got me? I said — joke over.' She stared at the stranger as hard as she could. 'If you don't tell me what's going on, and if you don't tell me where you've put your clothes, or who your fellow conspirators are — because if this *was* a joke it has now stopped being funny — I may start to get cross, you know.'

The warning apparently had no effect since the figure now seated on the edge of the bed remained motionless, staring at his feet in despair, as if they might suddenly speak to him; tell him how they had brought him to the cottage.

'My God!' he said in hopeless tones. 'My God — what have I *done* to merit *this*!'

'Well, whatever it is you have done, this is your very last chance,' Florence warned him, preparing to leave the room. 'I mean it.'

He stood up and stretched out a hand to hold Florence back, first by the arm and then by the wrist.

'No, you are not to leave me. Do you hear? I will not have you leaving me.'

'Let go!' Florence commanded him, feeling real fear for the first time.

'No. No, you — you are to stay here. I mean this.'

'Will you please *let me go!*'

He dropped her wrist and sank back onto the bed, a look of utter hopelessness on his face.

'This has gone way beyond a joke. I really think you must come up with some sort of explanation, and then I can help you.'

'I have no explanation, madam,' the young man replied. 'This is either a fanciful delusion — or else I have gone from the silence of nothing to a peasant's cottage, or — ' He brightened suddenly. 'Perhaps this is a folly of some sort, some place where you pay a soothsayer or an old prelate to amuse the ladies on their country walks?'

He looked suddenly and engagingly hopeful, but then, seeing the unreceptive look in Florence's eyes, he stopped.

'This is not such?'

'No, this is not such,' Florence told him firmly. 'No, the only folly here is you, young man.'

'I cannot think then . . . ' He looked round in despair at the very pretty bedroom as if he had never imagined to find himself in such a place.

'I tell you what *I* think,' Florence told him in brisk tones. 'I think you're simply suffering from

26

what is commonly called a hangover. I'll make you a strong coffee, get you some paracetamol, and then we'll search for your things,' she continued, as if talking to a small child. 'After all, they have to be here somewhere, and then you must be a good boy and go home.'

Florence turned towards the door, Punch by her side. She opened it and stepped into the garden. It was pouring with rain once more. She bent her head against the weather, and leaving the young man behind in the cottage she ran back to the house. She would make a good strong pot of coffee, get him to eat something, and then send him on his way.

Back in her kitchen once more, she reached first for the coffee, then for her cafetière, after which she put out a packet of paracetamol and a glass of water. To these items she added home-made rolls, some salty farm butter and a pot of home-made jam. It was not until she had finished setting the table and was once more crossing the lawn, this time with an umbrella, that she realised she felt quite oddly excited.

★ ★ ★

When Amadea's telephone rang once more, it was past ten o'clock, but the number dialling told her it was her mother, yet again. She shook her head. What *now*?

'Hallo, Ma,' she said in as kind a voice as was possible given that she still felt vaguely hungover.

'Amadea.'

'Yes, Ma.'

27

There was a short pause.

'I, er, I'm afraid it's me now.'

'You now what, Ma?'

'Not feeling well, love. I have, I have — a migraine.'

'Not got wasted again, Mum?' Amadea joked.

'No, love, not whatever it was you just said, no, just a rather bad headache.'

'But you don't get headaches; you always say you don't get headaches.'

'No, I don't. No, I think this is not just a headache, no, this is a migraine. Pure and simple, a migraine.'

'How do you know?'

'Because — because I can see spots in front of my eyes and I feel quite sick.'

'Oh, I am sorry.'

'That's all right, it'll go. They don't happen often, thank goodness. But it means I can't see you for lunch today, Amy. Do you mind? I'll give you a ring tonight.'

'OK.'

'I am sorry . . . '

'Don't worry. I'll find something to do. Really.'

Amadea replaced the phone. Damn, damn, damn. She had no food in the flat. She would have to go shopping. She turned and looked at Chopin, who was busy cleaning his paws.

'How bizarre is that, Fred? Ma of all people standing me up, not like her at all. Perhaps she's got a hangover? Now that's a notion.'

She frowned, hearing Rob Greer banging about on his balcony. Realising that he must be back from France, she went out on to her own and called down to him.

'Rob?'

'Amy?'

'You're back from France?'

'No, actually, Amy, I'm still zere, chérie.'

'Shuddup. Can I come down for a coffee?'

'As long as you bring some wiz you, I am clean out of ze café.'

Amadea immediately shut her eyes as Rob opened the door to her, wearing his usual weekend gear of T-shirt and tracksuit bottoms.

'Miss Fontaine, and with coffee too.'

'Take me to the cafetière,' she murmured, stretching out her hands and closing her eyes as if she was blind. 'I am not looking down until I see a coffee pot. Seriously, I am not. I am medically unfit until I have sipped of the black stuff.'

Rob, ever game, obligingly led Amadea through the chaos of his sitting room to the chaos of his kitchen, where she slowly opened her eyes, placing her hands on her hips and gazing around her overdramatically.

'There is no hope for hospitals if this is the way doctors keep their kitchens, Dr Greer, do you know that?'

'Amy, Amy, please,' Rob said reproachfully. 'I am only just back from France. Soon everything here,' he glanced unemotionally round his kitchen, which was filled to the brim with everything from piles of dirty holiday clothes to stacks of dirty saucepans, 'soon, everything here will be as white and shining as the gates of heaven.'

'Hmm.' Amy picked up a greasy frying pan and moved it out of the way of the kettle. 'You know what I think, Rob, seriously?' As she spoke she gave the pile of clothes on the floor a hearty kick to push them towards the washing machine.

'No, but judging from the way you're kicking the washing it's bound to be something interesting.'

Amadea turned and gave him a mocking look.

'Just tell me about France. What did you get up to? Tell me anything to take my mind off where I'm standing.'

Rob looked at Amadea a little hopelessly. Even with her dark hair pinned up any old how, her eyes seemed to fill her heart-shaped face, and her slim figure in its white cut-offs and matching tight white T-shirt was everything that a man could wish for, or dream of. The only trouble was, as far as Amadea Fontaine was concerned, he knew that Dr Rob Greer was just a friend.

★ ★ ★

Florence surveyed the rain-sodden young man now standing in her kitchen. He was looking more than bewildered, he was looking frightened.

'Why am I here? What is this place? I can remember nothing.'

He looked around him, the expression on his face still that of lost despair.

'Look, young man, I know you're not yourself but you really have got to crisp up a bit, you

30

know? This is a house. Remember what houses are? Places people live in? And this, here, is my kitchen.'

'You are a cook?'

'Well, yes, I suppose I am, or rather have been. Yes, I have cooked a great deal during my life, as a matter of fact.'

As he frowned at her response, Florence took stock of her situation yet again. She knew she should have marched the stranger out of the cottage, down the drive and off her property, not taken him into the house.

'If you are indeed what you say, I would ask you to be courteous enough to cook for me something that will tempt my appetite.'

Florence frowned. 'Do you have to talk like that all the time?'

'How should I speak?'

He looked so hurt that Florence quickly bent down to her saucepan cupboard and took out a frying pan.

'Very well. Bacon, our own eggs, sausages and some tiny Italian tomatoes, will that do you? After which I'm dreadfully afraid, rain or no rain, you are going to have to be on your way, young man.'

She struck a match and applied it to the gas ring.

Whoosh! With a howl of singular terror over went the stranger, arms flailing in the air, feet slipping on the marble tiles, cafetière sent flying across the table, all in a split second.

As he fell, the side of his head caught the edge of Florence's chopping block.

'Oh my God!' Florence dropped to her knees beside him. 'Oh my God, oh my God!'

But wherever God was, he could not hear her, and neither could the young man.

2

Rob was leafing through one of Amadea's carefully arranged glossy magazines. He was in her flat because, a few minutes earlier, Amadea had announced that she could not stand another minute in his.

'Do you know something? I have just realised I don't have to visit downtown Swinton to see how dropouts live, Rob. I have, after all, visited your flat.'

It was as if she had not spoken, because Rob was busy reading, and he now gave a contemptuous laugh.

'Oh come on!' He pointed to an illustration in *Top Interiors*. 'Who in their right mind would put a broken bust on the floor where everyone's going to trip over it? And as for all those perfectly arranged boxes of pebbles on the coffee table . . . ' He shook his head.

Amadea took the magazine from him and put it back in its place on her own coffee table.

'Look, stick to flicking through the *British Formulary*, why don't you?'

The telephone rang. Amadea cradled the receiver under her chin while she used a nail file. Multitasking was a mild obsession with her. She could paint her toenails, clean her shoes, wash up, all while taking a call.

'Ma?' She pulled a face at Rob, and mouthed '*my mother*' at him.

'Not so surprising, most people have had one, I think you'll find,' Rob murmured.

'How's the migraine? What do you mean it's gone? That was quick. So do you want me to come across for lunch — ' At least that would save her shopping. 'No? You want me to stay where I am because you're coming to *Swinton* in an *ambulance?* Are you hurt? . . . No, you're not hurt, but you're in an ambulance. I mean what kind of migraine have you *got?* What do you mean, it's not you? . . . What young man you've had staying? . . . What do you mean, 'not exactly staying'? You *said* he was staying — he came for an interview about a gardening job? But *you* do the gardening! You don't have a gardener . . . He came across to see you about hedge-clipping? And he fell and hit his head while you were giving him a cup of coffee. Well, that's not your fault.' Amadea threw the nail file down and covered the phone. 'She's afraid this gardener might sue her,' she said to Rob.

Rob paused, raising one cynical eyebrow. 'Ask Mrs Fontaine if she's rich?'

'Rob Greer, my neighbour, you remember Dr Greer? Well, he says to ask, are you rich?' Amadea looked across at Rob. 'She says no, she's not at all rich.'

'In that case tell her to relax. Poor people don't get sued.'

Rob picked up *Top Interiors* and started to flick through it again. It took his mind off how beautiful Amadea was looking, despite the fact that she was wearing no make-up. Actually he liked her better like that, not so uptight, not so tense, hair all over the place, tumbling down her back, her neat features already a little brown from the good weather they'd been having. He stared hard at a particularly boring stone bench, to take his mind off Amadea.

Amadea was still talking to her mother, but her tone had changed to one of kindness.

'Look, you can't blame yourself, Ma, it's not your fault, really. Don't worry, just ring me when you get to Swinton.'

She finally put down the phone.

'Why she had to go with him in the ambulance I wouldn't know.'

She picked up her nail file again and started to file her already perfect nails. 'Oh my God, Rob.' She looked up, biting her lip.

'Mmm?'

'Rob! God, Rob — '

'Demi-God Rob might be a little more suitable.'

'No, but don't you see?'

'I might well do, if you tell me what to look at.'

'No, no, don't you see — it's obvious, seriously.'

'It is?'

'Yes, seriously, seriously, I've got there in one. I think Ma cancelled me going over because — because she has a toy boy!'

Rob looked at her and smiled his mischievous, warm smile. 'Good for her.'

Amadea paused in her enthusiastic filing and frowned at him. 'You would say that.'

★   ★   ★

35

Jamie always found it hard to leave home during the school holidays. Leaving Dylan behind was so difficult. Dropping him off at nursery was not so bad because he was only one of many being dropped off, but leaving him behind with Mrs Jenkins, her kindly neighbour, was agony. Jamie would always stand in the forecourt of their block of flats and wave up to him, while Mrs Jenkins waved one of Dylan's hands at his mother standing below them in the road, which Dylan allowed, while at the same time sticking the four fingers of his free hand firmly in his mouth.

Today, however, Jamie had no reason to feel bad, because it was Sunday. Nevertheless she did feel bad, because they were due to visit her mother. It was not that it was a long journey; it was actually quite a short drive, out of Swinton into the countryside, down small country roads to the newly fashionable village of Shotcombe. So, no, it was not the drive — it was her mother.

Jamie stood back and surveyed Dylan with as critical an eye as she could, trying to see him as someone else might. She had dressed him in the smartest clothes she could afford, London clothes that were made in France and supplied through a chic mail order catalogue. Even so, she thought she could see her mother's expression as she stared down at Dylan, half pitying, half resentful. Her grandson, the leftover from Jamie's wild youth. No matter how smartly he was dressed, Jamie was sure that her mother would look at him as if he was wearing dirty jeans and wornout trainers.

'Come on, kid.'

She picked up her nappy bag and umbrella in one hand, holding tight to Dylan's hand with the other, while at the same time wishing from the bottom of her heart that she could actually look forward to seeing her mother, instead of dreading it.

She could at least enjoy the drive. It took them through narrow country roads and past signposts which either pointed the wrong way or had long ago lost the greater part of the name of any village. In this way the sign to Shotcombe read only 'Shotc', the last part having snapped off before even Rosa Charlbury had moved into her small, square village house with its perfectly black railings, its white-painted façade and its entirely correct Farrow and Ball 'studio green' front door.

'Hallo.'

Rosa Charlbury was elegant, prematurely white-haired, and classically beautiful. She opened the front door before Jamie and Dylan had time to close the black-painted iron gate that bordered her small front garden. Jamie knew by this that she must have been waiting for them long before their arrival. This should have flattered Jamie, but it only flustered her, making her feel as if she was actually late, instead of dead on the button.

'Hallo, Mummy.'

They kissed the air either side of each other's head in the approved fashion, and Dylan smiled shyly up at his grandmother.

'How are you?'

Jamie had long ago given up any hope of her mother addressing Dylan by his first name. There was a very good reason for this. Her mother was not only ashamed of her daughter being a single parent, she hated Dylan's name.

'I suppose,' she had said when told the name of her newborn grandson, 'I suppose we're lucky he's not called Glastonbury.' This was a less than oblique reference to the fact that Jamie had met Dylan's father at the Glastonbury Festival five years ago. That their meeting had resulted in a fatherless baby being born seemed to justify Mrs Charlbury's dislike of both pop festivals and single parents.

Jamie's father had been bright, handsome, and a charity worker. He and Jamie had loved each other, for a short while, but she had never had any intention of marrying him, for the very good reason that she knew his only goal in life was to go to Africa to work in famine relief.

They had lost touch, as people do, and eventually, because she either could not believe it or did not want to believe it, Jamie had discovered that she was pregnant. Dylan had been unplanned but not unwanted, and sometimes the unplanned, in demanding commitment, can become a source of delight — and that, as far as Jamie was concerned, was Dylan.

They were sitting in the small, chintz-covered sitting room. The room had no view until you stood up and then you could see the splendidly neat garden in which her mother so delighted. The herbaceous border would soon be coming into its own, a border that was always, rightly, her mother's pride and joy. Meanwhile there were magnolias blossoming, and bulbs set in clumps around the edge of the lawn, just as there were pots of hyacinths on the sitting-room window sill, and in the centre of the small mahogany dining table at which they would soon be seated.

'For the life of me I can never remember the name of the company you work for,' Rosa stated, as she handed Jamie a long-stemmed glass of sherry. 'Someone in the village was asking me, but I just couldn't remember. I said, 'Somewhere in Swinton and it has a funny spelling,' but that was all I could remember.'

'It's called Psemisis.' Jamie had taken off Dylan's coat and was now watching him with nervous eyes.

Please, please help him to behave! There was so much that could be wrecked in her mother's sitting room. China ornaments, little boxes from Halcyon Days, a small collection of antique thimbles, endless treasures that needed dusting, but not touching. 'Now, don't touch, sit,' she told Dylan.

The handsome little boy sat on the edge of the large chair, his eyes round and innocent as he stared at the small train in his hand before placing it firmly on the carpet and pushing it up and down.

'No, Dylan, sit!'

'Do you always address him as if he is a Labrador?'

'I don't want him breaking anything . . . '

'You were always so good at sitting still. You

39

were the stillest of children, everyone remarked on it, you know.' Rosa Charlbury sniffed lightly and sipped at her sherry.

Dylan was now back on his chair, and obliging his mother by running the train up and down the arm instead of the carpet.

'So how is — what's it called?'

'Psemisis.'

'Yes, how is it? Still finding your job interesting? Still calling yourself whatever it is you call yourself there?'

'Jamie.'

'Yes, still calling yourself that, are you? What was wrong with your own name? What was wrong with Lucinda, I would not know.'

'It was too upper class, Sheila Pryor, my boss, thought. Because I lecture to students so much, they thought it would be better if I sounded a little less like a toff.'

Jamie smiled. She hadn't minded Sheila insisting on changing her name. She had actually found it quite funny, and in the event quite purposeful. Nowadays you had to be careful to seem as ordinary as possible, particularly if you happened to be lecturing on something that was extraordinary. It was just how it was.

'What is it that you do? People in the village are always asking me that too.'

Jamie sighed inwardly. Every fortnight they had the same conversation. She knew that it was her mother's way of telling her that she thought what Jamie was doing was both inferior and unsuitable. By making her daughter repeat the details of her life every fortnight she was punishing her, over and over again.

'I'm a genetic scientist, Mummy.'

'Oh, that's right. A scientist. You know no one has ever cured or discovered anything of significance from experimenting on animals, don't you?'

'I don't do that sort of work. I am involved in research that does not use animals. I keep trying to tell you that — to reassure you.'

'I am old, Jamie. That is what comes from being old, you need everything repeated. I didn't have you until I was over forty, remember?'

Yes, Jamie did remember. She could hardly forget since her mother always reminded her of it, every time she saw her.

Rosa Charlbury put her sherry glass down, and stood up as if the very memory of Jamie's birth had been too much to allow her to stay seated.

'I am just going to put the sprouts on. Shan't be a moment.'

Jamie looked round the sitting room. It was dust-free, completely neat and tidy, filled with china ornaments, and it made her want to scream. The clock ticked loudly. It was as if it was mocking her. As if it was saying to her, 'There will be another whole three hours before you can get up to leave. First lunch, and then tea, and then at last at five o'clock — but not before — you can leave.'

The misery of it all struck Jamie afresh. Her mother's life encased within the four walls of the chintz-covered, china-ornamented village house. A life that had seen her marry at the age of thirty-nine, give birth at forty-one, and be left a widow at forty-five. Jamie had no memory of her father. She glanced towards his photograph sitting on her mother's small mahogany desk in its statutory silver frame. Evidently her father had been a very handsome man, the managing director of a large retail company, flying all over the world on business. He had died very suddenly, from deep-vein thrombosis probably caused by all the air travel he had done. Unfortunately he had been much older than Rosa, and had enjoyed, or not enjoyed, a previous marriage, not to mention other children, which meant that he had left Rosa and their small daughter badly off.

Although she would have loved to have known her father, nowadays Jamie always thought that being the only daughter of a widowed mother had acted as the essential stimulus to achievement. She liked the fact that she had always had to earn her own living; that both she and her mother had depended on her doing not just well but brilliantly. If her father had been rich she would not have had to try so hard at school, would not have gone to university, would not have been ambitious. She had been hardly more than a teenager when she had cut out a quotation, 'Embrace your reproaches, they are blessings in disguise.'

Lunch came and went with Dylan bravely and silently trying his best to cope with his grandmother's food.

'Does he not like sprouts?'

'Ye-es. He likes sprouts, don't you, Dylan? It's just that he's more used to broccoli.'

'Doesn't he like jelly? I thought he liked jelly. He ate jelly last time he was here. I thought he would at least eat jelly.'

'He is getting used to it. He just doesn't know it very well yet.'

Jamie stared at the game birds on her wooden place mat. What a stupid thing to say: nobody 'knew' jelly, jelly was not a person.

'Strange, little boys always used to like jelly.'

Rosa always said that too. Jamie now found herself staring miserably at Dylan's jelly. What must he think of her, always bringing him to a place where he was forced to eat jelly?

Anyway, why did her mother always make jelly when she must have noticed by now that Dylan didn't really like it? Why else would he eat it so slowly? Worse than that, why didn't Jamie tell her not to *make* jelly?

There was a simple answer to that question. She did not tell her mother not to make jelly because she liked a quiet life. Besides, to tell her mother that Dylan did not like jelly would not make any difference to what was served when they next visited. Her mother would merely pretend that she had forgotten, and produce a jelly anyway.

'Jellies and honeycomb moulds are becoming quite fashionable again, you know, particularly fruit jellies, jellies made with fresh fruit.'

Jamie nodded silently, her eyes sliding over to the clock on the mantelpiece as her mother

43

went to make coffee. Still only half past two!

'Can I help you?' she called out to her mother while grabbing Dylan's plate, replacing it with her own clean plate, and bolting down mouthfuls of the wretched jelly stuff.

'No, dear, really. I am better on my own, thank you.'

Jamie stared at the immaculately set table. Better on her own? And some.

★ ★ ★

When at last, after several tours round the garden and intermittent discussions about the state of the flower beds, the work Rosa was doing on the village committee and the closing of the village shop, five o'clock arrived and the small mahogany clock obligingly announced the hour, Jamie found it hard not to spring to her feet and run.

Dylan, thank God, had behaved himself. He had remembered to ask to go to the bathroom, he had sat quite still, and he had even eaten a little jelly. Jamie sighed inwardly with relief as she took out an envelope and placed it on her mother's desk. It was her 'something towards the housekeeping' envelope, filled with a small amount of cash to help her mother out. Nowadays they did not even refer to it. She merely left it on the desk, inside the Coutts leather folder, and presumably her mother spent it, wildly, on things like jelly.

Jamie looked round for Dylan, but he had

gone and there was only Rosa left in the room staring at the all too probable reason for his disappearance.

'Oh *no*. What has happened? Oh *no*.'

★ ★ ★

Amadea was looking confused. She was not used to her mother being anything except her *mother*, and mothers, as everyone knew, were meant to be found in the kitchen, standing by the kettle, waiting to make people coffee or tea, or rolling out pastry, or collecting apples to make chutney.

'What spooked him so much that he fell?'

'I only lit the gas . . . '

They were seated in the all-too-dreary out-patients' area of St George's Hospital, Swinton. It was not a good place to be, filled as it was with the kind of people at the sight of whom you immediately tightened your grip on your handbag.

'So, you lit the gas and he fell, hitting his head on the side of the chopping block?'

'He took a frightful bang to the head — it's left quite a gash.'

'What is his name, Ma?'

Florence looked away. 'I, er — I don't know actually, Amy. I really don't know.'

'But I thought you said you were interviewing him for cutting the hedges.'

'Yes, I was, but he came to me via his advertisement in the *Blackstone* magazine. Regency Services, I think his firm was called,' Florence added, improvising quickly. 'Yes, I

45

think that's what it was called.'

'Which explains his strange clothes — I don't think.'

'Well, people nowadays do dress strangely, Amy. Anything goes. Not like in your grandmother's day when it was all so much easier. Navy or grey for spring, light summer frocks and white cardigans and shoes, and tweed for the winter. There was a sense to it, I sometimes think, no agonising choices, and clothes lasted so much longer.'

Just like the linnet who housed herself in Florence's potting shed every year, Florence was doing her best to distract Amadea. If the linnet spied you, she would make the most wonderful feints to draw your attention away from where she was building her nest.

'Seriously, Ma, he must have some documents on him. A credit card, something, he's bound to have something,' Amadea persisted, sounding slightly querulous even to herself.

'Why? When you think about it,' said Florence, staring ahead of her, 'we don't all have to be card-bound — being card-bound is bad for you, I should think, like being egg-bound.'

Florence felt vaguely flattened as she noticed that Amadea did not smile at her joke. Perhaps that was why she said 'seriously' so often? Because she didn't like jokes.

'I expect they'll bring him round and find out who he is. He'll know who he is all right. Seriously, most people do.'

Amadea gazed around her. God, what a place to find yourself in on a Sunday afternoon. She should be back at the flat watching an old film and — well — enjoying herself, not sitting with her mother in St George's outpatients' in Swinton.

Perhaps her mother could sense how she was feeling because she gave her an apologetic look, and put a sympathetic hand to her arm.

'It's very good of you to come, Amy, really it is, very good of you to be with me. I do appreciate it, love, and Rob too, very kind of him.'

'Well, it's not my kind of thing, really, but Rob's very good with this stuff. I think he's making it his speciality actually. He deals in head cases and nutcases and all that.'

Amadea swung her legs backwards and forwards as she had always done since she was a child, and as she did so Florence felt a rush of guilt.

'Look, you go — ' She was about to say 'love' again, but quickly changed it to 'Amy'. 'You go, I'll wait for Dr Greer . . . Yes, I'll wait and you go, that would be best, I think.'

Amadea immediately stood up, trying not to look relieved. 'If you're sure?'

'Of course, Amy. You've done quite enough. Thank you so much for coming.'

With mutual relief mother and daughter parted, and Florence settled back to wait for Dr Greer to come and find her. Half an hour later, he finally appeared.

'Mrs Fontaine.'

They shook hands.

'Dr Greer.' Florence immediately fell silent,

dreading what he might be about to say.

'The patient is severely concussed, and there is bruising and a minor laceration to the right temple, consistent with falling against a sharp object.'

'That would be my chopping block — '

'As soon as he regains consciousness we will scan him. In the meantime I suggest you return home.'

Rob smiled at her in his professionally reassuring way, and then found himself smiling rather more genuinely, because Mrs Fontaine was obviously such a nice woman. Very well, she was middle-aged, but she had a head of thick dark hair which she wore up, held in place by side combs. She was wearing clothes that she must have worn for years, but they were neat and clean, and sort of innocent, like the straw basket she was carrying. Looking at her more closely, Rob couldn't quite believe that the strangely costumed young man she had brought in was actually Mrs Fontaine's toy boy, but you never knew with people; there truly was nothing stranger than folk, and if working in a general hospital didn't teach you anything else, it taught you that.

'Thank you so much for taking the time to come down and see me.'

Florence turned to go, but Rob stopped her.

'If you don't mind me asking, Mrs Fontaine, how are you going to get home, if you came here in the ambulance?'

'Oh, don't worry about me; I'll get the local train. The walk to the station will do me good,

48

and I can get a taxi the other end.'

Rob watched Florence leave the main concourse of the hospital and walk briskly out into the rain. It was a few seconds before he realised that it had never occurred to him to tell her to ring Amadea and get her to drive her mother back to her house.

Late the following afternoon he phoned Florence as he had promised.

'The patient has regained consciousness, and this morning's scan shows no fracture to the skull, but it seems the sharp blow to the temple has resulted in amnesia, which may yet prove to be only temporary.'

Florence, knowing that the patient had already been suffering from amnesia before the fall, stared round her kitchen. 'What will happen if he doesn't get his memory back?'

'There are a number of drugs that are sometimes used in such cases.'

'And if that doesn't work?'

'Well, if no one claims him, he'll just be clocked into the system.'

Florence straightened up. She didn't like the sound of someone being clocked into the system. 'Can I see him?'

'No visitors at the moment, Mrs Fontaine.'

'He must need some fresh clothes. Could you ask Amadea to fix him up with some fresh clothes? His are really rather eccentric. They might give the medics the wrong impression.'

'Certainly I will ask Amy — '

'Tell her I will pay, of course.' Florence was about to ring off when she thought of something else. 'He can't be an illegal immigrant, I shouldn't have thought, because he speaks such perfect English.'

Rob stared at the telephone for a few seconds after he had replaced it. He could not tell Mrs Fontaine that the stranger's so-called perfect English was one of the things that worried him most. With his 'sirs' and his 'by your leaves' he was most definitely not what even his best mate could call normal.

Rob picked up the phone again but this time it was Amadea's work number that he dialled.

'She wants me to *what?*'

'Your mum wants you to kit out the gardener who hit his head in her kitchen. Remember the gardener with the memory loss? He needs kitting out with what my stepmother for some reason still calls 'clobber'.'

'Oh, come *on*. She can't be serious.'

'She is quite serious.'

Amadea sighed. 'What else?'

'Nothing. She just wants him kitted out with some clothes, simple stuff. You know, tracksuit bottoms, trainers, a top with *Chicago* written across it . . .'

'Not everyone wants to look as if they've just sold their last copy of the *Big Issue*, Rob.'

'Do I detect a measure of cynicism in your voice?'

'Give me a break, Rob, I'm snowed under. Dogsbody Fontaine is my nickname here.'

'In that case, don't worry, leave it to me. I'll get some stuff for him. Cheers.'

Amadea frowned as Rob replaced the phone

without saying anything more, and shook her head. Poor man, if he didn't look like a missing person now, after Rob had chosen his clothes he certainly would.

★ ★ ★

Jamie had become a skilled speaker, well able to hold any restless young audience's attention. This particular day her talk was broadly based on an explanation of the Circadian rhythm, set by the body's internal biological clock, a clock which allows organisms to adapt to the daily cycle of light and dark.

'These Circadian rhythms are controlled by clock genes, a mechanism that contains the genetic instructions to produce protein, the levels of which follow rhythmic patterns, controlling actions such as sleep and rest, awareness and activity, body temperature, heart activity, blood pressure, the amount of oxygen consumed, and countless other functions.'

Inevitably, as happens when you have given a lecture many times before, Jamie found herself going on to autopilot. Perhaps it was because she had reached the point where she spoke about the effect of the rhythms on the heart that she found her mind going into flashback.

Her involvement with Dylan's father had definitely involved her heart, her whole heart and nothing but her heart, hadn't it? It had, but at the same time she had to admit, looking back with total honesty, that she had always imagined that her involvement with the handsome student would be only a mid-summer fling. *Go wing a fling* had practically been her motto but then she had been left holding Dylan and winging nothing, only dedicating herself to working even harder, making sure that she kept their heads above water. Anything else had become quite out of the question.

To say the least of it, Dylan was now the centre of her life. She imagined he would always be everything to her, that no one else would now, ever, come close; she was as certain of this as she was certain that she had never, ever been the centre of Rosa's life. Rosa was the centre of her own life, which was probably why she had married so late. She found it impossible to think outside the box of her own life. In Europe they called it radical individualism, in Swinton they called it extreme egoism, and Jamie called it being mad about yourself. Rosa was in love with Rosa: there seemed to be no room for three or even two in her world.

'And it isn't only the human race that is controlled by Circadian rhythms,' Jamie heard herself continuing. 'Mice have body clocks, as do fish, fruit flies, plants, fungi, and even the simplest of algae, known to scientists as cyanobacteria.'

Of course Dylan had to go and break one of Rosa's best boxes on Saturday afternoon, and it had to be the one to which she was most sentimentally attached, the one that had meant the most to Rosa, the one that she had looked at *every day of her life* since she had been given it.

'I will commission another one for you . . . '
Jamie had kept saying while Dylan, duly
retrieved from the loo where he had gone to
hide, stood by, anguished.

But nothing would assuage Rosa's all-too-
apparent hurt. It had been the final straw as far
as Dylan's grandmother was concerned. First
there had been the silly little boy's quite evident
reluctance to eat her home-made jelly, next his
inability to stay as still as a graven image, his
constant irritating fidgeting, and finally his
seizing *the* box, her precious, precious memento,
and dropping it. A disaster, the whole afternoon
had been a disaster, and Jamie had arrived back
at their flat in a state of catatonic shock, while all
the time knowing, as sure as there were stars in
the sky, that they would have to repeat the
experience in a fortnight's time — although not
perhaps the breaking of the box, please, please
God, not that.

'Excuse me?' a voice from the middle of the
room asked, one hand shooting into the air. 'I
wonder if you could stop there.'

Jamie stared at the owner of the hand. 'I'm
sorry?'

'I was wondering if you could stop there.
Because I don't quite follow.' The young
questioner was now standing up. 'If I understand
it, you are saying that all we are is — all we are is
an orderly construction of cells run by an
internal body clock, is that right?'

Jamie hesitated, sensing trouble.

'Because if this is so,' the questioner
continued, 'that will surely mean that we should

all feel the same, which we actually don't.'

'What is meant by that,' Jamie began, knowing all too well that she was sounding prim but not knowing how to stop herself. 'What is meant is that human beings can all react in the same way.'

'But that doesn't mean we all share the same emotions, surely? Or is that what it means?'

'You have to think of our genetic structure as a sort of template for the way we are, rather than looking for emotional specifics. On the plus side, we're soon going to be able to identify the genetic structure that gives us the diseases that would otherwise kill us, which is the field in which I specialise.'

'Yes, but does that mean you're going to be able to identify and classify genetically how we feel and why? That's what I'm really on about — because if that is so, you can count me out for a start.'

Jamie waited until the ripple of slightly shocked laughter had died down, and then she cleared her throat, determined to continue.

'The point about genetic structure is that it is a form of programming. The reason why birds and butterflies migrate, swallows never get lost, and peregrines return to their feeding grounds at exactly the right time is because they have genetic programming, dating back to time immemorial. In-built natural computer knowledge is what we now know they have.'

'But is emotion also controlled by our Circadian rhythm?'

Jamie tried to sound patient, despite the fact that the young man was obviously set upon making her late for her next appointment.

'I imagine yes, it could be. And this could enable us to put our knowledge to good use. We could cut down on the divorce rate by identifying the right kind of relationships, and even control domestic violence.'

'What about sex? Will it control that? No, hang on,' as the other students gave a shout of laughter. 'No, it's a perfectly serious question.'

'And I am taking it perfectly seriously.'

'If you say you're going to be able to identify what's wrong with us, the sort of people we are, tick the genetic box and away you go — then love goes right out of the window. It has to, surely?'

'It might change the nature of love, I grant you. But genetic science is concerned only with the good of mankind. Its object is our betterment, not our destruction.'

'I think it's going to take all the fun out of everything. We're all going to be wandering around like sleepwalkers, aren't we? Perfectly genetically controlled, no emotion and, frankly, no fun.'

The questioner sat down to mild applause and laughter.

'Well, let's hope we keep the fun. Let's hope too that, with a little bit of foresight, we'll control the bad bits and hold onto the fun.'

Jamie continued with the lecture, and since it was one she knew in her sleep, she allowed her mind to follow the student's line of thinking. He could be right, of course. What if it were true? What if emotion became irrelevant? Then everything they were trying to prove, everything they were busy trying to improve, would become mechanical, a set pattern. In making everything predictable, would it all become as grey as the sky outside? Did they need the chaos of love to make life beautiful? After all, Dylan had been born out of the chaos of love, and was he not beautiful?

★ ★ ★

Rob stood back and stared at his patient, as it struck him yet again that the man standing before him in his new clothes was almost absurdly handsome. A face as white as ivory, large deep-set dark eyes, long-fingered elegant hands, and a positive mane of lustrous dark hair. He was tall, with a physique that suggested an artist rather than a sportsman, especially now that he was dressed in his new clothes — clothes that were nevertheless in direct contradiction to his looks. It was as if someone had found an angel and decided to mock him by making him wear the most ridiculous clothing they could imagine. Sensing his discomfort, Rob put a comforting hand on his arm.

'It's all right, old thing, everyone looks like this. But frock coats . . . ' He glanced over towards the discarded brocade coat, the breeches and the boots. 'They're for after six only now, I understand from *Vogue*.'

The young man stared at him. 'If you could only tell me whom I might be, sir?'

'The jury is still out on that one,' he said

carefully. 'At the moment you're John Smith. So I suggest we stick to that, but only for the moment. Does John Smith ring any bells, by any chance?'

The young man shook his head. 'I know nothing, sir. Nothing of whom I am, or why I am here.'

'To take the more positive route, let us suppose you *are* John Smith,' Rob told him in a kind voice. 'And then let us suppose you're here to get better from an illness.'

'But all these people.' He nodded towards the curtains that Rob had drawn around his bed in order to dress him. 'They are old and dying, and so it seems to me that I must be dying too.'

'No, you are not dying, and you're certainly not old.' Rob paused. 'I tell you what,' he said suddenly, 'I'll get you put into a side ward — that might help. So many distractions here, it's enough to confuse anybody.'

He stepped out between the curtains, only to find Florence standing in front of him.

'How is he, Dr Greer? How is the poor young man?'

Rob moved down the ward, well away from John Smith's cubicle.

'He is stable, although still suffering from amnesia.'

'I forgot — Amadea said you bought him something to wear. I must pay you, really I must . . . ' Florence immediately started to rummage in her handbag.

'No, no.' Rob put a firm hand on her arm.

'Really. There's no need.'

'It was meant to be Amadea who bought them, not you,' Florence said, feeling embarrassed that Rob had been landed with the task.

Rob was already moving away from her. He shrugged his shoulders.

'You know Amy, Mrs Fontaine. Amy is always snowed under, Psemisis and she are an item.'

'But to take you away from your work . . . '

'I was off duty. And anyway, it's better that I should buy them than Amy, Mrs Fontaine. You know what she's like; with her taste you'd be bankrupt in no time. Besides, Swinton is not Brighton, you know. Metrosexuality hasn't reached us yet.'

Florence's smile grew a little easier as Rob continued.

'I'm going to have our John Smith — that's what we're calling him, by the way — we're going to have him moved to a side ward. It's too busy here.'

Florence followed his glance. While Rob's eyes were used to the chaos of a mixed ward, his companion dropped her eyes in a way that suggested she would not be so insensitive as to stare.

'Do you really think you can help him?' Florence nodded towards the still-curtained bed.

'I hope so.'

'But supposing you can't? You said something about going into the system. That he would be taken into the system?'

'It's difficult with cases like this, very difficult, to follow a patient right through. It's one of our problems in the health service, follow-through. Hardly ever happens.'

Florence turned away. She had only one hope left for the poor young man who had shipped up in her guest cottage at the weekend, and that was that he would somehow come to and remember who he was.

'I was thinking he might have been mugged or something like that, before — before he hit his head in my kitchen,' she suggested as Rob walked her towards the lifts.

Rob nodded. 'Don't worry about it too much. You can be sure we will do our best for him, Mrs Fontaine.'

Florence watched Rob Greer's face as the lift doors closed. He had not sounded all that hopeful. Her grip on her handbag tightened. She resolved that, whatever happened, she would not let that poor young man get swallowed up by the so-called system. After all, what would become of him, especially if he didn't even know who he was?

★ ★ ★

As soon as he heard her footsteps in the flat above him, Rob was upstairs and knocking on Amadea's door. Just as quickly, Amy opened the door to him and Rob immediately found himself wishing that she hadn't. In a light floral caftan of a kind she often changed into when she returned from work, she was looking far too ravishing.

'Are you going out?'

'Do I look as if I'm going out, Rob?'

Amadea shook her head and turned on her heel, but only after giving him one of her best drop-dead-twitto looks.

Rob put a bottle of his finest Chilean Merlot on the table, and held out a hand.

'Corkscrew, Nurse Fontaine.' Amadea passed him one, and he looked at it with distaste. 'Why do women always have the worst corkscrews ever invented?'

'Why do you think? To discourage men from drinking their wine.'

Over the second glass they dropped the banter and got on to the subject of John Smith.

'The fuzz have taken a mug shot of him, but quite honestly I doubt if you would recognise yourself from one of those. I always think that by the simple device of taking better photographs of missing persons, more people would actually be found.'

'Right! Great idea!' Amadea looked momentarily impressed. 'Get someone like Patrick Demarchelier, someone really good, to snap the missing people, and bingo! You would halve the missing persons files.'

Rob nodded. He hadn't meant to take it that far, but that was one of the fascinating things about Amadea. She always took everything and everyone too far — except him, alas.

'I expect someone will turn up, once they've done DNA, fingerprints, dental history, Uncle Tom Cobley and all. Someone's bound to claim the poor fellow. Trouble is he's so good-looking, if I took a nice snap of him and put it on the internet he would be claimed by half the world.'

'Not a bad idea. What's the website?'

Rob stared at Amy.

'No, seriously,' she continued, mischievously. 'We could auction him. What a sensation that would be.'

Rob shook his head. 'You know what you are?'

Amadea stared provocatively at him for a second. 'What am I, Dr Greer?'

'Completely heartless.'

For a second Amadea looked hurt, and then she nodded her head, almost proudly.

'Yes, I am,' she admitted. 'I am completely heartless.'

'Because?'

'Because that is the only way to be, Rob. The only way to be.'

'Come on.'

'No. Look at you, you're always saying you're never going to get involved with your patients. Now I am saying that I never want to get involved with life again. It's too ... ' She wrinkled her pretty nose. 'It's just too *involving*. As far as this life is concerned, I want to stay free as a bird.'

'I only *say* I mustn't get involved with my patients because if I do I will not be a good doctor. To be a good doctor you have to be determined to remain detached. Becoming involved will not do you or the patient any good. But that doesn't mean I won't work my legs off to try to get them better; or seen by the right people. And as to you staying free as a bird, just

61

make sure that you don't get distracted and fly into a window pane, Amy.'

But he spoke to her back, because Amadea had gone to put on a fresh CD and did not seem to have heard.

3

Florence could not put the memory of her uninvited guest out of her head, and yet at the same time she knew she must not keep ringing the hospital because it would not be taken well. She tried to concentrate on her normal routines — the house, the garden, Punch, the hens — but the worry was always there. Would John Smith be put into alien hands and end up languishing unclaimed in some national health ward? After a lapse of some days she finally gave in to anxiety and rang Rob Greer.

'The news is good, Mrs Fontaine, in that he is physically healthy, but I'm afraid he has been officially diagnosed as having a total memory loss. This may be due to the concussion, or he might have been suffering from it before.'

'Oh dear.' Florence was flooded with guilt. 'Oh dear, oh dear,' she said again. 'I feel it is all my fault.'

'It was an accident. An accident pure and simple. They happen, and we try to put together the results of accidents, but that is what it was, an accident. No one's fault, not yours, not mine, not his, just an accident.'

'I suppose so,' Florence agreed, but she couldn't keep the sadness out of her voice. If only she hadn't asked him in for breakfast, it would not have happened. If only she had done the sensible thing and sent him on his way, the poor young man would probably be perfectly all right.

'He will be examined later today by Mr Jorgen, who is a specialist in this field.'

'Someone out there must be missing him, wouldn't you say?'

'I would say so, Mrs Fontaine.'

The emotion in Florence's voice surprised Rob so much that the thought occurred that Amy might have been right and that John Smith might indeed be Mrs Fontaine's toy boy.

'I think he should be moved to somewhere like Swinton Clinic, somewhere he could have round-the-clock supervision.'

'The clinic costs hundreds of pounds a day, Mrs Fontaine.'

'Very well.' Florence looked across at some of her family silver sitting on the shelf on the other side of the kitchen. 'Very well,' she said, taking her courage in both hands. 'Put him in the clinic and I will pay for him myself, out of my own money.'

Rob did not like to ask Mrs Fontaine how exactly she was going to find the money to pay for someone to stay at her expense in the clinic. It was not his affair, yet he knew from Amy that her mother had not been left well off after her father's death. It seemed that her father had spent every last bean, leaving Mrs Fontaine with only her house and a tiny private pension.

After Florence had rung off, Rob dialled Amy's number at work to tell her the latest in the John Smith saga. It seemed to him that it was fast becoming something of a soap opera.

'She's doing *what?*'

Rob could not help smiling into the telephone as he heard Amadea's reaction to his news.

'Something got into your ears, Amadea Fontaine? I just told you your mother's insisting on having John Smith admitted to the clinic. She's offered to pay for him to be treated there from her own private purse.'

Rob put his fist up to his mouth to stop himself laughing, because he sensed he had just lit a match and set Amy's stack on fire.

There was the slightest of pauses.

'She can't know how much that place *costs?*'

Rob attempted to sound innocent. 'Well, yes, I think she does, Amy. I did hint to her that it's several hundred pounds a day.'

'She can't afford that!'

Amadea put the phone down and stared about her. Her office was just the same: the windows still had glass in them; she was still wearing a green skirt and a white jacket, so it must be true. Her mother was going to pay for her toy boy, a nameless young man who had lost his memory through bumping his head in her kitchen. She was going to pay for him to be put in Swinton Clinic. Now she had heard everything.

Amadea dialled her mother's number, but the phone only rang and rang and rang. She redialled, but it still only rang and rang and rang. Nevertheless she hung onto it, imagining Punch barking his head off, and wondering all the time where her mother might be.

★　★　★

65

Florence took the Georgian silver out of the old zip bag and placed it in front of Mr Hoskins, while at the same time keeping a watchful eye on Punch. In response to the 'NO DOGS' sign on the shop door, she had reluctantly left him tied up outside.

Mr Hoskins picked up the items one by one.

'Very fine, very fine,' he murmured, staring at the hallmarks on each piece as he held his glass up to his eye. 'Oh, and this, this is quite beautiful.'

It wrung Florence's heart to see the pieces on his counter, but she knew that human beings had to come before everything. Besides, she was somehow sure that Henry would think that she was doing the right thing.

Florence went on watching Punch as Mr Hoskins murmured his compliments about Henry's family silver.

'My husband's family had been very well off in their time, but of course times change, and the bottom dropped out of land,' Florence told the old man conversationally. 'You know how it is,' she said, one eye still firmly on Punch. 'Times do change.'

'Yes, times do change.'

Florence turned as she heard Mr Hoskins put down his eyepiece.

'The bottom has not just dropped out of land, Mrs Fontaine; it has dropped out of silver too. Even if I take this silver off you, fine as it is, it is worth hardly more than a piece of pottery nowadays. It has gone, silver, Mrs Fontaine, quite gone. A piece of pottery, I tell you, would be worth more than this.' He picked up a graceful Georgian milk jug. 'No one wants silver nowadays. They don't want the care of it; they don't want the look of it, any more than they want brown furniture, as we in the trade call it. They only want white. White everything: furniture, plates, sheets, towels, clothes, everything is now white. As long as it goes into the washing machine, and nothing to polish, or they can throw white paint over it, that's all they care about, and that's a fact. The most I could give you for all this would be . . . a few hundred pounds.'

Florence stared at him. 'A few hundred pounds?'

'Only a few hundred pounds.'

That would purchase one day for John Smith in the Swinton Clinic, or perhaps only half a day.

'Very well, Mr Hoskins, whatever you will give me I will take.'

'I will write out a bill of sale for you.'

He did so, opened a drawer with a key and handed her the money, carefully counted out. Florence put it in the now-empty zip bag, and then turned back to check on Punch. But the dog was gone.

★　★　★

Rob was watching Amadea with some amusement. He had never seen her so put out, not since someone had dinged her car door and driven off without leaving an address.

'How can she even *think* of footing the bill for this young man?'

67

Rob stared at her blearily. He had been on duty for so long now, he would not have been surprised to find out he was already asleep. 'It's not a question of actually thinking, it is something she is determined on doing, Amy. And I don't think John Smith is your mother's toy boy, really I don't.'

'*What*, then?'

'I think she just feels guilty, you know? Because he fell over in her kitchen.'

'But why is it no one can find this so-called Regency Services that he is meant to come from? It's a cover story, I'm sure of it. She's covering for something else happening.'

'Why would your poor mother make up a story about a man coming to cut her hedges, Amy?'

'Because she doesn't want to admit that she picked him up somewhere, or got him off the internet.'

'Your mother doesn't have a computer, Amy. You told me that. You said she was a Luddite, hated machines, wanted everything made by hand like William Morris. That's what you've always said.'

'Well, obviously she has changed. And now she has a crush on a young man and doesn't want to admit it. These things happen, I've read about them.'

Rob's eyes were shutting, even Amadea had noticed. She kicked the sole of one of his trainers.

'Has no one told you not to wear grey socks with trainers?'

'No, as a matter of fact when you're dealing with head injuries, and people who don't know who they are, that's not often something that comes up in the conversation. 'What colour socks do you wear with your trainers, doctor?' I don't think so.'

Amadea bent down and started to pull off Rob's trainers one by one, after which she removed his socks. Rob kept his eyes firmly shut.

'And as for your socks . . . ' She shook her head.

'They are quite washing-machine fresh — I just put them on.'

'They are *so* the wrong colour. Here — beer.'

She kicked his bare feet this time and pushed a bottle of beer towards him, but before she could turn back for a glass, Rob had reached forward and seized the bottle and was drinking from it.

Amadea placed the glass in front of him. 'Surely you know you shouldn't drink straight from a beer bottle? Rats do things to the necks of beer bottles that I wouldn't like to think about, Dr Greer — even you know that, surely?'

'I have asked you time and again to stop calling me Shirley.'

'Only if *you* stop making such bad jokes.'

Rob closed his eyes again.

'Rob. Please stay awake.' Amadea pushed his arm. 'You must help me. How am I going to stop my mother getting involved with this man?'

'You're not. You're not going to be able to stop her doing anything. She's a grown-up, a middle-aged woman. She can keep the young man in the Swinton Clinic as long as she wants, or at home as long as she wants. That is entirely her affair — if it is an affair, which I, personally, very much doubt.'

'But suppose he never recovers? Supposing he never remembers what he is, or who he is, rather, supposing he — well, just stays in there, not knowing who or where he should be, what then?'

'Well, if he's anything like Rip Van Winkle, Amy, he could be in there for a hundred years, and that would be quite hefty on Mum's credit card.'

'But, Rob, he could be feigning. He could be anything, a fraudster, a drug baron, anything.'

'Certainly. Or he could be someone who fell over in your mother's kitchen.'

'He could be a serial rapist, or a murderer. *Anything.*'

'I know. It's serious. I mean, he could be a lawyer.'

'It *is* serious, if only you would stop making jokes. This is seriously serious, Rob, if only you could see it. Women, older women, get fixations on young men. Sometimes they even stalk them.'

'He has no police record, that I do know. He's not even on a CD.'

'Your jokes are just so not funny.'

'It's a habit. When I'm overtired I make jokes.'

'And when you wake up, and when you come back from holiday, and before you go on holiday.'

'It's the reason I am so popular.'

Rob leaned his head back and closed his eyes once more. He was popular with everyone but Amy. Everyone, but everyone, liked Rob Greer,

70

except Amy. The problem was, since she lived in the flat above him, she was more than difficult to forget. In fact forgetting her was impossible.

*　*　*

Florence ran up and down the narrow high street outside Mr Hoskins's shop accosting strangers, so desperate was she to find Punch.

'Has anyone seen a sheepdog? Has anyone seen a sheepdog?'

People stopped and looked up and down as helpless as she, and then shrugged their shoulders. She ran to where the old police station used to be, and then, realising that the new police station was in quite a different direction, she turned round and ran there too. At least the zip bag that had carried all the silver was now empty, so running was not so hard. When she reached the new police station, she was just in time to find it shut.

'Have you seen a sheepdog? Black and white, medium-sized? He has a name tag on his collar,' she kept saying desperately to everyone she stopped; but they just looked sad for her, and although their eyes reflected nothing but compassion, she could see that they thought she had been careless somehow. People who lost their dogs could not have been looking after them properly, or else they would not have been lost, would they?

She couldn't face going home, so she called in at Dottie's cottage.

Dottie, small, dark and businesslike, took one

71

look at her and removed the large ball of wool that she always carried under one arm, and speared it with the knitting needles that were never at rest.

'My dear,' she said in her broad Devon accent, 'you look like you've been dragged through a hedge backwards, and then back through again.'

Florence stood on the doorstep. It had started to rain again. In her hurry she had left her umbrella in Mr Hoskins's shop, her hair was falling out of its combs, and she thought her heart was going to break.

'Dottie, I've lost Punch. I tied him up outside Mr Hoskins's shop, and I kept my eye on him the whole time, until I had to take the money and sign for it and then, when I looked round, he was gone!'

'Someone's taken Punch?'

'Or perhaps untied him, do you think?'

'How appalling. Look, Flo, I'd love to offer you a cup of tea, but you'd best go home directly.' She glanced back at the kitchen as if there was someone in there, which there wasn't. 'It was on the local news last night, an outbreak of dog-napping. I expect you'll get a call any moment, demanding a ransom.'

Florence stared at her. 'I never thought!'

'Why should you? Look, if I was you I would get on home. Mark my words, you'll be getting a call this side of soon, if what I heard on the telly last night is true. There's a spate of this pet-napping.'

To Florence the house without Punch was like a graveyard. She sat down suddenly on one of her old painted kitchen chairs, and put her head between her hands. How could she have let this happen? How? If only she hadn't gone into town with the silver, if only she had left Punch behind . . . but he so loved an outing. He always stood in the back of the car, never sat, always looking out of the back window, as if he was keeping an eye out for anyone who might be about to tailgate her.

After a minute or two she stood up and went to the kettle. She must force herself to do something, just must. She had hardly filled the kettle when the telephone rang. She ran to it, but it was no dog-napper. It was Amadea.

'Ma.'

'Amadea.'

'I have to talk to you about John Smith.'

'Who?'

'John Smith.'

'Sorry?'

'The man — who — fell — over — in — your — kitchen. John Smith?'

'Oh, yes, yes, of course. Yes. How is he?'

'He is the same, just the same, Rob says. He has recovered from the blow to the head, so his condition is *not* your fault, get it? *Not* your fault. But he still doesn't know who he is, and he still talks in that peculiar way.'

'Oh, poor chap.' Florence glanced round the kitchen, her foot tapping.

'The thing is, Mother dear — '

'I do so hate it when you call me that — '

'Hang on, I *am* trying to help you, Ma, and see your point of view and everything, but I really do think you should stop imagining that this man's state of mind is your fault. He was obviously off his rocker already when he came to be interviewed by you, and the fact that he fell over in your kitchen was not your fault.'

'Yes, you just said that, dear.'

'And I hate it when you call me 'dear'.'

'Sorry, love. Look — '

'No, Ma, you look. This is how it has to go. You have to forget about John Smith, he is not your responsibility. He has passed into the system, and become none of your concern now. He will be taken care of by the State, good care too. Rob says they are wearing seven-league boots nowadays, as far as these kind of cases are concerned. There are so many different treatments, you wouldn't believe how many.'

'Amy, please — '

'So you've got to promise me, *got* to promise that you will have nothing more to do with this young man, OK? Promise?'

'Amy — '

'No, Ma, no more Amys, promise me.'

'I'll promise you anything if you will only get off the phone!'

Florence slammed down the receiver and started to pace the kitchen. She walked up and down it, up and down it. She was sure that she had missed the dog-napper's call, and all because of Amy and her nagging. Nag, nag, nag, that was all she ever did! God, and they said that older people nagged. Amy's nagging was worse than — worse than — worse than . . . She stopped. She couldn't think what Amy's nagging was worse than. At that moment the telephone rang.

She ran to it.

'Yes?'

'We got your dog. Name on the collar is Punch. Obviously you would like him back. So, how much are you prepared to pay?'

Florence's eyes went over to the zip bag with the precious silver money in it.

'How much do you want?'

★ ★ ★

Amadea put down the telephone and turned to Rob with a relieved smile.

'She has promised not to have anything more to do with him,' she told Rob in triumphant tones, only to find that Rob had fallen asleep yet again.

She pushed his well-muscled arm, and as she did so it occurred to her that Rob was quite well made; and not bad-looking either.

'My mother has just promised not to have anything more to do with John Smith,' she insisted again.

'I suppose that is good news.'

'Of course it's good news, Rob.'

'Well, they're not just going to let him go when he's obviously in such a bad way, talking like something out of the Ark, and wandering about dressed as a Regency buck. No, he will be taken care of, don't worry.'

But Amadea was no longer interested in John Smith. She was too busy folding up Rob's socks.

'Trainers, either white socks, dark socks, or — ' she said sternly, handing Rob his shoes one by one, and then hiding the socks behind her back — 'no socks. Just trainers. But never, ever grey socks.'

Rob stood up. 'I'll put that on my computer. Memo: no grey socks with trainers.'

'Yes, do.'

Amy was looking so serious now her thoughts had turned back to sock colour that Rob knew he had to go.

'To tell you the truth, I shall be sorry to see the back of John Smith. He has such a strange way of speaking. Just because I didn't understand a word of what he was talking about, it didn't stop my enjoyment.'

He swayed towards Amadea, so far over her that she was forced to catch hold of him, at which he shut his eyes and rested his head on her shoulder and started to make loud snoring noises.

Amadea sighed but did not remove his head.

She patted his shoulder affectionately. 'Oh Rob, you're so tired, anyone would think you were a doctor.'

★   ★   ★

Florence stood at the rural bus stop. It was pouring with rain yet again. She had at least found another umbrella. A car passed by, but it didn't stop. Another car passed by, and it too didn't stop. The rain became heavier, splashing her shoes and tights, splashing her coat. She

76

waited, reluctant to believe that the caller had been a hoaxer, glancing at her watch every now and then and looking up and down the road. At last a car stopped. She stood still. She would not run towards it. It might be a kerb crawler, or someone out to mug her. The door of the car opened slowly. She wished to goodness she had thought to bring someone else, Dottie, anyone, and had not come on her own. Then she saw the sight for which she had been so desperately longing. Punch! She ran towards him, but the man holding his lead put out a hand to stop her taking hold of it.

'This is none of my business, believe me. But I have to ask you to hand me the envelope before I hand you the lead. And believe me, it's not for me. It's for someone else.'

Florence held out the envelope and as she did so she thought she could see Henry's face, the way it was when they used to have tea on the terrace. He had always loved the silver tea set. It had been handed down for generations, so treasured.

'Quite thin the silver now,' he would sometimes remark, 'but still with us.'

Oh dear, what would he say? Selling the silver to get back Punch? But then she thought she could also hear him say, 'It's people, not things, that matter. People, and animals of course.'

'Right, I've counted it, you can take him.'

Florence ran down the lane towards her car, Punch running beside her on his lead, barking happily. Oh thank God, thank God! He jumped into the car beside her, and Florence drove home in a state of euphoria. She had only just let herself into the house, closed the shutters and run into the kitchen to give Punch some much-needed water, when the telephone rang once more. She eyed it for a few seconds before reluctantly picking it up.

'Ma? Mum?'

'Oh, hallo, it's you again, Amy.' Florence sighed.

'Are you all right?'

'I am fine, why?'

'You don't sound yourself.'

'What do you want, Amy?'

Amadea stared at the telephone. It wasn't like her mother to sound so off-hand.

'I just wanted to make sure that you knew you had promised me not to have anything more to do with John Smith, and that you will definitely not put him in the Swinton Clinic. Promise?'

'Of course. I couldn't anyway. I haven't any money, Amadea. No money at all, really. Couldn't, even if I wanted to.'

'Oh well, that's all right. I was worried, when Rob said — '

'I must go, Amy. Punch needs feeding, and I haven't shut the hens up.'

'Oh, all right, be like that.'

Amadea laughed good-naturedly and put the phone down. Well, that was all right then. No more worries there. Her mother had seen sense.

★ ★ ★

Jamie looked up at the handsome man who was staring down at her. She knew him from

78

somewhere, but she could not have said where.

'I'm sorry?'

'Rob Greer. Remember me? We met at Amadea Fontaine's New Year's Eve party.'

'Oh yes, yes, of course.' Jamie stood up and held out her hand. 'How are you?'

'National Health Service tired is the only answer to that.'

'Yes, of course, you're a doctor.'

Rob waited for the usual remark that followed this announcement, but for some reason Jamie Charlbury did not make it.

'Do you know, you have just won a hundred points, Ms Charlbury.'

'I have?'

'You have.'

'Because?'

'Because you did not say 'job for life'. I say 'I'm a doctor' and back comes 'job-for-life'.'

Jamie laughed. 'Try being a genetic scientist.' She pulled a face and put on a funny voice. ''A whoey whatey who?''

'And next?'

'You first.'

Rob paused, considering.

'Next, after 'job-for-life' comes 'You people have ruined the National Health Service, ruined what was once the pride of Britain.''

'Yes, yes, of course, that must be fun.'

'A jaw-breaker! Every time I'm faced with it I get carried out holding my aching sides.'

Rob looked down at Dylan, who was blowing bubbles at the bottom of his sundae glass with his straw.

'This is your chap?'

'This is my small person — Dylan Charlbury.'

Rob waggled his ears at Dylan. 'Bet you can't do that?'

Dylan shook his head and looked away shyly, unsmiling.

'Start again time,' Rob said to Jamie, looking rueful. Then, seeing the new football beside them, he went on, 'OK, so — want to come to the park and kick a football?'

He was asking Jamie really, and they both knew it, despite the fact that he was actually addressing Dylan.

'Yes. Thank you.'

Rob looked at Jamie. 'Hey, not just handsome but has manners too? What have you done to deserve this?'

They both smiled, and Jamie stood up holding out her hand to Dylan, and taking hold of the new football in its net.

'I hope you've enough energy for five?'

'I shall make sure I have.'

As they walked to the park, Rob said casually, 'I don't know whether I should talk to you about this, but since Amadea is your PA maybe you should know. She is in a bit of a state about her mother. Thinks her mother has become obsessed with this young gardener who came to do her hedges, or some such. I only mention it in case Amy brings it up at work, because I am actually looking after the young man, at the hospital.' Rob glanced at Jamie to see if he was boring her. Realising that she was more than interested, he went on, 'When I say I'm looking after him, I'm actually keeping a weather eye open, to see what happens to him. He's a bit of a strange creature, talks in riddles, and quotes bits and bobs from books. Sounds like Shakespeare. What happened was, he fell over in Amy's mother's kitchen, became concussed, and when he came round he appeared to have forgotten who he was. That's all we know at the moment, and I'm only telling you because I think, and don't tell Amy this, that her mother may be telling a porky about how he came to be in her house lying on her kitchen floor. I think there's more to it than that, so we really have to stand by for events.'

'I understand, but what a thing to happen! Let's hope he gets better, yes?'

Jamie threw back her head of thick, long, blond curls and sighed. It seemed that there was always something happening, every day something new and difficult; but on the other hand why wouldn't there be? Life was all about things happening.

'I wouldn't have mentioned it, but it occurred to me that since you two work so closely together, it might be helpful.'

'It is.'

They had reached the park, so Jamie let go of Dylan's hand, then took the football out of its string bag and placed it on the grass.

'Wow!'

Rob watched the ball Jamie had just belted rise curving into the air and land with a jolly bounce.

'Your mum is not just a pretty face,' he told Dylan, and then, catching up his hand, he and

81

the little boy ran after the black and white football.

Jamie followed them, keeping her distance, so that they would not think they had to include her in the game, because when all was said and done, enough was enough.

She stood watching them, smiling. Life was still happening, and not all of it was complicated.

★   ★   ★

Florence always admired Dottie's ability to carry her knitting under one arm, ready to start, the moment there was a slight pause in the proceedings. When Dottie got going, small indeterminate garments seemed to lengthen in front of Florence's eyes.

At this moment in time, Florence was sitting with her neighbour on her small patio watching the movement of the clouds, while wondering obsessively, over and over again, what she should do about John Smith.

'John Smith?' Dottie sniffed. 'Really, the young take some beating, don't they? Couldn't they think up something a *little* more original to call the poor young man?'

'I suppose it's better than giving him a number. And, after all, there are thousands of people called John Smith who are rightly proud of such a very English name.'

'Nonsense, stuff and nonsense, Florence. If a beautiful young man fell over in my kitchen I should insist on calling him something delightful, such as Edward Ardizzone or Titus Ogilvy, something like that — not *John Smith*. Poor chap, when he comes to and remembers what he's really called, he'll feel so grey and nondescript when he realises what they chose to christen him.'

'What do *you* think will happen to him, Dottie?' Florence asked, still staring up at the movement of the clouds above them.

'What do I think? I think he will probably get better, that's what I think, but you know me, optimism is my forte. It's the knitting, you know, always making things, keeping busy. And the alpacas of course, bless their defensive hearts. All these things, busy, busy, busy things, keep you optimistic. There's always tomorrow to look forward to when you're busy. It's just how it is. *Carpe diem* — ' As Florence stared at her she added, 'Live for the day? Something like that anyway.'

Florence nodded. 'I *thought* I was busy until I went to that hospital, Dottie.'

'And then?'

Dottie poured them both another cup of tea with her non-knitting hand.

'And then I realised, all those poor people, some of them through no fault of their own, they all needed someone, and this young man, he might need someone until his mother or someone finds him. I mean, perhaps it was meant when I found him in my cottage?'

'I thought you said he came to cut your hedges?'

'I lied, Dottie. I lied because I didn't want Amy to start bossing me around, or telling me

83

off. As it is she thinks I'm going daft.'

'Of course, only understandable.' And then, as Florence stared, 'No, no, only understandable not that she thinks you're daft, but that you don't want to be told off. No, no, quite right, Amy would start thinking you've gone round the twist if you told her you just found a young man in your guest cottage and took him in.'

Florence couldn't help noticing that Dottie was knitting at a much faster pace, so she knew that her friend too must be thinking that Florence was indeed daft.

'So, you found him in your cottage, and you asked him in for a coffee?'

Florence nodded, and at the same time her mouth went a little dry. The incident sounded so much worse now that Dottie was raking through it.

'Yes, I did. I took him in and I offered him breakfast, but only after I realised he was rather strange, talking in such an archaic kind of way, and at the same time — it seems a silly thing to say, but at the same time — he did seem very gentle.'

'How did you realise he was very, er — what did you say?'

'Gentle.'

'Why did you think he was gentle?'

Florence shrugged her shoulders. 'Well, because he was so gentle-looking, I suppose.' She turned increasingly panicked eyes on Dottie. 'You won't tell Amy, will you?'

'No, of course not,' Dottie reassured her, knitting even faster, her fingers now positively flying. 'I don't tell anyone anything any more, you know me. The only people I tell anything to nowadays are the bees. You have to tell your bees everything or they get very angry indeed. They pride themselves on getting the news first, really they do.'

Florence nodded, accepting Dottie's eccentricities possibly more easily than Dottie could accept that Florence hadn't elected to call the police when she had found a strange young man in her guest cottage.

'Alas, now I can't afford to give poor John Smith even a day or two in the Swinton Clinic, because of the dog-napping.' She reached down and patted Punch, who was making it his business not to leave her side.

'That was a close-run thing, Flo, truly it was.'

'I just hope they won't come back. The police say those sort of people never come back.'

'Well, we won't think about that now, will we,' Dottie stated in a firm tone. 'What we *can* think about is what to do about this John Smith. Why don't you just visit him in hospital?'

'Well, well . . . because I promised Amy I wouldn't, I suppose. And I did, I did promise her, but it was just when Punch had been napped, and I wasn't thinking straight.'

'Oh tishy toshy!' Dottie gave a robust laugh. 'Tishy toshy, and hang a bell on it while you're at it. Promised Amy, indeed! You don't have to be held to that, Florence Fontaine.'

'Oh but I do — I was in a bit of a state, well, more than a bit actually, but you know Amadea.'

'Yes, yes, of course I know Amadea, and a

fine-looking gel she is too; but as for keeping a promise you made in the heat of the moment, no, that's like that man who promised God to become a monk when he was frightened in a thunderstorm.' As she saw Florence trying not to look puzzled, she stopped knitting and clicked the fingers of one hand. 'Oh, you know, you know, that man. And then there was the play.'

There was a pause during which Florence was sure she could hear the wheels in Dottie's head turning faster and faster as she searched desperately for the right name. It was a regular occurrence.

'Luther! That's the man. Luther. That is what your promise to Amadea was like, it was just like Luther's promise. A promise made in the heat of the moment is not a promise, Flo dear. Truly it is not. Ask anyone. You had a gun held to your head. That kind of promise doesn't count.'

'Are you sure?'

Dottie frowned, once more searching for an answer; finally she came up with one.

'Of course I'm sure. Besides, Amadea never even fetched up for her birthday lunch, did she?' Dottie gave Florence a sly look.

'She wasn't feeling well . . . '

Dottie's knitting needles were once more clicking faster than ever, but the derisory snort she gave rose above the sound.

'She wasn't feeling well? That, translated into English, or Amadea-speak, means she had other fish to fry.'

'Oh well, you know the young . . . '

Dottie gave a wry laugh.

'Yes, dear, despite not having any children I know the young all right. And I can't help noticing that the moment I feel a bit dicky I suddenly seem to have more relatives under the age of thirty-five than Abraham himself!'

They both laughed and Dottie noticed with relief that Florence had a bit more colour in her cheeks. Poor woman, she had been through quite a lot in the last few days, and really none of it her fault. All right, not ringing the police when she found the young man was sort of natural since everyone knew that they never came out anyway. And all right, she should never have taken this unknown vagrant, or whatever he was, into her house and offered him breakfast, but no one could legislate for the poor chap falling over and hitting his head. And then to have Punch kidnapped for a ransom . . . The poor woman, it was enough to make anyone a little pale around the gills.

'Yes, but Dottie, what do you think will *really* happen to John Smith now?'

Florence couldn't help returning to her current obsession although she was aware that Dottie must have been hoping that they had finished with the subject of John Smith.

'Realistically, I think they'll toss him back on to the street, and hope for the best. Back where they reckon he belongs, I expect.'

'Do you think they think he's — what do the police call it? — a dosser?'

'Either that or he's a jogger who should have used sat nav.'

Florence laughed. 'But surely they won't just

send John Smith on his way without a memory?'

'Depends what they think is wrong with him, like that poor — '

'There must be other things that can be done, rather than just turning him out on to the street,' Florence hurriedly went on, because Dottie's vagaries were sometimes very difficult to follow, and at other times impossible.

'You said the police have already photographed him for the Missing Persons files?'

'But that's what I mean, supposing no one claims him?'

'I told you — I reckon he'll just be left to wander the streets.'

'The funny thing is he speaks perfect English,' Florence mused. 'Well, over-perfect really. As if he has learned it. And he speaks it in such a very old-fashioned way.'

Dottie made an understanding sort of noise, because she could not think what to say to this, and much as she loved Florence a large part of her wished that she would forget about the useless stranger and turn her thoughts to practical subjects such as whether or not she was going to sell her house, and what she was going to do with the rest of her life, because she was still a long way from three-score years and ten.

'You know what I think I should do, Dottie?'

Dottie looked up from her dropped stitch, only to find her heart sinking as she saw the look in Florence's eyes.

'I think I should bring John Smith here, to my house. Put him back in the guest cottage where he started. After all, it might bring back something, mightn't it?'

'I suppose . . . ' Dottie's fingers were flying once more as she tried not to look startled.

'Well, it could, couldn't it?' Florence enthused. 'It might help bring back to him who he is, and how he got here in the first place.'

'Very well. And then?'

'Well, then we could find his relatives and all that kind of thing. They could help him back to being all right again. After all, here is a kind of paradise, isn't it? At least we think it is, don't we? Nothing but quiet, and birdsong, no noise, no pollution. It is a kind of paradise here, isn't it?'

'It is indeed,' Dottie agreed robustly. 'But suppose he doesn't like the countryside? Not everyone does.'

'He must have liked something about it for him to have ended up in my little cottage, I should have thought.'

'Well, that's a point. But how will he come here if they've stuck him in St George's?'

All of a sudden Florence's eyes were shining with the thought of the adventure that might lie ahead of them.

'We'll go and get him, Dottie, that's how.'

'We?'

'Yes, Dottie, we. We will go and get him, and together we will bring him here.'

'But we'll need people to sign him off, or whatever they do in hospitals. And supposing he's dangerous? A murderer, or a rapist, or just quite mad?'

'I don't think he is, Dottie. Truly I don't. I just think it would be so terrible if such a beautiful young man was turned out on to the streets. He won't know where he is, or how to go on. Without money, or a name, what chance will he have? They might deport him by mistake, or bonk him on the head and sell his body for spare parts. Anything can happen nowadays.'

For the first time in what seemed to Florence to be years and years, even centuries, Dottie removed the knitting ball from under her arm, stuck both needles into it and placed it on the table in front of her.

'You're right,' she told Florence in a calm voice. 'We must bring him here. After all, what kind of people are we, if we don't?'

They both stood up. Florence's cheeks were now rosy, and the expression in her eyes so determined that Dottie, who knew her only too well, realised immediately that there would be no stopping her now; and what was more, she herself did not care to. They would not be able to live with themselves if they just dismissed the poor young man as being out of sight, out of mind.

'Henry always said, 'When in doubt, do *something* rather than nothing.' That was his motto in life.'

'And Henry was quite right. Now come inside and let's have a little drop of something stronger than tea.'

Florence followed Dottie inside her small farmhouse, which sat to the side of the Old Rectory. Dottie led her into her chintz-covered sitting room and poured them both a glass of red wine.

'*Le bon vin rouge*,' she said in a commendable French accent. '*Santé!*'

They raised their glasses to each other, then Dottie disappeared to the kitchen to fetch some nibbles. It was only a few years since Florence Fontaine had lost her husband, and all too soon after that her only son. It did not need a psychiatrist to tell her old friend why she was taking such an interest in this young man who had walked into her life from out of the blue.

Maybe something would come of it, something good. After all, good things did sometimes happen. She hurried back to her sitting room with a small flowered plate on which she had arranged a selection of home-made cheese nibbles.

'Flo dear, I made these this morning. Only tiny, but I think you will find they go nicely with the wine.'

★　★　★

As for Mr John Smith, he lay in hospital in a state of benign confusion, oblivious to the debates his unexplained presence was causing while mystified by his current predicament. When he was awake, he was not sure that he was, and yet this very insecurity made him more determined than ever not to return to his previous condition. Perhaps he was afraid that if he questioned his present state he might find himself somewhere he did not wish to be, in a condition he was vaguely coming to recognise as so negative that even to be as he was at that moment was preferable.

This time, however, he could not help noticing that there was a change in the light that he saw with his eyes. This time when the light faded he fell asleep. This had not been the case before, since the light had never changed — or rather, the dark had never become light.

There was another difference, and a most notable one. When he slept he dreamed, vivid, joyous dreams. In these dreams there was often someone with him, someone who filled him with a feeling he had not previously known. But when the light changed again, from darkness into brightness, he would awake reluctantly from his dream, and with a suffocating sadness realise that with his awakening all memories had vanished.

Then, too, strangers would come to his bedside to question him, but he had nothing to say to any of them, and he had no idea why they were there, since he had no recollection of anything helpful or relevant to his current situation. As he lay staring ahead of him, these strange, frightening and oddly dressed beings came and went, bending over him, talking at him, moving him, prodding him, sitting him up and turning him over, but it all meant nothing, because he was helpless to know why he was there, or who they were. What they did to him was as meaningless as the talking box with its flickering coloured picture in the corner of the room.

However, despite his confusion he had noticed one change; he had developed a feeling, a sense that became more acute as the dark time approached. As the light faded he noticed his pulse quickening. It was as if he *wanted* the darkness, as if the dark contained something for him, which it did, for as he fell asleep he saw quite clearly the image of someone he had once loved.

4

'I believe he *will* recover his memory,' Florence kept saying to Dottie, as they donned suitable outdoor clothing and climbed into Dottie's old Land Rover. 'He just needs lots of tender loving care, wouldn't you say?'

Dottie could not say what she really felt; she was far too kind. But because she herself also believed that good could come out of bad, she had convinced herself that a little bit of innocent excitement could lift Florence's spirits out of what must have been not just a slough of despond but a sea of despair. She had been trying to encourage Florence to embrace life before it ran her over and she ended up like some old barn, covered in moss and ivy. Perhaps this young man would be the catalyst.

They had prepared the guest cottage for John Smith, putting in clean towels and new soap, and turning down the bed upon which Florence had originally found him lying.

'I'll help you pay for him, of course,' Dottie told Florence. 'After all, an extra mouth to feed is no picnic, Flo.'

'Now, Dottie . . . '

'No, Flo, no 'Now, Dotties'.' She held up a firm hand as if she was a policeman stopping traffic. 'I mean it. You're a poor person and I'm not, and I know your pennies are a lot shorter than mine, and so no ifs or buts please. I know you are flat to the boards with the old doh ray mee.' They both climbed up into her much-loved noisy old Land Rover. 'Besides, I want to help, do you see? Makes a change from knitting, putting a young chap to rights. Makes a helluva change, I can tell you. I mean I'm very fond of the pugs and the bees and all the rest of them, all lovely people, but their conversation can be somewhat limited, believe me.'

Florence smiled her gratitude, silently accepting, while at the same time she found herself looking back at her house and hoping against hope that the dog-nappers would not visit while she herself was napping John Smith.

'It'll cost you a mint, anyway, putting him up,' Dottie went on matter-of-factly, as she started up the engine. 'Young men eat so much more than young women. Well, no, to put it another way — young women don't eat at all, and by contrast young men never stop. And if he does remain in this peculiar state, not knowing who or where he is, the whole adventure could end up costing you a small fortune.'

'He didn't exactly fall out of an aeroplane, Dottie.'

Dottie sighed as Florence turned her large, kind grey eyes on her, and they both laughed as Dottie swerved to avoid a pheasant.

'Not an aeroplane, no, Flo, but he could have fallen out of a lorry and forgotten to roll up in the accepted manner.'

'He is no criminal, that we do know.'

Florence stared calmly ahead at the now rain-sodden country road.

Dottie glanced at her passenger as the old car lurched past fields of grazing sheep, and trees bending and swaying in the light wind.

'Get on with you, Florence Fontaine. We know nothing of the sort, and you know it; and you also know — that's half the fun!'

★ ★ ★

Rob Greer was waiting for them in the smokers' hut in the hospital car park.

'Any longer and I'll be as high as a kite,' he joked. 'Nicotine doesn't half linger on the air. First time I've inhaled so much stale cigarette smoke in years,' he continued, as the two women came hurrying towards him. 'I'm afraid we'll have to move fast before the police catch up with us.'

'He's joking,' Dottie muttered to Florence, seeing the look on Florence's face. 'Doctors make jokes like that, it's self-defence, apparently. It certainly makes me feel defensive.'

They found John Smith sitting silently in an armchair in one corner of a shiningly white private room, the spring sunshine filtered to a tolerable shade of brightness by a Venetian blind. He was doing nothing: reading nothing, looking at nothing, listening to nothing. He was just sitting in a standard-issue hospital dressing gown over a pair of equally standard pyjamas. He looked very handsome but also very dead, so dead in fact that until Rob leaned over him to listen to his breathing Florence suspected he might actually *be* dead. Then she saw his eyes open, and he turned his luminous gaze upon her.

Florence smiled and went up to him and touched him lightly on the arm, while Dottie stood by the door, beginning to appreciate exactly why her friend should feel so protective towards this young man. He was what people used to call a *dish*.

'You knocked your head in my kitchen, do you remember that?' Florence asked.

He stared at her a little helplessly for a second, and then suddenly lay back in his chair and covered his face in what was now, to Rob, a familiar gesture. He remained like that for a few seconds, while Florence wondered what to say next, Rob wondered what had inspired Mrs Fontaine to want to take on someone in John Smith's condition, and Dottie wondered how long it would take before Florence realised she had bitten off more than she could chew.

'I don't live very far from here,' Florence heard herself saying. 'In fact as the crow flies — '

'Somehow you are familiar to me,' the young man interrupted her, frowning.

'That's good,' Dottie put in briskly, nodding to Rob. 'That's good, isn't it? If you can remember Mrs Fontaine here,' she went on, to John Smith, 'then maybe you will remember something else?'

'Why do you say that?' he wondered. 'What is it that I might recall? I do not understand your meaning.'

It was Dottie's turn to go up to him now. She stared at him suspiciously. She had a strong belief that liars always blinked, which meant that she now made a point of looking straight at him,

97

promising herself that if he blinked or looked away she would know he was a sham. He did neither.

'I was wondering whether you might have remembered your name?' Florence asked him.

'My name?' he interrupted. 'I cannot have forgotten my own name.'

'That's certainly the impression everyone seems to be under. You're booked in here as 'John Smith'. Everyone thinks you're a pop singer.' She paused, hoping this might somehow have prompted him to correct her, but he remained silent. 'I thought perhaps, since you seem to remember me . . . '

He shook his head, and this time it was Florence who found herself staring at him.

'I surely cannot have forgotten my own name?' he repeated.

'That is precisely what seems to have happened, young man, and the sooner you can remember it, the better we will all be, and that is certain,' Dottie told him, pulling the front of her cardigan together.

'Why, pray, do you look at me in that way, madam?' he asked, clasping both hands together under his chin in a prayer-like gesture. 'You look at me in such a quaint fashion.'

'Do I? I am sorry if it is disconcerting, please forgive me.'

'We are all looking at you in a funny way,' Florence told him, 'because we are all hoping that quite soon you will remember who you are.'

'It's relatively simple,' Rob told him. 'The reason you are here is that you had an accident when you were in this lady's kitchen, as she just told you.'

John Smith turned towards Florence. 'I was in your kitchen? Why — what are you? A cook perhaps? Why would I be in a kitchen talking to a cook?'

'No,' Florence returned, patiently. 'No, I'm not a cook and why you were in my kitchen — well, that's another story. What I'm trying to say is that the reason you don't remember any of this is because you banged your head. That's the whole point, you see. The doctors have been over this with you time and time again, but *because* you banged your head you don't remember your name. You don't remember that you and I have met — and that — '

'Forgive me, madam, but I fear you are wrong. Rather more correctly perhaps I should suggest to you that you do not exist, that you exist only in my mind. I imagine that I must be imagining you, and because I have imagined you, you are imagining me — in your own imaginings, imaginings that are only possible because I have imagined you in the first instance,' he ended, a note of triumph creeping into his voice as if what he had just said made perfect sense.

'I don't think that is necessarily so,' Dottie put in briskly, while at the same time trying to be as careful as she could not to upset someone who was so patently unstable.

'It is not necessarily so, I must agree.' He stopped her, holding up a long-fingered hand. 'Necessity has nothing to do with this. Allow me to explain for one moment and you may understand. I am in a reverie. This — all this — is not a reality. It is simply an imagining. A dream, if you will. Your dream, of which I am a reluctant part. Why, see the way you are dressed. See beyond this window. Enormous boxes on wheels, huge birds in the sky, thousands of people clothed in such strange and ugly garb, lights that shine like suns in the darkness. To you, because you are part of this unreality, these things are as they always are. These things are normal to you in your nightmare imaginings, but they are fresh to me for I have never seen such things; and because of this I am indeed certain that I dream. This must also, in some way, go to show why I have no name, and why I too am dressed in these strange garments: it is because none of this is real. None of this is in fact occurring; of that I am now sure. I say, I insist, this is your nightmare, into which you have drawn me. I am part of your nightmare. Soon you will wake up and I will have disappeared.'

For a moment Florence found that she almost believed him. It was as if everything within the room and without was just as he had described, distant and dreamlike, irrational and weird, until she remembered the philosophical puzzle with which Henry had loved to tease her.

Do we dream our dreams? Or do our dreams dream us?

His tease meant that she would often go to bed determined to dream, while at the same time wondering, puzzling, was she real, or was all her reality just a dream, herself a part of the dream that was being dreamed?

100

'Here we are all by day — ' Henry used to misquote. 'By night we are hurled by dreams — or are they the reality?'

As Florence found herself quoting these lines in answer to John Smith's meanderings, and Rob looked at his watch, determined on hurrying them all out of the hospital as soon as possible, the young man turned to Florence and, standing up, caught her by the hands.

'Robert Herrick,' he said quietly. 'I think that is who — Robert Herrick.'

'I don't understand. You've remembered your name is Robert Herrick?' Dottie asked, confused.

'Yes, yes, Robert Herrick, I think that is who.'

He gave them all a sudden and brilliant smile and started to pace the room, smacking one balled fist into one long-fingered open hand.

'Here we are all by day,' he declaimed. 'By night we are hurled by dreams — each one — each one into a sev'rall world! Robert Herrick! Ah-ha! I have remembered something. I am sure that is right.'

'I don't understand,' Dottie said again, watching him pace. 'Are you saying you're called Robert Herrick? Wasn't Robert Herrick some sort of a poet?'

'Some sort of poet? Robert Herrick was a genius. Herrick was a Master,' he said again, his face alight with the realisation that he had remembered the verse.

'Did you hear me quoting it? Was I quoting that out loud? I didn't realise I was actually saying anything out loud. It was on my mind, I suppose, because — because Henry, my husband, was forever quoting poetry.'

'I think that is from *Hesperides*,' the man said as if he hadn't heard her, turning away to stare at the blind-covered window. '*With something, something, something thousand such enchanting dreams, that meet/To make sleep not so sound, as sweet.*'

'You seem to be remembering quite a lot. This is good.'

Rob and the two women looked from one to the other excitedly.

'I hope to remember more, madam. Better that I have forgotten my own name than to forget the muse that drives us all.'

'Then maybe, if you can remember bits of verse like that, maybe this means your memory *is* coming back? What else do you remember?'

He turned and looked at Rob silently for a long moment. Then he closed his brilliant eyes and tilted his handsome head back.

'What I have remembered is who I am,' he said, in a very quiet voice. 'I have remembered that I too am — a poet.'

'So if you're a poet, do you sign yourself Anon?' Rob asked, eagerly. 'Is that why you can't remember your name, because you prefer not to have one? Do you prefer to remain anonymous?'

'Bring me a quill and some vellum, and I will write you anything you care to ask of me.'

Rob drew the two women aside.

'I think he may well be play-acting. In fact that makes me sure of it,' he whispered to them, before turning back to his patient.

102

'I'm afraid the National Health Service only do forms, and the odd biro — the very odd biro.'

'I can prove I am a poet! I think I have remembered that I am.'

Rob took Florence outside the room.

'Are you sure you want to take Robert Herrick home with you? You could be landing yourself in a difficult situation. He could bore you to death with his poetry!'

'You don't think he's dangerous, do you?'

'I am not a specialist, but not many of our patients go around demanding I bring them a quill and some vellum when they want to write something, Mrs Fontaine. As a matter of fact yesterday evening I lent him a pen, a Pentel actually, because he said he needed to scribble some lines.'

'And?'

'And he went into one of his 'what-is-that!' routines — you know . . . as if he'd never seen a pen before. I showed him how it worked,' Rob continued. 'We went through the whole procedure again, but soon enough it was back to 'Bring me a quill and some vellum.' '

'I see.' Florence persisted, 'So were you able finally to show him how to use the Pentel?'

'Sort of, but when I finished there was some more of the 'what-is-that!' routine. Then — and this seems to be the key — and then he finally accepted the pen as normal, because obviously it was all part of his *reverie*.'

'So you think this is his play-acting, or do you think he imagines he is in a dream? He really couldn't keep this up as play-acting — not for this long. Why would he? What would be the point?'

'Try free board and lodging? Great acting can often result in exactly that.'

'No. No, I really believe he thinks he's in some sort of dream. If he's lost all recollection of absolutely everything — I think that's only natural. You wake up and you have no memory. No memory of anything. Nothing of not just *who* you are but *what* you are, and who and what everything around you is. In a catatonic state of amnesia, which we have to suppose he is in, it would surely seem as if it was all imaginary.'

'I'd have thought if that was the case you'd need to be able to remember what a dream *was* . . . except I suppose the subconscious could still be working, cueing in key recognitions.' Rob paused, considering. 'You are awake. You are asleep. You are dreaming.'

While Florence was outside with Rob, Dottie had decided to do her bit to try to get the young man to snap out of whatever state he was in or, perhaps, pretending to be in.

She picked up a crumpled blank sheet of paper and studied it, turning it backwards and forwards.

'Has the muse failed to visit Mr Herrick?'

'The muse has deserted me.'

He sank down into his chair, and stared unseeingly in front of him as if all inspiration had vanished with his memory, his face a picture of despondency.

'I think you should allow yourself a little more

time, don't you? You are still suffering from amnesia . . . '

'Time is no friend to those whose inspiration has vanished, time is not a friend to anyone — no one embraces till the end of time, time takes all kisses, time takes all time, it eats itself; time is the victor, we the vanquished — '

'Amnesia means a loss of memory, not a loss of time,' Dottie told him in her brisk matronly voice, interrupting the dismal flow from the chair as she began to clear up the rest of the blank crumples. 'Look, I understand that this must be very difficult for you, because as Dr Greer says — '

'Forgive me, but what you say makes no sense. It has no import. It can have no effect on this, the present state of the matter. What shall occur to us is written in the stars. We are as sleepwalkers. The celestial powers laugh down at us — and why should they not? Seeing us as bees struggling in honey, doomed to drown in the sticky mess of our own creation.'

'That's one way of looking at it, I suppose,' Dottie agreed, dropping the last paper crumple in the waste basket, then, and for no reason she could think of, straightening up to run one hand down the front of her home-knitted cardigan to make sure that the buttons were all still done up.

As a matter of fact, what he had just said was so much against her own beliefs that if she had not felt understandably wary of doing so, she would have liked to argue with him.

'Talking of the destiny that shapes our ends — '

In response to this he gazed at her blankly.

' — people fall into two schools of thought about this subject,' Dottie continued firmly, 'as to whether or not we're controlled by our genetic structure emotionally as well as physically, or whether environment and self-determination are our metaphysical mentors. From what you have just said, it would sound as if you belong to the latter group — or perhaps an even older school of thought — the predestination thing, that everything we do or think is predestined, that we have no free will. That no matter what we do or choose to do, it's already taken care of. Whereas the way I feel — '

'The future lies not in our stars but in ourselves?' he wondered suddenly.

'*Julius Caesar!*'

'Shakespeare's Caesar?'

'I did *Julius Caesar* once. At school.'

He stared at her. 'You performed? In a *play?*'

'I was Mark Antony.'

Dottie again checked that the buttons of her cardigan were all done up, but for no better reason than that she felt oddly wrong-footed by her admission.

'No, my lady, you are a *lady*, you could never be an actress.' He gave her a suddenly deep look. 'You have too much of innocence about you to act in a play, to live outside the decent world, to travel from one town to the next, never resting, to end your days buried outside the perimeters, in ground that is not hallowed.'

'No, well, perhaps you're right.' She opened the door to the corridor outside. 'Look, I think if we are going we'd better do so this side of soonish, before he starts in on the quill and vellum routine again,' she told Florence in a lowered voice.

Rob and Florence returned to the room at once.

'I am willing to have you discharged,' Rob told John Smith. 'Mrs Fontaine is going to take you back to her house for rest and recuperation, following which you may well regain your memory.'

'I would like to return to my beautiful world,' he implored them.

They all stared at him.

'What sort of world was this?' Florence couldn't help herself asking, while Dottie sighed, thinking to herself that Flo had quite enough on her plate without asking more questions. They really should get going.

'A world more elegant than this, madam. A world full of grace and beauty — not this nightmare.'

'Look,' Dottie cut in. 'Where we're going to take you is better than here, truly. I can put my hand on my heart and tell you it is really beautiful. You'll like it as much as anything you have ever dreamed of,' she finished in a convincing tone, because that was one thing of which she was quite sure. Where Florence and she lived was quite beautiful, cut off from the rest of the world, a secret haven of which few people knew.

'If you'll excuse me, I have to do my ward rounds,' said Rob.

'Of course, of course.'

The two women hurried the young man out of the back entrance and into the car park. Rob closed the door behind them, shrugging his shoulders. He only hoped that John Smith was not going to prove too much of a handful for the women. One thing he knew, and that was that they had no idea what they were taking on, which was probably just as well.

* * *

Outside in the car park Florence and Dottie were encountering a strangely novel phenomenon as John Smith stared blearily at Dottie's old four-by-four before stepping into it.

'What, pray, is this — a horseless carriage?' he asked, swaying slightly.

Dottie raised her eyes to heaven. This was taking loony talk too far, even for her. But then, seeing the bewildered look in Florence's eyes, she too stepped into the car.

'Yes, that is exactly what it is, a horseless hackney carriage,' she offered, feeling silently grateful that Rob had given the patient a small shot of Valium.

'They all move without horses.' He stared out of the window. 'None of these carriages have *horses*.' He shook his head at the cars, nose to tail, the exhaust fumes, the rigid faces of the drivers, before murmuring faintly, 'This is hell.'

'You said it, love,' Dottie called back over her shoulder to him, trying to find an opening to turn into the endless line of traffic. 'You try driving in it!'

Moments later Florence was glad to see that the Valium had taken effect, for the patient had fallen fast asleep, his chin sunk onto his chest, his thick dark hair flopping forward in vaguely heroic style.

'Well, he is well and truly yours now, Flo,' Dottie announced, over the sound of Classic FM playing gently on her car radio.

'Not really mine, Dottie.' Florence stared out of the window. 'But I wonder that he has no family — a mother, someone, who will be missing him.'

'He may be orphaned, duckie. A lot of people are, you know. I was orphaned from an early age, which everyone thought was tragic, but when I see what trouble parents can make for their children, I find myself counting my blessings, really I do.'

'They put out photographs on these websites and suchlike,' Florence mused. 'Perhaps someone will see his.'

As Dottie drove out of Swinton it seemed she knew just why Florence's voice had become subdued.

'You're thinking about John Smith's mother, aren't you?'

'As a matter of fact, yes.' Florence shut her eyes for a moment. 'If she's alive she's probably imagining that he's dead, or has been in some terrible accident — not fallen over in someone's kitchen and lost his memory.'

'No point in putting yourself in her position.'

109

'No, I suppose not.'

'So what's next, Flo? Come on, you must have a plan?'

'My plan is to get home. And yours?'

'Precisely the same, love. Precisely the same.'

Unfortunately the traffic down to the South West was heavy, as it seemed to be all the year round now. In the event they finally arrived at the Old Rectory just as it was getting dark. The car breasted the last rise in the long gravel drive and both women were only too thankful that they had arrived back safely after what seemed to them now to have been a bit of an adventure.

The Old Rectory looked for all the world like a beautifully designed set for an eighteenth-century play: the full moon rising and lighting the fine old house, and the gardens where bats scavenged in the increasingly warm air, and owls swooped in silence on their prey, set about the house in careless cottage style, filled with the soft scents of early summer.

As Dottie's old car swayed and bumped up the pot-holed drive, a large dog fox stood momentarily caught in her headlights.

'Look at that so-and-so!'

Dottie drove hard at the fox, but the fox, unafraid, stared at them nonchalantly, his green eyes glinting, his long pink tongue hanging lasciviously out of one side of his mouth. Then he trotted casually away, to disappear, apparently unperturbed, into the shadows of the night.

'God, how I wish I had my gun!' Dottie stared after him in fury as Florence gaped at her.

'Oh Dottie, you couldn't shoot a fox, could you?'

'After what he did to my hens last month? I could take a cannon to him.'

'And I thought you were a pacifist?'

'I am until it comes to foxes,' Dottie growled.

Their passenger still seemed to be fast asleep as they eased him out of the back seat and towards the house.

'I think we should get him to bed, don't you?'

'Not much else we can do with him, except toss him in the lake.'

The two women draped John Smith's arms around their shoulders and made their way up to the house in necessarily slow fashion.

'If anyone saw us, heaven only knows what they would think,' Dottie went on, panting slightly as they finally reached the front door.

'Thank heavens he can at least walk a little, or we could never manage.'

'Do you think he can undress himself?' Dottie wondered. 'Or are you going to do it?'

Florence stared at her old friend. It was not something to which she had given any thought.

'Oh, I don't think that's necessary, do you, Dottie?'

'Well, at some point, Flo dear, he is going to have to have his clothes taken off him, but don't let's worry about that until the time comes.'

They walked slowly through the house, to the sound of Punch barking, and emerged in the back garden. They were actually at the door of the guest cottage before their patient started to wake up.

'Where am I?' he asked in a sleepy voice.

'You're home,' Florence told him.

He paused, opening his eyes wider, and taking his full weight on his feet, he straightened up, easing their burden.

'You're no lightweight, young man,' Dottie told him, panting and holding her sides. 'Really, you may be slim as a trivet, but bantamweight you are not.'

He did not seem very interested in the fact that they had both been shouldering him, but looked around him in the darkness, sniffing the air almost in the manner of a human hound, letting his nose tell him what other kinds of animals might be about.

'I have been here before,' he finally announced, peering into the darkness. 'Some time I have been here before, I know it. This is not a place without some kind of memory for me.'

Dottie sighed inwardly. Oh *dear*. Here we go again! She was increasingly afraid that Florence was having her wire quite firmly pulled.

'Yes, you have been here before.'

'And now you're here again, dear,' Dottie told him in a suddenly tired voice.

She was dying for a drink. It had been a long afternoon, and a little drop of tiddly at heaven knows what hour of the day or night it was would be more than welcome.

'You might remember the cottage, perhaps?' Florence prompted him, but the young man had flopped down on the bed, only to fall back fast asleep.

Dottie stared down at him thoughtfully.

'I think we should at least take his shoes off; and his trousers, Flo dear.'

'You're right, Dottie. David always used to say that waking up after a late night still in your clothes felt like some sort of terrible punishment.'

She smiled, remembering David's first hangover, the first time he wore black tie, the first time he was caught climbing in the kitchen window, his funny handsome face trying to assume an innocent expression.

'Yes, we should at least try to undress him, Flo,' Dottie agreed. 'It is going to be a bit of an exercise in diplomacy though, two older ladies undressing a handsome young man — let's hope the vicar doesn't burst in.'

They slipped the patient's clothes from him while keeping him diplomatically covered with a sheet.

'Gracious, that was so discreet.' Dottie straightened up, looking justifiably proud. 'I don't think a bunch of nuns could have done that more tactfully.'

They both looked down at their sleeping patient. After a few seconds Florence leaned forward to brush the hair from his forehead. They were about to leave the cottage when Florence turned back.

'Oh dear, Dottie, he hasn't cleaned his teeth.'

She looked momentarily mortified, while Dottie sighed over-dramatically.

'Cleaning his teeth is a bridge too far, Flo dear, really it is. I think we've done very well, considering,' Dottie said with some satisfaction as they gently closed the cottage door and negotiated the lawn back to the terrace and so into the house. 'I mean I can't think when I last undressed a man,' she went on. 'Well, I can as a matter of fact. It was in 1987 — when we were living at the farm. And it was Percy, dead drunk from a Farmers' Union meeting. His legs felt so heavy they could have been felled elms, really they could.'

Florence frowned, still thinking of the young man in the bed, for with his dark hair outlined on the clean white starched pillowslip she could not help feeling that he might have been David.

'I think we should give him a proper name, don't you, Dottie?'

'If you really want to . . . ' Dottie frowned, dreading what Florence might suggest.

'How about Edward — Edward — Green, say?'

'He looks quite like an Edward,' Dottie agreed. 'And Green is not too startling for a surname after all, is it?' she continued, feeling a great deal more the thing as she realised that the yard arm must have fallen, or was it the sun that had to move over it? At any rate she knew she could now look forward to mixing her evening drink.

Florence kissed Dottie goodnight by the front door, giving her a warm hug as she did so.

'You've been Trojan,' she told her old friend.

'I know,' Dottie agreed, before driving off a little too fast to her cottage as a dry martini seemed to be not beckoning but calling aloud to her.

What will be, will be, she told herself as she went through to the kitchen to wake up her pugs. All of them yawned, owl-eyed and still sleepy, reluctant to leave the warmth of the Rayburn for the cool of the outside.

While the pugs were moving busily around the bushes and flowers, Dottie herself hurried down to the bottom of the garden, determined, as always, on telling her bees the latest news.

'It is obvious that Florence has taken in this young man as some sort of replacement for her poor dead son, which could be disastrous. We must hope and pray that it is not.'

⋆　⋆　⋆

For her part, Florence stood on the step outside the French windows leading into her sitting room. Punch had heard her arrival and was barking, urging her to come and let him out, but she delayed for a moment, looking around her as if seeing everything for the first time, or as if, like some traveller returning home from abroad, she was only now able to appreciate the beauty of her surroundings. The moon had climbed ever higher in the sky, illuminating the countryside with a light of such brightness that there was hardly a part of her garden that she could not see. There was a young man asleep in her guest cottage. Life was both the same, and very different, which was good. She had needed it to be.

5

When the newly christened Edward Green awoke the next morning he felt completely at peace. He was lying on a crisp white linen sheet, beneath an equally crisp white bed covering of sorts. The room in which he lay was decorated in pale yellow colours, made more luminous by the rays of sunshine that were filtering through gently moving curtains. Outside he could hear birdsong: thrushes, blackbirds, all manner of birds. As he lay in the room with its bare polished floorboards and shuttered windows, he knew he was no longer in hell — and if not in heaven then at least in an adjunct of it, a sort of anteroom where moderate sinners might wait to be called to explain and then to atone for their various sins.

He had no desire to move. He knew time was passing because the direction of the light changed as the earth spun slowly in space. The curtains moved imperceptibly as the late spring breeze grew gradually calmer, and the warm sun began to penetrate the room further. As the morning aged, and the warmth grew to the heat of the day, so the birds muted their song, and the place where he lay fell to absolute quiet, eventually broken only by music, an instrument playing somewhere outside, a sweet sound like the song of the birds, confirming God's presence in the garden.

Entranced by the sound, he raised himself from his bed and went to the window to look down on to the gardens below. In a distant flower bed he could see a figure half hidden among the roses, identifiable only by the overlarge straw hat she was wearing. In the centre of a perfect sward of grass stood a fine, large apple tree. Sitting on a bench that encircled the tree, the dark-haired woman who had come to his rescue in the hospital was playing some sort of wind instrument, while at her feet, listening, looking, fascinated by everything around him, sat a small black and white sheepdog.

The musician was quite unaware of his presence, apparently enwrapped in the music she was making, while the other figure moved slowly among the flowers, removing deadheads and occasionally stopping to savour the scent of a particular bloom.

'Well, I must say, this is new.' Dottie turned to Florence, waving her secateurs appreciatively. 'How long since you played?'

'I know.' Florence shifted slightly in her garden chair, and stared ahead of her. It was difficult to explain to Dottie of all people why, now, after all this time, she had decided to take out her clarinet and play. It was as if she was a girl again, or as if David was still alive and they were about to play a duet together. 'I just felt like it, I suppose,' she said. 'Ridiculous isn't it? Do you mind?'

Dottie shook her head, frowning.

'Of course I don't mind, ducks. No, but I'm

impressed you still play so well. Mind you, you always did have an exquisite lightness of touch. Henry always said that.'

'Did he?' Florence looked surprised.

'Yes, he did. So I suppose it's all still there, somewhere, just waiting to be awoken, a bit like the garden in spring.' Dottie was staring at the flowers with a sudden dreamy look, her voice taking on a much lighter tone, so that Florence looked closely at her, but hardly had her tone changed than the expression on Dottie's face shut down once more. It had been only a fleeting moment, but for some reason it raised Florence's spirits, gave her hope that things *could* change, they might . . . she didn't know what — they just *might* change, they might all change, now that summer was coming.

'Music. It's a bit like riding a bicycle. Or getting back on a horse. It must be the same with painting,' said Dottie.

'Depends why you stopped in the first place.'

'Tell me more about this mysterious young man.'

'You know everything, Dottie.'

'I want to know more than everything.'

'I don't know any more than you do. I suppose I am just hoping that I can — we can — make him better.'

Dottie seemed to accept this. She turned her attention to the clematis she was cutting back.

'You used to paint as well as play, didn't you?'

They both knew why she had stopped.

'Yes, I did. But I was, am, only a Sunday

painter. I could never paint to order. I am an amateur.'

'I see,' Dottie agreed, seeming to acquire not just a new patience but a determination to try to understand. 'So since you can't paint to order, you won't paint at all, is that it?'

Florence sighed.

'I can't paint any more, Dottie. People always either laughed at my paintings or ignored them. And — after — you know, after, I haven't been able to go on. I just didn't have the energy. Besides — daubs, just amusing daubs, that is what most people thought of my paintings. They thought I was — what do they always say? Oh yes, they thought I was *churning out* another daub.'

Dottie frowned up at the clematis, towards which she was now feeling quite confrontational.

'So, the fact is you *haven't* been painting, not that you *can't*?'

Florence picked up her clarinet and prepared to play some more.

'In some funny way I think you mostly paint for someone else, to gain their approval, or something like that,' she said, frowning down at her fingers, which she had now arranged along the clarinet. 'And once they are gathered, well, the heart goes out of you and it all seems rather pointless.'

Dottie sighed inwardly. Florence was still an attractive woman, but the light that had shone from within, giving her the luminosity that is so necessary to a woman's beauty, seemed to have been extinguished when first her husband and then her son were gathered. Perhaps it was inevitable.

As to Florence herself, she wondered silently why it was so difficult to explain what was in one's heart. How could she explain to Dottie that, for years now, blue sky had seemed grey, red dresses offensively loud, and even the colour of the earth in her flower beds only drearily brown? She realised that the impulse to play had now faded, so she turned to put the clarinet away. As she did so, she saw a figure at the cottage window, standing in the morning sunshine, looking around him as if he did not quite know what to make of where he was.

'Good morning,' Florence called, as he left the window and opened the cottage door. 'I'm Florence, and you — you are Edward, I believe.'

'You are Florence?' he replied, astonished. 'And I am — *Edward*?'

'So I gather,' Florence told him with quiet authority. 'Did you sleep well? I think you must have done, seeing the time.'

'Thank you,' the newly christened Edward replied slowly. 'I slept very well. Indeed, it seems I have slept the sleep of the blessed.'

He blew on his hands one by one, an odd gesture.

'Have you done something to your hands?' Dottie asked, viewing his behaviour with immediate suspicion.

'The water in the faucets was *hot* — why was it hot?'

'You haven't scalded yourself, have you?'

'Nothing to cause distress.' He stood in the

doorway, gazing out at the garden. 'This is the most beautiful of mornings, a feast to both the soul and the eye, would you not agree?' he called to Dottie.

Dottie turned slowly from her snipping and pruning and smiled doubtfully, because it was immediately obvious to her that this poor young man must imagine that he was a poet.

'It's a simply lovely morning, yes,' Dottie agreed, adopting the kind of nursery voice that she hoped was appropriate when dealing with people who have lost whatever plot they might once have had.

Edward turned to Florence. 'Tell me, what corner of paradise is this?'

'Our corner of paradise,' she stated simply. 'Our house.'

'Of course. My father's house has many mansions.'

'I would hardly call this a mansion. Look — would you like me to get you something to eat, Edward?' Florence moved forward to steady him as she saw him lean against the doorframe.

'Forgive me,' Edward told her in a low voice. 'I feel I may faint, such is the exquisite nature of my feelings. To be in hell one moment then in heaven the very next is — as you may imagine — taxing in the extreme. Words cannot express the sensation.'

'Of course,' Florence replied. 'You've had quite a hard time of it. It's only natural for you to feel a little strange.'

Edward turned his large eyes on her, and the expression in them was so profoundly sad that it

121

was almost shocking.

'It was you and that lady, I remember now, who rescued me from the pit of hell. All those poor souls groaning in the darkness of that place as they tried to sleep, each one's bed set so close to another's there was hardly room to move between them.' He stopped for a moment. 'I know now, madam, that hell is not, as the Bible would have us believe, a place of flames and torment. It is infinitely more subtle, a place of such ugliness that those consigned to its tortures walk about as if already dead.'

His eyes widened.

'Perhaps you'd like a nice cold glass of lemonade?' Dottie asked, assuming a purposefully crisp voice.

'I'll fetch one. You sit down here with Edward, Dottie. I will fetch the lemonade, and something to eat. Edward must be ravenous.'

Florence took herself off to the kitchen, leaving Dottie to settle herself beside him.

'Well, well, well,' she said in a kindly voice. 'You've had a very bad time of it, but now you're here, with us, away from — what is it you call Swinton? Oh yes, the pit of hell — but now you are away from it and here with us, you must learn to relax. R and R is what is needed.' As he stared at her, she added helpfully, 'Rest and recuperation?'

'I do not understand you.'

'Well, very few people do. Hardly understand myself.'

Dottie patted him on the arm, realising as she did so that Florence was right: he was obviously a sweet and gentle chap, but right off his trolley, poor dear. She herself knew that delusions were inclined to fall into set categories, and that if Edward, as they were now calling him, had suffered some sort of trauma which in turn had caused his amnesia, it would have stayed with him right through his concussion, because a mental trauma was like a broken arm, and amnesia was like, say, a fever, and just because you were feverish did not mean that your arm mended itself.

After Florence had set a tray of lemonade and home-made biscuits in front of him, the two women walked up the garden a little way from where he was seated.

'We must try and *humour* him. I'm sure Dr Greer would agree that if we try and make the poor young man come to his senses — break the spell, as it were — we might harm him.'

'I agree,' Florence said, while not taking her eyes from him. 'I've left Punch inside on purpose because I suddenly thought he might not even like animals.'

Dottie stared at her. 'Flo. You've hit the nail on the head, but the wrong way round. We *should* bring Punch out here and see if he *can* cope. If he can, Punch will surely do him nothing but good.'

'He seems so awfully frightened of everything at the moment . . . '

'I'm a firm believer in animals bringing about cures. What about all those autistic children who start to talk once they are given an animal to look after? No, be brave, bring Punch out, and let's see what happens.'

Florence felt oddly touched by Dottie's enthusiasm.

'Do you really, truly think we should?' she asked, lowering her voice even more.

'You said a moment ago that he was frightened of everything. Let's start by seeing if he is frightened of young Punch, and work our way forward from there.'

'Dr Greer said he was frightened of television . . . '

'Well, that just shows good taste.'

'He doesn't care for the phone either, doesn't even know what it is.'

'So — no telly, no phone — perhaps we're actually looking at a truly sane person, Flo Love? Well, never mind that, eh? We'll put on the answering machine and we'll shove your telly away in a cupboard, and we'll take care to monitor the visitors. We don't want some idiot turning up unannounced and undoing all our good work. We will make everything as near to heaven as is humanly possible.'

Dottie smiled, because Florence's face had lit up, and she suddenly looked like a child about to play a brand new and exciting game, something they had never played before — which, now she came to think of it, they possibly were. They were both about to pretend that they were living in paradise, where happiness always ruled and nothing untoward ever happened.

'Do you think we really can create a sort of heaven for Edward?'

'Of course we can, ducks. Remember how

your Henry always said that was what this place was all about. And what are you smiling at now, pray?'

'Nothing. It's just quite exciting, that's all.'

Florence was actually smiling because she had suddenly realised that this was the first time she had seen Dottie go for twenty-four hours at a stretch without her knitting.

★   ★   ★

While Florence busied herself making lunch, Dottie sat down again beside Edward in the shade of the old apple tree. His borrowed shirt was open so that it was impossible not to appreciate his physique. Although it was not a modern physique — there were no large muscles shaped from constant working out — neverthe-less, lit by the warm sun now climbing high in the sky, he looked momentarily as if he had stepped out of a myth. Dottie thought it was not impossible to see him as some kind of hero returning from a mythical Greek odyssey.

'This is truly a heavenly morning,' he murmured.

'Of course,' Dottie replied, plunging her hands into her gardening apron and looking around her. 'What else did you expect in paradise?'

'Truly said. And do you know that when I awoke I even heard the sound of music?'

'Oh you did, did you? Well, that was Flo's idea. She wanted you to be woken by beautiful calming music.'

'It was exquisite.'

125

'Mozart does tend to be exquisite.'

'I do not know his work.'

'He was a bit of a boy wonder was our Mozart, bit of a fly-by-night, a ladies' man.' She smiled. 'But he wrote wonderful music.'

'So it would seem.'

'You mustn't concern yourself with such matters,' Dottie reassured him. 'You must just take each day as it comes.'

'I shall.'

Edward closed his eyes momentarily, only to open them again slowly, and it seemed to Dottie that he wanted to reassure himself that he was actually still where he was, that the garden of the Old Rectory, the apple tree, perhaps even Dottie herself seated near to him with her hands still stuck into her serge gardening apron, were none of them a mirage. It seemed to her too that Edward was already changing, a little of the rigidity gone from his body, his eyes less blank.

'Ah — swallows,' he said, gazing above him as half a dozen of the birds wheeled high in the skies. 'But then of course there would be swallows.'

'Yes, this is a paradise for birds. There's never been anything here to harm them, you know, no sprays or weedkillers, nothing like that.'

'Not even this dog?' he asked, as Florence re-emerged with Punch into the garden.

Punch immediately ran up to Edward barking, but when Edward, obviously unafraid, put out a hand to him, Punch stopped immediately and wagged his tail.

'You know all about dogs?' Dottie asked

126

Edward, and she nodded approvingly, at the same time raising her eyebrows at Florence as if to say, well, that's all right then.

Florence disappeared into the house to get on with preparing lunch.

'Do you . . . do you remember anything at all of — of your previous existence, Edward?'

Edward looked up from stroking Punch, and his eyes moved from Dottie's kind, clear-skinned, open face up to the skies and back again to the dog who was now sitting at his feet, leaning against his legs.

'I do remember waking in hell,' he said slowly and precisely. 'Although what took me there I do not know, and truly that is hell, I tell you, to be sentenced without knowing your crime. After that I know only that I was lost. I had no mind, no strength, no memory and no purpose, and around me was only death, corpses and death.'

'I see,' Dottie replied, breaking up a small piece of bread that she had found in her apron pocket and throwing it out to some blackbirds and thrushes who were keeping their distance, eyeing them with overt interest. 'And that's all you remember of recent events?'

'I would hardly describe them as events. No, it was a journey into the unknown, a place where there was no sense, no humanity, no reason. It was as if I was part of some terrifying vision, perhaps frozen in paint by some genius of another age, and yet this painting was alive.'

'I'm trying to imagine a little of what you have gone through.'

'Of course.' Edward nodded.

127

'Who exactly do you think I am, Edward?' Dottie asked, trying to make it sound as casual as possible.

'You are some sort of saint,' he said, his expression quite serious.

His speaking goodness made Dottie feel momentarily ashamed, before another, more disturbing thought occurred to her.

Supposing this person they all thought was damaged was actually playing a game on *them*? Suppose he was using the whole experience as some sort of weird research? He could well be a writer wanting to find out what would happen to someone nowadays who was cast away by society — not on some remote island in an ocean somewhere, but in the very midst of so-called civilisation. She was sure she had read of such cases.

Whatever the truth, Dottie resolved that from now on she would make sure she was on her guard, always watching for some sign of elaborate deceit, some sign that Edward was a fraud. Goodness knows, poor Florence had been through enough without being taken in by some cynical trickster out to make a quick buck. Worst of all would be if he ended up selling his story to a newspaper. How everyone would laugh at the ease with which Florence and Dottie had been deceived!

'So, now that your senses are beginning to return,' Dottie mused, trying to keep the tone light rather than inquisitive, 'what more do you remember? What I mean is, can you remember anything of what you do; or who exactly you are

— prior to — well, prior to . . . before, really,' she petered out lamely.

Edward frowned and the expression in his eyes changed as he tried to remember. 'I wish I could, but however hard I try . . . ' He shook his head. 'Nothing comes to me, except perhaps in sleep.'

'Very well. Now, what you have to remember is that the whole purpose of *this* place is for you to do exactly as you feel. If you feel like sleeping, you sleep.' Dottie looked round at him and, seeing that he was smiling, she shrugged her shoulders. 'I'm afraid nowadays it might be called 'chilling out'.'

'Chilling — out,' he repeated, considering. 'That, it seems to me, is an admirably fanciful phrase. To step out of the heat, to bask in the shadows of a tree as fine as this, to be warmed by the sun yet cooled by the shade. Yes, those are fine things. I will do as you say, I will chill out. Beginning, if you will allow, beginning with taking a sleep here under this magnificent tree.'

'And I shall fetch you a chair in which you may do so.'

'You will do no such thing. I shall carry the chair.'

After she had settled him in Henry's favourite steamer chair under the branches of the old apple tree, Dottie wandered back into the house to give Florence a hand with the lunch.

'I still can't get over you playing your clarinet this morning,' she said as they sat together chopping vegetables at the kitchen table.

'Don't make too much of it,' Florence said, looking up and smiling. 'I'm not about to take

129

up busking in Swinton, if that's what you think.'

'Henry always told me that you were far too talented to be a jobbing musician, let alone a busker.'

'I just thought it might help Edward.'

'Henry said when you were young your father wanted you to follow in his footsteps, but then . . . '

'Then I met Henry, and his career came before mine, and always would. He was a fine, fine musician, and I knew we couldn't both be away on gigs; particularly not once the children came along.'

'How anyone with such a gift as you possessed can just turn their back on it is beyond me. I can't even play 'The Trotting Pony'.'

''The Trotting Pony', now that is difficult, particularly the left hand.'

They both laughed, and soon the meal was prepared, but when they looked out into the garden and saw Edward and Punch both asleep under the old apple tree, they decided to put off lunch for another hour, while Dottie went home to feed her cat.

Florence walked with her down the long drive, stopping off by the lake, where she crossed the small stone bridge onto one of the islands to sit in her favourite spot underneath a willow tree. As she sat and watched the swallows swooping down for insects and water, she found herself wondering what exactly had inspired her to play her clarinet for the first time in what must be years.

She examined the morning's sequence of events.

She remembered very clearly that she had woken to a beautiful day, that she had felt lighter, and then the next thing she knew she was sitting on her bed with her clarinet case. She hardly remembered the act of opening the red silk-lined box even though she knew she must have done so, but she did remember cleaning it through with its special pyramid-shaped brush, choosing a new reed from the small ebony-coloured holder tucked in a pocket of the case, moistening it and fitting it into the mouthpiece. After that she had gone downstairs and sat in the kitchen with her clarinet on her lap. It was still only a quarter to seven of that lovely late spring morning when she started to sort out her music, shot through with a strange determination to play the piece that had caused her to fall in love with the clarinet in the first place.

So she had known exactly what she had wanted to play, but had not known why.

She supposed it must have been for Edward — poor young man — because why else would she have chosen to sit outside in the garden opposite his open bedroom window if it was not to bring him gently back to consciousness? That, and the fact that it had been the last piece she and David had played together.

She got up and walked quietly round the lake, watching the large mirrored carp swimming lazily among the thick reeds and bulrushes, and hearing the loud sucking noises they made as they fed, and remembering how the unheralded appearances of their big pink mouths across the surface of the water had always made David laugh. She had let the image remain buried, but now it came galloping back to his mother, and it was not alone — along with it came the sounds and the smell of the sea.

★ ★ ★

It all seemed so long ago, but in human terms it was only a few years. In the late summer following Henry's sudden death, they had gone on holiday, just the three of them, staying in a rented house, and for the whole month the weather had been glorious and the swimming and surfing exceptional. None of them, not Florence or David or Amadea, had wanted the holiday to end, until the weather changed abruptly and they were forced to endure three days of rain and wind. Finally, as the last suitcase was put in the car and the sun came out, Amadea had seen the chance for one last swim, not least because they would pass their favourite beach on the way home.

'Half an hour?' she had pleaded. 'An hour at the most? One last swim?'

With some reluctance Florence relented, deciding to follow suit and take a short swim herself.

There was a good sea running, with a full tide seemingly still well away from turning, and not many people on the beach because it was early in the day and the water was cold enough to deter the less determined swimmers. With the waves running high and fast they had several exhilarating runs before Florence and David called it a day. Amadea was following them. David had reached his mother when he saw her anxious face.

'Where's Amy going?' Florence asked, beginning to run back down the beach. 'She's gone back in.'

Now both of them looked, shading their eyes against the bright sun — which was when they saw Amadea, now far too far out to sea.

'Why did she go back?' Florence shouted. 'She knows we have to leave!' She was starting to panic. 'She must have got carried along by the tide! Or the current! What are we going to do?'

She turned back to see if there was anyone else on the beach.

'I'll go and get her!'

David was running down the beach as Florence raced over to another couple.

'Can you go and help him?'

The man had stood up and started to run towards the water, while all the time David was swimming strongly out towards Amadea.

'He can't manage by himself! Not in this sea!'

By this time Florence too was swimming out to them.

'Here! You're going to have to take her from here!' David yelled.

'Why?' Florence had shouted, taking hold of a now-petrified Amadea. 'I need you to help me! I can't manage by myself!'

'Go on! Go back!' he urged her, changing direction as he did so.

'Where are you going? What are you doing!'

'There's a boy in the water! And he's in trouble!'

Before Florence could protest any more David was gone, swimming as hard as he could towards another figure struggling about fifty yards away in the increasingly turbulent sea. There was nothing Florence could do except swim back-stroke as hard as she could, tugging Amadea behind her. As she left her gasping for breath on the beach, she turned back to the sea.

'Where's David?' she cried. 'I can't see him! I can't see David!'

All she could see, all anyone could see, was water, a wall of waves crashing down and sucking at the shore, the tide fast receding in a vicious turn. Florence began to run back into the waves but she was blinded by the spray, which was now being whipped off the sea by a direct headwind. Stumbling in the undertow, she fell over face down, struggling quickly to her feet with a throat full of salt water as she tried once more to get a sight of her missing son.

'David!' she yelled. 'David — where are you?'

A man ran up to her, his face stark with shock.

'My son!' Florence begged him.

'He went in after the girl, and then he went in after my kid. He held him up until I reached him, and then — and then . . . '

He stopped, collapsing on the sand.

'Where is he now?' Florence cried, dropping down beside the exhausted man. 'What hap-pened? Where is my *son*?'

She remembered shaking the man, who avoided her eyes, stumbling towards his wife who was cradling the rescued child in her arms. Florence remained where she was, her feet rooted in the shifting sands, desperately calling to David. But no one answered her calls, and all that could be heard was the sound of the waves rising and falling in increasing fury, while the sky darkened, and the wind whipped around her, as if it was determined to take Florence's cries and throw them to the far horizon where no one knew her, or cared who she was.

6

Because the house lay at the end of a long lane, a lane that in turn led off a minor country road, where it stood surrounded by undulating green fields, the first thing visitors would say was that they were sure they had come upon a small corner of paradise.

All that first morning Edward slept under the apple tree, and when he awoke it was only to take himself off for a leisurely stroll around the gardens, observing the wildlife and admiring the fine display of roses. Horses and cows were grazing in distant pastures, and apart from birdsong and the hum of the bees there wasn't a sound to break the spell. Wherever he looked, shading his eyes against the welcome sun, Edward's eye fell on beauty, and as he observed the delicate colours of the late spring flowers and inhaled their dizzy-making scents, or admired the magnificent trees that dominated the pastures, or observed the bright light sparkling on the still waters of the lake, he gave thanks to God for his redemption, knowing that he must indeed have sinned greatly to have spent time in such a hell as he remembered before he came to his present paradise.

Beyond that, his mind was still a total blank. He had started to accept it as some sort of punishment that had been visited upon him for a reason he had yet to discover.

He stopped in the shade of the fine chestnut tree that graced the paddock and sat down, leaning against the trunk.

'Is something wrong?' Florence wondered as she joined him on her way back up from the lake. 'When I left you, you seemed so happy. Has something upset you?'

'Only my fears.' He turned his startling eyes on Florence. 'It is not so much a fear as a knowledge.' He paused. 'I know that some time I shall be taken away from this place of peace and beauty, and while I realise that the awareness must serve to heighten my present happiness, it also makes me sad.'

'No one is going to make you go anywhere at the moment, truly they are not.'

He looked at her. 'You do not understand,' he protested, standing up. 'It will not be for you to decide what will happen to me.'

'I promise I will not let you be returned anywhere against your will.'

He shook his head. 'You are a woman, you can have no such power.'

Florence could almost hear Dottie's voice warning her that she might be getting in too deep, but it was too late now.

'Woman or not, I can and will promise you that. Now come back to the house. You will be better there.'

She walked him back to the terrace and settled him into a chair, before going to the kitchen, which was where Dottie found her some time later.

She frowned as she noticed Florence's anxious expression.

137

'I'm afraid Edward's taken a few steps back.'

'Why — what's the matter with him, poor soul?'

'He's started to get himself into a stew about having to leave here — '

'How ridiculous, he's hardly arrived. Besides, no one's going to send him back against his will, least of all you.'

Florence turned away, but Dottie caught her arm.

'Come on, Flo, tell Dottie. You're looking . . . let's say, a bit thoughtful?'

'I was miles away when you came in. I'm not really on the ball at the moment.'

Florence glanced at Dottie and then returned to staring into the middle distance, gazing at the view beyond the kitchen window, where the green of the grass seemed to be melting into the line of trees, and beyond that more fields, and Dottie's farmhouse, itself surrounded only by the horizon of the pale blue sky.

'I had a dream,' she finally confessed, and, as Dottie remained diplomatically silent, she went on. 'I haven't been dreaming much lately, which has been a blessing, I must say — but now . . . ' She stopped.

'Your nightmares have returned?'

Florence smiled. 'No, not exactly. I think what has happened is that taking this poor young man in, giving him a place to rest and recover, has awakened things I thought I would never ever dream about again.'

'This dream you had, was it a nice dream or a horrid nightmare?'

138

'It was nice, really.' Florence stood up suddenly and gazed across the lawns. 'I dreamed of Henry, and David, of course.'

Dottie sipped at her wine, careful not to look interested.

'Splendid man, your Henry,' she said eventually, avoiding any comment about David, because he had not been what anyone would call splendid so much as pretty perfect. David was one of those human beings who, when they are gathered, force everyone else to wonder why it could not have been them to have been taken rather than an angel such as David Fontaine.

'Funny thing is, if I had dreamed of Henry before, say a few months ago, I'd have found it — well, I'd have found it quite difficult. But today — now — I don't. I dreamed we were both young again, and it was — all right, and — we were all together, all of us, the whole family. And it was all right.' Florence knew that Dottie would know what she meant by that. She turned to her. 'Everything was fine.'

There was a short silence.

'You know Edward is not the only person who thinks this place is paradise, don't you?'

'It is particularly beautiful on days like this when the sun is shining — '

'Or when all the bluebells are out — '

'Or when the swallows first arrive — '

'Or when it snows — '

'Or at any other time,' Florence added with a smile. 'As a matter of fact something else occurred to me, as I was sitting here — first awake, then asleep and dreaming, and then awake again.'

'What occurred to you? Shall we sit for a minute?'

They both sat down and Florence dropped her voice, wanting to confide in Dottie but not wanting Edward to overhear.

'Well, I read this book recently. About Agatha Christie. How much do you know about Agatha Christie? Did you know about her famous disappearance?'

'I saw that film they made about it,' Dottie admitted, frowning because she could not quite see where this was going.

'This book was much, much better. Point is she said she was suffering from amnesia, and when her husband went to collect her in this hotel up north — she thought he was her brother. But she had no recollection of anything else at all. No idea of who she was or where she'd come from. Then someone had the idea of putting her under hypnosis, a proper qualified psychiatrist who practised hypnosis, and the truth came out. As well as her memory coming back.'

'Do you know anybody that fits the bill?'

'As a matter of fact I do. This friend of ours — well, he was more Henry's friend really, but he's a proper hypnotherapist. I just thought, I don't know why, I just thought he might be able to help.'

★ ★ ★

140

After they had all taken a leisurely stroll that evening, and Edward had retired to the cottage, Florence prepared for bed, only to be startled by a phone call from Amadea.

'Anything the matter?' she asked, glancing at the clock and trying not to sound worried.

'Just wanted to come and see you, that's all.'

'You sound upset.'

'I am upset, but I can't talk about it on the phone.'

Florence's grip on the telephone tightened as she instantly wondered if Rob Greer had told Amadea about Edward.

'It's a little difficult just now, Amy,' Florence stated, trying not to sound guarded.

'I don't want to stay or anything, I just want to chat.'

'Just call before you leave,' Florence suggested, finally giving in to the idea.

'Better still,' Amadea capped her, 'ring me before nine tomorrow morning if it *isn't* OK. OK?'

For some reason Florence forgot. Perhaps it was the extra mouth to feed, the eggs to be collected, everything and nothing, but the truth was she quite forgot until Dottie, who was keeping an eye on Edward, burst into the kitchen.

'Amadea's arrived,' she said. 'Wearing yellow!' she added inconsequentially, as if that made her arrival even less welcome. 'We must hide Edward.'

Florence dropped her carving knife back on the board.

'Don't worry, I'll deal with her, Dottie,' she said quickly. 'Edward's in the cottage, asleep. Lock the door, keep an eye on him, make sure he doesn't come out, could you?'

'I'll put my chair in front of the door like a Russian babushka.'

Dottie left at such a trot that it seemed to Florence she had never seen her friend move so fast in her flowered frock and cardigan — indeed, she looked for all the world like a large painted ornament come to life. Only seconds later Amadea was stepping elegantly across the gravel towards a visibly flustered Florence.

'Darling, what a — lovely, er — surprise.'

'It can't be that much of a surprise, Ma. I told you I was coming. You knew I was coming — I rang last night.' Amadea stared at Florence, who, standing in the drive and wiping her hands on her apron, found herself staring right back. 'I did, I told you I was coming,' Amadea insisted.

Florence kissed her warmly. 'I know, I know, all my fault; it seems I must have forgotten. Indeed, I had forgotten, but now I have remembered. How lovely to see you!'

'Mike and I have busted,' Amadea announced without more ado, shaking her head semi-tragically and gulping, while at the same time staring up at the summer sky through her sunglasses. 'He binned me.'

Florence opened her mouth to say something, but realising she could not find words to express the huge relief she felt on hearing Amadea's news, she quickly closed it again. No one except perhaps his mother and father, and Amy, had really liked Mike Brinton. Rich he might be, successful he might be, but sensitive and kind he most certainly was not. Unfortunately Amadea had been unable to see beyond his Porsche and his good looks.

'He only sent me a 'dear Amy', would you believe? After all this time, he wrote me a 'dear Amy'.'

'I'm really sorry, darling.'

Amadea stared at her mother for a few seconds, before starting to laugh.

'Good effort, Mrs Fontaine, but not good enough.' She sighed. 'You never really liked him, did you, Ma?'

'No, that's not true, Amy. I never really knew him.'

'Just as well, eh?' Despite her laughter, Amadea looked wan but resigned. 'Might I be allowed to come in for a minute?'

'Oh yes, yes, darling, of course.' Florence gave her a quick hug. 'I'm sorry I completely forgot you were coming.'

Amadea sighed. 'You're getting absent-minded. As it happens it doesn't matter because I'm not coming in for long. I only came by for a drink.' As she followed Florence into the house, she went on, 'Crispin up the road has asked me to dinner and to spend the night. All very above board, as his mother is staying too, but dinner with Crispin sounds just the right kind of treat to cheer a person up, especially when she's just been binned. That's me, not his mother.'

Florence poured a glass of wine. 'I have to

admit, Amy — now you mention it, I have to admit — '

But that was as far as she got, because Amadea interrupted her, sighing. 'I know you have to admit you didn't like Mike — wow, don't I wish those words didn't rhyme. Anyway, you reckon I'm well rid of him, I expect?'

'I'm really sorry you're hurt.'

'Oh, forget hurt, Ma — try humiliated.'

'It isn't fun, however it happens. Getting a kick in the teeth is never fun.'

Happily Florence was saved from anything further, because after drinking a glass of wine rather too quickly for her mother's liking, Amadea turned her attention to doing her lipstick and looking at a text message at the same time.

'Oh sugar! Hardly here and now got to go. That was Crispin. He wants me over straight away. 'Bye, Ma. Lovely to see you.'

Amadea whisked herself out of the kitchen, out of the hall and into her car, just in time to miss Dottie and Edward appearing equally suddenly from the garden. Florence turned at the sound of them, trying not to look flustered.

Dottie pointed at Edward's back. 'Big failure . . . could not stop you-know-who. He was desperate to come and find you,' she explained, shame-faced. 'For some reason he thought you had gone. I told him you were here. Told him over and over again but it was no use, he had to see for himself.'

Florence was still standing in the porch, nervously watching Amadea all too slowly

144

brushing her hair before putting her car into gear.

'Should you not tell that thing to go away?' Edward turned to Florence, an expression of unvarnished disgust on his face.

'We're obviously not a car man anyway,' Dottie observed.

Happily, perhaps at last satisfied with both lipstick and hair, Amadea drove off.

'There we are.' Florence nodded from the now-empty drive back to Edward.

'If you will excuse me,' he said, starting to move past her, 'I wish to take a walk.'

'No, Edward, it's not time for a walk.' Florence caught him by the arm. 'Much better to come and sit in the garden,' she told him firmly.

Dottie nodded vigorously in agreement. 'That's the ticket. Be a while before you can sashay all over the countryside on your own, young man. Now, my turn to make dinner, Flo, so off you go. Have a stroll in the garden while I cut up the pie and toss some salad and make some mayonnaise.'

Edward looked round, first at the guest cottage up the lawn where he had been found and then at the flowers and trees. He shook his head slowly while Florence watched him intently, as if he was a child taking his first steps, threatened by every sharp edge.

'I feel as if I am in a place where I should not be, and yet I never want to leave it,' he confessed.

'That's understandable.'

'What has happened to me? I can't remember

145

anything. Surely I should remember *something?*' he asked suddenly, sounding strangely normal.

Florence patted the old bench under the apple tree, inviting him to sit down, but he remained standing, looking around him with a lost expression on his face.

'There are no set rules for memory, selective or otherwise. Sometimes one remembers one thing, and other times — well, something comes shooting back. Memories can be brought back by all kinds of things — someone's hair colour, a much-loved book, a favourite tune. Those are the sort of things that bring back memories, sometimes most vividly, sometimes slowly, in a piecemeal kind of way, edging their way back,' Florence replied.

She was well aware that for her there was very little that did not bring back memories. Recently her whole life had seemed to be nothing but memories.

'But why don't you know about me already? Surely you should know if I am here in your house?'

'As I keep trying to explain to you, this place is only a beginning. This is . . . well, I'm not sure of the best way to describe it so that you understand what it means. Perhaps you should think of being here as like being a traveller, say, in a waiting room. Yes, you are in a pleasant kind of waiting room until you find out who you are — that might be a good way to approach everything, wouldn't you say?'

'I am in a waiting room, waiting to find someone.'

He pushed his hands through his long, dark hair and frowned down at Florence. It was not a petulant gesture, rather more a sign of concentration, as if he had just made a new determination.

'Does that seem too difficult?' she asked him.

As he nodded his head, an expression of misery in his eyes, Florence went to him and, taking his arm, walked him to the old wooden bench under the apple tree, from where he, in his turn, now stared up at her.

'I think, no, I *know* I have lost my reason,' he said with sudden authority, the timbre of his voice changing. 'I'm mad. My God! I am, I'm mad.' He spoke in a sober, dull voice, while at the same time Florence saw that the look he was giving her was frighteningly sane.

She maintained as muted an expression as possible, but it caught at her heart that Edward must now be coming to some sort of understanding of his situation.

'Oh dear, Edward. Why? Why do you think that?'

'If I am mad how can I possibly be expected to answer you?' he snapped.

'I think people who are so-called 'mad' are the last people to realise it. No one could be altogether mad and know that they were, could they?'

'I know something is wrong, something is terribly wrong with me. What is happening to me now makes no sense. If I am asleep and dreaming, then perhaps it is all a dream from which I will wake up. But if not? If I am awake then why do I know not who I am, or where I am?'

'I promise you, you're not asleep and dreaming. The only way you can be dreaming is if I don't exist, and you're dreaming me. But I do exist, that's a fact. This place exists, and because this place is real and I'm real, you must be real too.'

'But what I have seen, surely those things were not *real*? I know I've told you before that I have seen things of which I should have no knowledge, so they must be things I could not possibly imagine except in some sort of hallucination, sights from hell, as if in a painting. Then you brought me here.'

He sighed, as if he was suddenly released from terrible pain.

Florence felt touched by the panic she could see in his eyes, and yet she knew she must remain firm.

'You're going to be all right, Edward,' she assured him. 'If you can trust me to look after you, I promise you — you're going to be all right. There's no need to be afraid, really there isn't.'

He stared at her. 'Are you my mother perhaps? Is that why you brought me here, because I'm your son?' he asked, a mixture of hope and longing in his voice.

Florence shook her head. 'No, but I could be, and that is all that matters for the moment.'

★   ★   ★

Now seemed as good a time as any to put Edward in the hands of Henry's old friend Pierre

Lavalle, the hypnotherapist, but only after Florence had checked with Rob Greer.

'The thought had occurred to me, as a matter of fact, and right from the start. I'm not trying to queue-jump, but it did seem to be an obvious route. I said as much when he was in the clinic, but they're all into this drug therapy protocol now. They consider hypnosis old-fashioned, and because it isn't fashionable of course they bad-mouth it. They say it's unreliable because it allows autosuggestion by the patient and manipulation by the therapist.'

'I think they should keep fashion out of medicine.'

'Couldn't agree with you more, Mrs Fontaine. Speaking for myself, I hate holding consultations in my mini-skirt.'

Florence laughed. 'So it's all right if we proceed?'

'Fine, absolutely. You go ahead. Who knows what might be uncovered?'

⋆   ⋆   ⋆

Pierre turned up a few afternoons later, driving up to the Old Rectory in his ancient but immaculate Humber Super Snipe. Although the Humber was always in near-pristine condition, the same could not be said, alas, for its owner, who gave Florence the impression that he had parachuted into the garden. On this particular afternoon he was wearing white clothes: a long white linen overshirt, white linen trousers and yachting shoes. The fact that he was extremely

149

tall added to the startling impact he made as he stepped towards the house, his white hair sticking up in feathery plumes.

Florence greeted her old friend with a kiss, and a long, long hug, which immediately told Dottie that they had not seen each other since Henry's funeral. Then, taking him by the arm, she led him to the side gate and from there round the garden to explain as best she could the condition of the man he was about to examine.

Pierre listened intently, nodding all the while and saying very little, until Florence had finished.

'Interesting . . . ' Pierre paused. 'Very interesting, but I doubt very much that this is due solely to a bump on the head, although of course it does happen. In severe cases, a blow to the head can cause blindness, not memory loss. Sounds to me as if there must be another reason altogether for this poor fellow's memory loss, and let's just hope that a course of hypnosis will help unlock him. If, I say *if*, it works it can be like a door opening wide, or a gate, sometimes even a sluice gate — when released, the waters of memory literally gush through.'

While they were in the thick of their discussion, Dottie was doing her best to explain to Edward what was going to happen.

'This friend of Florence's, Pierre Lavalle, is coming to speak to you, to give you some reassurances. But he has to speak with you, not just *to* you, so we will leave you two together.' As Edward looked apprehensive, she went on. 'No, no, don't worry. You should trust him. He's a

150

nice man. He makes people more . . . ' Dottie paused. 'He makes them more *peaceful*. Whatever happens, I promise you will be much happier after you have talked to him.'

'I need peace, my peace I give unto you,' he murmured, looking ahead and frowning.

'That's the ticket,' Dottie agreed, also frowning and at the same time thinking that really, compared to human beings, animals were not at all complicated or difficult.

She had advised Florence to introduce Pierre to Edward outside. 'You know, like dogs, so much better to introduce them in the open air.'

So Pierre came out on to the lawn, and Dottie, seeing his white clothes, round cherubic face and shock of white hair, thought with approval that a mad person might easily have mistaken Pierre for a heavenly messenger. After a minute or two, patient and hypnotist disappeared together into the small study off the hall, both of them now seeming all too eager to talk, leaving Florence and Dottie to cross their fingers and hope for the best.

It was only a matter of minutes, once Pierre had settled his patient down and entertained him with some interesting talk about the hell Edward had experienced before arriving in paradise, before the hypnotist's new patient fell soundly and peacefully asleep on the sagging study sofa.

Pierre stared for a second at his startlingly handsome patient.

'You are fast asleep, Edward,' he said. 'You're in a deep, deep sleep and while you are in this sleep you are going to empty your head of all

151

your present memories, of everything that has happened to you right back to the time you fell and injured your head. Do you understand me?'

'I understand,' Edward replied, in a calm voice. 'I have no recollection of any such events.'

'That is good,' Pierre replied, checking the tape in his recorder and beginning to take his usual notes. 'So let us find out if you can remember who you are. What's your name? The name given to you at birth.'

'Edmund. My name is Edmund Percy Gains.'

'And what age are you, Edmund?'

'Thirty-three years and four months.'

'Where were you born?'

'Why, in London of course!' Edward laughed. 'I am surprised you have to ask me that.'

'I wonder why that should be?'

'Because of who I am, naturally. Is that not a good enough reason?'

'Because you are Edmund Gains.'

'Naturally I am Edmund Gains,' Edward agreed. 'I am the eldest son of Sir Roger Gains. Or to give my father his full title, Sir Roger de Gains. We are of Norman descent, the square-headed Normans and not the fair-headed Saxons.'

'Right. That is excellent. You're Edmund Gains, son of Sir Roger de Gains, and you were born in London just over thirty-three years ago — that would be in nineteen seventy-two.'

'Hardly.' Edmund frowned. 'That is an error of judgement on your part. Or just bad mathematics. How could I be born in the future? More than two hundred years from the day of

152

my birth? You cannot have realised what you were saying, because I was born on the twenty-ninth day of March, in the year of our Lord seventeen hundred and twenty-one.'

★   ★   ★

As Edward lay, still serenely hypnotised, on the study sofa, Punch stole in to see him, and promptly climbed onto the old couch and fell fast asleep at his feet. Meanwhile Pierre went in search of Florence and Dottie to report his findings. He found them enjoying the afternoon sunshine out on the terrace.

'This has all the hallmarks of a classic case,' Pierre began. 'Although to my mind no two cases can ever be the same, it is a classic case in the sense that the patient is in what's called a mental regression. This is when the mind imagines itself to be back in time, and the patient along with it. It's a syndrome we come up against regularly, one that leads patients to believe that they have lived a previous life when in fact what the mind is experiencing is an enormous déjà vu.

'When we've had a déjà vu it's very difficult not to believe that we have actually lived through an experience before, even though our rational side tells us this is not possible. When we have a déjà vu, a part of our brain suffers a time delay — a microsecond, that's all it needs and all it takes, just enough for the part of the brain that sees things to be just that microsecond ahead of the part of the brain

153

that *identifies* the things that we are seeing.

'It is purely a matter of being out of synchronisation. One part of our brain is just a fraction behind the other parts, for who knows what reason? Fatigue? Heat? Or perhaps some trauma? Anything you like. And so here we have the same thing in this sort of patient, only on a much, much larger scale. The patient is convinced he has lived before and can give a minute account of that life, down to the smallest detail sometimes.'

'How can that be, though?' Dottie wondered. 'How can they know a previous life in detail if they haven't actually lived it?'

'Good question, but believe me it's possible. They can have absorbed things, things they've heard or read or been told and forgotten all about — usually things heard in childhood, small fragments of disconnected facts and histories that the subconscious mind starts to put together as a whole. It starts to make a story out of it, create a character, someone who remains locked away somewhere in the patient's brain, until for some reason or other these fragments become a whole, and the patient becomes this other person. Sometimes they only become this other person at certain times, as in a form of schizophrenia. Edward/Edmund is possibly the former type of patient; over the years his brain has collected and collated all this information and turned it into the character he believes he is under hypnosis. Furthermore, I imagine this belief may well have been triggered by a blow to the head. In most of the cases I deal with, the patients have no idea of this other personality and are apparently in full possession of their memories and their mental faculties when properly awake, although this is not the case here.'

'It seems to make sense to me,' Dottie said happily. 'Makes me feel quite jealous, as a matter of fact. I wouldn't mind thinking I was the Empress Josephine or Elizabeth the First for a short time. Could be quite exciting.'

'But — but, say, in the case of Agatha Christie, Pierre, she wasn't in full possession of her faculties when she was awake, was she?' Florence asked. 'I mean she'd no idea who she was. It was only under hypnosis that the truth came out and her memory returned. There was no imaginary other person — well, there was, but it was someone known to her. Her husband's mistress, wasn't it? She believed she was her husband's mistress, her former best friend.'

'I take the point, Florence, but it is demonstrably the same syndrome. It just so happened that Agatha Christie's person was a real person, someone she had sublimated, or wanted to become in order to make her first husband love her again. I don't think Edmund Gains is a real person, not for a minute, but for some reason he's a real person to our Edward, someone he has buried away in his subconscious, perhaps someone he read about in a book when he was a child, or a person of his own invention, someone he would rather have been. Of course it's early days yet, and I'm sure we're going to discover much more about his invention,

155

Edmund Gains, as the time passes. I'm sure we shall discover who the real Edward is and why indeed he wants to pass himself off as this fellow Edmund Gains. It could be something in his childhood. It almost invariably is. We'll probably find his father or his mother wanted from him the one thing he could not give them. Or that his father or his mother did one thing, and he had wished for them to do another. We all shut our lives away in a series of mental cupboards, do you see? And what people like me have to do is find the keys and open up all the doors.'

'I still don't quite follow, Pierre,' Florence persisted. 'When Edward's awake, he's in confusion. He has no idea of who he is, or where. The people you're talking about seem to be leading perfectly normal lives, and then regress back to their fantasy lives only under hypnosis. Is that what you are saying?'

'Straightforward cases do present themselves like that. Obviously with Edward we have a complication, and that is the amnesia. That's what makes this case more difficult, but basically it's the same syndrome, and I feel sure that after such a good and fruitful start we'll very soon reveal the real Edward — rather than this eighteenth-century poet fellow he imagines he is.'

'He thinks he's an eighteenth-century poet? Is that why he perked up when Florence quoted poetry to him in his hospital room?'

'If that is what happened, it would make sense.' Pierre turned to his briefcase and took out his notebook again and scribbled in it. 'He

156

imagines, it seems, that he is a poet of some repute, named Edmund Gains, born in March seventeen hundred and twenty-one.'

'Good heavens,' Florence said quietly, looking up into the skies above. 'How extraordinary! That must be why, when we chanced upon poetry, he really came alive for the first time. To tell you the truth, with the weird way he talked when I found him — I thought he must be on something, or just . . . well, mad really.'

'Only understandable, but the detail of these 'memories' is really quite remarkable, you know. I can never get over the way the mind absorbs all these things. Quite extraordinary. I will call again in two days.' He turned at Florence's front door. 'For the moment I have to tell you that I am quite excited, truly I am. If we could get this young man to refind his true persona, Florence, our living will definitely not have been in vain.'

Florence and Dottie saw him to his car. It was only when they were inside the house again that Florence came to a sudden halt.

'How do we wake him up again? Oh dear, Dottie, I forgot to ask Pierre!'

She fled out into the drive again.

* * *

Jamie stared at her home help, who was looking both embarrassed and confused.

'How long has he been like this?'

She shook her head doubtfully. 'I dunno. He was fine one minute and the next — well, he started to look all queer. Said he could see things

157

on the walls, things crawling on the walls.'

Jamie's hand dialling the doctor's number shook so much that she had to restart it twice.

'It's Jamie Charlbury, 34 Beanacre Square, yes, Swinton, yes. It's my son, Dylan. He has a very high temperature, over a hundred and three. I was out, but when I got in the help told me he had been like this for some time.' She paused, listening. 'No one can come out? I see . . . Bring him in? But — but I can't, he's delirious, quite obviously delirious . . . How do I know? He keeps complaining that white rats are crawling up his blankets. But — but you still want me to bring him in? Very well . . . I see. No, thank you. No.'

Jamie replaced the phone. Oh God, oh God, she couldn't move him, she couldn't take him in, more than that, she *wouldn't* take him in. She tried to think what to do next, then picked up the phone again.

'Could I speak to Dr Greer, please?'

'You can, and you are.'

'Oh Rob, I'm so sorry to call you. It's Jamie. I am so sorry, but are you very busy?'

'I'm so busy I can't tell you, I have just finished shaving and I'm exhausted. No, just kidding, I'm at home, Jamie. I have a few hours off. Why? Want to go for a Starbucks?'

'No, I want your opinion, Rob. It's Dylan. He's really ill, the surgery insists that I bring him in, but I don't want to move him, in case . . . I mean I don't know what it is, he keeps saying he can see white rats on his bed . . . '

Rob was round at the flat in a minute. He took

158

one look at Dylan, felt his forehead and started to wrap him up in a blanket.

'We must take him to St George's. I'll get him seen to at once,' he told Jamie in a low voice.

'What do you think it could be, Rob?'

'Could be all sorts of things. But we don't want to take risks with young Dylan, do we? I'll drive you both.'

'Is it — could it be . . . ?'

Rob shook his head, knowing what she was thinking.

'We won't go there, Jamie. What we will do is go straight to St George's. Time is of the essence with children. As we both know, they get sick quickly, and happily they recover quickly.'

He carried Dylan down the stairs and out to his car, and Jamie followed him. Her mind had gone on hold, as if it was frozen, and she seemed to be seeing them both from above, something that had happened to her once or twice before, like when she said goodbye to Josh at the airport, or when she had to tell her mother she was expecting Dylan — moments like that.

What would happen if Dylan died? She would have nothing to live for, nothing at all. He was her whole world; more than that, he was the reason she had not allowed her heart to break when his father left and went to Africa.

★   ★   ★

Still Edward remembered nothing. He remembered nothing from his past and, just as Pierre had told Florence and Dottie, he remembered

159

nothing of the hypnotherapy session, not even meeting Pierre and going to the library with him. When he had been under hypnosis, Pierre had persuaded him that when he came to, the last thing he would remember would be sitting in the garden, and that was exactly what had happened: he found himself back sitting in the sunshine under the apple tree, as if he had drifted to sleep in the dappled comfort of its shade.

'I am becoming more and more intrigued,' Pierre told Florence as she walked him to his car for the second time. 'Edward is hanging on to Edmund and he's certainly very tenacious as far as this other persona goes, but something he said made me think that we might be going to succeed.'

'Are we allowed to know?' Florence ventured. 'Or would that break patient confidentiality?'

'Yes, it would, and no, you are not. Just cross your fingers — hard, because it could all become quite exciting.' He stopped, looking round at the old house, the charm of the gardens, the soft English light. 'You know, I have many cases brought to me but none as complicated and — well, I can only say romantic as this. A man loses his memory and believes he is not just someone else but someone very interesting, and not only that — '

'Yes, go on!'

'No, I mustn't tell you. It would spoil it for all of us, and make it difficult for you too.'

'I *can* keep a secret, Pierre.'

Pierre smiled. 'No one can keep a secret,

Florence. Everyone tells just one other person. Besides, a secret is a burdensome thing, God wot.'

'Gracious, Pierre!' Florence gave a light laugh and touched him on the arm. 'You are beginning to sound just like Edward! It must be catching.'

This time they both laughed, and a minute or two later Pierre drove off. Florence watched the car disappearing. There was something about cars leaving your house, the tail lights receding, the occasionally waving hand, that made you feel both peaceful and at the same time unaccountably sad, and just at that moment Florence felt both. Perhaps it was because a part of her wanted Edward to stay as Edmund? Did a part of her wish for him to go on thinking that he was in paradise with her and Dottie as his friends? Perhaps it was because this lost young man brought back memories of her own loss; not Henry but David. She had always accepted that he would not come back to her; what she could not accept was that she would never see him again, in some other place.

Edward was different. Perhaps because of an over-powerful imagination, he seemed determined to return as Edmund Gains — a long-dead poet; which, while not exactly an example of madness, was certainly strange. She sat down in her old rattan chair and Punch planted himself beside her, so that she could stroke him. It was one of Punch's most charming attributes that he knew when someone needed him.

Did John Smith alias Edward alias Edmund

Gains simply arrive out of the blue? And if so, why? Was it because he had become so sure that he was this poet of long ago that on the anniversary of, say, his death he had been determined to find out more? And in so doing had he somehow lost all his original identity?

Florence stared ahead disbelievingly, before deciding to take a bath and change her clothes for supper. Thank God Dottie had gone home or she might have been tempted to talk it all over with her, and that would have been fatal. As it was, she knew Pierre was becoming more and more excited by his sessions, so she knew there would be more news, news that might clash with her own ideas or news that might discredit everything, most of all Edward. He might, after all, be a fake — a jolly good one, but a fake nonetheless. Indeed, everyone knew that some people would go to any lengths to attract attention. In order to cope with their mental problems, some would set about injuring their bodies. Perhaps taking on someone else's identity might just be a cry for help?

★   ★   ★

'He's still this chap Edmund Gains,' Florence told Dottie in a voice that she was struggling to keep from sounding sadly resigned. They were sitting in the kitchen finishing up their lunch. 'In fact it seems to me that he's more convinced than ever that's who he is. Pierre told me yesterday that he himself is finding it hard not to believe Edward *is* Edmund, so convincing is he

162

under hypnosis. Apparently it's the details into which he goes — you know, such things as Herrick having terrible taste in clothes, and everyone teasing him about a pair of yellow stockings that make him look like a cockscomb.'

'This is getting a bit spooky, Flo, don't you think? Might we be thinking of stopping soon?'

'Do you think we should, Dottie?'

Dottie thought for a moment. 'Gracious no,' she said stoutly. 'We are made of sterner stuff, aren't we? We fight on till the last, of course we do. Mustn't give up before the finishing line.'

★ ★ ★

Now he was involved, Pierre was more than ever determined to pursue his own line of enquiry.

'Now then, Edmund,' he said to his patient a few mornings later. 'Tell me about your reputation. You told me in an earlier conversation that you enjoyed a certain degree of fame. Can you remind me? I've got a bit rusty about poets and their works — in your time.'

Edward, his eyes closed, smiled. 'When I say considerable repute, it is, to be sure, a somewhat idle boast,' he replied. 'But my jest is born out of a desire to impress, because I dare suppose I am not as famous as I would like. I'm not famous in a way of which I could boast — like that jackanapes Tom Gray, or some such rhymers as Robert Herrick — but I am already of some renown, believe me, albeit in much smaller circles. I am most fortunate to have a fine and generous patron in Lord Harlington, a man of

163

letters and a connoisseur of the arts, unlike the poor Hanoverian — '

'George the Second.'

'Alas, that wretched Act of Settlement, how much it churned our innards, how it gave us meat for revolution!' Edward gave a huge sigh. 'If only Queen Anne's son had *lived*.'

'This patron of yours, Edmund, is he someone you like?' Pierre continued, gently prompting.

'I have had several patrons, but my favourite is Lord Harlington, a man of singular distinction. His munificence towards the artist is known to all, as are the great gatherings at his houses. I am most fortunate in that it has fallen to me to be his private poet, a position I am honoured to have held since he heard me reading my verses. My lord is not, however, a fop; he worships women with all the passion that I reserve for my poetry. I live only for my verses. Live only to enchant my lord and his coterie, to make magic in their ears as they sip their wine and eye the women.'

'You write poetry only for Lord Harlington?'

'He has an iron hand on the back of my breeches now that I live on his estate and versify only for his delight, and that of his family. But he is a good master, unique and engaging, and since his estates are many, I enjoy blessed solitude, until such times as there are solemn occasions, when my lord will request me to write in celebration, or in dolour. Naturally, since I am like all versifiers a knave at heart, I will also write on occasion to please him. Such pleasantries as sonnets to Lord Harlington's favourite horse, not to mention his many dogs. And then of course there are, for his private eye only, poems praising certain delicate attributes of the fair companions that have pleased him.'

'But there is still time left for you to pursue the muse?'

'Most certainly or I should not stay. Besides the blessed peace of the estate, I am well paid, well housed and well fed. I am free to compose my own verses whenever I so desire, and I do desire. There is nothing I desire more than to compose one line — just one line — that might linger on after my passing. However light, however gossamer, to have a line pass into the blessed language that is English, the native flower of our tongues, heady with the music of our ancestors, delicate in meaning, in sound as blessed as the green of our meadows.'

'Are there many who think and feel as you do?'

'Never more so — not just in my own opinion, but in the view of others. England has the finest poets in all Europe, and we are assured a welcome wherever we go ... '

'I'd love to hear some of your verse.'

'I am flattered, sir,' Edward replied after a slight pause. 'But my situation at the moment is not ideal.'

'Couldn't you be persuaded to recite just a few lines? One couplet perhaps?'

Edward sighed and leaned his head back as if considering the notion.

'No,' he replied finally. 'I'm working on a new

165

ode at this very time, but it is still rough and unformed. Besides, I am not sure whether I shall even complete it. It has a tone more melancholy than my normal voice.

> *'My soul sighs — and a heavy torpor hurts*
> *My heart, as though of Lethe I had drunk.'*

There was a long pause.
'You wrote that, Edmund?'
'I did indeed, sir. I wrote it, one heady summer afternoon, in the grotto at Lord Harlington's house, overlooking the lake. The birds were singing, the bees humming, and around me was a sight that was very heaven.'
Pierre gazed round the room. No need to note down those few lines anyway.

''*My soul sighs — and a heavy torpor hurts . . .*'''
'Gracious, it sounds just like 'Ode to a Nightingale',' Dottie said drily, her heart sinking, because this surely proved their Edward, or Edmund as he liked to call himself when hypnotised, was a fraud, if not both a plagiarist and a fraud.
'Keats's working title was apparently 'Ode to a Songbird'.'
'How does it start exactly?' Florence frowned.'
'O for a beaker full of the warm South', isn't it? Then

> *'My heart aches, and a drowsy numbness pains*
> *My sense, as though of hemlock I had drunk.'*

166

Pierre corrected her. 'That's the opening stanza.'

They all stared at each other for a second, wondering exactly what this meant. Florence was the first to break the silence.

'You think Edward's subconscious has been plundering Keats and that he's imagining he wrote this?'

Pierre looked thoughtful. 'It is perfectly possible.'

'Or it could all be part of his imagined persona, the persona that has taken on Edmund Gains, and Keats's poetry?'

'All I know is that I am talking to Edward who in deep hypnosis has revealed that he *thinks* he's this poet chap.'

'For the sake of argument,' Florence continued, 'suppose he does take on the mantle of Edmund, because he may or may not have boned up on him at some time and become obsessed by him, etc., etc. What this session has revealed is that, in Edward's mind, *Edmund* wrote that poem first.'

Pierre gave Florence a wry look. 'So Keats was a plagiarist?'

They all laughed.

'No, Pierre, not necessarily so. But he might have heard or read this other poet earlier, and to put it politely — been, let us say, *inspired* by it.'

'Much more likely Edward in his fanciful imaginings vaguely remembers Keats's poem and approximates it in his subconscious, I am afraid.'

'I agree with Pierre, Florence. I don't think that young Keats had any need to go pilfering.'

'I'm not saying that he did, but it just might be — if Edmund Gains was a real person — ' Florence began again, before coming to an abrupt halt.

'No, no.' Pierre's tone was kindly. 'We're not dealing with some magical case of re-creation here, just a simple run-of-the-mill regression. I would guess that Edward's a well-educated fellow, a chap who'd have read Keats. Keats was, and still is, very much the sort of poet to stick in the heads of romantic young men, and Keats was and is very quotable, particularly 'Ode to a Nightingale'. Although people usually suppose 'O for a beaker full of the warm South' to come from one of the other odes — the 'Ode on a Grecian Urn'. But I digress.'

'No matter, but alas, you don't seem to be getting very much further, do you?'

'As a matter of fact I think we're making pretty big strides here,' Dottie put in.

'But you haven't yet advanced him from his state of total amnesia. Mentally he's just as blacked out as ever. I'd have thought that after this many sessions he'd have started to recollect *something* about his real self — who he really is.'

'Good point. I hadn't really considered that yet. But you're right — I've been too intrigued by the amount of detail this chap has about his brilliant alter ego. But as I have said before, I don't think I've ever come up against a case history with quite so much highly detailed information.'

'Was he married?' Florence asked suddenly.

'As Edmund, that is. I mean, was. Was. *Was* Edmund married?'

'I haven't come across a wife so far, but there doesn't seem much mention of a woman in his life. I should be quite surprised if there is one. He seems almost sexless.'

Florence turned to Dottie as they were seeing Pierre off.

'What is that expression Amadea's always using — oh, I know. Yes. *As if.*'

'Oh,' Dottie groaned, 'I do rather hate that, really I do. But — as if *what* exactly, Flo?'

'As if a young man as beautiful as that wouldn't have women in his life! What a perfectly ridiculous notion.'

Pierre had started to close his car door, and then pushed it open and climbed out again.

'Oh, by the way, I forgot to tell you — Edmund Gains. According to Edward, he not only lived in London, apparently he also came to live near here, very near here in fact.' As Florence and Dottie drew nearer he added, 'Harlington Hall ring a bell? The National Trust have just reopened it to the public, I hear.'

Florence stared at him, remembering that Pierre had only recently moved to the area.

'Have we heard of it? Harlington Hall is only a few miles away. You can walk to it from my side gate, the paths lead up through the fields and woods.'

'Forgive me, I am spatially agnostic, never know where I am until I've arrived and someone says, 'Hallo, Pierre.''

'This is so exciting, that he mentioned

169

Harlington Hall,' Florence insisted, and she put her hands on top of her head as children do when they are surprised, or thoughtful. 'It is just so exciting.'

Pierre drove off, well pleased with the reactions to his discovery, as Dottie followed her friend back into the house.

Florence had changed over the last few days. Not just her voice now seemed to have a much lighter note to it, but her step too — even that seemed lighter. Dottie watched her face as Florence clicked her fingers sharply, as Pierre had taught them to do to bring Edward back, but only after they had led him to his favourite seat under the old apple tree.

Perhaps it was fanciful, but to Dottie it was as if God, or Henry, or David himself, had sent this young man to Florence to take David's place for a few days, or weeks, or however long it might be. Whatever the reason, it was jolly good while it lasted and she was as caught up in all the excitement as anyone.

'You know we're not going to be able to keep young Amy in the dark for very much longer,' she told Florence as they walked down the drive to Dottie's cottage.

'No.' Florence smiled at her, all of a sudden looking young and mischievous. 'No, of course not, but best not to involve her before we have to, don't you think?'

They both laughed and parted from each other in high good humour.

7

Jamie stared at Rob. 'What are you telling me?'

'I am telling you it is a virus.'

'And?'

'Nothing can be done. You can do nothing for a virus, nothing works, not antibiotics — nothing, as you know.'

'Could it be meningitis?'

'He has some symptoms but not all, so no.'

Jamie sank down on the bench outside the ward, as Rob went to the coffee machine. She spent so much time dealing in certainties at work, and now she realised just how difficult it was for her to deal in such uncertainties as an unknown and untreatable virus.

Rob gave her a coffee. 'My stepmother calls this wartime coffee — it's warm and it's wet, but not much else.'

'You must tell me, has his temperature gone up even more, Rob?'

'No,' Rob lied. 'As you know, temperatures mean nothing more than that his body is fighting the infection.' He paused. 'I must stop saying 'as you know'.'

'I do know that a very high temperature can cause damage to brain tissue.'

'Look, don't let's go there.' Rob put an arm round Jamie's shoulders. 'I know Dylan's going to get better because I won't let him do anything else, so that's all *you* need to know.'

171

'How do you know?'

'Because — I just do. Dylan has to get better, for you, because he loves his mum. So he will.'

But Dylan didn't get better, and his temperature rose so alarmingly that even Rob's paediatrician friend Luke Petrie started to look white to the lips.

'We're all doing what we can, Ms Charlbury, believe me. I've been on the phone to my colleague at St Edward's in London, and we are really putting our heads together. Why we can't bring his temperature down, I don't know.'

After twenty-four hours of such anxiety Jamie had the look of someone who had been sleeping rough. Rob's heart ached for her, and once he was on duty again he went regularly to the children's ward, always hoping, hoping against hope, that the news about the little boy would soon be better, because that was all you *could* do with a virus.

When he was off duty for a few hours and back at his flat, his stepmother rang.

'How's your friend's little boy, Rob?'

'He's been better, let's put it that way.'

'Can I visit?'

'You don't know Jamie and Dylan.'

Rob's stepmother sounded tolerant if impatient when she replied after a beat, 'I asked you, can I visit him, Rob? Not whether I can get to know him.'

Rob hesitated, and then, remembering Jamie's distraught face, he relented. 'I don't see why not. Yes, of course. Of course you can.'

He replaced the telephone and after a bite to

eat and a bottle of beer drunk from the neck, he returned to the hospital, the children's ward, and Jamie. He beckoned to her.

'Would you mind if my stepmother visited Dylan, Jamie?'

Jamie stared at him as Rob tried not to look embarrassed.

'She'll only sit with him. But she will need to be alone, can't have anyone else in the room.'

'They've said no visitors.'

'Mmm, I know, but since it's my stepmum, I think they will give her a pass.'

Jamie nodded dumbly. She had stopped seeing everything as if photographed from on high, and now felt as if everyone was speaking to her from the top of a mountain.

'Of course, let her come. But she mustn't disturb him.'

'Oh, she won't disturb him,' Rob reassured her. 'Far from it. She'll just sit with him quite, quite still. That's what she does, that's all she does.'

Jamie nodded, intent only on returning to Dylan's bedside, while Rob went outside the hospital to ring his stepmother on his mobile.

'Will nothing bring his temperature down? Can't you do anything?' Jamie asked, stopping one of the nurses for what must be the hundredth time, but she only smiled and hurried on. As far as Jamie was concerned, she might as well have shrugged her shoulders.

Less than an hour later a slim, white-haired woman wearing cool linen clothes and carrying a large houseplant emerged from the lifts. Walking with a brisk light step and accompanied by Rob, she went straight up to Jamie and introduced herself.

'You don't know me, Jamie, I am Teresa Greer, Rob's stepmother.' The expression on her lightly tanned face was one of calm rather than anxiety.

Jamie saw her, heard her, but such was her fear for her son that the words seemed to have no meaning. It was almost as if she had forgotten that Rob had said his stepmother might visit Dylan.

'You are Rob's stepmother,' she heard herself repeating. 'Rob's stepmother,' she said again.

'Yes, he said that you might allow me to visit Dylan.'

'Dylan is very ill. He should have no visitors.'

'I will do nothing more than sit with him.'

Jamie came to suddenly. Hell, she didn't know anything about Rob Greer's stepmother; she might be a madwoman intent on harming Dylan.

'Are you sure you're Rob's stepmother? What I mean is, how can I be sure that you are Rob's stepmother?'

'Because here is Rob.' The woman gestured. 'Here is Rob, and he will tell you who I am. I am Teresa Greer, your stepmother, am I not, Rob?'

Rob nodded and, taking Jamie aside, he said, 'I promise you that my stepmother will do nothing more than sit beside Dylan for a few minutes, perhaps ten at the most, and I will stay with you, here, while she's with him. It will do no harm, might do some good.'

Jamie nodded. 'If you think — ' she muttered. 'If you think I should, then let her sit with him, but only for a few minutes.'

He looked at his mother and nodded. 'Sit down,' he said to Jamie, and put his arm around her shoulders. 'Sit down and wait here,' he repeated. 'She will just sit with him, that's all. I promise you — that is all she will do.'

Such was her state, Jamie was hardly aware that Rob had his arm around her; she merely stared at the door of the room where Dylan had been put in temporary isolation. For some reason she found herself gazing up at the clock on the wall opposite them. It was a plain white hospital clock, a clock that ticked silently, its red second hand seeming to move more slowly than any clock in front of which she had ever sat.

'Why doesn't she come out?' She turned to Rob sounding angry, even to herself. 'Why doesn't she come out now? She has been in there at least five minutes.' She pointed up at the clock. 'Too long!' She stood up. 'I'm going in there. I'm going to tell her to come out.'

Rob put a restraining hand on her arm. 'Just give her a few more minutes,' he begged. 'Really. Just a few more minutes.'

'Yes, but what is she doing in there? Why does she want to be in there? This is ridiculous, I am going to go in and get her out! What possible good could your stepmother do, any more than my own mother?'

She stopped, realising she had not even told her mother.

'Please, just give her a few more minutes.'

'No.' Jamie shook her blond curls. 'No, I will not leave her in there with Dylan. I'm sorry,

175

Rob. I know nothing about your stepmother and not much more about you, now I come to think about it, except you're a friend of Amadea Fontaine's. That's all I know about any of you.'

She started to tear herself from Rob's restraining hand.

'Please,' Rob went on begging. 'Just let her have a few more minutes.'

He looked at Jamie, and realising that fury was mixed with her panic, he said reluctantly, 'I suppose I should have told you, Jamie — my stepmother is a healer.'

'A *what*?'

'A healer. My stepmother, Teresa Greer, is a healer.'

Jamie stared at him. 'You are a *doctor*, Rob, and you believe in *healing*?'

'It is *because* I am a doctor that I believe in healing.'

'But you — you can't.'

'Why not?'

'Because you're a fully qualified doctor, just as I am a genetic scientist. We believe in medical science, not healing.' Jamie stopped, realising that what she was saying sounded absurd. 'You know what I mean.'

'Yes, I do, but I also believe in using *everything* to help people get better, so long as it has no side effects. Healing does no harm. Sometimes it works. I've seen it work.' As Jamie still stared up at him, he repeated, 'I believe in every single form of healing. I believe we must help patients every way we can.' He stopped as

176

he saw Teresa coming out of Dylan's room. 'And here is my stepmum now, so you can relax. See, I told you she wouldn't be very long.'

He smiled with sudden pride as he saw his stepmother, and with relief, as he took in what she had in her hands.

Teresa Greer stood in front of Jamie. She was still holding the house plant she had brought with her to the hospital, but with a radical difference: now the plant was dead.

'You can go in,' she told Jamie. 'He's fine.' Jamie stared from her to the collapsed plant. 'Dylan has had a virus, and now I'm happy to say the plant has it.'

She said goodbye to Rob and started to walk off.

'But, but — ' Jamie hurried after her. 'But is he better?'

Teresa turned and smiled at her. 'Put it this way, I should be very surprised if one small boy won't be going home with his mum very, very soon, Jamie.'

★   ★   ★

With each of Pierre's visits Edward seemed to be less frightened that he was going to be sent away from the Old Rectory. It was as if the hypnotherapy was calming him, as if by letting his secondary personality loose under hypnosis Pierre was calming the unknown submerged personality.

This particular morning he seemed happy to accompany Florence down to the lakeside studio which Henry had built for her, many years before.

'Are you sure you want to come?'

He nodded happily.

'I am going to sort through some paintings in the little studio over there,' she said, pointing to the other side of the small lake.

It was the first time she had done such a thing since Henry's death, and even as she began to sift through a set of her drawings she wondered what had inspired her to cross this emotional Rubicon. But it seemed she was not to be given the time to find an answer, for she suddenly got the feeling that she was being watched intently. Turning round, she found Edward, his expression hovering between despair and longing.

'Who is this man? He is, I think, an artist. Are these his paintings?'

He was staring at a portrait of Henry that Florence had painted many years before when the studio had first been built. It showed a thoughtful, kind man, full of tolerant humour.

'He was an artist. He was a musician, but he . . . ' Florence hesitated, not wanting to mention death in case it upset Edward. 'But he is no longer with us,' she volunteered finally.

'He has now passed on to a better place.' Edward nodded. 'If there is one.' He stared at the paintings and drawings, lifting them up and examining them carefully. 'He was a fine artist with beautiful line and strong, vigorous execution. I should have liked to meet this artist,' he continued. 'I like this work. It is noble and beautiful, and beauty excites me in such a way that I feel I could love this person as a friend, if only because he loves God's world so much.'

'God's beautiful world that we are intent on destroying . . . ' Florence muttered, half to herself.

Edward lifted one of the paintings and turned it towards Florence. It was a painting of the house and a much wilder, less tamed garden. A painting like the portrait of Henry, executed long, long ago when Florence was first married. It was a painting from when she and Henry had spent days, weeks and months undisturbed by anything more than his practising for a concert tour, while she painted. Long ago days when they had sat together, holding hands and listening for the first sounds of summer, waiting for the arrival of the first ducklings making their brave way across the grass to the lake, watching for the small black moorhen chicks with their bright beaks to dart in and out of the reeds.

'You have tears in your eyes — you are unhappy.'

Florence shook her head and turned away from the sudden, really rather sane anxiety she could see in Edward's eyes.

'Far from it. Quite the opposite, as it happens.'

★　★　★

Florence Simpson had been a talented musician when she met Henry Fontaine, but from the moment he dated her she knew that her life would be his life. It was not fashionable, it was not modern, but it was a fact: nothing else

179

mattered to her except Henry, and that was how it would be. Happily she was not the only one. Henry knew that his life would be hers too. As is normal when two people, however likely or unlikely, fall in love, no one approved of Florence marrying Henry. She was too young for him, not intellectually up to him, would prove a menace to his already successful concert career; or she might put her career before his, or influence him in the wrong way, quarrel with his manager or disagree with his repertoire — Henry's friends told each other with disinterested complacency, before sitting back to watch their predictions come true.

Florence's friends, on the other hand, thought Henry far too old for her. They saw at once, and with blinding certainty, that the age gap would be too great, that he would be old before she was even middle-aged, that he would become tiresome, take over her career, probably force her to give up her music, make her have children, domesticate her against her will. Altogether Henry Fontaine was not what they would choose for their divinely funny, light-hearted, free-spirited Florence.

Of course everyone, from both sides, was completely right.

Henry and Florence were not at all suited to each other. He *was* too old for Florence Simpson, and she *was* too flighty for Henry Fontaine. Everyone was right, and everyone was wrong, for the truth is that when two people love each other, wrong or right seems hardly to

180

matter; all that matters is that they do love each other.

Florence's parents having died when she was quite small, and her grandfather when she was a teenager, she was led up the aisle by Henry's best friend and manager, Dick Saxon, the man whom Henry's friends and relations were convinced would be the first she would remove from her new husband's life.

Far from wishing to lessen Dick's influence over Henry, Florence set about making him their best friend, godfather to their children, and a constant in their life. To the day Henry died, despite Dick having long ago retired from being his manager, he remained their best friend — charming, kind and intent on being there only when needed.

'You are proving them all wrong,' he once said to Florence, his voice grave, his tone purposefully pompous, and all the while Florence could see that behind his thick, horn-rimmed glasses his eyes were twinkling with a more than slightly cynical appreciation at the truly unexpected turn of events. 'All the knockers have been proved wrong. What you and Henry have, few people enjoy, and that being so it is best to do as you do and not let the barbarians in. Keep them at bay, beyond the gates. They'll only seek to destroy what you have, take away little bits of you, put about rumours which are untrue, but which you can't deny because you have no idea what they are. No, if you are happy, stay alone, and consider the rest of the world well lost, and that includes me.'

Perhaps because she was younger than both Dick and Henry, Florence took his words very much to heart, and set about making their lives at the Old Rectory as private as possible. She devoted herself to their happiness. She soon found her hands full, for with Henry away on tour for weeks at a time, it was up to her to take responsibility for so much; and yet when he came home she had to make sure to hand over the reins to him quickly, as though he had been there all the time, so that he would still feel part of the place.

So, quite naturally, it came about that they lived their lives on a constant high of expectancy. Either Florence was expecting Henry home at any minute, or, with heavy heart, she would find herself waving him off on yet another tour; but with their children away at weekly boarding school, during their precious weeks together they could love each other whenever they wished, pretending they were quite alone in a world of their own making, which in so many ways they were.

They shared a mutual love of animals, nature and art, which meant that it was not long before Henry had built Florence her little studio over-looking the lake, and not long again before, at his prompting, they both took up painting, only for Henry to give it up.

'You gave up your music for me, so now I will have to give up my brilliant painting future for you,' he said, pretending to pull a long face.

It is always impossible to believe that two people can make each other happy, and stay that way. Impossible because no one can prove happiness, any more than they can prove love, but the truth was that Henry and Florence had made each other completely happy.

* * *

'Dylan better then?' Amadea asked.

'He is on the mend, thank goodness. Turned the corner, but not quite out of the woods yet.'

Amadea looked round as Sheila Pryor came into the room. She smiled her best smile at Jamie's boss, knowing that this was not a conversation she should be overhearing, but not quite knowing how to get off the telephone.

'Oh, good. Jamie? I'll ring you later.'

Sheila, smart as new paint, slim and supercilious, because there was no point in being Sheila Pryor if you were not all of those things, gave Amadea a long look, allowing a well-judged pause to elapse before she spoke.

'What was it then, what did Jamie's baby have?'

'Child, actually, he is a child. He had a virus, Sheila, a nasty virus, but he is getting better.'

'A virus.' Sheila sighed elaborately. 'When isn't it a virus?' she asked. 'Either on screen or off?'

'This friend of mine, Rob Greer, was wonderful apparently, quite wonderful. I can't tell you how, because you will think I'm a sandwich short of a picnic,' Amadea went on, busking it, because she could see from Sheila's steely gaze that Jamie's continuing absence was as popular with Ms Pryor as a broken fingernail.

183

'The work is piling up, you know, Amadea.'

'Yes, I know, Sheila. Jamie has been off message for the past few days.'

'Off message? Thirty-two emails unanswered? I call that off the wall, Amadea. Psemisis is not heartless, but competition is such that the oil well of goodwill can run dry when it comes to absenteeism.'

'Jamie calls me several times a day. She's regularly in touch.' Amadea tried to look nonchalant, but knew she had succeeded only in looking guilty.

'There will have to be some sort of hurry-up scheduled p.d.q. Psemisis Europe is about to descend on us, and that has not happened since I joined in the early noughties, believe me. We are on red alert, Amadea, and we could do without absences due to viruses. I need all that recent data to be in place yesterday, do you understand?'

'In place soonest, Sheila.'

Amadea had never thought she would be thankful for the tidy desks policy at Psemisis, but at that moment she was only too glad of it, for without it Sheila Pryor would have seen exactly how much work had actually piled up, and it would not have been a pretty sight.

She glanced up at the clock. It was nearly lunchtime. A good excuse to call round and see Jamie, who seemed to have gone on hold since her little boy fell sick. Knowing that all calls at Psemisis were recorded, and all emails were networked to a main computer, she went outside with her mobile to ring Jamie and warn her she was coming round after office hours. There were certain matters to which she needed urgently to attend.

★ ★ ★

As soon as the door opened, Amadea was struck by how different Jamie's flat was to her own. Not pale grey and white, not duck-egg blue and grey, not spare, no stones beautifully arranged, only baskets of toys, bright red curtains, Scandinavian rugs, and shelves full of children's books.

'Hi, Amy, come in, come in.'

Jamie stood aside and Amadea walked in, with the look of someone who had just stepped out of a lift into a world of which she had no previous knowledge, and where she might not be able to make herself understood. She tried to seem unhurried and unfussed, and then, realising that she had failed, quickly made up for it by thrusting a large basket of flowers at Jamie.

'Had to call round and bring Dylan something, not to mention Dylan's mum, of course.'

'You shouldn't have, but I'm awfully glad you did.' Jamie put the basket on the coffee table. 'Come in and see the patient for yourself. He's a bit weak still, but someone you know is reading to him.'

Amadea tiptoed into the room indicated, a brightly painted, cheerful room with trains on the curtains and covers, and a large teddy bear seated on a chair in one corner. Seated on the bed was someone really rather familiar.

185

'Dr Rob Greer, I presume?'

Rob smiled in his usual relaxed manner and, holding a finger to his lips, he pointed to the little boy under the covers.

'We're nearly off to sleep,' he whispered.

'No, I'm not,' came a voice from the bed, and they both smiled. 'I want *James the Red Engine* now, please.'

Rob pointed to a small child's chair. 'Sit in the Noddy chair,' he commanded Amadea, 'and prepare to be enthralled.'

Amadea sat down, almost obediently, and before long she was reluctantly hearing of James the Red Engine's adventures. Even so, as Rob embarked on yet another story of a railway engine, she couldn't help feeling that Jamie had somehow stolen Rob from her. Rob was her friend and neighbour, not Jamie's friend and neighbour. She hadn't said a word about Rob to her, nothing about having made such friends with Rob that she could call on him when Dylan was sick. Now it seemed that he had become some kind of surrogate father.

She frowned. She liked Jamie. She liked Rob, so it was good, wasn't it? Two people she really liked becoming good friends, perhaps even something more? Of course it was. It was good. She was glad for both of them. Of course she was, she was really glad.

'I say, Rob, much as I want to hear about Henry the Green Engine, I have a very important date at the wine bar. Ta-ra. Night, Dylan! Night, Jamie. See you at the office asap, yes?'

★ ★ ★

When Jamie finally arrived back in the office a couple of days later, Amadea was at pains to bring up the matter of her friendship with Rob Greer, if only to demonstrate how pleased she was for them.

'I am so glad dear old Rob helped you with Dylan. You must have been terribly worried.'

Jamie looked at her. 'I will always, *always* think he saved Dylan's life — it was just such a blessing that I remembered meeting him at your flat and exchanging numbers with him. I keep wondering what would have happened if I hadn't.' She touched Amadea lightly on the shoulder. 'I owe you so much, Amy, really I do.'

Amadea glanced down at her notepad, at the top of which was written in large letters *SHEILA FIRST THING!*

'The thing is, Jamie, there is a bit of a blast on with the boss of all bosses. Sheila has been howling for you for some time now.'

'I was at the hospital worried out of my skull,' Jamie continued as if Amadea had not said anything. She smiled. 'Then Rob suddenly produced his stepmum, and . . . ' She lowered her voice. 'And she is, of all things, a healer, and Amy — it was she who did it. She only went and healed Dylan. She came in carrying this plant, and she transferred the virus to the plant she had brought in, and — Amy, it *worked!*'

'Well, there you go.' Amadea turned back to the screen, convinced that not just Jamie but also Rob *and* his stepmother were several dozen

187

sand-wiches short of a picnic.

'No, it really, really worked.'

'Well, there you go,' Amadea said again lamely. 'So . . . so miracles do happen, even in Swinton. And,' she glanced down at her notebook again, 'and Sheila does want to see you quite urgently, Jamie.'

'Yes, miracles really do happen, Amy, they really do.' Jamie turned at the door. 'And what's more, Rob told me that even the young man your mother is so sweetly nursing at home, the one who was concussed, apparently even he is getting better by the day.'

Happily for Jamie, she had left the room before she could see the expression on Amadea's face.

★ ★ ★

Florence stared at the façade of nearby Harlington Hall and, despite her previous knowledge of the little estate that ran for miles only a short walk from her own house and garden, she found herself once more enthralled by the building's simple, elegant symmetry. The Hall was built in a classical Georgian style with just an element of individuality, and its stone façade was perfectly suited to the surrounding countryside. It was large but without pretension, ideally sited, the sort of country house to which a Georgian gentleman would retire to escape the dust, noise and mayhem of the capital in the hot, summery weather. At the Hall he could stroll in his gardens, admire the growth of his trees and make yet more plans for his arboretum.

The ancillary buildings were set well away from the house. The milking parlour, stables, staff cottages and estate manager's house stood discreetly behind pale brick walls and old hedges, while in front of the Hall fine lawns swept down to a ha-ha, and a stone terrace allowed a spectacular view over the deer park that lay below.

Behind the house the formal gardens were laid out in a series of outdoor rooms. There were rose beds, water gardens, a walled garden and herbaceous borders, and a secret garden had been created in a deep, dry hollow hidden by a circle of grand trees.

As Florence joined the first tour of the day, a luxury made possible by her deliberately arriving half an hour early, she could not help imagining Edmund Gains standing on the fine flight of stone steps that led up to the half-glassed front doors, sitting on the balustrade of the terrace that overlooked the park, or wandering among the many follies and grottoes that were set about the gardens. Hands clasped behind his back, head tilted slightly as he gazed at the beauty around him, his head would be full of the verses he was about to write.

Indeed, the truth was that there was no escaping Edmund. He was everywhere, looking down at her from an upstairs window, walking through the woodlands, riding through the park — she even saw him lying in a four-poster bed, his long frame discreetly draped with a coverlet, just as *Edward* had been when she had found him in her own guest cottage.

'Ah now, let me see . . . ' said a perfectly intonated English voice behind her as Florence crossed the hall. 'You must be — ' Dick clicked his fingers. 'No, don't tell me, you are — you are Florence Fontaine?'

She turned to face the voice and saw an immaculately suited middle-aged man, bespectacled and perfectly groomed, pepper-and-salt hair brushed back from a high forehead, his waistcoat adorned with a fine gold watch chain, a fresh red rosebud pinned in his lapel.

'And you are?' she asked, immediately taking up the game. 'You are — no, I had it — it was on the tip of my tongue. I did know it. I did. But, no, it's gone.'

'Dick Saxon.'

'I was just about to say that!'

They laughed and kissed each other.

'Have you finished the tour?'

Florence nodded towards the fast disappearing group.

'Yes, nice little group from Sussex. They only really come for the tea, but at least they were sweet enough to pretend they were interested.'

'There is nothing quite like one of the Nat Rusty guides showing people round. Henry always said the really interesting things about a house involve knowing why there is such a very large hole in the hangings above the Queen's bed, and other tasty titbits.'

Dick's smile was as engaging as ever, and his manner as mildly exaggerated, and the look in his eyes as warmly appealing.

'How long since you visited? Before my time, of course.'

Since Dick had been living on the estate for only a few months, they both knew the answer to that.

'Not since Henry was gathered,' Florence said quietly. 'We used to come up here and walk in the woods together, and of course we visited the house when we first came to live at the Old Rectory.'

'In that case follow me, and I will pin your ears back!' Dick said, stepping aside to allow Florence to go ahead. As he did so, Florence looked flattered and pleased. She had grown so used to stepping into the gutter, or crossing the road to avoid odd-looking types, that she had quite forgotten what it was like to be with someone like Dick.

'Do you know,' Dick went on, 'I was particularly thrilled to hear from you — because, judging by the looks on people's faces when I brought the subject up, I don't think anyone has ever asked us about Edmund Gains before. I had no idea who you were talking about when you rang, but I do now. So *exciting*. Tell me, how come your friend is so interested in him? Very little really remains of Gains's work, you know; and even less of his life, poor fellow. Even here all we have is a couple of very, very slim volumes in the library.'

'You have some of his works here, Dick? Some of Edmund Gains's poetry?'

'Yes, I was thrilled to discover that they had been catalogued. I'm afraid I can't let you take them away, but we can have a jolly good deco at them. Apparently Gains is not quite Shelley and not quite Keats, who both came along after him.' He opened a heavy brass-handled wooden door for Florence. 'And of course, as a poet in residence Gains can't have had the easiest of times, always being asked to scribble down a snatch of stanzas about one of Lord Harlington's doggies. Can't have been the easiest of tasks, I shouldn't have thought. Probably why that sort of poetry is always called 'doggerel'!'

'Very good — and, who knows, probably true too!'

Florence laughed as Dick leaned across and pushed open yet another heavy brass-handled wooden door, this time leading into the library.

'Still, I think you will be fascinated, if not by the commissioned stuff then by the non-commissioned poems. Some are really rather good, at least to my untutored eye.'

Dick fetched the library steps as Florence gazed round the beautifully light room with its gold-painted cages that housed floor-to-ceiling volumes of inestimable age and interest.

'Are there any paintings of Edmund Gains, Dick?' she asked him, as he reached from halfway up his steps into the appropriate shelf.

'Do you know, I never thought to ask.' Dick climbed slowly and elegantly down the steps, holding not one but two slim volumes. 'By Jove, this is going to be such fun, ferreting around after a dead poet. What a lark! But I'll leave you to it. Nothing worse than someone looking over your shoulder.'

Each book was no more than twenty-five or thirty pages, and after making sure Florence was seated comfortably at the library table, Dick returned to his office leaving her alone to browse.

Each poem sat on a single page, the longest ones singing the praises not of Lord Harlington's mistresses but of his best horses. Since writing a series of poems extolling the virtues of a line of undistinguished horses would try the talents of even the finest poets, Florence was unsurprised to find that the verses were, to say the least, uninspired.

The dogs fared better, the lines in praise of their delightful characters coming to life with verve and charm.

'So you liked dogs better than horses, Mr Gains?' Florence murmured out loud. 'Or perhaps you knew them better?'

But best of all were Edmund Gains's verses in praise of women. Their audacity and their spirit made her smile. It seemed some things in life remained unchanged. One thing was certain: Edmund Gains knew that Lord Harlington was enthralled by the opposite sex, so if he wanted to keep his position as poet in residence at Harlington Hall he had to write romantic, sensual verses in praise of the beauties whom my lord admired, however temporarily.

An hour or so later Dick let himself quietly into the library.

'Good, aren't they? Particularly the ones about the fair sex?'

He stood at Florence's side, and nodded down

at the book that she was closing.

'I expect you feel as hungry as a hunter?' he went on, pulling out her chair for her as she stood up. 'In fact I know you must, after your walk across the park. In recognition of this I have had Mrs Bradley make us some of her famous sandwiches, and if you think that a sandwich is just a sandwich, believe me, you are about to be proved wrong.'

Dick's prediction was correct. The sandwiches were not as other sandwiches. They were filled with produce from the estate, and they seemed to cry out to be relished.

'And now for some of Mrs Bradley's famous Tiny Cakes. Children love them.'

A tray was presented, filled with the smallest petits fours and éclairs, and served with Italian coffee.

'That is as lunch should be, isn't it? I can say that because I didn't make it,' Dick enthused. 'Just tuck and bite. I never tire of it. It fills my being, shoots me past the snoozing hour of three fifteen until tea o'clock, at which point I feel so right with the world I even forget to look forward to my dry martini at seven. Now, however, for the pièce de résistance.' He paused, his eyes sparkling, and indicated several large portfolios. 'I had another quick ferret while you were immersing yourself in the works of dear old Ed Gains because I remembered that, four or five Lord Harlingtons ago, a record was made of everyone who worked in the house. It became something of a tradition here, but one which was stopped after the First World War because most

194

of the men listed did not return.' He stopped momentarily. 'There's a sign in the main gardening shed, you know, all the names recorded and the dates — one man returned here to Harlington. Only one.' His eyes clouded over. 'Imagine to yourself, I often do . . . only one.'

Florence was silent, thinking of all the actresses who had been employed by the politicians to mount platforms in every village and town, to sing and joke the young men out of their civvies and into army uniforms, and from there into the trenches where no music played, and no girls laughed.

'At any rate, back to our Edmund G.' Dick smiled. 'It occurred to me that, among all the drawings — a great many of them are nothing more than cartoons really — there just might be *something* from long, long ago.'

Once again Dick left Florence in the library, to examine the portfolios containing drawings and sketches. Most of them, as he had warned, were merely moderately talented family sketches of the servants and others who worked in the house or on the estate. Not a sign of the resident poet Edmund Gains.

And this in a period that gave us so many talented painters, she thought, struggling not to feel disappointed. It had, after all, been only a hunch. She glanced at her watch. Dottie was at home looking after Edward so she had a little more time.

She pulled another portfolio towards her. This one did not contain drawings or sketches but a small collection of tatty leather-bound house books awaiting repair and restoration, records of life in Harlington Hall during the eighteenth and nineteenth centuries that some of the owners had obviously been at pains to keep up. Florence began to read in the desultory way that people do when they are really waiting for tea, and pretending not to be — until she came across an entry written by a young woman, who soon revealed herself to be a daughter of the house, and the book her journal:

Pappa has introduced another young man to our household, to entertain himself and our guests. He is to be 'poet in residence'. I think it is fanciful, but since Mamma hires soothsayers to impress visitors I suppose we must be thankful that he is not a Druid bestrewn with mistletoe ready to sacrifice us, but merely our very own versifier, who it is said shall write us verses about anything we so desire. Privately I have to say that should his verses be one quarter as good as his most excellent looks then the desire for poetry might well have to give precedence to another form of desire altogether. He is divinely tall, as handsome as Adonis, and sweetly shy. He is called Edmund, and already dear Emily — sweetest sister and one must suppose our own artist in residence — has expressed a wish to draw him, so fetching is his appearance and physical demeanour. Mr Gains demurred, saying that having his likeness done made him uncomfortable and too conscious of his own self, that such things were a vanity and intrusive on an artist's soul and injurious to the muse, turning his thoughts away from his art. Furthermore, he had learned from an Italian acquaintance who was also a poet that many great artists believed the moment anyone drew or painted their likeness the sitter's own artistry withered, as if their very soul had been drawn. We were most impressed by this notion and thus quite understood Mr Gains' reluctance, particularly since he had expressed himself so eloquently and politely, excusing himself with the utmost grace. Later my dear sister told me that she intended to draw Mr Gains whether he liked it or not. I told her that if this was so she must do it privately so as not to disturb our poet's muse or endanger his soul, and although we both shared a small amusement at such a notion dear Emily agreed. I shall wait to see the result of her secret labours.

As soon as she had read the entry, Florence began carefully turning the precious pages of the journal in search of the possible drawing. If Emily had achieved her objective, there was a slight chance it might be found within the covers of the humorous young lady writer's journal, since it contained many other sketches and thumbnails of visitors with the Hall's children and pets, as well as plenty of fine drawings of the house and gardens, and encouraging lines from

197

the Bible, not to mention quotations from Shakespeare and other poets. But where oh where was the sketch that sister Emily might have made unbeknown to Edmund Gains?

'Have we found something that excites us?' Dick had returned. 'Research is so exciting, it lifts one up and carries one along on such a — well, a high, there is no other word for it. It is a high.'

'What I have found is that, as you said, Edmund Gains lived here and wrote here, and I have also discovered that someone who lived here intended to draw him, but that is all I can find.' Florence showed him the entry in the commonplace book. 'Wouldn't it be wonderful if we could find the drawing that Emily here did of him?'

'Nothing in the other portfolios? How disappointing.'

'No, nothing. Even so, I know so much more than I knew this morning, Dick.' She glanced down at her watch. 'You have been so kind, but I must get back to my visitor.'

'I shall continue to root about for you. I promise I feel as excited as you, really I do.'

'Whatever I can do to help here, just tell me, Dick. You will, won't you?'

Dick paused by the great doors that opened out on to the parkland.

'There is one other thing, as it happens.' He turned to the vast marble table that carried all the National Trust literature, guides to the house and books about the Harlington family. 'We are starting up an annual fête champêtre in aid of the gardens this year. Everyone is being urged to come, the whole neighbourhood. It should be fun. You bring your own picnic and we put on entertainments.'

Florence looked down at the tickets he was handing her.

'The theme this year is the eighteenth century, the Age of Reason. White wigs and costumes are greatly to be encouraged, and there will be music and dancing, naturally.'

'You're too generous.' Florence smiled.

Dick grinned. 'I know,' he agreed, starting to laugh.

★   ★   ★

When Florence returned to the Old Rectory, Dottie was hovering about the hall with an anxious expression on her face.

'Guess who has come back to haunt us?'

'I know, I know, I saw the car.'

The two women looked at each other.

'Who can miss Amadea's car?' Dottie stared gloomily out of the half-glassed doors to the drive where the car was parked. 'The colour's so bright you have to wear shades to look at it.'

'Shades?' Florence gave a sudden laugh. 'Oh Dottie, that is so funny, 'shades' is such a dated word.'

'Yes, it is, isn't it? But you know, it still sounds cool, even now. She's in her room, by the way, and not in the best of moods.' Dottie nodded towards the second floor.

'Who told her? Not Rob Greer?'

'No, that woman she works for who has a man's name.'

'And?'

'And she took the rest of the day off, apparently, to come down here and — you know . . . '

'And give me what for?' Florence looked rueful.

'And stick her nose in where it's not wanted is what I was going to say.'

Florence put a hand on Dottie's arm. 'Stay with me, will you?'

Dottie nodded. She had been going to stay with Florence anyway, wouldn't have dreamed of doing anything else — they were in this together, after all.

'I will stay with you through thick and thin, my dear Flo. I know what the young can be like when it comes to bullying. My nephews, dear as they are, on a bad day give me the most awful gip. Come on now, I've got tea ready. Edward and I have been having a marvellous set-to about iambic pentameters, too risqué for words. If anyone gets wind of it — well, scandal!' In the kitchen as she poured the tea, she went on, 'So tell me, did you have any success with our alternative personality, dear old Edmund Gains of the poetic outpourings?'

'Oh Dottie, *such* success! I've read his poems about horses and dogs, and there's even mention of Edmund himself, in a diary written up by one of the daughters of the house.'

Florence picked up her teacup, but before she could get any further she saw the expression on

Dottie's face change as Amadea came into the room, tossing her hair back and running her fingers through it.

'Hallo, Dottie, again. Hallo, Ma, again.' Amadea kissed the air around Florence's head.

'Hallo, Amy. This is a surprise.' Florence looked up at her pretty daughter, reserve in her eyes, as she waited for the lecture about Edward Green.

'Tea, dear?' Dottie asked, her expression already one of benign authority.

'Thank you.'

Amadea sat down opposite the two older women, and they waited as she sipped tea and nibbled a home-made biscuit.

'So, this young gardener is staying here, I gather.'

Florence looked at Dottie and pulled a little face. 'Well, yes, he is,' she admitted, carefully.

'You took on this young man after all, Ma.'

'Well, yes, I did, Amy.'

'Right against my advice.'

'Was it, dear? I don't remember your mother saying you had advised her against it.'

Dottie's face was all innocence. Even so, Amadea changed her tack and, ignoring Dottie, said to her mother, 'I was really worried about you being on your own here, out in the country, with this young man, if you must know.'

'Very kind of you, Amy, but I'm not on my own. Dottie is here, as you can see — and Pierre Lavalle, your dad's friend, who is a qualified hypnotherapist, comes across every day to see Edward, as we now call him. We think we are

201

beginning to sort out the poor young man, and what is more I think we may actually have some success.'

Florence felt all the excitement of the afternoon draining from her. She had been so enthralled by what had happened at Harlington Hall, all she had wanted was to come back home and chew the cud with Dottie. Instead she was now finding herself on the back foot, having to cope with Amadea.

'I was just saying to your mother, Amadea,' Dottie put in over-brightly. 'I was just saying that the R and R has really done dear Edward a great deal of good. That together with the fact that Pierre is analysing him.'

'*Analysing* him? How on earth much does that cost?'

The two women stared at Amadea and seconds later both, as one person, simultaneously said, '*Nothing!*'

'In that case he must be useless.' Amadea shrugged her shoulders.

'And since when did you take a course in psychiatry, young lady?' Dottie wondered.

'He's not analysing him as in psychology and being on the couch, Amy,' Florence told her gently. 'He is hypnotising him.'

'Oh, don't tell me!' Amadea exclaimed. 'What has gone *wrong* with everyone? First I have Rob Greer and his stepmother healing Jamie Charlbury's child of a virus with the aid of a plant.' She paused. 'And now I come home to find you two have some weirdo hypnotising another weirdo.' She shook her head. 'I think everyone's gone mad, I do really.'

There was a long pause, during which Punch scratched his ear loudly, and Amadea pushed him to stop, and Florence found herself sipping her tea a little too quickly.

'Amadea?' Dottie said at last. 'Do you believe in angels?'

Amadea finished doing her lipstick. 'No, I do not believe in angels, Dottie.'

'So you wouldn't know that unlike the rest of us angels can fly, because they take themselves so lightly?'

Amadea shrugged her shoulders again, just as Punch gave a small, pleased bark and Edward walked into the room.

Florence and Dottie stared at him, their hearts sinking. This was definitely not the right moment for Edward or Edmund or whoever he was to make an entrance.

'Hallo, Edward — would you like a cup of tea, dear?' Dottie asked, still too brightly for her own taste.

Amadea turned and saw Edward for the first time.

'Who is *this*?' she asked, turning to her mother, and laughing suddenly before turning back to Edward. He was looking irresistibly handsome, if, Dottie noted, her heart sinking, more than a little vague.

'Who are *you*?' Amadea demanded.

'I am Edward,' he told Amadea with quiet authority, at which both Florence and Dottie exchanged relieved looks. 'Edmund' was obviously, however temporarily, on hold.

'I am Amadea, Edward.'

Edward stretched out elegant fingers and shook Amadea's multi-ringed hand.

Florence and Dottie stared. Amadea's expression had changed in a matter of seconds. She was now smiling so sweetly she looked not just pretty but beautiful.

'How nice to meet you, Edward.'

'Very nice to meet you too, Amadea.'

They both smiled, and as they did so Dottie turned back to the stove and the boiling kettle, rolling her eyes heavenwards. 'Now who doesn't believe in hypnotism?' she muttered.

Florence too turned her back on them, and she also lowered her voice. 'Did you hear that, Dottie?'

Dottie looked at her.

'Edward spoke quite normally.'

8

'You'd like to come out to Repton's Bistro, wouldn't you? It's only down the road.'

Dottie came into Florence's sitting room just in time to see Amadea giving Edward her most dazzling smile.

'Are you all right?' she asked Edward.

'He's fine, really.'

Edward stared at Amadea as Dottie hurried out of the room to find Florence.

'I think when I get to heaven,' Florence announced, looking up from her labours, 'the first thing St Peter is going to ask me is to go round to the back door and chop eternal parsley for him.' She paused. 'As a matter of fact, now I come to think of it, I must ask Edward/Edmund to rewrite that poem 'Werther had a love for Charlotte/Such as words could never utter;/ Would you know how first he met her?/She was cutting bread and butter.' I will ask him to change it to something about first seeing 'Florence chopping parsley' — except it is so terribly difficult to rhyme parsley with anything except *ghastly*.'

'I just overheard Amadea saying she was going to take Edward out to some bistro or other,' Dottie announced, paying no attention at all to Florence's wonderings.

Florence was silent for a moment. 'Well, she would be, wouldn't she?'

205

'How can we stop her?'

Florence looked thoughtful. 'We'll say Pierre forbids it, which he probably will if we ask him.'

'Of course, why didn't I think of that?'

'Come and talk to me, Dottie.'

'In two or three seconds. First, I really must scupper the rather overt plans of our resident nympho — '

Dottie fairly flung herself back into the sitting room, where Amadea was now alone. Dottie looked round, worried.

'Where's Edward?'

'He's taken himself off outside on the terrace. He wants to gaze at the sunset or something. He's very otherworldly, isn't he? And doesn't seem to know a thing about gardening either.'

Dottie ignored her and went to the window. When she saw that Edward was sitting under the old apple tree gazing at the sky, she gave a small, imperceptible sigh of relief.

'Amadea.' As Amadea did not look up, she repeated her name. 'Amadea.' She cleared her throat. 'Kind of you though it is to ask Edward out for supper, I'm afraid it is just not on, old love. You see, he's undergoing rather a sensitive time, and Pierre, your father's friend Pierre, does not think it a good idea that he has anything to do with the outside world just now.'

Amadea shrugged her shoulders. 'Don't worry, Dottie, Edward doesn't seem to want to go anywhere anyway, just wants to sit around talking about his poems.' As Dottie tried not to react to the news that in their absence Edmund had obviously swung into action, Amadea joked,

206

'Better warn Ma, Dottie. Wouldn't surprise me at all if Edward was to turn into a sitting talent.'

She picked up her expensive bought-on-a-credit-card handbag.

'What time's supper?'

'When your mother has it ready and not before,' Dottie stated, realising too late that it sounded just a little too pointed, but Amadea laughed with sudden good humour.

'You're in a very strict mood, Dottie. Would you rather I went back to Swinton before dinner?'

Dottie pretended not to hear and hurried out to the kitchen to help Florence, while Amadea, having no inclination to chop either onions or parsley, let alone peel potatoes, went back out into the garden.

'I have just recalled the meaning of your name,' Edward confessed, standing up as he heard her approach. 'How very remiss of me not to have remembered that Amadea means 'loved by God'. I knew it must be something heavenly because we are after all in paradise, a paradise made more heavenly by your presence,' he added graciously, waiting for her to sit down before reseating himself.

'Sweet of you to say so, kind sir.'

Amadea sighed inwardly. Her before-supper entertainment was obviously going to be a straight choice between disapproving Dottie and loony Edward, but at least it took her mind off having been binned. They were both silent as Edward stared ahead at something only he could see, and Amadea wondered not just what to say next, but how to say it. She knew she was sitting with a loop-the-loop artist, what she *didn't* know was what to talk to him about.

'Do you like to versify?' he asked politely, after the short pause had extended into a lengthy silence.

'No, not really, but I do like poetry.' She searched wildly in her mind for someone she liked. 'I like William Blake for instance. Very much. Yes, I like him.'

Amadea gazed around her at the soft summer evening. It was at just this time of year that her father had delighted in reading poetry out loud, often sitting out on the lawn peering at the words by the light of a lantern, while moths flew about the flame, and she and David had sat listening to his mellifluous voice.

Probably because she was feeling on the back foot, for once, instead of turning quickly away from the memory, she examined it minutely, because it didn't seem possible now that all that had actually happened, that they had all been together, and that now they were both gone — her dad and her brother, as if they were actors in a play that was no longer being performed, the curtain fallen, the costumes put away, the lines long forgotten, except perhaps by them, wherever they were.

Sometimes, when she was in Swinton, trying to live the life she knew the young were supposed to live, Amadea would find herself wondering if any of her idyllic childhood had happened at all. All those moments of shared happiness, all that laughter, were they perhaps just something she had imagined?

Edward was staring at her. 'If you like William Blake you may well enjoy Edmund Gains,' he stated. 'You know 'At the Gate of Paradise'?'

'Yes, of course,' Amadea lied quickly, because she thought she caught a flash from the luminous dark eyes at the mention of this work; and besides she wanted to help the conversation along. 'Edmund Gains is brilliant.'

Edward considered this for a moment. 'No, I don't know who you mean.'

'But you've just asked me if I knew that — if I knew Edmund Gains's verse?'

'I cannot have done.' Edward stared into the distance as he considered the possibility. 'Why would I? How could I? I have no idea why I would. Why would I know someone called Edmund Gains? I don't think I have ever even heard such a name.'

Shaking his head in perplexity, Edward stood up and strolled away from her, hands clasped behind his back, away into the growing twilight as if he were a shadow vanishing.

Amadea watched him for a few seconds, and then hurried in to speak to Florence.

'He's really weird, Ma. I mean first he's asking you if you know someone's verse, and then he says he doesn't know who you're talking about. I tell you, he ought to be in a safe place.'

At her pronouncement both Florence and Dottie looked round.

'He is in a safe place, Amy,' Florence told her evenly. 'He's here with us.'

'But what about you, are you safe?'

'Oh, I think so, Amy. After all, it seems the worst habit he has is quoting poetry.'

'I'm not sure that's particularly catching, is it?' Straight-faced, Dottie glanced from mother to daughter and back again.

Amadea sighed as she looked at her watch. Both Dottie and her mother were impossible, and, in a mad world, that at least was for sure.

'Supper ready yet? I have to get back to Swinton tonight, God is visiting.' As Florence frowned, Amadea went on, 'Psemisis Europe is in town. All present and correct, you know?'

'I'll hurry everything along.'

Florence turned up the heat on the gas stove, but as she did so the memory of Edward's fall returned. It had been terrible, and yet for some reason she could not regret it.

★   ★   ★

Pierre Lavalle was now beginning to believe, however reluctantly, that Edward/Edmund might be schizophrenic.

'Are you sure?'

'No, of course I'm not sure.' Pierre shook his head. 'But everything you have just told me only goes to confirm what I have begun to fear. The fact that the patient comes in and out of the past into the present, only to regress again into the past, all seems to coincide with such a diagnosis. In which case . . . ' He looked at Florence. 'In which case hypnosis is never going to be the answer, I'm afraid, and you and I know it.'

'I don't want him — ' Florence was about to

say 'put back into hospital' when she stopped, because the idea was just so abhorrent to her.

'I did tell you about the verses I found at Harlington Hall?'

'Yes, you did.'

There was a short pause during which Florence realised that the fact that she had found verses by Edmund Gains was perhaps not going to change Pierre's diagnosis. He was obviously, and reluctantly, coming to the conclusion that the only explanation for Edward imagining he was Edmund Gains was that he was suffering from a dual personality.

'Some people have been found to have as many as fifteen different personalities,' Pierre went on.

'Yes, yes, I do know, I saw a film about it once . . . '

'Then you also know that they can treat people like Edward/Edmund with really sophisticated drugs nowadays.'

'Yes, yes, I know. I just don't want Edward becoming a medical guinea pig. And I — and I mean if they start delving about, they might find he is not only sure he is Edmund Gains, but Christopher Marlowe, Lord Byron, and the entire dictionary of English poets, and where would we be then?'

'We can leave him as he is for the moment, but not for ever,' Pierre warned.

Florence nodded, not looking at him. 'No, no, of course not. Quite apart from anything else, it will not be possible.' Pierre looked at her. 'I have made up my mind to sell the house — I am

211

rather short of pennies, I'm afraid. Should have done it years ago, as a matter of fact.'

Pierre nodded and together they strolled down the drive to his car.

'I don't want to worry you,' Pierre said, having kissed her on both cheeks in avuncular fashion, 'but the truth is, Florence, Edward could become dangerous. I don't say he will, but he *could*. There is a possibility he might have assumed this gentle persona, this poet's personality, in order to cover up his own more violent persona. This often happens. Or it can happen the other way round: a human being who is terrified of something or someone will regress into a violent personality, in order to defend his too-gentle nature. The human mind is so terribly complex. This is why I would advise you, no matter what your own plans may be, to consider taking poor Edward back to hospital, to a psychiatric wing, to find more expert help than I can possibly give him. I think it may prove to be the only solution.'

'Yes, yes, but not quite yet, surely?' Florence gestured around her. 'I mean how can I take him away from all this when he might be suffering from nothing more than a mild form of amnesia? Would you like someone you don't know, and who doesn't care for you, to take you away from here and chuck you in a hospital ward just because your mind may be temporarily on hold?'

'No, of course not. I'm only saying that this situation cannot go on for ever, that's all. I doubt that Edward's condition will cure itself.'

Pierre looked down at Florence, and the look

in his eyes was affectionate, yet he knew that she needed to accept that all he was doing, all she was doing, was really only delaying the inevitable.

Florence let herself back into the house and was about to step into the garden and bring Edward round by the snap of her fingers, when she stopped. She would have to tell Dottie what Pierre had said. Dottie would know what to do. She always had more sense than Florence.

'Let's just give him a few more days in paradise,' Dottie announced, after a fractional pause during which she too had to push away the realisation that Pierre might be right.

★　★　★

The following morning there was a wholly new and unexpected threat. Edward had decided to go for a walk.

'I am going to those Elysian fields I see over there,' he told Florence in firm tones, grandly waving one elegant hand towards the neighbouring fields. 'The woods and fields of Elysium beckon.'

'Wait there, just a minute, I will come with you.'

Florence dashed back into the house to tell the ever-patient and nowadays ever-present Dottie.

'Edward wants to go for a walk — around the estate.'

'Oh dear.'

They stared at each other. It was a beautiful day, the sun was shining, presumably God was in his heaven, and certainly all was right with their particular world, but up to now they had done such a good job of keeping Edward protected from everyone, and everything, they dreaded that he might become disturbed after an encounter with the unfamiliar.

'Best go with him, stick to the paths, and double back once you get to the view from the Temple of Diana.' As Florence glanced up at the clock, Dottie continued, 'It is so early still, there will be a good hour or two before anyone else appears. Besides, if you stick to the view from above, Edward will only see people very, very small. Matchstick people shouldn't distress him too much. So, just stick to the woodland paths, and I am sure all will be well. Why shouldn't it be?'

The first part of the walk up to the famous gardens passed without event: indeed, the almost unnatural quiet of the woods made it feel as if they were trespassing in another part of paradise. Then they drew into the thick of the closely planted forest where the woods suddenly seemed to be inhabited by a whole new world that lay hidden from the rest of humanity, a world that echoed with the calls of birds, with the sudden movement of deer and rabbit. Once or twice, when Florence suspected that another human being might be approaching, she took a diversion along one of her secret routes, paths they had all known and loved since the children were small.

'Why are we hiding?'

Edward's dramatic expression, the seriousness

214

of his face, the look in his eyes, made Florence smile.

'Because it is something that children do,' she told him, remembering how she had always asked David the same question when he had suddenly dodged behind a tree, or taken refuge behind a bush.

Finally they emerged on to the small patch of grass on the hill above the Temple to admire the sight that had never failed to take Florence's breath away, and which she knew could never disappoint.

Her already silent companion stared wordlessly at the vision in front of them, the sweep of landscape decorated with ornamental temples and follies, the majesty of the many great trees, the beauty of the planting, the shape and movement of the lake, the ancient footbridge, the spire of the old church set so perfectly inside the great gates.

She turned to Edward, about to explain to him how the garden had been created; then she stopped, realising just in time that he must consider what was spread out before them, below them, around them, to be merely part of the fantasy that they had all been at such pains to recreate for him. He must imagine the view was yet another room in heaven, and why not? She remembered David turning to her before they left on that fatal holiday, and saying, 'It's our little glimpse of paradise, isn't it, Mum?' So, now she came to think of it, he had seen paradise, with her, perhaps before he had even arrived there.

'No *feeble soul is mine*,' a voice beside her said quietly. '*No shaker in a storm troubled sphere* —

'*Here heaven's glories shine* —

'*And alike shines faith, protecting me from fear.*'

'That is beautiful,' Florence said, after a pause. She turned to him. 'Would that be another . . . Edmund Gains?' she asked, testing him.

'Yes, it is Edmund Gains,' Edward replied. 'Of course it is Edmund Gains.'

'He published a great deal under Anon. He was obviously quite shy? Or modest perhaps?'

'Fame devours poets,' Edward agreed. 'Poets should remain in the shade, only their poetry should shine in the sunlight.'

'Really, Edmund? That is interesting.' Florence dropped in the name as casually as she could. She knew that she was taking a risk but in view of the urgency of the situation she had decided this was as good a time as any to go for broke. 'From what I've heard, your poetry is very good.'

'You've heard tell of me?' Edward looked at her in amazement. 'Most unusual, I have to say, and yet I am flattered. Perhaps, if you will permit me, I could compose something in praise of you, and your wondrous beauty.'

'That is not exactly how I think of myself . . . '

'Modesty only enhances beauty, just as conceit destroys it.'

'I would love you to compose some new verse, but not about me.'

'The Elysian fields and the views of this other house in God's heaven have much inspired me.'

As they walked back Florence fell silent again, thinking it best to leave Edward to his thoughts. Amused, she let him wander beside her with his hands clasped behind his back and his head inclined, perhaps pondering the work he was about to create.

Now and then she would glance in his direction, taking advantage of his concentration. It took little imagination to see Edward as a real poet in an age when intelligent people were in thrall to the ancients, loving the vision of an Arcadia filled with gods and goddesses, when belief was not limited by science, but extended by the idea of a perfection which man could attain if only he could just stretch out his hand to grasp it.

'I am lacking in manners, my company as grey as the bark on that tree,' Edward announced, turning round and offering her his arm. 'I have plenty of time to spend in composition, and yet here I am walking along with my head in the clouds when I should be delighting in your presence.'

'I'm fine, really,' Florence replied. 'I like being quiet, it does not trouble me.'

She stopped, realising that she was beginning to sound like Edmund.

'I find your company delightful and there are so many things to be discussed. First of all, tell me, if you will, about the life you have led. It was not wasted in an idle marriage, with some confounded wretch spinning around you a web of misery when he should have been enchanting you?'

'No, no, I was happily married. Very happily. No, but one thing you must understand,' Florence began again, thinking what she was about to tell him might well need prefacing. 'You won't want to stay here for ever, you know.'

'Oh but I shall, I shall never want to leave — never. I know it.'

They walked on, Florence effectively silenced by his happiness, and filled with sadness by it too. Edward sang quietly to himself, as children do.

'That is a very long song, Edmund,' she observed eventually as they drew near to the back gate leading to her garden.

He turned his large, dark eyes on her, and for the first time she saw genuine humour in them.

'It is a very long song,' he agreed. 'It was composed to tease King George. He has a habit of falling asleep and snoring at the very moment a song begins. Two of my friends composed this song by way of a wager between themselves. The wager was this: if His Majesty awoke before the end of the song, then one of them would lose his money, while if he continued to sleep the other would.' He laughed. 'The king never awoke, and the song became famous as a lullaby. All the nurses sing the ballad to their babies, who, like the king, prefer sleep to song!'

Then he stopped, frowning.

'Something the matter?'

'I don't know why I said that,' he answered in a matter-of-fact voice. 'Where did that come from? Why did I say that?'

Florence stared at him, realising that his other

218

personality had reasserted itself. She walked on, feeling frightened for him, and at the same time certain that Pierre was right — Edward needed more professional help than they could offer him.

★　★　★

Jamie stared at Sheila Pryor. She knew things had not been too good the past few days, since she got back to work. She had felt a bit of an atmosphere building up, and why wouldn't she? Everyone at the company got tense when Psemisis Europe was in town. They did not always bring a scythe in their briefcases, but occasionally out it came.

'I beg your pardon?'

Sheila looked directly at Jamie, determinedly employing her most detached manner. When it came to these situations she knew she had to pretend that there was a glass wall in front of her, and that she could see and hear the person she was dismissing only at a great distance.

'I am afraid I have to ask you to clear your desk, as of now — or rather in the next twenty minutes, Jamie.'

Jamie felt as if she must double over, the pain was so intense. It was literally as if she had been kicked in the stomach. Then she clenched her hands at her sides, resolving to hold onto the things that really mattered.

She held onto the memory of Dylan being cured by Rob's mother, and she held onto Rob visiting them at the flat, sometimes three times a day. She held onto Rob reading to Dylan every evening now. She held onto the fact that Dylan, although still weak, was actually getting over the wretched mystery virus. Those were the things that mattered, really mattered, not Psemisis.

'May I ask one question, Sheila?'

'Go ahead.'

'Why me?'

'MD Psemisis Europe made the decision. Unfortunately you gave him and his team the wrong impression. You were not sufficiently prepped for the interview, they felt you were woolly-minded and lacked the kind of commitment twenty-four seven that they expect here. That, and the need to cut back of course, is why we have to let you go.'

'My son was sick, Sheila, really ill. He was hospitalised, no one knew what was wrong with him. It was terrifying.'

'I know, Jamie, and believe me I understand, but we're trimming from each department, and someone has to go ... ' She shrugged her shoulders, suddenly feeling like a cigarette though she hadn't had one in years. 'Someone will snap you up as soon as your foot hits the pavement out there. Really they will.'

Jamie breathed in and out. She had always suspected that Sheila, in common with many heads of department, secretly, or perhaps not so secretly, hated single mothers, pregnant women, working mothers and anyone else who still had their reproductive organs. Sheila herself had never married. She took lovers. She was probably typical of a certain kind of career woman from

220

time immemorial. She preferred her job to her life. She could offer the commitment management required in terms of hours, and the fact that she had not a single idea of any originality in her head was obviously neither here nor there.

'Someone in *Swinton* will not snap me up, Sheila, and you well know it. My life is here. My son is at nursery here, my flat — ' She stopped. 'And anyway, you can't do this to me, I have a contract.'

'I think you will find Psemisis Europe can do this to anyone they choose, Jamie.' Sheila had started to look vaguely bored, as if the conversation had already gone on too long. Or perhaps Psemisis had a line in everyone's contracts to say that they were allowed only two minutes' protest.

'I will get a lawyer on to this.'

'I should save your money. Really. I checked your contract last night, and the fact is you will get six months' pay, and by the time that runs out you will have found yourself a niche in another company, and you will be fine.'

Jamie stared at Sheila. She was making Jamie sound and feel like an ornament on one of her mother's shelves.

'Have I worked so hard — for this to happen?' she asked bitterly. '*So* hard?'

Sheila glanced down at her expensive wrist watch, and Jamie, knowing that this was the moment to leave, turned on her heel and left her office. She walked slowly down the corridor in a daze. Life came at you, it really did; and not just in ones but in twos and threes, and sometimes in sixes and sevens.

'You all right, Jamie?' Amadea turned from her computer screen. 'You look as if the old bag has bitten you in the ankle. If so I should go to Nursey on the fifth floor and get a tetanus jab. I'm told Sheila's bite can be lethal.'

Jamie looked at Amadea. She was pretty and single, and had not a care in the world. For a second she found herself envying her.

'I've just been told to clear my desk.'

Amadea stared at her. 'Very funny, I don't think.'

'No, it's not funny, Amy, it's true.'

Amadea stood up and went to offer Jamie a hug.

'My jaw has just dropped to the floor! They can't do this to you. They can't! What about all your research, what about all that? I mean no one works harder than you, Jamie, no one. Look, they've got the wrong man, I mean person. I'll go and tell them, they must have dropped a pin on the wrong name. They can't get rid of you.'

Jamie sat down suddenly, putting her head in her hands. 'Well, apparently they can, Amy, apparently they can.'

Amadea knelt down beside her. 'But what did the old cow say, what reason did she give?'

'She said I made a bad impression at my interview with Psemisis Europe. I have to clear my desk in the next twenty minutes.'

'But you're a single parent — they can't do this to you!'

Jamie lifted her head. 'They can, Amy, and they just have.'

Amadea stood up. 'That — that is so *bad*.' She walked up and down their office, punching a fist into her right hand. 'That is not just bad, that is wicked.'

Jamie watched her for a second or two, and then, breathing out determinedly, she stood up.

'No point in moaning, no point in doing anything. I've only got twenty minutes. Would you mind helping me pack up, Amy, before security arrives?'

'No, no, of course not — I'll run to the basement and nick some dustbin bags.'

Jamie stopped, and rallying suddenly, she called after Amadea, 'You won't have to nick them, they must be in my contract somewhere: 'six dustbin bags for desk clearance'.'

It wasn't until she was helping to pack up poor Jamie's effects, which were considerable since she had worked for Psemisis for over six years, that Amadea's indignation started to turn into a hard ball of anger. Jamie was a real friend and a massively tolerant boss, forgiving and warm-hearted, always seeing someone else's point of view, always looking at the big picture, never disloyal, never dished the dirt with anyone, just did the job and went home to her little boy.

'I can't stay here, not with them treating you like this,' she announced.

'Don't be silly, Amy. Just because I have been given the push doesn't mean that you need to jump out of the window after me.'

Amadea frowned. 'Actually,' she said suddenly,

223

'I don't like this place anyway. I like you, but not the company. I don't even like what they do. I never did like what they do. Not that your research isn't the tops, Jamie, but you know — the rest of them — they're a mixed lot like the rabbits.' She stopped, remembering this was one of her father's favourite expressions from *The Wind in the Willows*. 'Yes, all the people here, they're a really mixed lot like the rabbits, and anyway, I don't want to stay anywhere where they treat someone like you in this way.'

'No, no, Amadea, please, wait, you can't — '

But it was too late. Amadea had left the room in search of Sheila Pryor. She finally found her in the company cafeteria surrounded by her acolytes.

'Ah, Sheila, Miss Pryor rather.'

She stood smiling in front of Sheila's table, realising that she had not only never liked the company, she had always disliked Sheila. She was not just hard-boiled, she was Teflon-coated.

'A bit formal today, aren't we, Amadea? Or should I call you Miss Fontaine?'

'Maybe, yes, actually.' Amadea looked round the table, the smiling faces only adding fuel to her fury. 'I came up here to tell you, Sheila, that I am leaving. I am clearing my desk now, along with Jamie Charlbury. We are both going together. It's a show of sisterhood, as well as a protest. And I particularly want you to know that I do not care to stay a moment longer with a company who can dismiss a hard-working single parent out of hand, while at the same time displaying the logo *Psemisis — the company that cares for people*, and what's more — ' She stopped. 'And what's *more*, I shall make it my business to tell everyone I know about how little you *do* care about people.'

'You mean everyone you meet when you go clubbing? Or everyone you meet when you go shopping? Or everyone you meet when you're at the gym?'

This drew a ripple of laughter from the acolytes around the table.

Amadea stared at Sheila. 'OK, make fun of me, but remember, the day will come when you will have a taste of your own Psemisis medicine. You too will be told to clear your desk. I'm just sorry I won't be here to see it!'

She turned on her heel, and minutes later found herself helping Jamie carry the heavy black dustbin bags down the stairs and out to the company car park.

'Now what?'

For a second Jamie looked not just helpless but childlike in her vulnerability, as she looked from the dustbin bags to Amadea and back again.

'I always walk to work. The company encourage us to walk to work . . . '

'Do they? I didn't know that.'

Amadea looked so blank that they both started to laugh. They laughed and laughed until their sides ached.

'Come on.' Amadea picked up one of the bags and started to walk towards her car. 'I'll take you home, and then we'll make a plan.'

They began lifting the bags into the boot.

'You shouldn't have given in your notice because of me, Amadea. There was no need.'

'There was every need. I couldn't stay if I tried, really I couldn't. There are words for people like that Sheila Pryor, but my New Year's resolution was not to say any of them until after six at night, so they will have to wait. Just eight hours to go, and then — oh boy — watch the air turn blue.'

They loaded the last of the bags and drove the short distance to Jamie's flat, where they hauled them upstairs to the first floor.

'Come in for a coffee.'

They were leaning against the front door, panting.

'I'd love to, Jamie, but I can't.'

Jamie put her key in the front door. 'Glass of wine, then?'

'No, love, I can't. I always believe in doing things at once, you know.' Jamie looked at her questioningly. 'It's the car. I, er — don't exactly own it. I've suddenly realised I'll have to take it to Coronet Cars, and get the old so-and-so to take it back.' Now Jamie was staring at her. 'And that is just for starters.'

'You don't own the car?'

'No way. As a matter of fact I hardly own anything, everything I have is on a card. But hey, no card, no cares. I'll ring you in a day or two, probably come round and take a cup of coffee off you.'

Amadea tossed her head bravely and ran off down the stairs. Jamie went to the window and watched her reappear in the street below. If anyone had told her a week ago that Amadea would leave her job as a gesture of solidarity, she would have laughed at them, but the truth was that she had, and judging from her rather jaunty walk, she seemed suddenly to have freed herself from some kind of baggage.

Jamie turned back to the large heap of dustbin bags taking up her small hall and sighed. Now to cope with her own considerable baggage.

9

Amadea looked around her flat. What she had said to Jamie was true. It seemed there was hardly anything in the whole place that was not there thanks to a credit card. Furniture, china, clothes, sound system, everything had been bought on credit. What had she just done? She had walked out of her job, impulsively, hastily, and in a spirit of solidarity with Jamie. Oh my God, she had walked out of her *job*.

She sat down suddenly, putting her fingers to her mouth and pressing against her lips. She must have been mad!

She paused, trying not to panic, trying to be realistic. It was not the end of the world, she would not let it be the end of the world. Besides, she was glad that she had been mad, because it had made her feel so much better. She had stood up for someone else's rights, and, what was better, she had stood up to Sheila Pryor, whatever the financial cost, however many buses she would have to catch, however many credit cards she would have to spend months paying off, somehow, anyhow. She had at least stood up for justice, tolerance, and Jamie Charlbury.

For want of something better to do, she stretched out on her becomingly grey sofa and stared up at the ceiling. She had already handed back the car. Now she would have to set about selling stuff, and quite a lot of stuff. Stuff that she should never have bought, and which she realised would be worth considerably less than the mountains of money she had borrowed to pay for it.

For instance, what had got into her, for God's sake, to want to buy an expensive flat-screen television when she hardly watched the wretched thing? What had got into her that she had wanted a ladies' Rolex watch? There were clocks all over Swinton, and anyway, ever since she had bought it she had lived in fear of being mugged and had either to leave it at home or to wear it halfway up her arm so that no one saw it.

She sat up again, looking masochistically around for yet more examples of her foolishness. The glass dining table and clear perspex dining chairs? Oh please, she would get about two pence for them, and that was for sure; and as for all the clothes in her wardrobes, they were too bright for a car boot sale, and not trendy enough for a smart London resale shop. None of this would matter of course if she didn't already know that, besides Psemisis, there were only two other large companies in Swinton, both Japanese-owned, and neither of them likely to be currently in need of a personal assistant.

To confirm this she started to ring round the employment agencies. They all took down her details and promised to ring her if there was any work, temporary or otherwise, but Amadea could hear from their voices that this was so far from being a reality it was actually pathetic. Only one thing to be done: phone home.

'I was wondering if I could come home for a bit?'

She heard the surprise in her mother's voice as she said, 'Of course,' after only a fractional pause. Or was it reluctance that had made her hesitate?

Amadea replaced the phone on the coffee table that only this morning she would have found so smart, but which she now realised with shock looked strangely cheap. She could hardly believe what had happened to her. Less than twenty-four hours ago she had a nice flat, clothes and a car. All right, not much of it was paid for, but that mattered less than the fact that she had enjoyed them. Now she was out of work, at a loose end, and going home to her mother.

'God, do you realise I will have to get the train home?' she said to Fred, who sat looking at her, his beautiful Siamese eyes projecting one word, *food*. 'All right, all right, I'll feed you, but pretty soon you will have to learn not to eat prawns, even on Sunday.'

At that moment the sound of singing rose from the balcony below. Amadea opened her French windows and called down, joking, knowing it was Rob.

'Stop that racket!'

'Come down for a coffee.'

'Oh all right, but it'll have to be yours. I can't afford coffee, not now — '

Amadea practically bolted downstairs in her enthusiasm to see Rob. Rob's flat might be everyone's idea of a site of major pollution, but at least Rob was in it; and at least if she was with him she would not be on her own with her thoughts any more.

'Oh God, Rob.'

Rob stared at her. 'I keep telling you I am only a demi-god, Amy, not a god, not yet at least, sweet of you though it is to promote me.'

Amadea shut her eyes, preparing to go through their old routine.

'Take me to your kitchen, oh demi-god.'

Rob, ever obliging, took her by the hand.

'All right, you can open your eyes now,' he commanded.

Amadea slowly opened her eyes, and then widened them as she took in the scene before her.

'God, Rob — '

'Demi-god, Rob.'

'Sorry, demi-god, Rob, this is . . . ' She looked round. 'This is *weird*.'

Rob stared at her. 'After all this time, all this time you have spent moaning about my kitchen being a hard-hat area, that is all you can say? *Weird?* Not beautiful, fantastic, or just sensational, but weird.' He took her by the shoulder and started to push her from his kitchen. 'That's it, out! No coffee, not even a teeny-weeny cappuccino.'

Amadea made herself into a dead weight, refusing to budge, but he pulled at her arms so hard she had to move.

'No, Rob, please, please don't chuck me out. Please.'

'Out! Calling my kitchen weird, if you please. I'll give you weird, Amadea Fontaine.'

'No, please, don't chuck me out, please, not when *I*'ve just been chucked out.'

'I heard from Jamie, she rang me. You weren't chucked out, you walked out, I heard all about it.'

He stopped pulling at her, and Amadea returned to the kitchen.

'I did, I walked out because they sacked Jamie, and now I'm out of work and can't get a job.' She picked up a tea towel suddenly and wiped her eyes. 'I can't get a job, Rob, not even a small one. I've been out of work for at least two hours.'

Rob stared at her. He hadn't thought ever to see Amadea wipe her eyes on his tea towel, let alone have tears in her eyes. Amadea did not even cry at *Bambi*. He knew because he had watched it with her.

'You'll get a job,' he reassured her. 'Of course you will.'

'No, Rob, Jamie will get a job, not me. People like me, young women like me, are two a penny, if not three a penny. I've got to go home for a couple of weeks and try and think of what to do. The car has had to go back, and I'm selling everything I can on eBay — '

'Everything?'

'Yes, everything, what else can I do? Swinton is not exactly huge, and there are only so many jobs to go round. Let's face it, I fell on my feet with that job at Psemisis, but if something doesn't come up soon I'll have to go to London, and I can't afford to store my furniture. I can hardly afford to eat, that's why I have to go home.'

'I'll take your dining table and chairs off you, if that will help.'

Amadea put the tea towel down abruptly. 'Will you really?'

'Of course. They're great.'

'Do you really think so? I thought they looked a bit too spare.'

'That's what I like. Spare, minimal, that's what I like, and Jamie likes,' he added innocently. 'She suggested the makeover here. Really got behind me to throw out all the junk, pare down, and now you can see the room properly, so wasn't she right?'

Amadea looked round. 'Yes, yes, of course she's right. Very right. It looks fantastic, not weird at all. Shall I make us a coffee? Sorry for being such a wimp.'

Rob stared at her. It caught at his heart to see Amy crying, it caught at his heart to hear her apologising for being a wimp, but he refused to give in to his heart. Amy had hurt him too many times in the past.

'Come on, kid, one strong black coffee and you'll be dancing on tabletops again.'

The kettle having boiled, Amadea made the coffee in Rob's large brass cafetière. She could see that Rob liked her better for having walked out of her job, which was probably why he was prepared to buy some of her furniture. What she couldn't see was how he felt about Jamie. She poured the coffee into two mugs, making sure to add two teaspoonfuls of sugar to Rob's cup, and then sat down opposite him.

'Are you and Jamie an item now, Rob?'

'Not so that you'd notice, and not that it's any of your business, Miss Fontaine.'

'No, of course it's not,' Amy agreed, holding up her mug so that Rob could hardly see the expression on her face. 'On the other hand — '

'Yes?'

'It's not *not* my business either.'

'Oh, it's not not your business either, is it?'

'No. After all . . . '

'After all?'

'Well, after all, you are both friends of mine. And I have just given everything up for Jamie.' Amadea smiled mischievously. 'She owes me, and pretty soon, if you buy my dining-room set, you will too.'

'You're a minx, do you know that?'

'Yes, Dr Greer, I do.' There was a small pause. 'You don't by any chance need a nurse, do you?'

★　★　★

Florence, Edward and Dottie were enjoying a glass of wine on the terrace when Amadea bumped up the pot-holed drive in the old station taxi. She had not been able to face packing up the entire flat, part of her hoping that there would be no need, that pretty soon something would come up at one of the smaller companies in Swinton. She had sold most of her wardrobe with gratifying speed for a few hundred pounds, but instead of being sad she was now feeling oddly, happily light.

'Oh, look who's here again,' Dottie announced, and she found her heart sinking, for fond though

234

she was of Amadea, the poor girl always did seem to use up the oxygen, not to mention tire Florence. 'And with baggage, wouldn't you know?'

Florence went to meet Amadea and, bit by bit, helped her to carry her suitcases, not to mention the cat basket, up the stairs to her old room, which for some reason now looked too small to accommodate the cat, let alone Amadea. Florence pointed to the small desk.

'Your old desk,' she said for want of saying anything else.

'Oh, good.'

Amadea smiled wryly. Now she was not at Psemisis she doubted whether she would have much use for her desk.

She must have looked as lost as she suddenly felt, because Florence gave her a quick hug and said, 'Don't worry, love, everything will come right soon.'

Amadea nodded, not believing her.

'Lunch?'

'No, thanks, Mum. I think I'll just unpack and have a bit of a rest. It's been a long morning. At least I've been able to sell quite a lot of my stuff,' she said in a depressed voice, nodding towards her two suitcases. 'Rob Greer bought my dining-room table and chairs, and the man in the flat above was thrilled with the sofa. That's all that's left, really.' She paused, frowning. 'It's so strange how one's life comes down to so little.' She turned to her mother. 'It's weird being back, really weird. I feel as if I've just come home from school for the holidays.'

Florence smiled. 'I'm sure.'

'It won't be for long, I promise.'

'It can't be for long, darling. I have to sell the house. I can't go on living from hand to mouth.'

Amadea's heart sank, not because she didn't approve but because it suddenly felt as if every door was closing behind her and she would soon be completely alone, no mother, no Old Rectory, just her and her cat.

'No, of course you can't go on being poor, of course you can't,' she told her mother, trying to sound warmly understanding while fearing she might be sounding quite the opposite.

'It won't be easy to sell paradise, but it has to be done. Your father was a wonderful, kind man, but he was impractical, and when he married me I'm afraid he married someone as careless about money as he was himself.'

'Ah, so that's where I get it from — both of you,' Amadea said, pulling a wry face.

'I'm afraid so. Your father and I always lived high, wide and handsome, you know, always spending a little more than we could afford.' Florence shrugged her shoulders. 'But we enjoyed ourselves. We were happy.'

'Of course you were.'

Florence leaned forward impulsively and kissed Amadea on the cheek.

'You're very understanding, do you know that, Amy? Try and come down for lunch. Dottie is bringing a pie over, and I know Edward would like it. Someone nearer his age, poor soul.'

Amadea shut her bedroom door and gazed around her. She had put her address book on her old desk, and now there were the two suitcases beside her, and she was alone with them, she felt even more alone, even though she could hear her mother and Dottie and Edward talking on the terrace.

She opened the wardrobe doors and gazed in at the kind of things that mothers always keep. First party dresses, swimsuits, old straw hats, school magazines piled on top shelves and tied into bundles with pieces of ribbon; gumboots of different sizes, an old hockey stick, two old tennis rackets. Seeing everything so faithfully preserved took her back to when she was young, and at the same time made her feel strangely hopeless, a failure, as if she had not fulfilled her parents' dreams for her, as if all the things that they had kept confirmed their disappointment in her.

To overcome the sad feelings of regret that everything was yet again taking a downturn, she lay on her bed, gazing at the ceiling and wondering what to do with the rest of the week. There was something so unsettling about being at home again. Once you were an adult, being at home in your old room once more made you feel as if you were being forced back into school uniform.

She dozed off into a depressed sleep, of the kind into which you drift reluctantly, but from which you also never want to wake up.

She awoke later, feeling foggy, restlessly aware that what had woken her was the sound of Punch barking. For a few vaguely irritated minutes she lay listening, as if some distant radio were playing both too softly to involve you and too loudly to allow you to sleep. Eventually she swung her feet onto the carpet and went to look out of the window, indifferent to the weather, to the fresh green of the trees and to the birdsong, feeling only that she was in an emotional cul-de-sac, and yet not knowing quite why she was, or how she had got there.

The afternoon was hot, and there was a lazy Somerset feel to the air, not exactly sultry but unmoving, as if the air itself was waiting to wake up from its siesta. Birds dipped over the lawns, over the stream that ran down the side of the garden, and swallows swooped over the little lake. Amadea yawned, watching the scene as if detached from it, seeing it but not really wanting to be part of it, waiting for something to happen to bring her out of her torpor. There was someone in the lake, a man swimming, probably Edward. She shrugged her shoulders, turning away. She might as well join him for a dip in the lake. After all, what else was there to do?

★ ★ ★

It had taken only twenty-four hours for Jamie to become used to being at home. Not that she was a woman of leisure, by any means. She had to take Dylan to school and pick him up again, and without a job she had time to clean the flat until it shone; wash and starch everything from Dylan's shorts to the tablecloths, and dust and polish everything from the tops of the doors to the soles of her shoes, and that was all fine. What was not fine was trying not to think about Rob Greer.

'Is Rob coming round today?' was the first thing Dylan now asked when he woke up, and the first he asked when he came back from school.

'No, not today, maybe tomorrow,' was the statutory reply.

'You're getting to be a bad habit with Dylan,' Jamie joked when Rob called round that evening.

'And what about Dylan's mum?'

'Oh, you know, Dylan's mum is used to being on her own. She is an independent soul.'

'And now she is out of work?' Rob looked at Jamie.

'Same old, same old. You know, Dylan and I are used to being footloose and fancy-free. Best way to be, otherwise you get disappointed. I saw that at the office. Everyone being constantly disappointed by someone, and I thought that was the way not to be.'

'But that doesn't have to be a whole way of life, does it, Jamie?'

Jamie put her head on one side and smiled. It was a habit of hers that Rob found endearing.

'Are you trying to tell me something, Rob?'

Rob nodded and put his head on one side, mimicking her.

'Yup. I'm trying to tell you that I thought you might like to come and have dinner with me at this new restaurant on the edge of town — but now my nerve has failed because it's bound to be *disappointing*.'

Jamie smiled. 'I will book Mrs Tippett to sit.'

'And I, Ms Charlbury, will book a table.'

Amadea couldn't be bothered to unpack her suitcases, so she had changed into an old swimsuit she had found in the chest of drawers in her room. With a towel over one shoulder, her old school gymshoes on her feet, but still half asleep, she was sauntering down towards the lake when she thought she heard Florence calling.

'Amy! Amy!'

She could see no sign of her mother, so she continued walking towards the lake, where the young man whom she had seen swimming had now vanished.

'Amy! Amy!' her mother was still calling. 'Amy! Amy!'

Amadea stared. The young man had gone, the head of dark hair disappearing under the surface of the water. She started to run, hoping, expecting to see him resurface, but there was no sign of him. Upon reaching the bank she dived in and swam as fast as she could to where she had seen him last.

'Oh, for heaven's sakes, I thought ... I thought you were in trouble.'

Edward stared at her. 'Don't worry, I'm a strong swimmer,' he reassured her, and put out a hand to help her out of the water. 'You are too, I see.'

He was still staring, but not as hard as Amadea was staring at him.

'You are a strong swimmer, and I am a strong swimmer, and here is my mother who is also a strong swimmer,' Amadea repeated, as if she was talking in a foreign tongue, because she felt not just puzzled but utterly confused.

'Why did you think Edward was in trouble?' Florence held out a towel towards her.

'Why were you calling out to me? I heard you calling and I thought it was because Edward was in trouble. He disappeared under the water, I couldn't see him.'

'That's because I was swimming under water.' Edward looked pleased.

'And I was calling you because I wanted you to take Punch in with you. You know how he loves a swim.' Florence looked down at Punch, who was standing beside her on his lead. 'If I let him off he will jump in and try and rescue people.'

Florence laughed, but Amadea shook her head.

'I don't know. I don't know why I thought something had happened. I suppose I had just woken up and I was in a half-sleep, and I saw his head disappearing, and then it didn't seem to appear again.' She shook out her hair and frowned, shivering. 'I don't know what's got into me lately, really I don't. I think maybe . . . ' She shrugged her shoulders and turned for the house, a lump in her throat.

'Amy, Amy?'

Amadea never cried, and for that reason she didn't want her mother to see. Once in the house she ran up the stairs, turned on the shower in the bathroom and stepped smartly in. Maybe it was because she had just been thrown over, or maybe it was just a bad moment in her life, but she kept

241

getting the feeling that she was making a complete Horlicks of everything; worse than that, she had the feeling she had been doing so for most of her life.

'Come downstairs and have a cup of tea with me, Amy?'

The last thing she wanted was to go downstairs and have a cup of tea with her mother, but because she couldn't think what else she could do, Amadea, her face repaired, her clothes clean, her heart still heavy, trailed down the shallow, familiar stairs of the Old Rectory and into the kitchen.

Her mother was sitting in the faded chintz-covered chair that Amadea now seemed to remember her sitting in all her childhood; but now it seemed that David and her father were in the room with them, and they were all having cups of tea and chocolate cake and it was a Saturday sort of day, with the sun shining, and they had all been swimming in the lake, and not Punch but their dogs, all three of them, had been running up and down the banks barking their heads off, because it worried them to see everyone in the water laughing and splashing, but at the same time, unlike Punch, none of them wanted to get in.

'Sit down, Amy, while I get you a tea.' Her mother always did say 'sit down while I get you a tea'. 'Or would you prefer a hot chocolate?'

'A hot chocolate, please.'

Hot chocolate after swimming . . . Walking awkwardly up the stones of the beach until you reached the hut, and then dashing in, blue-lipped, teeth chattering, to grab a rough striped bathing towel and rubbing yourself hard to get warm, while hot chocolate was poured and Marmite sandwiches were unwrapped. It had been not just bliss, but heaven.

'I told you I must sell the house, but that doesn't mean . . . that doesn't mean we won't still be — we won't still mean a lot to each other.'

Florence's voice was only just penetrating Amadea's consciousness.

'Yes, of course, of course.'

She had no idea what her mother was on about.

'I just wanted you to know that I have no alternative, really I don't. Besides, this place has become too much for me. I have hung on here for as long as possible, but now I realise that I must let go. It would be best.'

Amadea was holding the mug of hot chocolate between her hands as if it had no handle. It was made of pottery, so it was heavy. When she turned it round Amadea saw it said 'Amy' on it and a date. David had given it to her for her birthday. She seemed to remember that it was her tenth birthday. She looked again at the mug. Yes, she had been ten.

'David was so artistic, he was even a good potter, wasn't he?' she asked her mother suddenly.

Florence nodded. David was good at everything he did; he was that kind of young man. Florence always imagined that had he lived he

243

would have grown into a renaissance person, musical, artistic, and generous to a fault. She sighed inwardly, but without grief.

'He could throw a pot with the best of them,' Florence agreed. 'Such a funny expression I always think — throwing a pot.'

'Do you still miss him? Do you still miss David?'

Florence looked at Amadea evenly. They had never discussed such a thing before. Amadea had certainly never brought the subject up.

'Not a day passes when I don't think of him, but now it is without sadness. He was taken for a reason. That was the span he was given, the length of his life, and I have accepted that. To do otherwise would be quite wrong. But sometimes when I see something, as you have just seen the mug he made for you, when I see his handwriting, say, on the flyleaf of a book, or catch sight of someone with his hair colour, then my loss catches at my heart quite as badly as it always has; but a moment later it is gone, just as he is. He was happy for his span, so I know I must be happy for mine. We are not put on this earth to be unhappy, of that I am perfectly certain.'

Amadea finished her mug of chocolate, and then stood up and went to the kitchen window, careful to keep her back to her mother.

'I wish I could feel like you, but I can't. I hated David for dying, you know, and I still do. I hated him for being such a hero, for coming to rescue me and the other little boy, for drowning like that, for breaking everyone's hearts. I wanted

244

it to be me, not him, because he was so much better at everything, just altogether much nicer than I could ever be. He was so much the perfect son, and I the imperfect daughter.'

Florence stared at Amadea's back, a troubled expression on her face, but she did not argue with her, or contradict her. They both knew that everything Amadea had just said was true, and they both knew that there was nothing to be done about it.

'You were different, that's all.'

Amadea nodded, silently, still staring out of the window.

'I've always thought that from the moment I was born I had disappointment written all over me, except with David. He never minded the fact that I was not up to him. Never minded that I was a lightweight, not musical, not a painter, nothing like you two, or him, just a plodder really. In fact I sometimes thought he liked me better for not being up to much — not in a bad way, but in a relieved kind of way, because with me he could be just a big kid, whereas with you two he had to be sure to be perfect.'

'I can see that.'

The expression on Florence's face was one of complete if troubled understanding.

'I've never stopped blaming myself for going for that last swim, for being the reason we lost David.'

'You were not the reason, Amy. Life was the reason. Life is dangerous, and David did what David always did — he went to someone's rescue. He was like Lord Nelson, he always wanted to be a hero, and he was. So that was good: think of that, he died the way he wanted to die, doing something heroic. There are people like that, and David was one of them.'

Amadea went to say something, and then turned away feeling as if she had lost the heaviest burden imaginable, but she would not cry, she just would not. She had cried too much, and for too long, all alone in her stupid flat, with only Fred for company, as the grief of the accident overwhelmed her.

After a long silence Florence said evenly, 'Be an angel and go and sit with Edward. I never like him to be on his own for too long. I always think he gets invaded by dark thoughts, thoughts that he can't understand. Besides, I expect he will like someone to talk to. He is very Edward at the moment, but don't be frightened if Edmund pops back out again, Edmund's very gentle too.'

'Sure, I'll go.' Amadea paused by the door. 'Edward does seem very different from when I first met him.'

'Yes. We see a great deal more of Edward than Edmund at the moment. But — you know, I worry, because what with one thing and another he can't stay here much longer. For one thing I'm selling the house, and for another Pierre doesn't think he can do much more for him. He thinks Edward really will have to go back to Swinton Hospital for what he calls 'proper treatment'.'

Amadea came back into the room. 'Yes, but

what *exactly* does Pierre think is wrong with him?'

Florence looked round at Amadea. 'He thinks he is suffering from dual personality syndrome, or something like that. His other personality, the one he has adopted, is a sweet gentle poet, but definitely not the young man we call Edward. Edward is someone quite different. For some reason we haven't been able to find out, he seems sometimes to become this poet from another age — you know, the way some people become Napoleon? Or Elizabeth the First? Or Queen Victoria?'

'But who is this other person, Ma? What do you know about him?'

'He's someone called Edmund Gains, and this is really the strangest thing, Amy: he was no one anyone had ever heard about until one day, under hypnosis, he came out with Harlington Hall, our Harlington Hall.' As Amadea's interest was well and truly caught, Florence went on. 'Of course, as soon as Pierre told me I went up to see our old friend, your dad's manager — remember Dick Saxon? Dick has just moved into a cottage on the estate and is helping out with the re-opening of the house, and he has actually found some of Edmund Gains's poems for me. They are riveting, but they have not got us anywhere, except we now know that for some reason Edward thinks he *is* him — his secondary personality is Edmund Gains.'

Amadea sat down again opposite her mother, and the expression on her face had gone from sorrow remembered to present excitement.

'But this is so fascinating. Someone from the past, living near here, being taken on by this young man who came to cut your hedges. What a story!'

Florence put up a hand to stop her, her spirits sinking as she realised that she had to be truthful with Amy, for there was no longer any reason not to be.

'No, Amy, Edward did not come to cut my hedges. No, I actually found him in the little guest cottage wearing fancy dress, and speaking as if he was straight out of an old play. I thought he was on drugs, just to begin with. I thought he'd — what is it you say? Oh yes, I thought he'd done his brains in in some way, poor young man, with one of those Ecstasy tablets or something.'

Amadea stared at her mother. 'He *didn't* come to cut your hedges?'

Florence shook her head. 'No. I made that bit up, I'm afraid, because I thought you'd get cross with me for taking him under my wing. In fact I knew you would.'

Amadea stared at her mother, and then she put her arms around her and hugged her quickly and spontaneously. 'Oh, but that is *such* good news, Mum.'

Florence stared at Amadea. 'What is good news, Amy?'

'Don't you see? This means you're human after all!'

Florence frowned. 'And what am I normally?'

Amadea looked mischievous. 'Only a plaster saint, that's all. Only someone I can never live up to. Only someone who's so good to everyone it

248

leaves nothing for the rest of the world to do.'

'Now where are you going?'

Amadea was by the door.

'If you really want to know, I am going to Google 'Edmund Gains, poet' on my computer and see what it comes up with. You never know, it might even say 'see Edward Green'. It's all so riveting.'

This time they both laughed. Amadea left, shutting the kitchen door behind her rather too loudly, which woke Punch and made him yawn and stretch, as if he thought he ought to be taken for a walk.

Florence stared ahead of her at nothing in particular, for once paying no attention to Punch's yawning noises. She had suddenly sensed, when she saw Amadea making a running dive into the lake, that some sort of emotional bubble was about to burst, but she'd had no idea what shape or form it would take. Now it had burst, she felt exhausted, relieved, flattened and drained. Things might start to look up now. Perhaps in trying to rescue Edward poor Amadea had somehow reversed the tragedy? Perhaps that act had brought things full circle? What her mother would never tell her, and what she was sure Amy had not noticed, was that Amadea had pulled on the same swimsuit that she had been wearing on that terrible day.

★ ★ ★

Jamie stood in front of the mirror and stared at herself. She was wearing an old linen jacket,

249

much pressed, but also new trousers — so they made the jacket look better, she hoped. Dimly, somewhere, she could hear Mrs Tippett letting herself into the flat, and Dylan running to meet her. She could hear it only dimly because she was feeling nervous, anxious, almost panic-stricken.

She knew she should go to meet Mrs Tippett and make all the 'Here's the coffee and there's the tea, and he can watch *Henry the Green Engine* once and that's all' kinds of conversation, but she could not bring herself to do so.

The simple fact was that she was more nervous of going out on a date with Rob than she would have thought possible. Rob was such a cool, funny guy, she was sure she would never be able to keep up with his banter. She would be boring, and worse, the evening would be tedious, as all first dates were.

Of course she had dated before Dylan came on the scene, but never since, and now she knew why. It was because it was too difficult, too risky to her self-esteem. Failure meant embarrassment and a draining of confidence, and would be far worse than not dating.

Her eyes strayed towards the phone. She would really like to phone Rob and tell him she had a headache, except to a doctor a headache would not be enough. No, it would have to be a migraine. Before she reached the phone, it rang. Jamie picked it up slowly and reluctantly as if it was about to burst into flames. It was Rob. He must have decided that he was the one who would have the headache.

'I've been a bit held up, so I'll meet you at the restaurant. Don't be late, will you? I'll think you're going to blow me away.'

Jamie went back to staring at herself in the mirror. So he had read her thoughts. She had been just about to blow him away, but only because she had not dated for so long that she had lost confidence in herself as a woman. It was that feeling of being rusty, and not knowing quite how to be, not wanting to be up for something, not wanting to be up for anything, and at the same time not wanting to be up for nothing at all. Perhaps he was feeling the same?

She turned away from the mirror. Oh, for heaven's sake, she was going to meet Rob, not the Phantom of the Opera. She had been going out to the park to play football with Dylan and Rob for days now. She had been having chats and glasses of wine with Rob, and Rob had been putting up with Dylan and her for hours at a time, so what was the big deal? There was none. He was Rob, and she was Jamie. They were going to have dinner, that was all. Just dinner.

But they weren't going to have just dinner, and she knew it. If they were going to have just dinner as mates, or friends, or whatever they were meant to be, then Rob would not have been phoning her, and she would not be nervous. No, this dinner date was different.

★　★　★

Rob stared at himself in the mirror. Jamie had helped him to turn his flat into a minimalist's

251

idea of heaven, and its effect had been to make him realise that he was not just an unmade bed in his habits but in his appearance. He no longer longed for Amadea. He missed her, but he did not long for her the way he had used to when he lay in bed waiting for the sounds of her return from some late-night date, worrying whether she would be back at all. Hoping, always hoping, that she would not stay out all night, which she sometimes did.

Now was different. He no longer had to wait up for Amy because she was gone, perhaps for ever, which was one of the reasons why he had been finding himself staring in the mirror so often lately. After all, when someone to whom you had been wildly attracted went out of your life, you had all the time in the world to stare at yourself, all the time in the world to wonder why she had never thought anything of you, never seen that you were actually a tall, handsome, articulate man with a ready wit.

'How would she see you as that when you look like you do?' he asked his reflection. 'Hair badly cut — clothes terrible. All right, you have abandoned the grey socks and left aside the frayed T-shirts, but for what? For an even more boring turned-down look that would not attract a woman of ninety-five. No, my friend, you need a makeover, and not tomorrow, today.'

He paused, still frowning at himself in the mirror. A handsome head, large green eyes, a straight nose and a mouth that smiled a lot were not enough.

'You know your trouble, mate? You look like

an overworked doctor, which is not that surprising since you are an overworked doctor.'

He sighed, his eyes sad. 'Time to make with the credit card, and throw myself on the mercy of hairdressers, clothes shops, catalogues, and anyone or anything that can or will help me, because if I'm meant to be taking young Jamie out to dinner tonight, boy do I need to hurry.'

★   ★   ★

So it was that Jamie, looking fresh, blond and more youthful than she had for some time, came into the restaurant to find Rob looking more handsome than he had probably looked since he was a young medical student who had never drunk more than half a pint of beer.

'Rob, you look great.' Jamie pecked him on the cheek.

'Jamie, you look great.' Rob pecked her on the cheek.

'What happened to your hair?'

Jamie sat down opposite him, staring at Rob's handsome head.

'I had it straightened.' He ran an embarrassed hand over it. 'I hadn't meant to have it straightened, but the young girl at the hairdresser's with the ring in her navel thought it would suit me.'

'Then, the ring aside, she has great taste.'

'Not in her navel she hasn't.' Rob shook his head. 'If only they knew what they were doing to their kidneys by going around dressed like they were Turkish belly dancers. Talk about the

253

expense to the National Health Service, and that's before we get to what rings do to the body. Glass of champagne?'

'No, no, really.'

'Oh yes, really.' Rob pointed to his own glass. 'I insist. I have done nothing but fight disease on behalf of humanity for the past weeks, and now is a moment to celebrate the gains rather than the losses.' He beckoned to the waiter. 'Another one of these please.'

Jamie looked nervously at the champagne when it was brought to the table. She was so unused to being spoilt, and she could not help wondering at the expense of it all. For a second it made her feel guilty, as if she knew that Rob could be spending the money on someone rather more worthwhile.

'No, really, your hair looks great, Rob,' she said again, and then, 'cheers!'

They clinked glasses and then fell silent, which was the moment when Rob gave her his widest smile, suddenly realising that she was feeling as shy as he, which made him feel much better and, for some reason, more shy. Hell, they knew each other, didn't they?

'As far as my hair goes, shall we move off 'great' and get to another adjective, like 'fabulous' or 'divinely handsome'? I quite like that last one, by the way.'

'You are divinely handsome,' Jamie agreed. 'Dylan's father was divinely handsome too,' she added, realising immediately that to say so at this point in the evening was a gaffe of the bigger sort.

'Ah, so I have competition from Dylan's father in the looks department, do I?' he asked, unable to keep the disappointment from his voice. 'Does he too have his hair done by the little girl with the ring through her navel?'

'Oh, no, absolutely not,' Jamie said, rather too quickly. 'In fact I wouldn't know where he has his hair done. It's so long since I saw him or heard from him.'

'Ships that passed in the night, were you?'

'Not that passed in the night, no, not like that. No, we fell wildly in love, much to our mutual astonishment, and then we went our separate ways, me to Swinton to work for Psemisis, while he had to go abroad. But we kept in touch, by email and texting and all that, as you do . . . ' Jamie stopped and rolled both her index fingers over each other. 'Blah, blah, blah. But he wanted to change the world, and I just wanted to earn my living.' She looked up from her glass of champagne, upon which she had been concentrating rather too hard. 'Yes, he had a passion to put something back, not to pass through this world and leave it in a worse state. He particularly wanted to help Africa in any way that he could, so off he went, and of course almost as soon as he had gone I found I was pregnant. But we had always agreed no strings attached, so I was determined, absolutely determined, not to hold him to anything. After all, it was my body that had become pregnant, not his. But nor would I, in inverted commas, do anything about it. So I had Dylan, and I sent him pics and texts, and then it all stopped.'

She shrugged her shoulders. 'These things happen, don't they? Dylan doesn't seem to have missed having a father, so far. I have told him all about Josh, and he knows that his dad loved him, and well — he seems a very cheerful little boy, quite confident, wouldn't you say?'

'He's everything a father or mother could wish.'

But they both knew they were lying. After all, Dylan had embraced Rob not just without hesitation but as if he had never thought a man would come into his life. Over the past days it had become quite obvious that small boys really enjoyed having much bigger boys around the place, and even as Jamie looked into Rob's eyes, searching for reassurance, she saw that her dinner companion was having some difficulty in accepting that Dylan might not prefer having a father to — not having a father.

'Let's have everything on the menu,' Rob suggested. 'No holds barred.'

Jamie held up the large card in front of her face to cover her feelings.

She had no idea why she had mentioned Dylan's dad. It was so stupid, and she had a feeling it might have spoilt the evening, but when she lowered the menu to ask Rob for advice and saw how he was smiling at her, with such understanding, she knew that far from being the wrong topic, it might have been quite the right one.

'Now it's time for you to tell me about yourself,' she said, after they had ordered and Rob had chosen the wine.

256

'You want me to tell you about myself?' Rob looked rueful. 'You should never say that to someone like me, Jamie. I am a confirmed egoist, and I love talking about myself.'

'In that case, off you go.'

So Rob took a sip of wine and began.

* * *

It seemed that he had been brought up in the wilds of Gloucestershire, before it became tamed. Rob and his brothers had wandered the Cotswold fields, fallen off their ponies, and fished streams and lakes with no sense of anything except freedom. Their father had been a country doctor, looking after a number of villages, in the days when doctors still made home visits, so it had been inevitable that Rob and both his brothers would go into the medical profession, one to become a surgeon, one a heart specialist, and Rob, the youngest by some years, aiming to specialise in head injuries. Their mother, a former nurse, had been only too happy to be a doctor's wife, so their home life had been an unendingly happy sequence of home-cooked food produced at very odd hours, and amiable chaos. Then she had died, quite suddenly, and it had all stopped. Their father remarried very quickly. His second wife was a family friend, someone who had been a friend to all of them, but so different from their mother that it was difficult for her stepsons to reconcile themselves to her. Nothing daunted, she spent the following years trying to bring order into the all-male

257

household, cooking nourishing food but insisting on serving meals on time, altogether dispensing a kind but firm discipline, until finally, after some Herculean struggles, she earned not just the respect of her stepsons but their love.

'Let no one tell you that cleanliness is *not* next to godliness,' Rob told Jamie, pulling a rueful face. 'My poor stepmum, how she put up with us all when she first married Dad, I don't know. She is, or was, or has to be, I realise now, a saint, and little wonder that my father loves her.'

'I only wish my mother had found someone else.' Jamie looked rueful. 'It would be an answer to this single parent's prayer. But she has been a widow so long I don't know whether she would know how to even go out to dinner with a man without telling him how to use his knife and fork. Everything in her house is so perfect that putting people in it makes it look messy. Dylan only starts to smile once he's left it. He runs, jumps, drives me crazy when we get home . . .'

'I know, it's the 'phew, been there, done that, now I can really live' feeling, so your mother has a positive purpose in Dylan's life.'

'Well — yes, I suppose she has.'

The conversation had come to a sort of halt again, and they both realised it. They had covered each other's family, they had covered Dylan, but the one other subject they had in common, and with which they were now left, was the one she sensed neither of them wanted to tackle — Amadea.

Jamie hesitated, knowing she had already put her foot in it earlier in the evening; and yet she wanted to tackle it, because she knew from Amadea over the preceding months that Rob had always been there in her life, but of course Jamie had never asked Amadea, or wanted to know, whether they had been an item. It had been none of her business. Now Rob looked at her, a quizzical expression on his face, knowing just what subject lay between them.

'So Amadea walked out of her job for you?'

'Yes.'

'That is so not Amadea, as she would say.'

Jamie hesitated. 'No, Rob,' she said slowly. 'Actually, you're wrong, that is just so Amadea.'

Rob looked at Jamie, and thought that for the first time on this first date he had really put his foot in it.

'How do you mean?'

'To understand Amadea you have to realise she is always at pains to appear just how she isn't.' Jamie laughed. 'Flighty, uncaring, living for the moment, but she's actually not like that at all. For some reason she has cast herself in the part, and now she is stuck with it; but the Amadea I know at work is just not like that.'

It was understandable that Rob did not want to hear that Amadea was not as he had come to think of her, but he could see from the expression of reflective affection on Jamie's face that he was going to be made to hear nonetheless.

'There is so much to Amadea that she is at such pains to cover up. She was always the first into the office, the first to bring you a coffee, just how you liked it. Always putting little posies of

259

flowers on my desk when she knew I was down, or Sheila Pryor had been bullying me. And never grumbled, you know? Didn't matter how much work I threw at her, she went at it hammer and tongs as if it was the best thing in the world. Sure, she liked partying, but she's young, why wouldn't she? And you know, losing her brother that way, that was not easy for her. In fact I don't think she has ever recovered from it, I really don't.'

Rob stared at her. 'I didn't know Amadea had lost a brother. She never said anything about losing a brother.'

'She wouldn't. Yes, she lost her brother a few years ago in a swimming accident. I only knew because I looked in her office diary and saw she had pencilled in 'David's birthday', and thinking it was some new boyfriend I made a joke about it, a joke which turned out to be about as funny as appendicitis — '

'Oh, that can be quite funny, always providing it's not yours . . . '

Jamie laughed. 'Anyway, now she's back home with her mother and her friend, and this poet person — who is a knockout, I hear.'

'Yes, he is, off the wall but very good-looking,' Rob agreed, the unwanted realisation coming to him that Amadea and the beautiful young man would be together often, that the weather was gorgeous and they would have a great deal of time on their hands.

Rob finished his glass of wine far too quickly, and motioned to the waiter to bring him his bill.

'So, home Jamie, home.'

Jamie nodded. 'Sure, but I think we'll walk.'

'No, no, I'll get them to call a taxi.'

'No, you won't. We're going to walk. It's a lovely night, and Mrs Tippett's not expecting us back until eleven.'

They wandered through the still-busy streets, and Rob put his arm around Jamie in the way that lovers do, and she put her arm around him, so that when they finally stopped and kissed, it was quite natural.

It was a lovely kiss, comfortable and sweet. They walked on, and kissed again, and again, and all the kisses were comfortable and sweet, and Jamie found herself wondering if now, at last, she might have found someone to replace her beloved Josh. And Rob found himself insisting that at last he had found someone to come between him and his completely unrequited love for Amadea.

They stopped outside the flats and Jamie put on fresh lipstick, and they both tried hard to look as if they had been having dinner in a friendly brother-and-sister way.

Mrs Tippett was a comfortably upholstered, small, white-haired woman who wore the kind of spectacles that look as if they are never removed from the wearer's face, not even at night. She eyed the returning diners with some interest.

'Dylan's been up all evening watching the telly with me. He wouldn't go to bed until you both came home.'

She stepped aside to show Jamie the unfamiliar sight of her son wide awake at eleven o'clock at night, then she beckoned Jamie to

261

follow her into the kitchen.

'He's never like this when you're out working late, just tonight. You know what I think, don't you?'

'No, but I think you're going to tell me.'

'I think that he's afraid of — you know — him.' Mrs Tippett inclined her head towards the sitting room where they could hear Rob and Dylan laughing. 'I think he thinks that you're going to marry that man and leave Dylan here with me . . . at least that's what he said to me earlier.'

Jamie stared at the babysitter. She had no idea whether Mrs Tippett was telling the truth, and they both knew it. It would be worse than anything to question Dylan about what he might have said. Jamie sighed. It had been such a lovely evening, up until then.

'How much do I owe you?' she asked flatly.

Mrs Tippett looked at the clock and sucked in her breath with some enjoyment.

'Well, we're into the extra hour now, aren't we, Jamie, and you know the agency rules?' She held up one hand and struck off each of her fingers as if they were skittles and she was throwing bowls at them. 'So that will be, let me see . . . Forty pounds.'

'Yes, of course.'

Jamie promptly handed over what now seemed, in the light of the mischief the older woman had just wrought, far too much money.

'I'll put you to bed, young man, and if I put you to bed you'll stay there,' Rob was saying as the two women went back into the sitting room.

After Mrs Tippett had departed in her usual galleon-in-full-sail manner, Jamie stood watching Rob pick Dylan up and hold him upside down, which was just what not to do at bedtime. But since it was making Dylan giggle happily, she suddenly didn't care.

'Now this is how it is: you will stay like this unless you go to bed and stay there.'

Dylan giggled and giggled, but finally gave in with 'I promise!'

Rob turned him right side up again and, with a look of triumph towards his mother, walked him into his bedroom.

It was a large sunny room, a room on which a mother had obviously expended huge efforts to make it just as a room for a boy should be. Hand-painted cupboards with pictures of animals, shelves full of books about trains and engines, and more trains and more engines, and a bed that was not just a bed but could double as a boat, as Dylan quickly demonstrated by pulling up the bedclothes to show the boat shape and the name on the side, *The Jolly Dylan*.

'You're a lucky little boy, aren't you, Dylan?' Rob stated, looking round thoughtfully. 'I never had a room to myself when I was young. I had to share with my older brother, and that's all I did share, the room — because he swiped all my toys, the swine.'

Rob glanced at the books. 'I'll read you one story and then it's lights out, and not a murmur, do you hear?'

Dylan nodded happily, but Jamie, watching from the door, knew that one story was not

263

going to be enough. He was too excited.

It was only when Rob was on his fourth book and Dylan had not given in either to sleep or to being on his own that Jamie finally threw in the towel and beckoned to Rob to follow her out of the room, shutting the door behind him.

'I'm going to have to break all the rules and put him in my bed,' she told Rob, with a look that wavered between apology and frustration. 'Wouldn't you know it?'

They both laughed, once again ruefully.

'Just as things were going — well.'

Jamie nodded. 'They can go well again, can't they?' she heard herself suggesting.

'They will, Ms Charlbury, they will,' Rob told her in a lowered tone. 'At least if I have anything to do with it, they will.'

They looked at each other.

'What a thing!'

He kissed her quickly on the lips and went aback into Dylan's room.

'Come on, young man, your mother has decided to break all the rules and take you into her bed, you lucky, lucky boy.'

He put out his hand and Dylan, his face flushed with the triumph of his tactics, reached out a warm, plump, childish hand and took the larger one in his.

'Can I have one last story in Mum's bed, Rob?'

'No, you can't have one last story — ' Jamie put in, but stopped when she saw the look on Rob's face. 'Oh, all right, just one last story.'

'Which way the master bedroom?'

'Through there.'

Jamie pointed, and finally led the way, opening the door on to a room that Rob, quite purposefully, had never entered.

Jamie had allocated herself a smaller room than Dylan, a fact which Rob instantly appreciated, and which he found touching. Nor was it the room of a married woman. It was very white, very clean, with stripped pine floors, no frilly dressing table or ornate mirrors, a plain cream table set about with a few jars, a chest of drawers, a hanging cupboard and white linen curtains. It was very much the room of a singleton, except for one detail, the leather-framed photograph by the bed of a dark-haired young man with large eyes and a sweet expression. Rob stared at it.

'Dylan's dad, Josh,' Jamie stated without embarrassment.

'He's very good-looking.'

Jamie looked away. Damn, damn, damn!

Not long after, Rob excused himself and went home, leaving Jamie with that most unappealing of feelings, namely a strong desire to kick herself in the shins.

10

Dick Saxon looked out of the diamond-patterned window of his idyllic cottage and sighed with the beauty of everything that he saw before him. The colour of the green, the smoothness of the water on the large lake sparkling before him, the swans moving not slowly but somehow inexorably across the surface. He was lucky to be alive on such a splendid morning, but better than that, much better than that, he knew it with every fibre of his being. Seconds later his telephone rang, sounding a great deal louder than he had ever heard it, due, he realised, to the extreme peace and calm of his little drawing room.

'I'm Amadea Fontaine, Florence's daughter,' a voice informed him, 'and I've been trying to find Edmund Gains, the poet of Harlington Hall, on the internet. I've come up with diddly squat, so my mother wondered if you, on the other hand, might have found something?'

'Ah, the daughter, how nice to hear you,' Dick said, smiling as he stared ahead of him, still savouring the quiet of the morning and the old-fashioned heavy black telephone receiver. 'As it so happens, I finished snapping the poems yesterday evening and after a long wrestle with my recalcitrant computer managed to zip them all into a file. I'm about to pop them over to you now. Is not technology a mighty thing? I must

266

tell you something else, too: while I was snapping them I read some of his private stuff again, and even though I'm inclined to be a fully paid-up philistine as far as verse is concerned, they struck me as really rather good, not at all amateur — in fact quite the opposite.'

'Perhaps he is responsible for all the poetry written by Anon?'

Dick laughed. 'Now there's a notion! It would mean headlines in the *Guardian*, Anonymous exposed at last! Splendid stuff, perfectly splendid. No, what I do know is that sometimes these poets in residence published their more risqué or anarchical verses anonymously, but only because they were frightened that if their patrons read them they might lose their stipend, or be thrown out of their grace-and-favour cottage. So with the wind in the right direction and a full set of sails, here goes: I am emailing them — although I must confess I might as well be abseiling them.'

Under an hour later Amadea had received and printed out the entire works of Edmund Gains.

'What on earth are these?' Edward asked in amazement when Amadea showed them to him.

'They are poems, Edward, written by Edmund Gains.'

Edward stared at her. 'Poems? But I don't like poetry.'

Only yesterday they had talked about fame and Edward had said, lightly scathing, 'So many poets and writers confuse fame with achievement. They are always too busy attending some salon where the hostess of the day will be

267

lionising them, instead of seeing to their proper duties, the nourishing of their genius. I have always nourished my talent, alone, in the country.'

Then he had stopped as if struck by the force of his own argument, and after a few seconds he had left Amadea for his room, where she found him later, staring into the middle distance, as if he was working out something very complicated, such as VAT on everything that had ever been produced in the world.

★   ★   ★

The following morning, for the first time in years, Florence had crept out to her studio, and started, hesitantly, nervously, to prepare her canvases, to sharpen her pencils, to think, to look, to see with eyes whose vision was now for some reason becoming more and more clear.

It was as if she had been climbing a terrible mountain, slipping and falling, hurting herself, bruised, body aching; sometimes parched with thirst, sometimes hungry, always alone — so alone, but worse, always pretending that she had to go on, because there was no going back. But now she realised, as the sun filtered into the room in which she stood surrounded by her work of long ago, that she knew something else: if you could be brought to turn and look around you, instead of always grimly ahead, there was a *view*. And it was a beautiful view. She herself was not in the landscape she could see spread out below her, she knew she was far too insignificant for that, but she was very much part of it. She was as much part of it as the wind that was rippling the lake outside, and the trees that were swaying gently; and to be part of it was quite enough.

She had promised Amadea, who had just left to walk through the woods to Harlington Hall to meet Dick Saxon, that she would keep a watchful eye on Edward until Pierre arrived for one of their sessions. She must not leave their poet to his own devices. She must keep an ear out for him at all times, babysit him, as Amadea had put it; so she could not stay too long in her studio but must return to the house, which turned out to be reassuringly and beautifully quiet. For a few seconds all that could be heard was the clicking of Punch's claws on the old wooden floors, as he made his way to his water bowl in the kitchen. Florence held her breath. Silence was what she had become used to, but the silence she had been used to was a lonely silence, and this was not lonely. It was a silence filled with contentment, with the ease of early summer sunshine, with the feeling that the sun had risen and was smiling on all of nature, giving it a wake-up call, telling it to hurry along and make the most of these precious days.

But she was forgetting their poet in residence!

She climbed the stairs to listen outside his door. Silence from within the room too. But this was a worrying silence. Had he slipped out when she was not looking? Had he tried to follow Amadea up to Harlington?

'Edward?'

Still no noise from within.

She opened the door.

Edward was seated by the desk, but not writing, as she had half expected. He was staring out of the window. Despite the sound of the door opening he did not turn. He, it seemed, like Florence in the studio, was in some sort of trance.

'Edward?' she said again, still a question in her voice.

At last he turned towards her, and Florence saw at once that there was something in his eyes, something she had not seen before.

'Are you all right?'

He waited before replying. 'Are you?'

Florence hesitated. 'I think I might be,' she said eventually. 'And you?' she asked quickly, because there was something in his face that caught at her heart.

'I think I could be,' he replied.

★   ★   ★

Dick Saxon was looking less urbane, and more thoughtful. He had found nothing more to link Edmund Gains to Harlington Hall, which while somewhat irritating was not the end of the world, because now Amadea was with him he had realised that the story of Edmund Gains might not be the only story they were investigating.

'Florence hasn't given me the picture in full, then?'

For a second they found they were staring at

each other, knowing that the same thought was crossing both their minds. Was Florence Fontaine, a lonely middle-aged widow, somehow fixated on this young man who had strayed into her life and been concussed in her kitchen? Or was the man in her kitchen a loony who had simply hit his head?

Dick frowned. 'He came to cut her hedges, you said?'

Amadea nodded, not wanting to tell Dick that Florence had lied about the young man's mysterious arrival in her guest cottage. Nor did she know how much Florence had told him.

'Yes.' She cleared her throat, intent on steering a careful course. 'Yes, apparently he came to cut her hedges. She offered him a coffee, and he concussed himself.'

'And since the fall he thinks he is this chap Edmund Gains, who we now know was once the bard in residence. So either he is mad, or he has become so.' Dick paused. 'Madness is most definitely infectious, of that there is no doubt at all. I found that out managing musicians — not your father, of course,' he added hastily.

They both laughed.

'I don't think any one of us at the Old Rectory is mad, yet — but I do think we have all become rather more involved with Edward and Edmund than we could ever have imagined we would,' Amadea told him in a thoughtful voice.

Dick made a rather doubtful 'mmm' sort of sound, before continuing.

'Great Scot, I don't think any of you are in the least bit mad, Amy, absolutely not. A little insane perhaps, but only because you have all taken on this poor fellow, but certainly not mad!'

Amadea looked glum. 'Whatever, but the truth is it can't go on for much longer. Ma's got to sell the house pdq.'

'That's a pity. Run out of wampum, has she?'

'That, and the fact that she has been coping on her own for too long really. I think she feels she needs to change her life, that she has been treading water since Dad died and David was drowned. Which means she will have to send Edward back to Swinton Hospital quite soon, which she is really rather dreading.'

'No — Swin*vile* is not nice, I do agree, and as for being left in Swinvile Hospital — well, it's not a place for a sensitive soul like Edward, I can see that.'

'No, that's it. And of course no one feels that more than Ma, poor old duchess. I know it sounds pathetic,' Amy went on, feeling oddly pleased because she seemed able to talk to Dick in a way she would not at first have thought possible, 'but every time I see an 'Edward' bit coming through, I get so excited — it's as if a door you have been pushing and shoving against suddenly opens. And you know Pierre Lavalle?'

'Ah yes, Pierre, good chap. He did such wonders for my fear of flying, I had to take a year's sabbatical in order to appease my lust for long-haul travel.'

'Well, Pierre has brought out this other person even more under hypnosis, while with us, for some reason, more and more 'Edward' is coming back, so much so that the 'Edmund' bit now

272

seems rather puzzled about 'Edward'. But you know, I might go back home now and find everything's changed.' She shrugged her shoulders. 'When I showed Edward the poems you emailed to me, he looked at me as if I was mad, but two hours later I found Edmund sitting at my mother's desk trying to pen a verse or two about the sunset. It's all so bizarre.'

'He does sound very much like a young man suffering from a dual personality. Not as uncommon as we would think, and it does seem the only explanation.'

'Someone told me that even a few puffs of the wrong kind of cannabis can do it, that it can bring out a paranoiac streak that you had no idea existed.'

'Oh, I expect they'll find peanut butter can do it before too long.'

Dick pushed his glasses up on to the top of his head, taking a long look at Amadea. She was not in the least bit like her gentle brown-eyed mother. She was considerably taller, slimmer of course, with a pair of mischievous blue eyes that were very much her father's. She might be a trifle modern in her manner, but he sensed that she had a vein of great decency, and that she was genuinely troubled, if not moved, by this young man's predicament. He replaced his glasses, at once coming to a new decision.

'I tell you what, Amadea,' he announced. 'I have an old friend coming to stay. Your mother has very kindly asked us and another mutual friend, Theo Mayer, to lunch tomorrow — a little bachelor party composed of Theo, myself and a chap called Walter Dexter. I am trying to get Walter interested in your mother's paintings, but Theo is a book chap — eats, sleeps and dreams old books. Who knows but he may have some angle on this fellow Edmund Gains?'

Amadea felt really grateful. Dick could see this and was touched by it. It wasn't easy for Florence to be the widowed mother of an adult daughter, but nor was it easy to be the daughter of a lonely, impoverished mother.

'Don't worry about a thing,' he told Amadea as they parted, he to stroll back to his office, Amadea to walk back to the Old Rectory.

★ ★ ★

Amadea would have taken his advice had she not arrived home to find her mother already at the front door.

'Such bad luck — Pierre has been taken to hospital, acute peritonitis.'

Florence and Amadea looked at each other, saying nothing as Amadea's mobile phone rang and she plucked it out of her pocket.

'Sorry, Rob, I'm not coming back to Swinton just at the moment. I will this side of soonish. Ring you back. 'Bye.'

She turned to her mother, and seeing the look of disappointment in her eyes she touched her briefly on the arm.

'Come on, Ma, we're not going to give up on Edward and Edmund quite yet, are we, even if we have lost Pierre.'

'No, you're right, Amy, we have to make a plan, Stan.'

It had been one of David's catchphrases, and they both smiled.

'As a matter of fact, Dottie has a plan, Stan, but . . . you know Dottie, she lives a bit in her head. Hasn't read a newspaper for years and years, and hardly listens to the radio. Takes the view that it's a waste of time to read about things she can do nothing about. Which is a point of view, after all.'

'Perhaps we should both go to the great woman herself and ask her what her plan might be?' Amadea suggested.

She had forgotten what a warm-hearted experience entering Dottie's farmhouse could be, an experience she had not known for what now seemed years. It was not just the smell of baking bread, or the rows of meticulously labelled home-made preserves, or the worn chintz, or the cats observing from window sills, or the old pugs curled up on cushions in front of the Aga. It was Dottie herself, breathing warmth the way a dragon was always rumoured to breathe fire.

'Sit down, sit down,' she begged. 'Just wait till I fetch you a glass of something and then I'll tell you my plan.'

Florence sank gratefully into her usual chair on the patio, while Amadea prowled about smelling the roses and pinching a piece of lavender between her fingers to better appreciate its aroma.

'Well now,' Dottie began, as they sipped their

chilled white wine. 'Since Pierre has been plucked untimely from our services, it seems to me that the best we can do, in the perhaps quite short period we have to decide about Edward, who by the way is . . . ?'

'With Dick Saxon back at the house.'

'Well, the best we can do is to try and think this thing out for ourselves. Now I know that Pierre was coming to the conclusion that Edward was suffering from some sort of dual personality, which may be the correct diagnosis. But there are other theories about these conditions, and since Pierre is *hors de combat* I have been delving into some of my old books. And it's quite interesting.' She paused, staring ahead. 'You see, in the very, very old days our ancestors believed that these conditions were nothing less than alien spirits occupying our bodies, sometimes one, sometimes two, sometimes many more. They believed that some terrifying incident could enable such a spirit to enter a human being, and that the only way they could get rid of one was to exorcise it, send it back to where it belonged.'

Florence and Amadea were watching Dottie with some interest.

'Now,' Dottie continued, realising that for once she had both their attentions. 'The problem with this is that nowadays no one will *do* them. They all funk exorcisms. I know because of poor old Edith Pargeter, in the last cottage to the right just before the pub, you know? Well, dears, she inherited a spirit from the twit who had lived there before she bought it. The silly woman used

276

to do table rolling, and so, as happens, she left someone behind. What a pest he was. Smoked the most beastly old shag I have ever smelt, slammed doors in her face, and once broke the loo seat. Edith was not amused. She rang round all the priests and the vicars and shamans and I know not what, but none of them would do more than bless the place, and that wouldn't get rid of the wretch, so she finally settled for shifting the bogeyman herself.'

Dottie paused, sipping appreciatively at her wine as she savoured Edith's victory.

'What did she do?' Amadea asked.

Dottie smiled. 'You won't believe this. She shouted at him.'

'*What?*'

'She did, she yelled at him. As I remember it she nearly went hoarse, but it worked. Every time she smelt his old shag in her bedroom she went after him hammer and tongs, and the same when he slammed the doors and all the rest. 'Get out of here, you smelly old ghost!' she yelled, time and time again, and do you know what? He only went! Mind you, it took months. But she won, in the end she sent him on his way, and she has lived peacefully at Pear Tree Cottage ever since, and that is the truth.'

'But we can't yell at Edward/Edmund, Dottie,' Florence said reasonably. 'He takes exception to the sight of a motor car. If we start yelling at him he'll probably pass out!'

'No, Flo, of course not, I'm not suggesting we yell at poor Edward. No, no, not at all. No, what I suggest is that we try and have him exorcised.

And that is my point, d'you see? I think the poor young man is being inhabited by this Edmund Gains. I've thought about it a great deal, and it all makes such sense. The fact that he is being occupied by someone who lived and worked at the Hall, so near to where we are — couldn't that be some sort of a pointer, wouldn't you say? That and the fact that he was found in Florence's guest cottage?'

'Yes, but how would we go about it, if it's true, I mean? How would we go about actually getting Edward exorcised?'

Dottie's eyes took on a sphinx-like look. 'I know of a goodly woman in Dorset, Mabel Minton by name. She is something of an expert in these matters. She is not on the blower, but I can ring her neighbour and she will take a message to her for us.'

'Does this mean that if we took Edward to see her, she could get rid of Edmund Gains?'

Dottie nodded her head solemnly at Amadea, whom she suddenly realised she liked a great deal more than she had used to do.

Florence sighed. 'Oh dear, of all the dilemmas to face, of all things to feel — ' She stopped.

They both stared at her until she continued.

'I hate the thought of Edmund being chucked out just like that, isn't that stupid? After all this, I really don't like to think of him being sent on his way. He is such a dear, gentle fellow.'

'Yes, Ma, but if Dottie's right, he is somewhere where he shouldn't be. Remember that, and it's up to us to find out where he *should* be, surely?'

Dottie's expression was uncharacteristically

firm. 'Amadea's quite right, Flo, and all I am saying is that I think Mabel might help Edmund do just that. It's a very strange world, the spirit world, but the thing is that it really exists, and only a fool would deny it. Would you agree with that?'

Florence nodded. 'Oh, I am with you there, Dottie. Yes, of course, I believe that, absolutely. I believe in spirits and heaven. I just don't know whether we should actually exorcise poor Edmund. I mean where will he go, if he is not here?'

'I expect you can ask Mabel that yourself, Flo. She probably knows how to handle that kind of thing, sends the personality somewhere more suitable, like back to Harlington Hall. Yes, that is probably what she will do, send him back to where he came from, don't you think?'

'That does sound a good idea.'

But despite her accommodating words Florence was still looking so doubtful that Dottie decided to plunge ahead with another story about Mabel.

'You particularly will like this story, Flo, because of Henry, you know?'

Dottie made sure that she once more had their full attention, because she did so hate to waste a story, and then she began.

'A highly talented pianist was having a bad time of it, and I mean a *really* dreadful time of it. It seemed no good would come of his playing this particular composer, whom he had selected as the most suited to his style. After a really terrible recital during which he had made a hash of everything, he decided to throw in the towel and give up playing the piano professionally. Before he could do so, he had to attend a supper party in his honour given by a devoted friend of his. The friend, perhaps as some sort of gimmick, had asked Mabel Minton to attend as a guest, despite the fact that she had not been in the audience. In the event Mabel sat next to the disheartened pianist, who during the course of the supper party was astonished to be told by her, in perfect musical terms, that one of the reasons he was having trouble performing this particular composer, was because his pedalling was all wrong. Naturally the pianist, feeling pretty affronted, asked on whose authority she could possibly know this. 'Why, the composer himself, of course. He wanted me to tell you not to give up,' Mabel replied. At any rate it transpired that the young man promptly, and very wisely, took the advice from the other world; and the result was that his career took off once more, and now he is able to tell everyone, including those asses the music critics, that he has his coaching from the very best authority!'

'Gracious, Dottie, you never told me any of this.'

'Only because there was no need for it. But the plain truth is that it is just that — the plain unvarnished truth.'

Florence frowned, looking back towards the house where she hoped Dick was still keeping an eye on her patient.

'I don't see what we have to lose, do you?' she said, looking purposefully at Amadea and Dottie.

'Nothing at all, Ma.'

'I'll be on to Mabel straight away then — make sure the old girl will receive you,' Dottie said, rising. 'It's not always easy with Mabel, I have to tell you. Fingers crossed.'

As Dottie went inside, Amadea turned to Florence. 'Exciting, don't you think?'

'Oh yes, Amy, it is, very exciting.' Florence put a hand on her daughter's arm. 'But don't you think it could be — well — dangerous too?'

'Who for? Edward or Edmund?'

'Either of them, or both of them.'

Amadea frowned. 'I think if we were going to see Mabel, because . . . because, well . . . '

'Because, say — we wanted to be frivolous?'

'Exactly; if we were doing it for fun, perhaps it might be dangerous. But that's not why we're doing it. We're doing it for philanthropic reasons, so it can only be good, surely?'

There was no time to tell if Florence was convinced, as Dottie had come back out of the house wearing her most triumphant expression.

'Mabel's neighbour popped in with my message, and it seems Mabel will see you and him tomorrow morning,' she told them. 'What a boon, the dear old darling has had a cancellation. The luck of it, I can't tell you. She's normally booked up for months ahead. Gets called away so much too, you know — hither and thither she goes. There are so many dilemmas now. People building over graveyards and I know not what. And then they wonder at the ensuing chaos, well, I mean — what *do* they expect? So — who will drive Edward to Mabel Minton's

281

house? I would say that Amadea was just the right person.'

'But would you want to, love?' Florence turned to Amadea.

'I would love to,' Amadea volunteered at once. 'Besides, you can't go, Ma. Remember — you've got Dick and his friends coming to lunch.'

'Oh yes, so I have,' Florence agreed in a suddenly distanced voice, her heart sinking at the idea of entertaining not one but three men on her own. She turned to Dottie. 'Would you like to join us?'

'Love to, dear, but I have the extraordinary general meeting of the Smalls Club.'

No one dared to ask what that might be, or indeed what it might entail. Instead they all diplomatically finished their drinks, feeling suddenly in a buoyant mood. After all there is nothing quite like a decision made, and in this case there had been not one decision made but two.

Amadea herself was honoured that the two older women had felt able to trust her, while all the time she secretly hoped that she would indeed bring Edward home a restored character. It would be so sensational if that happened. He would never have to go back to dreaded Swinton, and her mother could sell her house knowing that she had been involved in a particularly joyous adventure.

When Florence and Amadea returned to the Old Rectory, they were met by Dick Saxon. He wore a puzzled expression.

'What a delightful young man Edward is,' he

said, taking his leave of them in the drive. 'I can quite see why you got involved with him.'

He waited diplomatically until Florence had hurried into the house, and then turning to Amadea he lowered his voice.

'Not a sign of Edmund the whole time you were out, would you believe?'

'What? No poetry, no little quotes from Keats or someone?'

'Not a thing. No, just a very nice young man who seemed to be enjoying his stay — despite not being able to remember why he was here.'

It was ridiculous but Amadea immediately felt an overwhelming sense of disappointment. This, after all, might mean that there was now no need to take Edward to see Mabel Minton.

'Well, perhaps you've cured him, Dick?'

Dick laughed. 'Or maybe your mother's cooking has?' he asked light-heartedly. 'We're all so looking forward to having lunch with her tomorrow.'

Amadea waved him off down the drive, and then she too hurried indoors.

'Edward,' she called up the stairs as soon as she could. 'Edward, it's Amadea. Are you there?'

Edward peered down the flight of wooden stairs at her, frowning.

'I am here, but I must not be disturbed,' he told her. 'A sonnet is upon me, and I must go to wrestle with the Muse.'

Amadea nodded. 'Of course. Sorry, Edmund.'

She turned back and retraced her steps. There was still a need to consult Mabel Minton, but there was also, strangely, a growing hope that they might be able to banish Edmund for longer and longer periods. After all, if Edward had stayed in place all the time Dick Saxon had been with him, maybe Mabel would dismiss Edmund altogether. What a victory if she could.

★ ★ ★

The following morning Amadea borrowed her mother's old car and set off with Edward by her side. For most of the journey into Dorset he looked as if he had died and gone to heaven. He sang, he gazed about him, he smiled, he pointed out places of beauty, the interminable fascination of the differently shaped clouds scudding through the Dorset skies, the cows grazing in the fields, the sheep seemingly immobile on the hillsides. Everything gave him pleasure.

It turned out that Dottie's acquaintance, Mabel Minton, lived down an unmarked winding lane that led along the side of a hill until it resolved itself into a clearing that faced the pounding sea. At the top of the open land, nestling into the arm of a cliff, lay a fading ochre-coloured pebble-dashed bungalow named Madaoscar.

For a second Amadea found herself staring at the house plaque. Of course — Ma — after Mabel, then Da — after perhaps David, or Davina — and then Oscar. A bungalow obviously named after all the family.

'How charming,' she said, turning to Edward, but saw at once that her delightful companion of the journey had gone. Edmund was back in his place.

She felt unnaturally disappointed, then quickly pulled herself together. That was why they were there, for heaven's sake! To get rid of Edmund. However harmless, he was definitely in the wrong place, and would have to be sent back to where he came from so that Edward could have a life of his own, on his own.

'Good morning, my dears.'

Mabel, for it had to be her, stood before them in all her glory — and glory it was. She was not just a tall woman but a woman of immense height, dressed in a long gown of many colours; splendidly home-made, it sported large squares of everything from old tea towels to pieces of every kind of fabric, velvet and satin, cotton and linen. It was a dress that gave a new meaning to the idea of recycling.

Mrs Minton herself was handsome, in a baroque, Mediterranean manner, with a long sallow face topped with a closely cropped head of stubbly bright ginger hair.

'Come in, my dears, come in.'

'Hallo, I am Amadea Fontaine, and this is — '

'I know who this is, my dear. Come in, come in.' She took a firm grip of Edward's arm. 'You will want a nice glass of an ambrosial nature after your long journey, sir,' she told him, seeming to know at once that Edmund was very much in place, which Amadea found to be almost spooky.

However, whether or not Mabel had realised that it was Edward's other persona that was staring out at her, seeking reassurance from her firm expression, it did not seem to matter.

'You'll be in good hands,' Dottie had said as they had driven off, but Amadea had not known quite what she meant until now.

Now she did know, because far from being weird or not-of-this-world, Mabel Minton emitted a very real and human warmth. If Amadea could have put her finger on it she would have said, from the moment she met her, that it was obvious Mabel was someone who, from the moment she stood beside you, made you feel not just less taut, less neurotic, less worried, but altogether better. Like a horse whisperer, but someone who tended human beings. It was as if you suddenly knew why you had been put on this earth, and it was not to be eternally anxious, always striving, striving, striving — but to be part of this world, to listen to the internal rhythms of life and try to find where your place in it might be.

A jug of ambrosial juices of an indeterminate flavour was presented to them, and Edward, looking strangely boyish, stared around him at the many cats, of varying extractions, that were occupying so much of the furniture.

'So, who is at home today?' Mabel asked Edward.

Edward frowned. 'Working for Lord Harlington as I do, I am seldom, as you say, at home, madam. You must know that.'

'Why must I know that?'

Mabel stared at him, her head lowered, her eyes focused on his handsome face, looking into his large dark eyes as if she could read his thoughts, which all of a sudden it seemed to Amadea that she might well be able to do.

'Because,' Edward said in his careless, slightly patronising Edmund voice, 'because, madam, you are a witch.'

'So I am,' Mabel agreed. 'A white witch, a herbalist, a hypnotist, a dowser, a member of a holy order of people who have inherited the wisdom of the ages, a wisdom all but stamped out by the destruction of the monasteries, they being our first health service, free to all. Quite so. And you are therefore?'

'I am Edmund Gains, madam. Sometime poet in residence to Lord Harlington of Harlington Hall. I live in what is known as the House of the Soothsayer, behind the lake, and I compose verses for my lord and his lady.'

'I see.' Mabel sat back, looking intently at Edward. 'And how long have you been poet in residence at Harlington Hall, sir?'

'For some few years, madam. I am most popular with the ladies to whom I compose odes of a flattering nature, which they greatly enjoy. Sometimes 'tis an ode to their favourite bonnet, sometimes 'tis an ode to their beauty, to their silhouette, to anything that pleases them. And I do please them. Believe me, madam, I do please them greatly.'

'It would be only too surprising if, looking as he does, he did not,' Mabel murmured to Amadea, straight-faced.

Amadea smiled. It was true, because despite the distinctly unglamorous nature of Edward's T-shirt and jeans, his good looks were still quite striking. Indeed, in the gentle light of Mabel's old pink-and-green-glass-shaded Victorian oil lamps he was now, perhaps more than ever, convincingly Edmund Gains.

'My dear, will you leave us now?' Mabel said to Amadea, while staring intently at Edward. 'I have a feeling that it might be better — your aura is quite, let us say, exciting — and we do need to calm this gentleman.' At that moment the bungalow seemed to rock a little. 'Ah.' Mabel put out a hand. 'Did you feel that? A definite tremor. We'll be in the sea in another few years, ten at the most. Doubtless we shall need a sail and some oars to keep afloat. There we go again.' The bungalow shook. 'Dear me, the tide's definitely coming in. Perhaps it would be a good idea if you went off for a drive and came back when it is out? This goodly gentleman, meanwhile, can tell me all about himself.'

She nodded briskly at Amadea, who immediately let herself out of the bungalow and drove off towards the nearest village, feeling as she did so that she was somehow deserting her charge. She had no doubt that Mabel had some kind of special power. She imagined that she could see it in her eyes, and she knew that whether or not you liked to believe in such things, poor Edward Green, as her mother had named him, was or had been occupied by someone else, someone who had lived in another time.

She drove into the next village, parked, and started to walk down its quiet main street. It was at once obvious that it was owned not by many and various people but by one family. It was not just its uniformity, not just the quietness of it, it was the feeling that it had somehow been flattened, all its individuality carefully extracted from it. Despite its undoubted age and its decorous façades, it could as well have been a model village, the brainchild of some soap millionaire.

She sat down on a bench outside the post office and watched as children too small to go to school, but old enough to drive their mothers insane, popped in and out of the village shop struggling with sweet wrappers, their jaws working overtime, while their mothers walked slowly back to their rented houses, perhaps wondering to themselves how long the freshly bought bribes would keep them occupied.

At that moment the mobile phone in the top pocket of her jacket rang out in the quiet, and despite the fact she immediately answered she still attracted the vaguely appalled looks of the villagers passing by her bench.

'Rob who? Rob Greer?' she asked.

Such was the change in her circumstances over the past days, it was almost as if Swinton was another part of her life, long, long ago.

'Yes, Amadea, this is Rob Greer. Rob who lived downstairs from you, remember?'

'Still the same old Mr Sarcasm?' Amadea asked, careful to keep her tone light.

'Strangely enough, I am not in a sarcastic vein.'

'So how can I help you?'

'Quite easily. Have you still got that young man? 'John Smith' or — I can't remember what you rechristened him.'

'My mother rechristened him Edward Green.'

'Yes, him. Have you still got him in your custody?'

'Yes, why? As a matter of fact, even as we speak he is seeing someone who may be able to help him.'

'Oh good.'

'Why oh good?'

'Because I think I know who he is, that's why. No, to put it another way, I think I know who he *might* be.'

★ ★ ★

Florence looked around her. It was, praise be, a sunny day once more, so she had been able to lay her lunch table outside in the garden under the old apple tree. She had put together what she hoped would be a delicious menu, starting with a light sponge roulade filled with tomatoes, herbs and crème fraiche, followed by chicken in a creamy sauce cooked in the oven with a Parmesan and crushed organic crisp topping, then a lemon meringue pie served with home-made vanilla ice cream. There would be cheese of course, Somerset cheeses, and Bath Olivers, and 'That should keep several wolves from several doors,' she murmured to Punch.

Happily for her, since she was on her own, her kitchen was not too far from the terrace, so she could hop in and out of the French windows to the garden between courses.

She changed into a light yellow dress with

white flowers printed on it, and having given her hair a jolly good brush and put it up with the aid of some pretty combs, she felt as unbothered as any widow who is about to entertain three single men.

Only minutes later Punch alerted her, barking ritualistically long before the car could be seen driving slowly and carefully up the bumpy drive. Dick and his friends strolled into Florence's small hall, displaying all the relaxed charm and grace that single men have a habit of displaying when they know they are to be the guests not only of a generous hostess but an excellent cook.

Dick's two friends could not have been less alike. First came Theo Mayer, small, bald and beaming. She had met him before, with Henry. He was the kind of friend for whom, Florence guessed, other friends were always trying to find a girlfriend, despite the fact that he was probably far happier without one. Next was Walter Dexter, tall, handsome, grey-haired, and from the moment he walked into her house seeming inexplicably to fill it with a new warmth.

Perhaps it was the fact that, although Walter Dexter was handsome, he was donnish in manner. Whatever it was, as she put out a hand to shake his, Florence found herself saying 'How do you do' to him rather than 'Hallo', which was just so old-fashioned and fuddy-duddy she really could have kicked herself.

'Hallo,' was *his* response, as he proffered an admirably cool hand, but he seemed to know that she thought she'd made an ass of herself by sounding so stuffy, because he smiled as she coloured slightly.

'Let's go outside. I have made some proper Pimm's,' she murmured, feeling a little flustered.

They trooped out after her, and of course the moment they saw Florence's rose-filled garden they all beamed, and that was before she handed them some admirably strong gin-laced Pimm's.

'I thought this was going to be a pretty super sort of day,' Dick said, looking from side to side as he sat down and replacing his white straw hat on his head. 'I shall now predict that there are going to be a great many more super days this summer. You're a rose man, aren't you, Walter?' he added, nodding towards the rose-clad walls of the old house. 'He's a walking encyclopaedia, absolute mastermind about roses, you know,' he told Florence.

'In that case perhaps you can identify this old friend for me?' Florence asked, jumping up and leading the way across the lawn. 'It did nothing last year, but it suddenly decided to make itself felt this month, and I have quite forgotten what it's called.'

'One of my favourites, that is — Sombreuil.' He turned and called back to Dick, 'Beautiful, isn't it?'

'Very beautiful,' Dick agreed, and his eyes narrowed appreciatively as he watched Florence and Walter chatting as if they had known each other for years. He turned to Theo. 'Told you, didn't I?'

'Matchmaker, matchmaker, make me a match,'

Theo sang in a low voice, but Dick's smile only broadened.

'I am a genius, Theo, and you know it,' he said happily, and he tilted his hat back slightly so that the sun fell on his smiling face. 'Marvellous, everything is already quite marvellous. I knew it would be, just knew it.'

And that was before they all sat down and ate Florence's superb lunch, accompanied by a delicious chilled rosé wine.

'Ah, rosé, now that has come back into fashion, in contrast to Campari, which is still on the outs.' Theo drank appreciatively. 'Good.'

'Very good,' Walter agreed.

Theo turned to Florence. 'Walter has a vineyard in France, so that is quite a compliment, I can tell you.'

Florence started to clear the plates from the first course, setting them one by one to the side of the terrace, quietly.

'I am impressed,' she told Walter Dexter.

'No need to be, I do assure you. I inherited it from an aged aunt. At first, to tell you the truth, I thought it would be burdensome — '

'A fine thing. He was not thinking of us, was he, Theo?'

'No, he was not thinking of us, Dick.'

'But then, if I may be heard . . . ' Walter continued inexorably. 'Then I realised that I would be turning my back on something splendid — '

'The happiness of your best friends,' Dick chipped in.

'That, and the fact that someone else might

not look after it the way it had been looked after, the way it should be looked after, so I have kept it under my wing, if only to keep the locals — '

'And your friends,' Theo said, standing up to help Florence bring in more plates.

' — happy.'

'The seasons there, the people there, the food, it is all so exquisitely timeless — '

'And all that is before your friends arrive to entertain you with their marvellous wit . . . '

'Exactly, all before that,' Walter agreed, giving in at last to laughter.

'It is timeless here, isn't it?' Dick stated loyally. 'This particular corner of Somerset is timeless. No one knows of it, only a few of us, and we're not telling, so you mustn't.'

Walter now stood up to help Florence serve the second course.

'How many acres do you have?'

'I have three, but at least half an acre is taken up with the little lake, and then there is the vegetable patch, but I have to have help for that, although not for much longer.' She looked up at Walter, briefly sad. 'I have no more pennies, you see, I must sell. This is my last summer here.'

'How heartbreaking for you.'

'Yes, it is,' she agreed, going to sit down. 'But don't let's talk about it, let this be a happy day. After all,' she gestured round at everything, the blue sky, the flower-filled garden, 'in the winter, all this is what we dream of as we listen to the rain thundering on the roof and try to stoke the damp logs in the fireplace,' she added. 'All this colour, all this blue sky, all these birds, all this is the stuff of our winter dreams.'

'To summer dreams then,' Walter announced, suddenly holding up his glass.

They all raised their glasses in unison, smiling, and clinking them in the best tradition.

'To summer dreams.'

★　★　★

After lunch and in a necessarily mellow if not euphoric state, they all followed Florence down to the lake, to stand on the little bridge, to stare into the water, to appreciate the water lilies, to watch the pink rounded mouths of the carp as they occasionally rose to the surface.

Walter pointed across the lake to the pleasant brick-and-wood building facing down the water.

'And that is?'

Florence turned away. 'That is . . . ' She cleared her throat. 'That is nothing, just my studio.' She looked about her as if she had run out of things to show them.

'May we look in?'

She looked at Walter briefly, and then looked away again.

'You don't want to go in there, it's only paintings and things,' she said, embarrassed, but because she could see Walter was waiting for more, she went on. 'My husband, Henry, he had it built for me. So sweet of him really. But I haven't been in it much since he died, just to dust a bit. And then the other day I found I had to go into it, but you know, it's not somewhere someone like you, a gallery owner . . . I mean too awful to have to peer round the studio of an amateur painter and pretend enthusiasm.' She pulled a little face. ' 'Er, er, er, well, yes, I can see what you mean . . . ' ' People said that so much, Henry and I ended up calling my paintings I-see-what-you-means!'

She laughed, at the same time remembering how often she would retreat to the studio when things got too difficult up at the house.

'Even so, may we, though?' Walter persisted, nodding towards the little building. He turned back to Theo and Dick. 'May we if we promise, hands on hearts, that we will not say 'I see what you mean', even if we do? Come on, boys, promise?'

Dick and Theo put hands to their hearts, and their faces assumed serious expressions.

'We promise not to say 'I see what you mean, even if we do!' ' they chorused.

'There, you see?' Walter turned back to Florence. 'Now may we go into the inner sanctum?'

'It would seem churlish if I said no, so I can't,' Florence said, laughing, while at the same time feeling only relief that she had been in and tidied and dusted the place.

Nevertheless, good natured though the whole expedition to her studio was in intention, she could not quite banish the familiar feeling of wanting the floor to open up and swallow her the moment she saw them staring round at her amateur daubs.

Perhaps because they had promised not to say the dreaded phrase 'I see what you mean' the three men fell silent, staring round at what was unmistakably Florence's world. Since a great many paintings had been hung on the rails, they were able to start at the beginning and go on, like Alice in Wonderland, until they stopped. Walter started first, and finished last. Every now and then he put his glasses on top of his head and stared intently, closely, at the paint, until finally, when he came to the last, he turned to Florence.

'These are not daubs, Florence,' he announced.

'I am only a Sunday painter . . . '

'In that case Sunday is indeed a blessed day.'

'They are very good,' Dick mused, again making his way round the framed and hung paintings. 'Really, I would say, very saleable.'

'I haven't painted regularly for some time, Dick,' Florence assured him, as if she was afraid that he would ask her to get out her brushes and start in straight away.

'Never mind that, these are very good,' Dick said proudly. 'Very good. Henry must have known how good they were. Didn't he encourage you to sell them, or take them to someone like Walter here, or bring him to see them?'

Florence remembered how Henry had hardly ever called in at the studio, hardly ever viewed the paintings, except in a hurry, because he was always busying himself round the lake. At some point he would poke his head in the door and ask her to help him move a bench, or something of that nature.

'Oh, I don't think he ever thought of my painting except as a kind of hobby really. Something that got me out from under his feet when he was practising up at the house.'

'Well, there you are,' Theo said, his eyebrows raised, he too studying Florence's imaginative world of strong colours and endless movement, of fantasy birds flying over water, of bright flowers and brilliant figures on beaches. 'There is no accounting for taste, and this is certainly mine.'

As Dick and Walter moved outside once more, chatting animatedly, Theo slid up to Florence. 'Walter owns a very fashionable art gallery in Cork Street,' he muttered. 'And he knows a bit too, despite being a gallery owner!' He nodded encouragingly, at the same time pulling an over-serious face. 'I expect you've seen his advertisements in *Country Life*? Dexter's Gallery?'

'Dexter's Gallery? He's that Dexter?'

'Yes, Walter Dexter. He is the second Dexter. He inherited from his father, William Dexter, but not before he had served a long apprenticeship. Walter has a great eye, and is really very discerning.' Theo paused, looking Puck-like and mischievous. 'I think you might have been *discerned* by him, you know, Florence.'

'Oh, I don't think — '

'I do,' Theo said firmly. 'I was always very fond of your Henry, Florence, but I have to tell you that to my mind he determinedly kept your light under a bushel, out here. The fact he never let your paintings enter the house was a source of some puzzlement to me. If I had been married to you . . . ' He circled round the little studio, an admiring look on his face. 'Why, I would have trumpeted your talent to the world, and hung your paintings from the rooftops of my house; but darling Henry was too caught up with his own career.'

'Which was only understandable, after all. And you know, looking back, Theo, Henry was never, ever negative.'

'I know, and never interested either. There are so many men like Henry. It is the fault of my sex, the indulgence in the 'little woman' syndrome. You can do your tatting, or your cooking, or, as in this case, your painting — just don't show me, or talk about it, or worst of all . . . ' He lowered his voice to a conspiratorial level. 'Worst of all, expect me to be interested in it.'

They both laughed.

'Henry wasn't that bad, Theo.'

'Hmm,' was all Theo would say in reply, and he turned back and gestured towards the paintings. 'These may not be Constable, they may not be Berthe Morisot, they may not be Marie Laurencin, but they are not nothing either. Florence, believe me, they are not nothing.'

Florence looked round at her world and, viewing it now, through Theo's eyes, it seemed to her that she was seeing it for the first time. It was not a world that she herself fully understood, and perhaps it was only fitting that she did not; perhaps if she did understand it, it would go away, never to return. What she was beginning to grasp was that there were other people who perhaps did understand and appreciate her world, and, it seemed, she had just given them all lunch.

11

Rob had become obsessed. He knew it, and yet he could do nothing about it. The reason he knew that he was obsessed was because he was now standing outside Jamie Charlbury's front door, wondering if anyone was at home. Of course as soon as he had rung the bell he wanted to flee back down the stairs, pretending he had rung the wrong one, but Mrs Tippett was too quick for him. She had opened the door and was staring at him as if she knew he was there on a lying pretext, before he could even turn on his heel and run off.

'Ah, Mrs Tippett.' Rob gave her his most charming smile, but saw at once that it had fallen flat. Mrs Tippett was definitely not a Rob Greer fan. 'I know it's a funny time to call — '

'The family are out, Dr Greer. Being Saturday, they are over at Dylan's nan's cottage for lunch, the present Mrs Charlbury that is. I am house-sitting for them, such a lot of burglaries at the weekends now,' Mrs Tippett continued in a purposefully cold voice because she did not approve of gentlemen callers. 'Being that it's Saturday, Miss Charlbury does not like to leave the place unattended. Seeing what Saturdays are nowadays, and seeing what towns are too, for that matter. Used to be ever such a nice place, Swinton, in the old days, but now youth and the undesirables have taken it over, I doubt whether its own mother would know it.'

Rob was by now inside the front door, and still smiling, only this time it was at Mrs Tippett's back as she stalked away from him into Jamie's scrupulously tidy sitting room.

'I left my glasses here the other night, when I was visiting.'

'I remember.' Mrs Tippett sniffed as if the memory was not a pleasant one, as if she had always suspected that Rob was the sort of person who would leave his glasses behind in other people's flats, causing inconvenience and annoyance. 'So what would they look like, these glasses of yours?'

'Gold-rimmed with pink-tinted glass,' Rob replied quite truthfully. 'Aviator, small and round,' he finished. 'I was reading to Dylan in his room . . . '

He started to move towards Dylan's room but Mrs Tippett, as he had hoped, was there before him.

'I'll go,' she said, looking ever more officious, frowning at Rob as if she suspected he might be the sort of man who would come up as an unsavoury item on the local news. 'You wait there, I will search Dylan's room.'

She hurried off, and Rob too hurried off, but in the direction of Jamie's room. As he did so he was surprised to find his heart thumping not just in his chest but in his ears, so great was his fear of being caught by Mrs Tippett.

The room revealed itself to be as orderly and pure as when he had last been in there with Jamie and Dylan, with one marked difference:

there was no photo in the leather frame by the bed. He stared in frustration at the empty frame. No handsome face stared back at him.

He moved towards the bed, and on an impulse pulled back the covers. There too was nothing, except, unsurprisingly, a white duvet and a mountain of white pillows. Feeling a great deal more like a policeman than a doctor, he lifted the pillows, and immediately found what he had been looking for. He slipped it under his jacket, at the same time pulling out the Aviator sunglasses from his inside jacket pocket.

'Found them!' he called to Mrs Tippett. 'Thank you so much!'

He bolted out of the flat and down the stairs to hit the pavement running. He didn't stop until he reached his car.

There he sat for a few moments staring at the photograph. It was too good to be true. He had evidence now. Without it, his story would be nothing. But now he had evidence, it must, it had to lead to something.

Back in Jamie's flat Mrs Tippett looked round the sitting room suspiciously. Nothing had been moved. So where had that young man supposedly found his sunglasses?

She stared with practised ease at the sofas. She knew they were just as she had left them, because she always put the pointy bits staring up towards the ceiling, and Jamie always left them square. She knew that none of the drawers in the sideboard had been opened because she would have heard the noise, for the simple reason they always stuck. She knew that nothing on the coffee table had been moved, because everything was *exactly* as she had left it. The book on French Provençal villages was in the same place, the magazines in the magazine rack, the jug of flowers, everything just as it had been. So where, she asked again, had that young man found his glasses?

She moved towards Jamie's bedroom. Ah, the door had not been ajar when she had been sitting watching afternoon television. It had been closed. She pushed it further, and this time it was her heart that was beating faster as, with an imagination fed by stories of weekend robberies, she stared into the room. The bedcover was not straight! The pillows were askew, and the photo that was always in the frame by the bedside was no longer there.

'Oh my God,' she said out aloud to the white-walled room. 'He has only gone and taken Jamie's photograph of Dylan's dad!'

She closed the bedroom door hastily, and went back to the sofa and sat down. She could not wait until Jamie and Dylan got back from their day out, just could not wait. She would certainly never open a door to someone, even someone she knew, ever again. What a thing to happen! But she couldn't be blamed, she knew she couldn't be blamed, and, what was more, she would not be blamed.

★ ★ ★

Mabel stared at the sleeping Edward and shook her head sadly.

'It's a flop,' she told Amadea. 'I do have them, you know. The trouble is, I don't know why it is a flop. Just something I can't get hold of. I had a flop like this once in Scotland. This poor couple couldn't get rid of the previous owner of their croft, and nor, I am here to tell you, could Mabel Minton. Just couldn't oust him.'

'What do you think it is though? I mean — '

Before Amadea could continue Mabel beckoned her outside. 'Better if we discuss the patient out of his hearing. People can hear, and in Edward's case both people can hear, when they are seemingly asleep or unconscious. It can be quite embarrassing. Wives can start to inveigh against their husbands when they're out for the count, and then whoosh, the gent wakes up and there's all hell to pay, you may be sure.'

She walked with Amadea a little way down to the shore, and then stopped, staring back at her really rather precarious-looking bungalow.

'Quite honestly, Amadea — you don't mind if I first-name you? — no, of course you don't, your generation hardly have surnames, do you? No, quite honestly,' she continued, 'if I may confide in you, Edmund Gains is a bugger, really he is, and I mean that in the old-fashioned sense, not literally. He just will *not* shift, will *not* give over. I can only think he had the most monumental ego. He talked non-stop about his wretched verse until I thought I would have to throw him in the sea to shut him up.'

'The same thing happened with Pierre Lavalle. The moment he hypnotised him, it was Edmund, Edmund, Edmund.'

Mabel nodded, sucking in her cheeks, which made a sort of popping noise when she released them.

'Of course poor Edward's whacked now, absolutely whacked, which is what happens when the other personality wears you to a thread, you fall asleep from the sheer exhaustion of it. I don't seem to have been much help.'

'You have tried, and I really must thank you for that,' Amadea told her sadly.

She stared round the beach at the myriad colours of the pebbles that were one minute shiny and bright from the wash of the tide, and the next minute quite dull. As the tide had just receded, they were now looking a little as she was feeling. She did not know why, but she had pinned such high hopes on Mabel Minton coming up trumps and returning Edmund to wherever it was he had come from. Her disappointment was double because she knew that Florence too had nursed visions of Edmund being given a kick in the butt and sent on his way. Now it seemed that Edward and Edmund would have to go back to Swinton Hospital for treatment.

'Of course there's no charge,' Mabel stated. 'Not that I charge more than anyone can afford, just ask people to put things in the honesty box, but when I have a flop — which is, I have to tell you, rare — I don't even ask that. What a pity though, not to be able to help you.'

Of course Amadea was dying to ask her what she had done that had failed so spectacularly, but she did not dare, not just because Mabel's expression was one of such unmitigated gloom, but also because she sensed she would, probably quite rightly, get a flea in her ear.

'What a nuisance it all is.' Mabel shook her head again, and they began to walk back up the beach.

Once outside her front door, she paused.

'There is one other thing, which can sometimes help in these really rather unpleasant cases, and that is to try and find out more about this character Edmund.'

'How does that help?'

'It might if we could find his weaknesses, do you see? Such things as drink, or women, or drugs, something that we could play on. I know it sounds far-fetched, but a colleague of mine was once able to transfer a rogue personality to a bottle of Mouton Rothschild, 1932. I think that was the year. Yes, he lured the culprit out by opening the bottle, and when he dived into it he smartly put the cork back in. He drowned of course.' She sighed with sudden satisfaction. 'He was quite wicked, you see, in fact very wicked, so we didn't want *him* around any more. And then of course there was the case of the Wishstead Rectory. That was mine. There I was able to transfer several very, very naughty personalities into a tree. That is a standard transfer, of course — our ancestors knew that it was most effective.'

'I know Wishstead Rectory, do tell me more.'

Mabel smoothed down her multicoloured robe and looked momentarily cheered as she remembered what a success she had enjoyed with that particular case.

'It was when the Buckmasters were living there. A nice couple, not at all disagreeable. They called me in because they had tried everyone, only to be turned away. There are some schools of thought that believe that if a couple are unhappy then there can be manifestations, and that they must first look to themselves before calling in a member of the clergy or some such. I am not, as you may gather, one of those. Unpleasant things can be inherited, in a house, or anywhere else for that matter. As it happens, the previous owners of the Rectory had been very naughty — Ouija boards and suchlike nonsense — and had left behind the result of their highly irresponsible conjuring. I remember that it was a very cold starry night when, following my usual practices, they walked me to the gate of the Rectory. It was October, the time of shooting stars in our West Country, and the skies were quite, quite clear — I tell you this because the weather is relevant to the story, for the next morning they found an old tree in their orchard split in two, and burned black, as if it had been struck by lightning. We knew then, of course, that some very unsavoury spirits had been responsible for all the unfortunate happenings in the house; bad smells, and other most unattractive events. No, I have to say that was a great success, very happy-making. Druids always banish spirits to trees, as you no doubt know — preferably old ones; and of course no sensible person ever cuts down a tree without first apologising to it.'

Mabel gave a small sigh of satisfaction, and

307

turned the handle of her front door.

'So you see, what I am really saying to you, Amadea, is that if we could find out a bit more about this fellow Edmund Gains, we might be able to trap him. It is worth a go. Because you really don't want to send this nice young man back to Swinton Hospital, do you?'

Amadea looked round sharply at that, but before she could say anything Mabel raised one startlingly dark eyebrow.

'I know, I know, you're wondering how I know, aren't you, dear? I can read thoughts, you see. It's not very difficult; as a matter of fact quite a few people can read thoughts.'

For the ensuing minute Amadea found herself trying frantically to remember what her previous thoughts could have been and hoping that they had been vaguely proper. Mabel seemed to have read this thought too, for she smiled.

'It's all right, dear, don't worry, you have a very nice mind, and you haven't thought anything that I wouldn't have thought in your place, believe me!'

★ ★ ★

Jamie always dreaded meeting Mrs Tippett by the front door, or rather she dreaded the moment she put her key in her front door and Mrs Tippett opened it before she could finish. It was as if, by pulling open the door before Jamie could turn her key, the older woman was able to establish her authority over whatever happened, or didn't happen, in the ensuing minutes.

308

'Ah, there you are, Mrs Tippett,' Jamie said lamely, as she gently ushered Dylan inside.

'Thank the Lord you are home, safe and sound,' said Mrs Tippett, a pious expression on her face.

'Has everything been all right? I hope everything has been all right?'

'No, everything has not been all right, Jamie.' Mrs Tippett drew herself up to her full height while nudging her spectacles further up her nose, as if she was hoping they would climb up to her eyebrows. 'No, it has not, by no means.' She waited until Jamie had removed Dylan's coat and hung it up. 'That young man who came back with you the other night — after dinner?' She managed to make dinner sound like an orgy. '*He* was here.'

'Oh, and?' Jamie attempted to assume her most uninterested expression.

'And he rang the doorbell.'

'I see, and?'

Jamie squeezed past the home help into the sitting room.

'And I let him in!' Mrs Tippett declared dramatically, following her. 'I should never have let him in, I know that now, Jamie, but seeing he was your friend, I presumed it was all right. Yes, I let him in, because he pretended to have left his sunglasses behind, but of course he had done nothing of the sort. He was here to rob you,' she said, lowering her voice. 'Yes, he was here to rob you all right, and rob you he did. And of one of your most precious possessions.'

'So what did he do, Mrs Tippett?' Jamie could

no longer keep up the pretence of being uninterested.

'Follow me!' Mrs Tippett beckoned and Jamie followed her to her bedroom, where the home help flung open the door and pointed dramatically to the empty photo frame. 'He has stolen your photograph!'

Jamie gave a relieved laugh. 'No, no, Mrs Tippett, no, I took that out of its frame. Goodness, what a fright.'

Mrs Tippett looked disappointed.

'Well, be that as it may, Jamie, one can't be too careful nowadays,' she sighed. 'That will be twenty pounds, not counting the agency fee, that is, and that's another thing: agency fees are colossal.'

Jamie reached for her bag. And having paid Mrs Tippett and let her out of the flat with the usual injunctions, she turned back to the sitting room. Poor Mrs Tippett, she so dearly loved to see bad where only good lay. As if Rob would steal from her — except . . . She paused at the entrance to the sitting room. Why would he leave sunglasses behind when they had come back from dinner? She went to make Dylan's supper, and then stopped, suspicion overcoming her, and turned back to her bedroom.

The room was almost as she had left it — only almost, because the left-hand side of the bed where she always slept was newly disarranged. She went quickly to the untidy pillows and, lifting them up, looked underneath for the precious photograph. Nothing there but the sheet. She pulled the duvet back, searching frantically through the bedclothes. Nothing there either.

She went to the door and called Dylan. 'Did you move Dad's photo from under my pillow?'

Her son frowned, looked bewildered, and quickly turned back to the television. 'No, I never,' he murmured, hardly interested, since it was time for his favourite programme.

Jamie went back to her frantic searching, and failing yet again to find the precious photograph of the father of her child, she sat down heavily on the bed and put her head in her hands.

It was obvious to her now. Mrs Tippett had been right: Rob had taken the photograph, not from the frame but from under her pillow. She looked up, staring ahead of her at the pale cream wall. She couldn't believe it. Why would he do such a thing? She stood up, and started to pace the room. He must have known she would discover his theft. Was it because of jealousy perhaps?

But — but he seemed so nice! Only a really paranoid personality would do such a thing, surely? Or someone who was sicker than his own patients.

She lifted up the phone and started to ring his mobile number, but it was on answer and she did not have the gall to leave a message saying, 'Hallo, Rob, this is Jamie. Just calling to find out why you nicked the photo of Dylan's dad.'

Why? Why had he done it?

★ ★ ★

When Amadea drove them home, puzzlingly, Edward seemed much more to the fore than Edmund. As soon as they reached the Old Rectory he complained of an unnatural tiredness, and left her to go and lie down. Amadea followed her mother into the kitchen.

'Well, was it a success then?' Florence asked, her eyes bright with hope.

'No, Ma, sorry, it wasn't.' Amadea tried to look equivocal, but only succeeded in looking despairing.

'No?'

'No. Mabel could do nothing, I'm afraid.'

Florence brought out a bottle of wine, after which Amadea continued.

'She's really cross that she could do nothing to get rid of Edmund. He persists.'

'But he was so much Edward just now.'

'Oh, very much Edward, but you know how it is, he can be Edward, Edward, Edward, and just as we think we're winning, something changes and back comes Edmund.'

Florence nodded sadly. 'So what happened exactly?'

'I don't know. I left them together, as Mabel suggested, and went off for a drive. I suppose she tried all her usual — I don't know, she did whatever she does, but nothing happened. It seemed Edmund just would not budge. She says Edmund's a show-off, an egoist. Rather hysterical actually is what she indicated — before she woke him up.'

'Woke him up? Did she hypnotise him, then?'

'I don't know. I told you, I didn't stay, it didn't

312

seem right; but she certainly left him sleeping after some sort of exertion, so whatever she did do, she has certainly exhausted him. She said he would probably sleep the rest of the day and night. She says what she does always leaves patients exhausted, and that sometimes the second personality gets infuriated, that you have to watch for that. He or she, or they, become alerted, they know you're trying to get rid of them, so they go the whole nine yards.'

'Really? But Dottie says all she usually does is point her index fingers at people, which sounds innocuous enough.'

'I don't know what to believe, Ma. I'm just so disappointed.'

'Me too . . . '

They both stared out at the beautiful sunset beyond the kitchen window, thoughtfully sipping their chilled white wine.

'I've put the house on the market, and would you believe I have a buyer already? One day, on the market *one* day, and someone wants it,' Florence volunteered, breaking the resigned silence. 'They have lists of people who want to buy old properties, so heigh-ho, it will all be done and dusted before we know where we are.'

Amadea put an arm round her mother's shoulders and gave her a quick sideways hug, without taking her eyes off the view.

'That is good. I'm not surprised though, this place is so special. Remember how Dad used to say — '

'That it was no good telling him that when he

313

died he was going to heaven, because he already lived there.'

'Perhaps he's still here — and David,' said Amadea in a matter-of-fact voice.

'Of course,' Florence agreed without emotion. 'So whoever wants to buy it must leave them to enjoy it, while I move on.'

Amadea looked at her mother. 'You're quite determined, aren't you?'

'Oh yes, pet, really. I must. Even if I had enough pennies, I would still move on now. It's not just because tomorrow is another day, it's because we must always keep moving forward. It's just how it is. I shall never love anyone more than Henry, but I have to find myself now. I love to think that he too would want that of me, but — ' She turned to Amadea, laughing suddenly. 'I don't think he would at all!'

'Dad could be a selfish old thing . . . '

'Not selfish, no, never that, just of his generation. It's different now. Better, I think, now young men and women are closer in their attitudes. Young men are more understanding.'

'Perhaps. Edward seems very kind. But back to *Edmund* — Mabel thinks that I, or we, should find out more about the unwanted lodger.'

'But we've found out a great deal.'

'Not enough, apparently. We need to discover his weaknesses — not just his weakness for his own poetry, but everything. She had some great stories about — '

'I'm afraid it will have to be you doing that, Amy.' Florence looked momentarily embarrassed. She cleared her throat and, patting her side-combs, moved away from the window. 'I'm going away for a few days. It's all been arranged. Dottie is taking Punch for me. It's Dick and Theo's friend, Walter — he's asked me to go on a trip with him, a sort of painting holiday. He wants to encourage me, to get me painting again. Thinks I might have lost confidence in myself, which is rather sweet of him,' Florence finished, clearing her throat once more.

'But this is great news! Where are you planning to go?'

'We're going on a sort of special walk through the hills and byways of Somerset, following the same route as Coleridge and the other poets, that sort of thing. I am taking my easel and sketch-books. He is taking his camera. Just friends, nothing more, you know. Just a walk.'

Florence turned away quickly, and in doing so missed Amadea's smile, which was nearly as wide as the window in front of her.

★ ★ ★

Florence had not wanted to go into any more details about her proposed walk with Walter through the Quantocks. It was part of a sequence of events that long afterwards would prove to have been inevitable; even to have a strange logic all its own, as things that have to happen so often do.

Walter had called back at lunchtime that day. It seemed that Theo had noticed that Florence had a book that Walter had been wanting to consult for some time. It was one of Henry's rather specialised books on opera, and he had wanted to look something up in it, or so he said.

Of course they all knew that Walter had wanted to call back to see Florence again, but when people get older they are less overt about their motives, and certainly Walter could not have looked more diffident when he arrived.

'Theo very kindly said — '

'No, of course,' Florence said hastily. 'Absolutely. I knew just where it was in our little library.' She patted the cover of the book. 'Do you want to take it off with you now, or would you like a nice Pimm's and some lunch before you go?'

Florence found herself looking up at her unexpected visitor almost mischievously. It was that youthful look of mischief that made Walter relax.

'What do *you* think?'

'I prepared something earlier — it's in the studio. On such a beautiful day I thought it a shame not to go to the little house and sit out on the decking and enjoy the ducks and moorhens, not to mention the sunshine.'

Walter's heart sort of jumped as he realised that she had pre-planned everything, as if she knew that he had not just come to borrow a book.

'I hope you don't think it presumptuous of me?' Florence asked him conversationally, as they strolled down to her little studio. 'But I do think it fun, in England, to enjoy picnics immediately the sun comes out.'

'If this is presumptuous, I wish more people

316

were presumptuous,' Walter said, and he looked about him appreciatively. 'As a matter of fact, I was going to ask to see your work again, for professional reasons. You know, with my Walter-Dexter-Gallery hat on?'

Florence tried not to feel pleased that he had referred to her painting as her *work*, but the truth was she felt elated. She had long ago stopped even talking about her painting to anyone, let alone showing it to them, because they never took it seriously.

She had set out a small table, two chairs, a white tablecloth, and opened not just a large green umbrella for shade but also a bottle of wine.

'Isn't it funny how continental our life has become? We all drink wine with our meals, we eat the same kinds of food . . .'

Florence frowned. Walter was not seating himself at her undoubtedly inviting table.

'Do you mind,' he asked, carefully removing his straw hat and gesturing with it towards the studio. 'Do you mind if I take a look first, before we have a drink? I am a better judge when completely sober.'

'Are you quite sure you want to look again? You don't have to, really you don't.'

'I am quite sure I want to, in fact I am perfectly sure I want to, Florence.'

'Then you don't mind if I don't join you? I do get rather tense when people are looking at my —' She went to say 'paintings' and stopped. 'When people are looking at my work.'

Walter turned to enter the building, saying as

he went, 'Quite understand, perfectly understand. So many of my artists say the same.'

In his absence Florence poured them both a glass of wine and stared out at her little lake with its yellow and blue iris, its ducks dabbling, and its moorhens skittering in and out of the reeds. It would be her last summer here, and yet she had no regrets, and she could not have said exactly why. Perhaps it was because, looking back at the house, she could see herself alone in it. It was as if she could see herself looking out, all the winter long, on to the grey weather, listening to the rain pouring down, and she could see how small and sad she looked, with only Punch for company.

Walter emerged a few minutes later, and taking out his wallet he placed a card in front of her.

'I would very much like to sign you up for my new country gallery,' he said simply. 'Would you be interested?'

Florence stared at the immaculately designed card. 'Well,' she said after a few seconds. 'Yes, of course I would be interested. No, actually I wouldn't be interested — ' She stopped speaking. Walter raised his eyebrows. 'No, I wouldn't be interested, I would be thrilled.'

'Well, that is good. I have two other artists I want to show for the opening exhibition, both men, you may or may not be relieved to know. However, I thought 'Landscapes and Ladies' would be a good title, because, as you might guess, they have a great interest in the second, and you have a great interest in both.'

'Yes, isn't it strange, I paint women more than men.'

'Not really, if you live alone in the country you're bound to see more women than you do men. Besides, women are more decorative, and you're a colourist. I love your bright, vibrant world,' he added musingly, gazing out over the lake with slightly narrowed eyes. 'It reflects an optimistic nature, and a love of life. You can warm your hands on it. No, really, I raised my palms to 'Dottie with Washing' and I felt the warmth coming off the canvas. More than that — I laughed. Do you mind?'

'I've never really thought about it before, but since you ask me, I suppose I want people to laugh and smile when they see my work. I don't want them to feel worse, really I don't.'

'Well, that is good, because they won't, believe me. No, they will not only buy, they will *enjoy* your work when they hang it. It will be something they will treasure. You have fashioned your own world, and they can go into it, and look around it, and it will give them . . . not comfort, more than that, it will give them a boost, a shot in the arm. Truly.'

Florence let out a great sigh. 'You have no idea what that means to me, Walter.'

Walter shook his head. 'Sorry, Florence, I have every idea.'

She gave him a quick look and then dropped her eyes. To judge from his face, things were moving rather quickly, and they both knew it.

'I'll just get the smoked crevettes. Amadea,

319

naughty girl, had them delivered, you know. A present from her, so extravagant, but I've made some mayonnaise, and there's soda bread and — help yourself to some more wine, won't you?'

She disappeared quickly inside the studio, and this time it was Walter who gave a great sigh. He had known from the moment he met this gentle woman with the kind eyes that she was the one for him. She was everything he had never found together in one woman. Selfless to the core, kind and sympathetic, but not so saintly that she did not enjoy laughter, wine and good food. She was, in short, pretty perfect. And that was before he fell in love with her paintings.

All in all, it was really rather unsurprising when, later that day, he rang back not just to thank Florence for lunch but to ask her to go with him on a short walking tour through the Quantock Hills. It would take them through little-known but beautiful parts of Somerset; past Coleridge's cottage at Nether Stowey to where the Wordsworths, William and Dorothy, had lived at Alfoxton.

'Coleridge wrote 'Kubla Khan' in Somerset,' Walter murmured. 'Not that it will make much difference to tired or aching feet to know that.'

'When do you start?'

'Tomorrow.'

Florence suddenly knew that this was one of those moments when she must be decisive. 'If I can park Punch with Dottie — '

She could, and the fact that she was prepared to do so meant that Dottie also knew at once that at last life might be changing for the better for her old friend and neighbour.

'Bring him tonight. Can't wait to have him.'

Florence turned at the door. 'Ridiculous isn't it, but I feel so excited.'

'Course you do, and about time. Do you the world of good to get away from us all.'

For a second, anxiety came back into Florence's eyes. 'Do you really think I should, Dottie?'

'More than should, ducks — you must.'

* * *

Early the next morning, as her mother packed, and Dottie arrived to take care of both Punch and Edward — as she said, not necessarily in that order — Amadea set off on her quest to Harlington Hall.

It was a pleasant walk across the fields behind her mother's house, a walk that revived childhood memories of riding bareback on a fat little borrowed pony through the long grass and the buttercups, ducking under overhanging branches, always kicking on, kicking on, David in front of her disappearing, seemingly uncaring as to whether she was still behind him, leaving trails of laughter as his pony galloped out of control. Then they would stop at the crest of the hill and look down at Harlington's expanse of water, at its temples and its bridges, sighing with satisfaction as the early sunshine played about everything below, making it look newborn, just invented, a gift from the past to the spirits of the future.

Dick was waiting for her at the front of the house. There were, as yet, no visitors, so their voices sounded strangely clear on the morning air, and the very emptiness of the vast estate that lay around them seemed, invitingly, to be something only they knew about.

'I have been on the trail of old Edmund for some time, first with your mother, as you know, and now with you.'

He led the way to his small cottage, one of three that overlooked the lake, and stood back to let Amadea pass him as he opened the front door.

'Yes,' he said, as they entered an exquisitely furnished sitting room filled with the kind of antiques and paintings that would catch the eye anywhere. 'Yes, I have been on the trail of old Edmund, and although I have said nothing to your sainted mother, I have to tell you, Amadea, that what I have found out is more than passing strange. Coffee?'

'Mmm, please.'

Amadea sipped at the coffee and then sat down in the window seat that overlooked the gardens below, preparatory to listening to Dick with a suitably solemn expression.

'Shall I go on? Or do you know more?'

'We know nothing really except what Ma found, in the diary and so on. But then she got distracted by me coming back home, poor thing. That was all she needed.'

Amadea looked rueful and Dick laughed.

'She loves having you back.'

'I'm sure she does, like she would a cut finger!' Amadea laughed.

'No, she does,' Dick said seriously.

'At least she's sold the house. Fantastic offer, and on the first day too. Apparently the estate agents have lists and lists of people who want old properties with not too many bedrooms and a bit of land.'

'I'm not surprised, really I'm not. It is such a lovely place, with a well-worn aura, the right kind of aura.'

'Do you believe in auras?' Amadea looked surprised.

'Rather. Yours is delightful, by the way, and getting more settled by the minute.'

Amadea shook her head disbelievingly.

'There's something really strange about the people who live round here,' she said, after a few seconds. 'I keep meeting people who can read my thoughts — or — or tell me about my aura.'

'I have no excuse. I've only been here a few weeks. As a matter of fact I have always believed in auras.'

Dick looked ruminative, staring momentarily beyond Amadea but so far into the past that Amadea, realising he wanted to tell a story, nodded encouragingly.

'Do you really want to hear?'

'You bet your sweet aura I do.'

It was Dick's turn to laugh.

'Well, I had a most extraordinary experience, when I was much younger. I was sitting with a friend on his balcony, overlooking the towpath at

323

Strand on the Green, do you know where that is? No, perhaps you don't. Well — it's a very old and very pretty part of Chiswick, overlooking the Thames. There we were, enjoying a quiet pint, as you could in those days, garnered from the pub next door, when another friend stopped by the balcony, accompanied by an older man. Suddenly my host sprang up as if he had been scalded and went into his house, beckoning me to follow him, which I did, of course. 'You're not to let that man into this house, Dick,' he said. 'On no account, do you understand?' As you can imagine, I was rather embarrassed.'

'Well, you would be.'

'However, not wanting to upset him, I duly made our excuses and we sat inside until they were well and truly gone, after which I asked my friend what it was that he had seen. I shall never forget his reply. 'He has the devil's aura,' he said simply.' Dick paused. 'Naturally I thought he must be a bit hungover, or at the very least not feeling quite himself; but we went on with the day, and that was that, until some months later when I met my other friend again. I had not wanted to touch on the subject of his companion, and indeed was most anxious to avoid it, when he volunteered the following.' As Amadea leaned forward, a faint shiver running up her spine, Dick went on. 'It seems that he was working on a design exhibition with this man in a large — no, not large — vast hall in Wembley. They had hardly entered the place when he of the strange aura pointed up to the roof, miles above them, and said, 'I worship Lucifer, I

324

worship the Devil, and I can prove that he exists. Whenever I am in a place like this, a raven will appear.' Well, of course my friend shrugged off this sinister warning, as who wouldn't? But sure enough, when they came back from lunch with the rest of their team, there was consternation among all the organisers. High above them, beneath the dome of the roof and above the safety netting, a raven was flying around, and calling, it seems, down to him.'

'I've come out in goose pimples,' Amadea said, putting down her coffee, and glancing over her shoulder to make sure that the sunshine on the gardens outside was still real, and seeing that a tourist bus had just arrived, and a thrush was pecking at the green lawn outside the latticed window. 'As a matter of fact, if it wasn't you who had told me, I would not have believed you.'

'If it wasn't that my friend, up until then, had been not just an agnostic but an atheist, I would not have believed him either. But the truth is since then I can't help paying attention to people's auras. It's something they bring with them. It has a special significance for me now, as you may imagine. But, back to our friend Edmund Gains, who is the object of our interest at the moment.'

'Now you come to mention it, Edward Green has a lovely aura but Edmund's is a bit iffy,' Amadea admitted, frowning. 'I mean he's not nasty or anything, but he does go on rather. I feel sorry for Edmund, who is obviously brilliant, but I prefer Edward, and when he goes away and Edmund comes back, I do feel sad.'

'Of course you do, because he's not meant to be there,' Dick agreed warmly. 'Well, just wait till you hear what I have found out, because I think you will be quite pleased. It's such a super day; shall we take advantage of the sunshine and walk in the grounds while I tell you all about it?'

They went outside together and Dick, who obviously enjoyed what Rob liked to call yarning, started to talk.

'It's really very odd. You know, everything about Harlington is known. Everything, that is, about the house and the grounds, well, practically everything, and Theo, who is cataloguing the books, says as much. For instance, all the family lie in the churchyard over there, and there are all the usual monuments to them in the church; and over there is the pets' graveyard, as is traditional with families like this. But there's absolutely no trace of Edmund Gains's headstone, despite the fact that we know now that he not only lived here — but died here too. And yet he is not buried here.'

'I didn't know he died here?'

'Oh yes, he died here all right. Theo made the discovery in one of his old books. So, we now know he died here, and at a very young age, even for those days. He could not have been more than twenty-three or -four.'

'It's really getting spookier and spookier, isn't it, Dick?'

'Yes and no,' he went on, his eyes sparkling with enthusiasm, 'because yesterday evening I found Edmund's headstone. I literally stumbled across it.'

'Where?'

Dick pointed towards a temple that was set a little way back from the lake. 'There, I found it over there, behind the temple to Venus.' He looked down at Amadea, his eyes widening. 'So you see, not spooky at all. Could be really quite an amorous setting, don't you think?'

'Venus? Why would he be buried behind the temple to Venus?'

'One can only surmise that he was a naughty boy. But certainly it was most unusual for a Christian in those days to be buried in ground that has not been consecrated. As you probably know, your mother found the only other mention of him in Felicia Harlington's commonplace book.'

'I expect she told me, but so much has happened — I have forgotten.'

'Well, no one has been able to find an actual likeness of him, just this reference, and now it seems that the only other trace of him . . . is behind here.'

Amadea, in some excitement, followed Dick round the back of the small but beautiful classical building, where, in a small clearing, stood a headstone.

'I asked old Stalky to mow round this and clean off all the gubbins from the stone,' Dick announced proudly. 'He didn't want to. He's a bit 'suspertitious' was how he put it, even about coming up behind here. 'A lorst soul, this,' he said. 'Don't like going there one bit, Mr Saxon, lorst souls are not to be tampered with, I tell you.' Ah, but I see he's done it, bless him.'

Amadea leaned down to read the inscription. As she did so, the grass in the fields above them swayed in the slight breeze, and the leaves moving in the trees seemed to be rustling with pleasure at the soft nature of the day.

' 'Where sheep may safely graze',' Dick murmured, looking up at the gentle contours of the fields, the sheep moving imperceptibly. 'My favourite hymn, so English.'

Amadea was not much interested in Dick's favourite hymn, only in the gravestone, the inscription on which she now read out aloud slowly and without comprehension as it was in Latin.

'Oh dear, my Latin's not good enough.' She looked up at Dick, now commanding his attention.

Dick stared at the inscription. 'I think it says something about a man much loved by all.'

'A man much loved by all . . . ' Amadea repeated slowly. 'And here are his dates, and yes — you're right, he was only twenty-three. What did he do for them to banish him out here, away from the church?'

'He wrote verses, to order. But also, maybe, just maybe, he fell in love with Felicia, she of the commonplace book. Or perhaps worse, she fell in love with him, and her love was not returned . . . '

'Exactly. That is just what occurred to me. A woman scorned — not good! It must be something like that, or why put him behind the temple of Venus? Of course!' Amadea went on, snapping her fingers as she suddenly remembered. 'Of course, just before Pierre fell ill, I seem to remember Ma going on about Edmund having been murdered, but because he was under hypnosis we never really believed him, thought it was just a fantasy, really.'

'Now there's a thing,' Dick said, again raising one eyebrow slowly, actor-style. 'A poet murdered in his bed. Do we know how?'

'The rumour was ... ' Amadea began carefully. 'The rumour was an overdose of opium. But surely such a thing would and could only be self-inflicted?'

'Not if the opium had been deliberately doctored.'

'Ah! *Ah.*'

Together they returned to Dick's office, where he showed Amadea three more journals that had recently come to light as the result of restoration work in one of the smaller studies. They had been found hidden away in a secret hiding place, behind some bookshelves. Both journals were the work of Lord Harlington himself, and from first glance Amadea could see they were a record of his many trysts and love affairs.

'Bit of a boyo, wouldn't you say?' Dick remarked as he poured them both some coffee. 'Mind you, I suppose if you're a stinking rich aristo you have to find something to do with your spare time.'

'There are quite a lot of references to Edmund,' Amadea remarked as she leafed carefully through the thick, beautifully handwritten pages. 'He seems to crop up with monotonous regularity.'

'He does,' Dick agreed, 'because the custom was that when his lordship tired of a lady he would pass her on, as t'were, to his resident poet. Most of these ladies seem to have quietly, or not so quietly, become besotted with the gent.'

'Well, quite.'

'In fact everything in the garden would appear to have been lovely,' Dick continued, pausing for dramatic effect. 'Until his lordship found his daughter was one of Gains's conquests, and from then on we really are rocking, as you may well imagine.'

He handed Amadea the second of the journals, already open at a particular page. Amadea took it and began to read.

'Lord Harlington seems to have become not a little agitated by the fact,' Amadea observed as she read on. 'From what I see here, he begins to lose it quite seriously.'

'Yet he didn't dismiss his versifier, did he?' Dick turned over more pages, indicating certain passages. 'See, here and here, there are frequent references. No, no, he lets him stay, while fulminating night and morning into his journals. But then if you read on a bit you'll see why. He tries to get rid of Edmund in an underhand and somewhat half-hearted fashion, only for the daughter to intercede on the poet's behalf. As you see, in the very last entry concerning the matter the implication is that if Edmund goes, Felicia goes.'

'Which could be how he got himself killed,' Amadea said, closing the second journal and beginning to flick through the third.

'You think the butler didn't do it?' Dick made a mock gasp. 'You think it was his lordship all the time, miss?'

'I think that's what the smart money would be on, you know? I noticed references to the two of them enjoying some opium, and if Edmund was murdered, who had the best motive of all?'

'Good thinking, Watson,' Dick said, carefully removing his spectacles to wipe them on his silk handkerchief. 'I say — what a super yarn. I would think that this is going to do no end of good for business here.'

He smiled happily and Amadea did too, before turning back to continue reading.

Dick was right of course, it would be good for business; but alas, there was another side to it too, namely persuading Edmund of the lively love life and poetical inclinations to get the hell out and leave Edward alone to pursue the rest of his natural.

★   ★   ★

Rob had not been working hard, he had been overworking hard, so much so that as soon as he had some time off he found himself sleeping, and sleeping as if he would never wake. But as soon as he did wake he knew he had to drive to the Old Rectory and see Amadea.

As he drove up the drive, he was overcome with remorse at the idea that he had stolen possibly the only photograph that Jamie possessed of Dylan's father. He stopped the car.

331

He really should ring Jamie. He reached for his mobile and dialled her number, but the answering machine was on and he balked at the idea of leaving a message about such a thing. Anyway, how could he? He might be wrong. He might have remembered everything wrong; he might have had too many cocktails that evening. After all, when you were tired you could have presentiments, hallucinations, anything; and just at that moment it seemed to Rob he was permanently tired.

'Rob! You're here!'

Rob looked around and about him as he stepped out of the car, a deliberately blank look on his face.

'Am I, Amy? Really? Oh, so I am.'

'Fool.'

Amadea reached up and kissed him firmly on both cheeks.

Rob looked down at her. 'You've changed, Amy.'

Amadea assumed a blank expression, imitating Rob by looking about her.

'Have I? Really? Oh, so I have.'

She stood on tiptoe and stared over-deliberately at the top of Rob's head.

'Anyway, that's a bit strong coming from you. Look who's changed! You have completely changed — hair, clothes, the lot — and you look really cool, you know that?'

Rob started to follow Amadea into the cool hall, grateful for once to be out of the sunshine, but then doubled back to the car to fetch his stolen goods — with the result that when he found Amadea once more, she was in the kitchen having coffee with Edward.

'Edward — do you remember Rob?'

Rob's expression was purposefully innocent.

'No, I don't think we've met actually, have we?' Edward shook hands.

'No, we haven't.'

'It's always the same, you think you have met someone and then you realise you haven't,' Edward said, putting down his empty mug of coffee. He touched Amadea lightly on the shoulder. 'I am going across to see Dottie and Punch, be back for lunch.'

'I'll come with you.' Amadea quickly followed him out of the room, but before she shut the door she whispered, 'We don't leave him alone — for obvious reasons.'

'Hurry back,' Rob mouthed, and then he sat down on the old kitchen sofa, his briefcase beside him, at which point his mobile rang.

'Ah, Rob . . . '

It was Jamie.

'Hallo, Jamie.'

Rob did his best to sound light-hearted-old-Rob, but knew immediately that he was going to be a failure, since just Jamie's 'Ah, Rob' had made a sound as near to metal filings falling on the floor as he had heard in a long while.

'Where are you, Rob, if you don't mind me asking?'

'I'm at the Old Rectory, with Amadea actually, Jamie. At her mother's house, you know?'

'Oh great, you're at Amadea's house.'

Rob frowned at nothing at all, realising too

late that he had yet again given too much information, but not quite knowing why.

Jamie paused, clearing her throat, before continuing. 'I have to ask you quite a difficult question, Rob.' She breathed in, her emotions as hard-held as her voice was cold. 'My question is this. What *is* it about me that you so dislike? I mean what is it that you so hate about me that you should take it upon yourself to steal the one thing that means most to me in the world, besides Dylan, that is?'

'I — er — I . . . '

He couldn't quite follow up his 'ers' with 'don't know what you mean'.

'Yes, you err, you err, all right, Rob.' Despite every effort Jamie knew her voice was rising in fury. She took another deep breath. 'You know, I really thought you were a nice person, Rob. I mean, you were the first man I have met, since Josh, that I have really wanted to be with; fair enough, it was just as a friend — but it could have grown into something more, you know. It really could, but not now. I mean . . . ' She paused. 'I mean, I just can't believe that you did what you did, Rob. You come into my flat on the pretext of having lost your sunglasses and you steal my *photograph* of Josh. I shan't ask why, except to say that you must be paranoid in some way, truly you must. Sick, to be honest. You must be really, really sick. And you know — you know, I am just so sad, damn it, not for myself but for Dylan, because not only did I think you were a nice person but so did he.'

Jamie's voice had started to break. Realising

this, she quickly ended the call.

Rob stared at his mobile, and for a second or two that was all he did, as he asked himself why he was in this particular fix. Could he not have just told Amadea what he had seen? No, he could not, because Amadea being Amadea, and Rob being Rob, he knew they would both need to have proof. Besides, Edward had changed a great deal. The photograph was old, although the likeness was unmistakable. There was only one solution. He started to redial Jamie's number, then stopped, realising there wasn't much point in talking to a woman when she was that upset. Besides she probably wouldn't take his call.

He was still staring ahead at nothing in particular when Amadea came back into the kitchen.

'Hey, you're looking a bit pale beneath your tan, aren't you, Dr Greer? What happened?'

'I am actually feeling incredibly pale beneath my tan, Amy.' Rob snapped his mobile phone shut. 'That was Jamie, and she is far from being in a good mood with me. In fact I would guess that, ten to one on, she is ready to murder me.'

'And for why, Dr Greer?'

'For why?' Rob turned to his briefcase, and proudly removed the stolen goods. 'For this, Ms Fontaine.'

He handed the photograph to Amadea, who at first did not even glance at it because she was too busy staring at Rob's funky new look.

'Look,' Rob went on determinedly, because he knew Amy was still mesmerised by his newly styled hair, although from her expression he could not have been sure what she was thinking. 'Look,' he repeated. 'I know this photograph was taken some time ago, but tell me, please, am I right, or am I totally right? Surely this is your Edward Green, as you call him; or John Smith; or whatever it is we were calling the poor guy when your mother brought him in? Surely this is him? OK, he looks much younger, as he would be, but it is surely him?'

Amadea left off her silent study of Rob's face and hair and glanced down at the photograph. For an instant she looked up and Rob saw the shock in her eyes. Her grip on the photograph tightened and she stared at it, then, holding it much closer to her face, she moved towards the window. Her hands started to shake.

'Oh my God, Rob! I thought you were fantasising, or — or going in for wishful thinking, but *oh my God*, Rob! This is . . . oh my God, Rob.'

Rob held up a hand as if he was stopping traffic, not a torrent of words.

'I keep telling you to stop deifying me, Amy, although I have to admit I understand the impulse.'

'Oh my God, you — are — only — *right*. It is the *spit*. This is Edward all right, it is, it's Edward.'

Rob nodded, his expression one of gradually warming satisfaction as he saw Amadea staring at the photograph and then back to him, and then down at the photograph again, the penny dropping at long, long last. It had been worth everything, the robbery, even poor Jamie's fury,

336

just to see Amadea's reaction.

'Now who is looking pale beneath her tan? Your turn, methinks, my lady Amadea.'

'Stop it, Rob. You're starting to sound like Edmund.'

'Ah, 'tis catching indeed, my lady.'

Amadea shook her head and collapsed beside Rob on the sofa.

'No, but . . . I mean, Rob, do you realise what this *means*?'

She leaned artlessly against him, and as she did so, Rob leaned forward and kissed her lightly.

Amadea continued to stare ahead of her, seeming not to have quite realised what had happened, still gripping the photograph.

'This means that Edward . . . ' she said, slowly.

'Is not Edward . . . '

Rob kissed her again, just as lightly, because she was conveniently in the crook of his arm, and anyway he wanted to kiss her. She was looking far too delightful not to be kissed.

'No, he is not Edward, far from it.'

His attentions still did not seem to have registered with Amadea, because she stood up.

'He is most certainly not Edward.' Amadea turned back to Rob. 'But — but do you realise what this really, really means, Rob?'

'I do.' Rob stood up and drew Amadea closer to him, but she seemed too mesmerised by the photograph to be aware of him. 'It means that Jamie gets her partner back, Dylan gets his dad back, and I get to tell you how much I have been missing your racket in the flat above me.'

Amadea ducked out from under his arms and walked off down the kitchen waving the photograph.

'I just can't believe it, I just can't believe it.' She stopped suddenly. 'Rob?'

'Yes, Amy.'

Amadea frowned. 'Rob, did you — I mean — did you just kiss me?'

'Yes, Amy, as a matter of fact I did. Twice.'

'But, but we don't do that kind of thing — you and I, we don't do that kind of thing, do we? We're just friends, aren't we? We just do not do that, not you and me, Rob.'

Rob gave her his most innocent look. 'You mean, we *didn't* do that kind of thing.'

'But we do now?'

Rob nodded, slowly and deliberately, at pains to keep his face straight. 'Yes, Amy, it seems we do.'

Amadea nodded. 'Oh. Oh, OK. If you think that's all right.'

'I do, Amy, very much. Would you like me to kiss you again?'

'In a minute, yes, but first I just have to show Ma this pic. This she just will *not* believe.'

'She is not the only one,' Rob murmured, sighing happily, but he was talking to an empty room.

★ ★ ★

Of course Florence had known nothing of Rob Greer's dramatic new piece of evidence when, the previous morning, feeling oddly young and

338

as if she had just been let out of school, she packed up and left the Old Rectory.

The distance between her house and the Manor House to which Walter had recently moved was only a few miles, and yet when she drove up the short drive she found Walter already standing outside the old oak front door looking casually anxious, as if he had been long expecting her. As soon as Florence saw him she knew at once that he was doing his best to pretend that he was not looking out for her, like David had used to do when he was waiting to be collected from school.

As soon as she had parked her car, he came to the driver's door and opened it for her, before removing his straw hat as they kissed briefly on the cheek. Replacing it, he gestured towards the house.

'Come in for a coffee, or a glass of fruit juice, do. You must be *exhausted* after such a long journey.'

They both laughed lightly, and Florence followed Walter into the house where a jug of fruit juice had been left out on a tray. It seemed that Walter took a pride in thinking of everything.

Naturally, on the short drive over, Florence had done her best to talk herself into what she thought was a sensible attitude. She must not allow herself to feel either shy or gauche or, worst of all worsts — to appear over-eager. She would just try to be what Amadea called 'cool', and she would call 'natural'. Amadea would say 'go with the flow', and Florence knew that she would be right. She must let things happen in the sure and certain knowledge that what will be will be. But, of course, as soon as she pulled on the handbrake of her beloved old car, and saw Walter standing so anxiously by the front door, she knew she could forget all her previous resolutions.

'Do you want to see round, before we set off? If you're anything like me, you're always itching to go round other people's houses.'

'Love to go round.'

'Sure it's not dull?'

'Quite sure.'

'I'll lead the way if you don't mind, because since we knocked down the old stables and built the new gallery and dining-room complex there are unexpected steps in awkward places.'

The house was laid out in such a way that the converted barn, now an art gallery, was self-contained, but flowed easily into the house, and doors could be shut off or left open as needed.

'What a wonderful piece of design.' Florence pointed to the staircase leading to the restaurant.

'It's a copy of one in Milan. It's made of maple, a terrible extravagance — I should never have commissioned it, but when you are on your own you tend to become indulgent, because unfortunately there's no one to tell you off.'

'What a lovely room.'

As they stood in the middle of the wooden floor, Florence looked around the brand new gallery and gave a happy sigh, for it seemed to her that the walls were not just waiting and ready for people's work to be hung on them, they were reaching out to them.

'This is the studio with dining room above, and around the courtyard out there — ' Walter pointed through the window — 'out there I have converted three or four cottages to rent — but they will only be let to painters or sculptors, artists, potters and so on. We want to preserve the atmosphere of working studios around a courtyard, and of course, if they want, they can come here to eat in what will essentially be a private restaurant.'

'What a superb idea, to have a gallery, and cottages for artists. Gracious, they will be pampered poodles.'

It was Walter's turn to let out a happy sigh. 'It's been a bit of a fight to get it all passed, but now we are there I hope you will agree it has been worth it? Would you like to see the rest before we set off?'

'I would love it.'

The approach to the house and grounds with its banks of shrubs and climbing roses had been very pretty, but now she was inside the new building Florence could appreciate just how beautifully designed it all was, and yet how commodious. She had seen that the house itself, like hers, was not too big, but unlike the Old Rectory, it was not a low-lying building with long windows but a square late-Regency box with glass and iron porticos, and the studio complex was offset to the side so that it did not interfere with either the approach or the view to the house.

341

They walked through the gardens, which, although newly redesigned, already had a look of maturity about them. The tall hedges had been clipped to make alcoves into which were set busts on plinths. The individual 'rooms' of the garden, already set apart from each other, now had a new theme, and each was dedicated to a specific season.

'The spring garden is going to be my favourite, I think.' Walter looked reflective. 'Spring always seems so particularly beautiful in England, don't you agree?'

Florence nodded, realising that it seemed years since she had looked forward to spring, or anything else.

The dining room above the gallery was light and graceful. It was painted white like the gallery below.

'I think this is almost my favourite colour,' she told Walter, patting one of the duck-egg-blue chair cushions.

The fact was that everything in the entire house was elegant and restrained, and classical in a way that was a delight. Yet there was no feeling of overt masculinity: no endless black leather furniture, no vast abstract paintings such as are usually bought by corporations for their offices. In the drawing room velvet curtains hung behind carefully designed wooden pelmets, and faded Persian rugs lay on polished wooden floors. A large pair of porcelain birds on the chimney-piece, an armillary sphere on a brocade-covered table, and some leather-bound books between ancient bronze Chinese dogs completed the picture of a room that everyone would want to sit in whatever the season.

'Now I must stop showing off, and we must start on our great adventure. Roger is bringing the car round. Ah, here they are, even as we speak.'

As soon as Florence saw Roger she fell in love. The object of her love was not Roger but the old-fashioned Bentley convertible he was driving.

'Oh, what a darling person, what a princess of the road,' Florence exclaimed, standing back to admire first its shining blue exterior, and then, as Roger opened the door for her, its matching blue leather seats, and its fine hood. 'Just look at her preening herself in the sunshine. What a fine job you've done,' she ended, turning to Roger.

Walter smiled first at Roger and then at the immaculately presented motor car. 'Bit of a car buff, are you?' he asked Florence, obviously hardly able to believe his luck.

'Oh yes.' Florence glanced quickly up at him and then back at the car. 'Oh yes, yes, yes. I particularly love old Bentleys. They have such mature appeal. There is something about an old Bentley, or an old Rolls, that exudes the right kind of class, the right kind of glamour.'

She looked up at Walter, a rare look of mischief coming into her eyes again, and he laughed, taking the point.

'Roof down?'

'Of course.' Florence nodded, untying an old straw hat from the side of her suitcase and cramming it over her hair, while Roger piled the

343

rest of the luggage into the boot.

Walter settled himself into the driver's seat, Roger shut his door, and they waved to him as the car moved graceful as a swan down the drive to the country road beyond.

'What exactly is she? I mean when is her birthday?' Florence asked, breaking the contented silence, as Walter stopped the car at a crossing.

'She's a Bentley S 1 Convertible.'

'She is? Well, we have to face it, she is heaven on wheels.'

'I thought you might be many things,' Walter told Florence, shaking his head with delighted wonder, 'but not a car buff. I should have known better. Any woman who cooks as well as you do, chooses her wines as well as you do, and looks as good as you do, has to like beautiful motor cars.'

Florence lay back against the leather seating, surrendering herself to the feeling that she was somehow young again. It was ridiculous but she felt carefree for the first time for years.

'Do you know, you are so right to call this a motor car; not a car, because that is exactly what she is — a motor car, not a vehicle, not a car, but a motor car,' Florence murmured appreciatively, and she gazed contentedly at the beautiful morning, at the blue sky, at the empty country road which now lay ahead of them as they motored along at a pretty pace. 'Isn't Somerset wonderful? Empty roads, no one about, and no one knows about us either. It seems we really do have the county to ourselves this morning, Walter. Quite to ourselves.'

Walter tried not to let his heart quicken as she said his name. Somehow the way she said it, the lightness in her voice, made him feel more special than he had felt for years.

'Somerset has ever been known only to a few perceptive souls, people of discernment, people who like peace and poetry.'

'You mean like Mr and Mrs Coleridge and the Wordsworths?'

For a second Florence's mind went back to Edmund Gains, but then she shut him out. She would not take the last few weeks away with her, nor the last few months, or years. She was determined to empty her mind of the past, and throw away the key where no one, least of all herself, could find it.

★　★　★

The drive that Walter had carefully planned, with stops at small hostelries and private houses which catered to select people on a bed-and-breakfast basis, was to take them through the Quantocks and along the top of Exmoor. It would also take them past the sea.

'Are you good at walking?' Walter asked, incuriously, after they had visited the poet's cottage and were returning to the car.

'Oh yes,' Florence said, but she looked up at him from under her straw hat, trying not to laugh. 'Just so long as I have a motor car, and a good dinner to which to look forward, I am, I think, a perfectly brilliant walker.'

Walter did laugh. 'A good dinner and a motor

car is exactly what I need between walks. We shall, I think you will find, get on supremely well.'

'Of course,' Florence told him, almost complacently, and for a second time Walter's heart took on a life of its own, setting off at a quick canter, not to say a fast gallop, without so much as a say-so from him.

12

The ritual humiliation that was their fortnightly Saturday lunch with her mother had been changed to a weekday, as Rosa was going away at the weekend to see a friend in Scotland. Nevertheless it felt like a terribly dull Saturday, as life in her mother's house always seemed to, one way or another.

Thursday or Saturday, it really didn't seem to matter, since it had begun in the usual way with two glasses of sherry poured for Jamie and Rosa, and one of tomato juice for Dylan, who now knew to sit himself as still as a statue on the wooden stool provided, making sure not to swing his legs or slurp his juice, but to stare ahead of him as stiffly as a guardsman on duty outside Buckingham Palace. Above all he knew he had to remember that he was at his *grandmother's* house, where no bad behaviour was tolerated. Where, as a matter of fact, now Jamie came to think of it, no behaviour of any kind was tolerated. Where Dylan had to pretend to be as old as his grandmother, until they went home, when he would suddenly remember with surprise and relief that he was actually only four and would jump about and run into all the rooms as free as a young colt in a spring paddock let out of its stable for the first time in weeks.

The clock ticked, and tocked, and ticked and

tocked as Rosa stared from Jamie to Dylan and back again.

'So you've lost your job?' she asked finally.

'Yes.'

Yet another long silence followed as the three of them considered this statement.

'Well, that is a pretty kettle of fish, I'm sure.'

Jamie nodded, but only because she could think of nothing to disagree with in this old-fashioned statement. 'Yes, it is.'

'What happened?'

Her mother frowned suddenly at Dylan, as if he had done something to cause his mother to lose her job, or as if she somehow suspected that her grandson might be at the bottom of this loss not just of face but of income.

'What happened was that I was sacked. It was when Dylan was ill, and I had to stay with him.'

'Ah.' This, although honest to a degree, unfortunately gave Rosa Charlbury a chance to stare even harder at her grandson, the all-too-unfortunate product of Jamie's all-too-unfortunate love of music. 'So they don't like single-parent families, I thought as much. These firms have to say one thing, because of all these silly new laws, but when it comes down to it, they are just as they always used to be, disapproving of women with domestic ties. It's always been the same. Far better in the old days when women who wanted careers didn't get married.'

'But I haven't been married — so that should make it all right, shouldn't it?' asked Jamie, throwing caution to the wind, and looking and

348

feeling suddenly that she didn't care what her mother thought.

'Of course it's not all right that you haven't been married,' Rosa said, dropping her voice as if Dylan could not hear. 'You should have insisted on getting married before the child's father escaped under the wire.'

'His father is not the kind of man who would understand someone insisting on anything.'

'Nonsense, all men need to be dominated, managed, and indeed handled. Only a feeble sort can't handle a man,' Rosa said, forgetting this time to lower her voice. She stood up. 'I am going to put on the lunch — '

'You look very nice as you are, Grandma.'

Rosa turned round slowly to stare down at Dylan. 'I beg your pardon, young man?'

Jamie put out a hand and gave Dylan's hair a nervous flick.

'It's Dylan's new joke,' she told her mother as the boy ducked away from having his hair tidied.

'I see.'

Rosa did not smile, but turned slowly back with an expression on her face as if she had now heard everything. She left them both in her sitting room, a sad little duo staring ahead of them, mother and son as helpless as each other, not knowing which way to turn to make the wretched time go quicker.

As soon as they sat down to lunch, the torture continued. Jamie and Dylan realised that it was their least favourite meal, Irish stew with the fat in, followed by the inevitable slimy jelly. But as it happened, the jelly turned out to be fortuitous, for just as Jamie swapped plates with her son, her mother returned unexpectedly to the dining room to witness her daughter's culinary treachery.

'What are you doing, Jamie?'

Jamie stared up at her mother, suddenly realising that she just might hate her. 'Me? I am eating Dylan's jelly.'

Her mother reached out and took the plate back from her, and reset it in front of Dylan.

'Dylan must eat his own jelly.'

She stared in cold anger from Jamie to Dylan as Jamie promptly took the plate back and started to bolt the jelly in a deliberately unappealing manner.

'Dylan,' Rosa repeated. 'Dylan must eat his own jelly.'

Jamie stood up, swallowing the last of the wretched stuff in a childishly cross fashion.

'Dylan doesn't want to eat jelly. And I don't want him to be made to eat jelly,' she announced. 'I don't know why you can't be like everyone else's grandmothers and give him ice cream, or chocolate cake. Why can't you find out what he likes instead of making him eat things he hates? But you were always like that, weren't you, Mother? Always making me eat things you knew I hated. An accomplished sadist really, now I come to think of it.'

Rosa, still a beautiful woman, drew herself up to her full height.

'You will not speak to me like that, Lucinda.'

'I am a grown woman, and while I know that it is my duty to respect and love you as much as I

350

can, I am no longer going to stand by while you make Dylan eat things he hates. What is more, I think it is about time you stopped disapproving and started to try and love us, if you can. I know it's been hard for you, bringing me up on your own, and now here I am bringing Dylan up on my own — '

'*I* was married!'

'And so would I have been had Dylan's dad not had to go to Africa to try and save millions of babies from dying, as you well know, Mother.'

Jamie picked up her bag and, taking Dylan's hand, she left the dining room.

'Where are you going? May I ask, where are you going?'

'I am going home. Dylan and I are going home, and we are not coming back to see you, Mother, until you decide to give us a better time.' She turned at the door. 'I'm sorry I can't leave you anything this week, but that is how it is. Next time, why not come and see us? At the flat? We could give you a really fun time.'

'I never go to Swinton — '

'Time you did, Mother, time you came into the twenty-first century. Time you stopped being a widow. You're a very beautiful woman, you should come shopping, get a new look.'

Rosa breathed in and closed her eyes. 'You make me despair, really you do.'

She opened her front door for them and closed it, slowly and decorously, once they were outside. Jamie had seen, with some dread, the wooden expression on her mother's face.

'Sorry about that, kid,' said Jamie. 'I didn't

351

mean to quarrel with Grandma, but you know — it has been torture bringing you here.'

Dylan looked up at her, his face a picture of misery. 'I like Grandma.' He started to cry. 'I'll eat jelly, really I will.'

A lump came into Jamie's throat. Oh God, she'd fouled up yet again.

⋆   ⋆   ⋆

'I am very glad you came to me for advice, because I really am the best person to help, since I was in on everything from the first. What we have to do,' Dottie told Rob and Amadea, her knitting fingers flying, 'is to begin at the beginning.'

Rob tried to look impressed by this notion, and failed spectacularly.

'Sounds like a good idea,' he agreed, bossing his eyes at Amadea, who quickly looked away, trying not to laugh.

'Yes, that is what we will do, we will begin at the beginning — do help yourselves to more wine, dears. Yes, we will begin at the beginning and, like Alice, we will go on until we stop. You see . . . ' Dottie glanced up at her kitchen clock, which was telling her that it was way past ten. She felt oddly excited to be up so late. 'You see, while Dick is amusing Edward up at the Old Rectory, we can be quite frank here, just between the three of us. Darling Florence told a porky, didn't she? She said that Edmund, or Edward or whatever he was calling himself, called on her. But he *didn't* call on her, as we all know — she found him in her guest cottage. So, *how* did he get there?'

'He stumbled in?' Amadea offered.

'He was drunk and wanted a lie-down?'

'Tiss, tiss, Mrs Tittlemouse. No, no, no,' Dottie insisted, her knitting fingers still flying. 'We have none of us thought this story *out* enough.' She paused theatrically in order to assure herself of maximum attention. 'He got there by dint, it seems to me, of being lost, not drunk. No, he was lost in his other personality — when he lost himself it was as *Edmund Gains*, who, as we now all know, was a poet who lived and died on the Harlington Estate. So, it seems to me, *Edward* must have been known up there, at Harlington Hall, at some time or another. After all, Edmund Gains is an obscure poet, someone who was hardly known outside the area, so *Edward* must have been at the Hall himself when he started to go into this other personality. I tell you, it is the only explanation. And I told the bees this morning, and they agreed that this was quite the right line. They did, they agreed entirely.'

Again Rob and Amadea tried not to look at each other.

'It makes the kind of sense we've been trying to make all day,' Rob said slowly. 'But Dick has got no further than finding Edmund Gains's grave, and the reference in the daughter's diary — '

'Commonplace book — '

'Yes, that. But what could there be to find at Harlington Hall? Dick has turned the library and

353

the archives upside down.'

'What else is there?' Dottie snorted lightly. 'There has to be *something* else, young man, there has to be some other reason for Edward and Edmund ending up in Flo's guest cottage — we can't all have thrown away our song sheets now, can we?' Amadea and Rob frowned momentarily at that, but Dottie continued inexorably. 'No, what you two should do is to give that photograph of yours to Dick Saxon to take back to Harlington. Get him to show it around, see if anyone else besides ourselves recognises him.'

Rob looked briefly at Amadea before turning back to Dottie. 'You are one clever lady, you know that, don't you?'

Dottie nodded. 'Of course, no point in being as old as me if you're not clever with it. Now go on and give Dick Saxon your photograph, although not in front of the patient of course. I'll get in touch with Mabel Minton. She must be able to work some kind of white magic in a situation like this. The grave, the poet, the young man who was lost in Africa — it all finally has to make some strange kind of sense. There's so much we don't understand, but Mabel surely must do, she just hasn't been trying hard enough. Think, just think, so many senses we have lost, given away with the dreadful march of time. What I must do is to get another message to Mabel.'

'Sounds like a song title — 'Gotta Get A Message To Mabel',' Rob murmured.

Dottie went to her antiquated telephone and,

staring at the wall where she had scribbled down numbers, started to dial. Unfortunately Mabel's message service, a neighbour probably as old as Dottie's phone, was deaf, so the message had to be shouted, and then relayed back a few minutes later.

'The answer is in the affirmative,' she announced, looking deservedly triumphant. 'Her neighbour will drive Mabel — as you know, she does not drive — and she will meet you in front of Harlington Hall tomorrow morning. I say.' She breathed out. 'Wouldn't it be splendid if we could kick Edmund in the backside and send him back to where he belongs?' She paused, frowning, the expression in her eyes one of benign intolerance. 'Poets, really! My mother always did say they made a point of being out of touch, not to mention, as in this case, otherworldly.'

* * *

Jamie was trying to cheer herself up by cheering Dylan up, and failing miserably. Dylan had not enjoyed school, and he was now not enjoying his tea, and she could see that he would soon be not enjoying either his bath or his bedtime story.

'Dylan — what is the matter with you?'

He sat silently staring at his plate.

'It was school, was it, Dylan? Did you have a bad day at school?'

Dylan said nothing, swinging his legs under the table, to and fro, to and fro. Jamie wanted to stop him, but because she dreaded tears she said nothing. She finally removed his plate and took it into the kitchen, where wave after wave of remorse swept over her as she stared at his unfinished food, while the sound of his legs banging relentlessly against the wooden chair echoed around the flat.

If she was truthful, she had to admit that her remorse began with Glastonbury. Her behaviour had been impeccable, until she met Josh. She seemed to remember him telling her that his behaviour too had been impeccable, until he met her, and then it had happened: the mad impulses that instant desire brings about had been indulged not at the festival but afterwards, back at her flat. They hadn't been able to leave each other alone — and looking back, five years on, Jamie could not help wondering how she would feel now if she saw Josh again. Would the spark have gone? Would they both feel the same? To be faced with so many questions was dispiriting, so she picked up Dylan's plate and tossed the pizza with commendable accuracy into the dustbin, and went to fetch him.

'Come on, kid, let's go to the common and play football.'

Dylan glanced up at his mother, giving her that particularly flat look that children can give grown-ups when they haven't quite finished avenging themselves on them, for some unstated reason that they might or might not allow them to discover.

'Will Rob come too?'

Jamie sighed inwardly, long and hard. 'No, Dylan, Rob is away. He will not be coming too.'

She snatched at her bag and followed Dylan out of the front door, counting slowly not to a hundred but a hundred and ten, which she happened to know was enough to get her to the ground floor, and so out into the open air, and fresh thoughts of a less lowering nature.

★　★　★

For the first night of their tour, Florence and Walter were to stay at a joyfully welcoming bed-and-breakfast run by some old friends of Walter's. Florence had been assigned a large double room with adjoining bathroom at the opposite end of the house from Walter, which was splendidly tactful.

As their hostess left her Florence looked round the room and immediately appreciated that it was full of personal touches — a teddy bear seated in a small chintz chair near the window, flowers on the dressing table and the covered tables; not to mention the bathroom filled not just with guest soaps but bath toys.

The bed was made up with freshly ironed white linen sheets which on close examination sported not just a faded family crest but a few of the tiniest of delicate hand-sewn darns, which was somehow oddly satisfying. To top it all, there were lavender sprigs on the pillows.

Walter, knowing that dinner was not served to guests at the house, had already booked a table at the local hostelry, which was only a short walk up the road. A warm evening found them strolling in companionable silence up to the

Crown and Thistle. As Florence stepped into the convivial atmosphere she had the ridiculous feeling that she was a young woman again, that the past was not just behind her but that she had locked the door and thrown away the key; until she sat down opposite Walter, and knew it was impossible. She knew she was falling in love again, which meant that she would have to touch on everything to do with the past before she could even think of having a future.

'You first,' she told Walter later, as, having eaten, they shared the rest of the bottle of wine.

'Well, like you, I've been married before, but my wife did not die — she left me.'

'Ah.'

Walter's face was expressionless as he sighed lightly. 'Yes, quite — *ah.*' He sipped at his glass before continuing. 'I suppose it was easier because we had no children, but more difficult too, because I was left with nothing *except* my work. And work is fine, of course, because it keeps you going, but it is also not fine, because it stops you doing anything about your situation. You just pedal on, and on, and on, delighting as much as you can in the common task, but living only from one routine to the next. So, these last years, that's all I have done really. I've just kept working, working, working, always hoping, in the back of my mind, I now realise, that I would collapse, have a heart attack and — die, and so be finally set free from the treadmill.'

'It was that bad, was it?'

'Oh yes, it was that bad all right.' Walter managed to look both rueful and sad at the same

358

time. 'Yes, it was that bad,' he repeated.

Florence was silent for a few seconds, thinking.

'They say the one who is left alone is the one who never recovers. And in a way that is true when someone dies, but perhaps even more true if someone leaves you.'

Walter nodded. 'Looking back now, I realise that I loved her, but really, she never loved me back. I think if she had loved me, we would have had children and a proper family life; but as it was we just had what they call nowadays a glitzy life, flying from one glamorous location to the next, going through the rituals of supposed happiness. But that is quite definitely no substitute for domestic bliss, believe me.'

Walter found himself appreciating the fact that Florence had once again fallen silent. She did not jump in with some conversational bromide, as so many other women might. She merely stared at him in a troubled sort of way.

'It is difficult to get over someone leaving you. At least, that is what I have been finding . . . ' Florence paused again, silenced for a second or two by her own memories, but also because Walter had put his hand across hers.

*   *   *

Dick took the photograph back to his cottage, but, being all too aware of his new-boy status at Harlington Hall, he did not immediately rush round to show it to Theo as Rob and Amadea had asked. For the first morning it sat on his desk, the unmistakable face of the poor boy with the dual personality staring accusingly at him as he struggled to bring order to the paperwork surrounding it.

He was finally saved the trouble of making the call, when Theo himself knocked unexpectedly on his cottage door. Dick found him standing on the threshold, from where Theo launched straight into a conversation without more ado, as was always his habit.

'You're good with people, Dick. I seem to remember that at one point, years ago, you were made into some sort of expert in the field? Flying around like Batman, sorting out a company's troubles, wasn't that what you did?'

'I was, for my sins, but only for a very short while. Managing musicians like Henry Fontaine was like falling off a log after trying to find out why some company's staff were always leaving, believe me. I say, since it's five minutes past midday, how would you fancy a *very* old-fashioned drink?'

'So long as it's not just old-fashioned but *very* iced.'

Theo mopped his brow and looked round the cottage sitting room. Dick, with his usual flair, had already managed to make it look splendidly stylish.

'You have some very nice things, old chap.'

'Tut, tut, Theo, chaps shouldn't mention a chap's things, terribly bad form.' It was an old joke they'd been sharing since university days. 'So, Campari and soda with ice?'

'Bless you, that *is* an old-fashioned drink

— and pretty delicious on a hot day too.' Theo wandered over to the cottage window and looked out at the roses climbing up the old wall opposite. 'They tell me it's going to be another wonderful summer for roses.'

'That is good.'

Theo nodded. 'Yes, another wonderful summer for roses, that unique mix of rain and sun which they so love.' He glanced down at the desk, and, seeing a familiar face staring up at him, picked up Jamie's photograph of Josh. 'Ye gods, Dick, what are you doing with this?'

Dick frowned. 'I was given it at the Old Rectory — the young couple gave it to me. It's this chap Edward or Edmund, poor fellow with the split personality. The one that Florence has taken under her wing.'

Theo shook his head. 'I can't believe it! I came to ask your advice about one of these Gemini boys, and here you are with a photograph of the very one who has gone missing.'

Dick frowned. 'But — but, Theo, this — this is the young man who turned up in Florence's guest cottage, unannounced and uninvited, and they've been trying to get him sorted out ever since.'

Theo went to say something and then stopped.

'Well, I'll be jiggered, as our old gardener used to say, I really will be jiggered. This is definitely our Gemini boy who went AWOL a few weeks ago. I've been giving out snaps of him to all and sundry. Yes, all and sundry have been searching for the poor fellow too, practically got Interpol in on it. Missing Persons Bureaux, Loved Ones Gone AWOL charities, they've all had their Sherlock Holmes caps on.' He shook his head again. 'And you say that the lovely Florence Fontaine has had him at her place all the time? How perfectly marvellous, Dick. We were dreading that someone had taken ruthless advantage and kidnapped him for some kind of East European workforce. You see, he has no memory, nothing. When you think of it, anything could happen to these poor fellows if they end up in the wrong hands.'

With a delighted smile Dick snatched up Theo's glass and topped it up, this time with gin and Campari.

'I was about to ring you up and ask for your help in trying to find out who he is, which is why the young couple gave me the photie.'

'Well, well, this is really — really almost a shock.' Theo sat down, still staring at the photograph of his missing Gemini.

'Tell me, tell me all, concealing nothing, as my father used to say,' Dick begged him. 'I know nothing of your gardening force except they always wave and smile and laugh and send me on my way singing.'

Theo shook his head, breathed out heavily and replaced the photograph on the desktop nearby. 'Here's the story. To begin at the beginning, the Gemini Trust was started by the Duchess of Millington when it was discovered that one of her sons was suffering from multiple personality syndrome, as a result of having been bullied at school.' Dick stared at him. 'I know, I know,' he agreed in answer to Dick's silent question. 'Who would think that bullying at school could have such an outcome? But the parents were abroad on diplomatic duties and had no idea of what was going on, and the school, as is so often the case, were perfectly indifferent to the poor boy's sufferings until it was too late. At any rate the old duchess conceived the idea that if she could find an occupation that would suit all the boy's different personalities, even if he didn't find happiness he could find some kind of contentment. It finally transpired that the only thing that suited all three personalities was gardening; so she set up a trust for him and others like him. The strange thing was that her really rather wobbly plan worked. Her son is one of the few cases on record of such a disturbing syndrome having been cured. Finally all three personalities settled down and became one. Of course psychiatrists and medics pooh-poohed it, saying that he hadn't been properly diagnosed in the first place, but the main thing was it worked, and so the Gemini Trust was started, supplying help to the old estates while hoping to alleviate various mental disorders.'

'Brilliant idea, brilliant story.'

'I know, but of course now the trust has a much wider remit, working with people of all ages suffering from disorders caused by drugs and alcohol and so on. It is most successful, but of course we do lose people every now and then, and every now and then they are returned to us. Sometimes they even come back of their own accord; or sometimes, like Josh, they don't go very far, and come back via a brilliant set of circumstances. Well, well, well, good old Josh.'

Theo smiled, but Dick frowned.

'We know him as Edward, of course, or Edmund.' He cleared his throat. 'Was he, I mean was he, do you think, in that condition because of drugs or alcohol?'

'Josh? Good heavens no, nothing of that sort. No, his case was quite different. It seems that Josh went to Africa, to try to save it, as so many people are doing.'

'Big place to save, Africa.'

'So it proved for Josh, very big; but like all the young and idealistic, he was determined to do his bit before he grew too old and grey. And I gather he did do his bit, magnificently, but with disastrous repercussions for himself, for it was while he was out there that he started to suffer from that particular syndrome that makes certain people think that the situation with which they are dealing is entirely their fault. It happens to doctors and nurses, aid workers like him, all kinds of personalities. Finally he found himself caught up in a bit of a dust-up.' Theo stopped. 'Quite a bit of a dust-up, as a matter of fact,' he went on, frowning. 'He ended up being knocked unconscious, and either mistaken for dead or feigning death to escape being killed, no one quite knows. Anyway, he was thrown into a pit underneath a whole lot of chaps who were thoroughly dead. It was there that he was found, rescued and eventually sent back to the UK.'

'Bad news all round then?' Dick put in, carefully.

'Very bad news. He was discovered to be in tertiary shock. He'd lost his memory, lost his personality, become a sort of zombie.'

'Hardly surprising.'

'No, so what to do? Finally the charity for whom he had been working contacted us and asked if we could help, which of course we were happy to do. When he first came here he had completely lost his memory, or rather his mind had blanked out. As far as Josh was concerned, he himself did not exist. But then one of the men cataloguing the library befriended him, and for some reason Josh started to read up all about this Edmund Gains. He became a walking blasted encyclopaedia about the chap. He ate, slept and dreamed him, even started to dress like him, until it seemed he had replaced his own lost personality with this Edmund fellow. Not that it mattered to us — Josh was, after all, harmless and one more eccentric figure roaming round the grounds in the evenings or at the weekends made very little difference; in fact it added to the charm of the place. I even found the brocade coat for him — and the boots. He was delighted. But then, as I say, he went AWOL.' Theo shook his head and smiled. 'I can't tell you how glad I am that we've found him. I missed young Josh. Well, we all did. Now, about the fête champêtre — I was going to suggest that we give a book of tickets to everyone at the Old Rectory.'

Dick stared at Theo, realising that his old friend had lived with people like Josh for so long that their dual or multiple personalities, or other problems, were something he had come to

365

accept with equanimity, just as someone else might accept hair or eye colouring.

'I've already given them some, but wait a minute, don't you think you ought to get someone to ring Florence and arrange to claim Josh, or whatever you have to do?'

Theo stared at him. 'Why yes, of course. I'll send a Trusty up for him asap, you may be sure. Now, about the fête champêtre. You know what I think is inspired is that *everyone* comes. That is what I enjoy. The farmer and his wife, vicars, priests, shopkeepers, every kind of person from village and town, and bless them, this year the theme being the Age of Reason, they should look splendid.'

'Ah, the Age of Reason, if only it had lasted, how much more reasonable we might have been.'

They both laughed, and a few minutes later Theo rang up his office and instructed someone to collect Josh from the Old Rectory.

★　★　★

Earlier that morning Amadea and Rob had driven into Dorset to pick up Mabel Minton. Before they set out, Amadea's face had been alight with enthusiasm.

'Oh Rob, imagine if we could reunite Edward with Jamie, wouldn't it be just the best and most wonderful thing that ever happened?'

Rob had agreed, but only after a second's hesitation. He, after all, had his own ideas about what the best and most wonderful thing that could ever happen would be, but he was not going to tell Amadea — yet.

Mabel was ready and waiting when they arrived. If Amadea and Rob had known her better, they would have realised that she had on not just her best hat but her most determined expression. She climbed into the back of the car, gripping a large, old-fashioned, battered doctor's bag.

'This is a most interesting case,' she announced eventually from the rear seat. 'And of course now that you know that the poor boy belongs to someone, you are right to hurry things along. After all, there may be some traumatic emotional reason for Edward's hiding behind Edmund. Yes, indeed. I have brought my bag,' she finished mysteriously, but though Amadea and Rob would have dearly loved to ask what was in it, neither of them quite dared, both realising that Mabel would tell them only as and when she thought it necessary.

They drove along in the kind of heavy silence that always hangs over cars when no one wants to make a fool of themselves by discussing something too trivial, but no one can quite think what to say to introduce a momentous topic. Eventually Amadea broke the silence.

'Mrs Minton, we think, Rob and I think, we have found out who your patient is.'

Rob turned to look at Amadea. He liked that bit, the 'Rob and I' bit. He liked it so much that when he straightened up and stared at the road in front of him once more he seemed to feel a new kind of glow, as if his heart was a candle to which Amy had at last put a match; but if Amy and Rob had thought the fact that they knew Edward's true identity would find favour with Mabel, they were to be sadly disappointed.

'It's not who he is in *this* life that we are interested in,' came the royal reply from the back of the car. 'It's the person who is inhabiting him whom we have to get to know, and how we get him to go, that is the question that must occupy us. The poor host personality is of no interest in this matter; he is merely a flower upon whom the bee has settled and refused to move.'

When they reached the Old Rectory Edmund was once more in full flow, waxing lyrical with lines of poetry to which Dottie, since she found Edmund much less appealing than Edward, was paying only scant attention. At Harlington Hall, Theo, in company with a Trusty, was climbing into his car to fetch the young man he had always known affectionately as Josh.

'He's been trying to interest me in Robert Herrick again,' Dottie confided to Amadea, raising her eyes to heaven. 'But really, dear, there is only so much poetry one can take at such an early hour, I find.'

Amadea looked sympathetic.

Rob touched her lightly on the arm. 'I'm going to get my medic kit from the car — just in case something exciting happens.'

Dottie walked past him to Mabel, who was still standing in the drive outside, looking serious. Dottie's expression mirrored that of their visitor, because she was all too aware of Mabel's power, of her reputation; but more than that, of the solemnity of the task ahead of her.

They both knew that it was not something to be undertaken lightly.

'Ah, Mabel, how good of you to come, and at such short notice. We are indeed honoured.'

Instead of shaking hands the two older women bowed towards each other, rather in the manner of middle-aged cardinals greeting each other at some grand occasion. It was as if, despite sharing the same faith, they were determined to keep their distance, until such time when a miracle could be said to have taken place.

'I suggest we walk up to the Hall, that we do not take a motor car,' Mabel announced.

'I'm afraid I can't — dropped a weight on my foot last night.' Dottie turned rather thankfully for home.

In the event Mabel, Edward, Amadea and Rob made their way along hardly frequented narrow paths across the back of the estate and up into the woods, until eventually they reached the vista that Amadea had treasured since she was a small girl.

'It's called Heaven's View, did you know that?' Amadea turned to Rob, breaking the silence into which they had all momentarily fallen as they looked down at the vast lake below them, edged at discreet intervals by temples and follies built into the hillsides surrounding the water. 'David and I used to come up here on our ponies, in the early morning.' Her face was solemn as she remembered with instant clarity her brother's face glowing in the early light. 'David always used to say that he would never have to be told what heaven was like, he knew it already, because

369

he had been here and seen it.'

'David?'

'My brother. He died a few years ago, rescuing me from the sea. My fault, you know, going for a last swim? Stupid. But there was another boy in the water, and of course, David being David, he had to go in after him too.' She shook her head. 'Handsome hero dies saving young boy.'

She looked up at Rob, shrugging her shoulders lightly, and as she did so she realised that, for the first time since David's death, guilt had vanished from her, and she felt as light as the piece of white thistledown that had just floated past her to drift out over the lake. And that was before Rob put his arm around her, and held her for a second.

He was too tactful to say what he was feeling, which was that it was little wonder Amy had become so determinedly defensive, trying to pretend that the best way to deal with life was not to care about it too much. He eased her from his embrace and smiled down at her, seeing her wrapped in a new bright light.

'We'd better catch the others up,' Amy whispered, after he had kissed her. 'Before we start kissing too much.'

The other two, led by Edmund, who was still in richly poetic form, had indeed continued on their way. Turning to see whether they had caught up, Mabel held back to speak to Amadea, while beckoning Rob to pass them.

'Where is the grave of Edmund Gains?' she asked, in a dramatically lowered tone.

Amadea nodded ahead of them, up the

winding path. 'Behind that temple, marked by a stone.'

'You stay here then, both of you,' Mabel ordered with sudden authority, as she strode quickly away to catch up with Edmund. Just before she turned the corner she waved them yet further away. 'Stay away from here,' she called, 'and let no one pass you, or us, for the next few minutes.'

This was easier said than done, for only a few seconds later Amadea found herself looking anxiously down the hillside towards a small party of people making their way slowly up towards the same temple. Happily they were still some distance away; unhappily they were climbing at a comfortably steady pace up towards where Rob and Amadea were busily blocking the path.

'Stopping them isn't going to be easy,' Amadea said, turning anxious eyes on Rob.

'Leave it to me,' Rob told her. He touched her lightly on the shoulders, finding them once again tense and rigid, as if she was too used to carrying a great burden on their slender shape. He pushed quickly down on her back. 'Relax! I will use the full weight of my medical authority and stop them as they approach. This is one thing I can do.' He made a megaphone of one hand. 'Is there a doctor on the estate? Yes, there is, Dr Rob Greer — who is crazy about Amadea Fontaine.'

'Shush.'

'No, I will not shush, Amy. I want everyone to know I am wild about Amy, and — ' he held up a hand — 'I have a feeling that Amy is wild about me?'

'If you say so.'

'If I say so? That is no reply, and you know it.'

He started to get down on one knee, but Amadea stopped him. 'Not here, later.'

Rob pulled a long face. 'You are such a spoil-sport.'

'Listen, dude,' Amadea told him, also pulling a face. 'There is, as my teacher used to say, a time and a place for everything, and besides, there is too much going on right now.' She pointed up the hill. 'What is happening up there could be sensational.'

'No,' Rob insisted, singing. '*You're sensational —*'

He had hardly finished when a strange, wild sound came from the fields behind the temple. It was very soon recognisable as that of galloping hooves followed by huge activity in the lake water below them. Amadea turned, feeling suddenly breathless, as if she knew something tremendous had happened, yet could not have said quite what it was.

'I have a feeling that Mabel has done it,' Rob said, grabbing Amadea's hand and realising instantly that the same thought must have occurred to her because she was as white as her shirt collar.

'Do you think?' Amadea found herself whispering, so much in awe was she of what she thought might have happened. 'Do you really think Mabel has done it, Rob?'

'Either that or Harlington Hall has just experienced its first twister,' Rob joked.

'Uh-oh — we have company!' Amadea nodded

in the direction of the path.

Rob turned to view the group of visitors which had now grown closer to them, and immediately decided to take ruthless advantage of his medical training. He signalled them, using the same authority that Amadea imagined he might use to break up a clutch of gossiping nurses. 'I'm a doctor — ' he began.

The party stopped, then stared at him in a vaguely irritated manner.

'No one's perfect,' someone joked, eliciting a small ripple of laughter.

Rob at once threw the wag his best 'Have you seen the state of the operating theatre?' look, which appeared to silence him, and began again.

'As I said, I'm a doctor, and I'm sorry to tell you that there has been a small accident up there behind the temple. So, if you don't mind waiting here for a few minutes while I attend to it, we should not be too long; but we don't want anyone to be caused any unnecessary distress or anxiety.'

At that there was a general murmur of sympathy, and the small group of silver-haired, good-natured, casually dressed British tourists waited obediently as Rob and Amadea hurried ahead of them, rounding the corner of the temple where it seemed that Edmund Gains had been buried in haste over two hundred years before. It was here that they found Edward stretched out on the ground, apparently unconscious, his face so pale it looked lifeless.

Rob went to him immediately and started to unpack his black leather bag. Mabel, one hand resting against a nearby tree, her own black leather bag once more firmly shut, watched him.

'I'm afraid the poor young man passed out, Dr Greer, and is only now coming round. Exorcisms of this kind are well known to be a bit wearing for the host body, you know, and not just the host body.'

Mabel slumped against the tree, wiping her forehead with a small handkerchief with, for some reason best known to her, small rabbits embroidered on it. Amadea immediately went up to her.

'Can I give you a drink of something? Rob has some bottled water in his bag.'

'Could you, Miss Fontaine? I must confess I do have a somewhat dry mouth, and my pulse is a little unsteady. I can hear it pounding in my ears. The force, you know, even if it only passes near to you . . . ' Mabel shook her head. 'It still knocks you backwards.' Amadea handed her a bottle of water, and Mabel drank from it gratefully. 'Still, in the end this was not the worst case, you know,' she went on, frowning down at some strange marks on the ground. 'No, the very worst case I ever saw was in Italy. A beautiful young girl, she could only have been about fifteen, her slender arms held by two strapping young monks while the prayers of exorcism were being said, but the force inside her made her whole body spin round, and strong though those strapping monks were, they were helpless to stop the Catherine wheel that the poor young girl had become.'

Mabel went to a nearby log and sat down

374

suddenly. Amadea turned to Edward, kneeling beside him as he slowly opened his eyes, while Rob put his stethoscope to his chest and listened to his heart.

'Edward?'

Edward stared up at her, a dazed expression on his face.

'Edward? I'm not Edward, Edward's not my name.' He started to sit up, shaking his head and looking around him. 'Why did you call me Edward? And who are you?' he asked Amadea. 'Why am I here? Who are you?' he demanded again. 'Edward? My name's not Edward, my name's Josh — Josh Lewiston.'

Amadea looked across at Rob.

'Josh, of course,' Rob told him, eventually. 'Josh Lewiston.'

'Why am I here? Why was I lying down here?' he asked, trying to stand up, and failing. 'God, I feel as if I've walked a thousand miles. Am I ill, have I been ill?'

'No. Well, yes,' Rob told him, 'but the worst is over.'

'How do you know?' Josh demanded with sudden aggression.

'Because I am a doctor, that's why I know. You have been suffering from a sort of fever, but you're going to get better now.'

'Very glad to hear it,' Josh told him. 'Because I feel really screwed up. Not me at all.'

'Why not lie back on the grass for a minute or two, gather your strength a bit. You've been through rather a lot, you know.'

As Josh closed his eyes once more, Rob leaned

forward and kissed Amy long and hard. Since Mabel also had her eyes shut, Amadea quickly returned the compliment just as the party of middle-aged tourists, who had obviously grown restless, rounded the corner. Seeing the kiss, they all burst into happy applause, a sound which encouraged Mabel and Josh to open their eyes again.

'All's well that ends well,' Rob announced to their new audience as he helped Josh slowly to his feet, and Mabel shook herself as if she was a dog that had just been doused with water. 'The patient is now recovering, and will soon be as right as rain.'

Another murmur of satisfaction from the group and they began to walk on past. Josh, leaning heavily on Rob, took a few tentative steps, and Amadea helped Mabel to her feet.

'I say, you don't mind me asking, do you?' The last of the party turned back towards them. 'But is this anyone we should know?' he asked, staring down at the grave of Edmund Gains.

Rob nodded. 'Oh yes, you should know him all right.'

'Edmund Gains? Can't say that I do.' He leaned over the gravestone reading the words. 'It says here, and I will translate it from the Latin, that he was in love with the daughter of the house, and she killed herself when he died.' He straightened up. 'How tragic.'

'Yes, it was tragic,' Rob agreed.

'Yes,' Mabel stated, suddenly turning back. 'That would make sense.'

'Why would it make sense?'

Mabel said nothing, so the man, his curiosity now thoroughly aroused, thumbed his way through a book he was carrying.

'Oh, yes, I see, it's got all about him in here.' He read quickly, then looked up, waving his book at Rob. 'It seems that when the girl returned to find this Edmund Gains had been murdered and buried up here, she galloped her horse off this hill.' He pointed towards the lake. 'Drowned herself in the lake for love of him. Well, well, he must have been quite a guy.'

'Well, well, indeed . . . ' Rob looked across at Mabel.

'His ghost is said to haunt the temple here. In that case I think I'll be on my way. Don't want to hang around here on my own! *Brrh*.' He laughed.

'No, just a minute,' Rob said, calling him back. 'Does it say any more in your book?'

'My wife's actually. She's nuts about ghosts and stuff.' But clearly the man was as interested as the rest of them, so he obligingly read on.

'"The legend runs that Edmund Gains is trying to find Felicia, who was his great love".' He looked up from the book. 'So, the daughter of the house was his great love. Well, that would never do, now, would it? A poet and a daughter of the aristocracy?'

'No, but a good story nevertheless,' Rob put in.

The man nodded, and closed the book again. 'And like all ghost stories, it involves a tragic end. I think I'd better catch my wife up, before I meet a similar fate.'

Rob watched him go, then held out his arm to steady Josh.

'Time for us both to go back to the Old Rectory, mate, because I don't know about you, but after all this hassle I could murder a beer.'

★ ★ ★

Florence had arrived home from her little break with that particular feeling of guilt which always seems to accompany having enjoyed unlooked-for happiness. The guilt meant that she knew she must do her best to cover up her secret. She certainly did not want everyone to see how happy she was feeling. She felt she must do her best not to let people know, but it was impossible. She knew she glowed, she knew her eyes shone, she knew she could not stop smiling. Fortunately, however, the excitements of the day had been too arresting for any of her fears of discovery to be justified, because the news of the moment was that not only had Edmund been banished but that Josh alone had returned in his place.

Of course Theo had gone into a spin when his Trusty had returned to announce that Josh was not at the Old Rectory. Dick and he had hurried down to find out what had happened, only to discover Florence peacefully occupied in her kitchen, preparing a summer salad for any and everyone who cared to turn up for lunch.

'Dottie left me a note to say that Mabel Minton, Rob and Amadea have all gone up to the Hall to visit Edmund . . . '

'But Edmund Gains is already visiting, Florence,' Dick reminded her.

Florence frowned at the note, because Dottie's handwriting was just a little bit like beetles moving across the page. She picked it up again.

'No, sorry — to be rid of Edmund. I think that's what it says anyway.' She smiled at the two men, who were staring at her as if they had never seen her before.

'Anything the matter?' she asked, her eyes widening. 'Is my hair on fire?'

'No, no, of course not. So long as Josh is with them, he'll be fine, I should have thought,' Theo said, nodding his head, but adjusting his glasses, pushing them up his nose, and smiling, for no particular reason. 'Is that a new dress, Florence? It's very pretty on you.'

Florence stared down at her dress. 'This? No, this is quite old, in fact very old.'

'Very pretty . . . '

'Yes, very pretty.'

Florence looked first at Theo and then Dick and realised at once that they must both know.

'Glass of wine, both of you?' she asked quickly. 'And stay for lunch on the terrace? I'm sure they won't be very long.'

They went out on to the terrace, but before Florence could bring out a bottle of chilled wine, or set the places for lunch, Dick made an old-fashioned, Churchillian V-for-victory sign, and Theo and he laughed and slapped each other's hands lightly.

'Bingo, old chap, bing — go! We are the matchmakers, we are the people movers, we are the happiness bringers.'

Their childish celebrations were cut short as Florence came back out on to the terrace carrying a wooden tray bearing a very welcome bottle of cold white wine and three nicely chilled glasses. Silence descended as the three of them settled back to enjoy their drinks with the usual small sighs and murmurs of appreciation, Dick and Theo determined not even to think Walter's name in front of Florence, let alone mention it.

Some few minutes later the little party from the Hall returned.

'I think you're wanted,' Florence told Dick, nodding towards Rob, who was standing uncertainly at the doors to the terrace.

Dick stood up, reluctant to leave the party, but more than excited to hear what had happened. Rob and he headed quickly for Henry's old study, where Rob closed the door, suddenly aware that the tensions of the last few weeks had come to an end, and for some strange reason feeling a little flat because they had.

'Good news?' Dick asked.

'Excellent news, brilliant news, but so bizarre.'

Dick touched the frame of his glasses and removed his silk handkerchief from the top pocket of his linen jacket, then promptly put it back. He could not wait to hear, so he said, slowly and carefully, 'How bizarre?'

'Very, very bizarre indeed,' Rob assured him. 'Not that I saw it. I didn't see it happen, but happen it did. Mr Edmund Gains was, is, we hope, well and truly exorcised.'

Dick sighed with pleasure. It was all so fitting:

the setting of Harlington Hall, the poet, the whole story of the daughter of the house falling for Edmund, everything was perfect.

'I imagine it must have been, shall we say, a trifle Italianate in both feeling and operation?'

Rob nodded. 'You could say. I mean I've never had much belief in anything, although my stepmother is a healer and — well, strange things do happen. Healing does work sometimes, not always. I suppose what Mabel has done for Josh is only an extension of that.' Rob shook his head. 'It has certainly shaken up all of us guys.'

For want of something better to do, and because he still could not believe that what had happened had indeed happened, Rob waggled his eyebrows in Groucho Marx style.

'So tell me exactly the sequence of events. It all sounds too marvellous!'

They sat down in Henry's old study chairs, looking for all the world like two consultants comparing notes.

'As you know, Amy and I went to fetch Mabel, and together with this young man we must now call Josh, we took her to the site of Edmund's grave.'

'Was that her idea?'

'It certainly wasn't mine. So we were on the way there when Mabel ordered Amy and me to keep guard for her, and she continued on alone with the patient.'

'That is interesting. She demanded to have a hard-hat area as far as outsiders were concerned, did she?'

'So for us it was rather as if the recording

stopped before the end of the film. We will never know what Mabel did, but she sure did something. Next thing we knew, Josh was flat out on the ground and in dire need of resuscitation.'

Dick shook his head. The whole business was extraordinary, but since he had always taken care never to shut his mind to anything strange, he had no trouble believing that something had taken place that they would quite rightly never understand.

'The patient is now asleep upstairs, and in a weak state, which is only to be expected, but I checked him over as he came round, and everything seems to be functioning normally. I would say that all he needs now is rest and recuperation, and he should be back at Harlington Hall within a week — '

Dick put up a hand, and Rob stopped abruptly.

'Except now he is rid of his secondary personality, Harlington will not be the place for him, I shouldn't have thought. He won't want to be weeding paths and so on, will he? He might need counselling.'

Rob looked purposefully vague. 'I suppose I should have asked Mabel Minton about that before Amy took her home. We'll get a message to her tomorrow, but I think I know what she would say if we asked her right now.'

'What would she say?'

'Well, I think she would probably advise us to leave well alone — the circumstances are all so weird. What he remembers and when, if at all, is in the lap of the gods, I should have thought.

Although given the circumstances, that is perhaps not quite the right expression.'

'But what about Africa?'

'I would say that that's another no-go area.' He paused, thinking. 'I must now go back to Jamie and try and find some suitable way to bring them together. Although that is also an area where angels will for sure fear to tread — '

'Your experience has obviously left you ethereally inclined . . . '

They both laughed.

'He has still to meet his little boy.'

Dick's eyes widened. 'He has a *son*?'

'Yes, and I now realise he looks the spit of him too. No denying the paternity, whatever the circumstances, I wouldn't think.'

'So really — ' Dick's expression was suddenly solemn — 'our summer saga is far from over yet.'

'Far from over.' Rob's face mirrored Dick's. 'In fact, I would say the hardest bit is yet to come.'

'Oh lordy.'

'Yes, oh lordy is about right. After all, this scenario could go either way. One, it could turn out that the mother of his son has harboured long-held grievances and there will be bitter feelings to play out, endlessly, and perhaps even pointlessly. Two, the father may not want to own his son, because he doesn't know him, and perhaps will never know him. Three, they could become polite friends but nothing more, which might be worse for their little boy than if they had never remet. Four, they could clap eyes on each other, remember how little they meant to each other and hate everyone for trying to bring them together.'

There was a small silence, which Dick finally felt impelled to break.

'Or — or they could instantly realise they have always loved each other and be perfectly delighted with everything, and see that the sun comes up in the morning and the moon at night, and flowers still grow under our feet.'

Rob stared at Dick. 'Well,' he agreed, 'there's always that, of course. But first I have to return Josh's photograph to the mother of his boy, and that, as they say, is not going to be easy.'

★ ★ ★

Rob did not know that Mrs Tippett thought she had wrongly accused him of stealing Jamie's only photograph of Josh, so he was more than surprised when he called at Jamie's flat to find that the home help welcomed him in such an effusive fashion that she could have been a patient trying to get him to fast-track her operation.

'Dr Greer?' Mrs Tippett smiled at Rob in an ingratiating manner, because when all was said and done Dr Greer was an unusually handsome doctor. 'I'm afraid Jamie is not here. She and Dylan are on holiday. She has taken him to Cornwall for his half-term. Such a delightful little boy, don't you think, Dr Greer?'

'Dylan? He's great.'

Rob stared thoughtfully across the small, immaculately tidy sitting room. Jamie's bedroom door seemed to be further away than he remembered it.

Mrs Tippett eyed him, her head on one side.

'So, can I do anything for you, Dr Greer?'

Rob removed his gaze from the seemingly remote bedroom door and looked at her, frowning.

'Do you know, you could do something, Mrs Tippett,' he admitted slowly. 'I would kill for a cup of tea, no milk, no sugar, but kill.'

'Oh, I don't think there's any need for that, Dr Greer. So, just a piece of lemon? That's how I like it in the summer, no milk, no sugar, just a piece of lemon.'

'Excellent. Just how I like it.'

'You people deserve medals, really you do. I'm always saying that, really I am.'

Mrs Tippett moved towards the kitchen, and as she did so Rob darted towards Jamie's bedroom, where he at once replaced the photograph of Josh in its frame.

'There we are.'

Mrs Tippett set the mug of tea down in front of him, and Rob drank it thankfully, for the truth was he had just come off the wards, and he was so thirsty he could have drunk the whole world dry.

'Thank you so much, Mrs Tippett.'

'Do call me Audrey — '

Rob beamed at her. He would call her anything she wanted. 'Thank you — Audrey.'

Rob bolted his mug of tea and left, mission accomplished.

Not much later Jamie returned with Dylan

385

from their short break, suntanned and relaxed — until Mrs Tippett opened the door, because for some reason as soon as she saw her home help Jamie always felt as if she had never been away.

'That Dr Greer was here again,' Mrs Tippett told her. 'Since he's a doctor I gave him a cup of tea, I thought it only right.'

Jamie stopped throwing unsolicited mail in the wastepaper basket, and turned slowly to look at Mrs Tippett.

'Dr Greer?' she asked, incredulity in her voice. 'He was here?' She would have liked to have added, '*And you let him in?*' but remembering that she herself had denied that Rob had taken the photograph, she simply stared at the home help.

'Yes, he was here.'

'*Why* was he here?'

'I think he wanted to see you, but he had to make do with me.'

Mrs Tippett patted her hair and gave a preening look, then picked up her handbag, umbrella and copy of the local newspaper and, nodding towards the envelope on the desk, let herself out of the flat.

Jamie watched her crossing the square and pulled a face, then continued to sort through her letters.

'Hey, kid, guess what — we've been asked to a party.'

'Yeah?'

'Yes, fancy dress too.'

'What's fancy dress?'

386

'It's when you dress up as other people, and in this case you wear masks too, because it's a masked ball, so no one knows who you are, and you have lovely things to eat, and you dance to orchestras, and stuff like that.'

Jamie frowned down, rereading the last part of Amy's note encouraging her to come to the fête champêtre at Harlington Hall.

'I don't want to dance,' Dylan stated.

'You don't have to dance if you don't want to, but I'm sure it will be fun.'

'I don't want to go.' Dylan gave her a look from under his long lashes. 'Unless . . . unless Grandma can come too.'

Jamie's mouth opened as she realised what he was saying. Great. That was all she needed.

Dylan wandered aimlessly about the flat, as if he knew he had thrown his mother a googly and was quite prepared to wait for the outcome.

'All right, Dylan, I will ask Grandma, if that is what you really want.'

A long silence followed this announcement — until Dylan ran out of Jamie's bedroom, his face flushed and triumphant, waving the photograph of Josh.

'Hey, Mum, Dad's back!'

Jamie stared down at the photograph before handing it back to Dylan, who did not notice the tears in her eyes because he was too busy kissing it.

13

Amadea stared at Rob. Their summer saga, as they now called it, was turning out to be a great deal more complicated than they had imagined.

'What does Dick think we should do?'

'He doesn't want to give advice. He's far too wise to do that,' Rob said sadly.

'Pity.' Amadea smiled. 'That means we can't blame him when it goes wrong. What about Theo?'

'He says we should keep Josh away from Harlington Hall at the moment. He thinks going back there might reverse everything, and Ma doesn't mind him staying on here, with me and Dottie.'

'What about your mother?'

'My mother, Rob darling, for your information,' Amadea stated slowly, 'has just driven off with Walter Dexter in his beautiful old Bentley to Le Manoir aux Quat' Saisons, for some serious eating.' She shook her head. 'She and Walter are now an item, would you believe?'

'Who's Walter Dexter?'

'He runs an art gallery in London and has just moved to the Manor House in North Dunham, five miles away. It seems . . . ' Amadea hesitated. 'It seems he has fallen in love with my mother.'

'I'm not surprised. Your mother is a very pretty woman.'

'Dick told me he even wants to exhibit her.'

'That's taking love too far, surely?'

'I meant he wants to exhibit her paintings, stupid.' She slid out from under the duvet. 'We still haven't solved our problem, Rob,' she said, pulling on a long, white cotton kaftan.

'No, but we have solved a great deal more.'

Rob closed his eyes because Amadea's figure was not simply lovely, it was stunning. He must concentrate on something cold, very, very cold.

'Strange to think it all started here, really.'

Amadea gazed round the little guest cottage while Rob kept his eyes firmly shut.

'I wonder what would have happened if Ma had not offered to make Josh a cup of coffee, Rob? I wonder if we would have — well, I just wonder, really, if she hadn't felt sorry for him . . . '

'She would have thrown him out of here, and sent him smartly back up to Harlington Hall, where he belonged, and he would probably still be weeding and mowing the gardens, and becoming more and more obsessed with Edmund Gains. As it is, he's fast asleep in the house, unaware of the fact that we know more about his life than he does.'

Amadea sat down on Rob's side of the bed.

'The thing is, we don't want to give poor Josh a fright, but we don't want to take anything for granted either. We have agreed about that, haven't we?'

'You mean as in my driving off to Swinton with Josh — ' Rob glanced at his watch and leaped out of bed — 'taking him round to Jamie's flat and throwing him in the door.' He

389

started to pull on his clothes faster than he would have liked because he was due back on duty in less than two hours. 'I think that might be as bad an idea as any we have discussed.'

'Agreed, mein Führer.'

'On the other hand, we can't keep Jamie and Josh apart for ever.' Rob started to hop a little as he pushed his second leg into his trousers. 'Because . . . because they have a child, and we surely have a duty to try to bring them together.' He looked up from fastening his belt. 'On the other hand we could go to ACAS; after all, they're always on the side of unions.'

Amadea ignored his joke.

'On yet another hand, he might not want to know about Dylan, and he might not be in love with Jamie any more, might have found someone else, probably has found someone else. After all, it is such a long time ago, and they have both been through so much.'

'And Jamie might not have been in love with him in the first place, or *he* might not. It might just have been a summer fling.'

'And some.'

'And, and — Dylan might not like him.'

'Oh, I think he will like him. Dylan is longing for a man in his mother's life, believe me.'

'Maybe.' Amadea pulled Rob towards her. 'But he can't have *this* man in his mother's life, all right?'

'No, agreed, he can't have me because I am spoken for.'

They kissed long and hard, and then parted to gaze at each other.

'Oh God, I so wish I wasn't due back on duty.'

'Oh God, I so wish you weren't either,' Amadea reassured him.

She moved away from him, feeling her pulse.

'Crikey, doctor, you have a bad effect on my blood pressure when you kiss me, you know that?'

'I hope to repeat the treatment soon, Miss Fontaine, believe me.'

He reached out for her, but Amadea held up her hand.

'No — two treatments in a short time is not what's needed for this patient. What is needed,' Amadea reminded him, 'is a solution to our mutual friend's problem.'

Rob frowned. 'What we ought to do is go through his notes in a professional way, as if he was one of my patients. That's what I would do, in normal circumstances.' He took a pen and paper out of his briefcase and sat down on the edge of the bed. 'Right, let's think. We have here one young man who was obviously an idealist, and whose heart was in the right place. His heart took him to Africa where he tried to help feed the starving. He ended up becoming embroiled in a bloody feud, and being found alive in the strangest and most horrible circumstances. How was he found, by the way?'

'Apparently they were just about to tip all these dead bodies into a pit, when they saw a pair of trainers sticking out from under all the bare feet.'

'So trainers have their uses after all, even if

you do need to put them in the washing machine every five seconds.'

'Yup. They found him, and although he was unconscious and half starved, they got him to a hospital where he was cared for by a Belgian doctor, who eventually managed to send him back to England, where — '

'Equally eventually — '

'His GP found a place for him on the rehabilitation course at Harlington Hall.'

Rob nodded, staring at his list of notes. He read them through a second time, and then shook his head.

'There's something missing. What about his parents? He must have a family out there somewhere?'

'No, apparently not. According to Dick and Theo, his parents were killed in an accident when he was tiny, and he was brought up by his grandmother, who is now dead. So, no, there is not something missing, Dr Greer. I have told you everything. He is to all intents and purposes an orphan, and that is that.'

'So how did this orphaned young man meet Jamie Charlbury?'

'Ah yes, that is interesting, as a matter of fact.'

'Yes, really very interesting, Amy, because he happens to have fathered a child.'

'Apparently all that happened after he left for Africa.'

'No, Amy, before he went to Africa something else must have happened.' Rob glanced at his watch again. 'Something else must have happened which led to Dylan being born. You know — ' his expression was deadpan — 'the birds and the bees, the coming together of two kindred souls who fall in love and . . . ?'

'Oh, stop it! Yes, of course they fell in love. Of course they did, at Glastonbury. Jamie was in the tent next to his, and she asked him in for a drink, and — well, you know the rest.'

'Glastonbury.' Rob threw the biro back into his briefcase. 'Of course, that is the key. We will take them both back to Glastonbury and see what happens. That is the only possible answer.'

'Jamie might not want to go.'

'Of course she will want to go.'

'Why 'of course'?'

'Because I will make sure that she gets invited.'

'How will you do that?'

'Most unusually, by getting someone to invite her.' Rob leaned forward and kissed Amadea again. 'Bye, honey — don't wait up for me, will you?'

Amadea quickly kissed him back.

'Go, go, before I start getting ideas, and don't forget to send my love to Psemisis — *not*!'

★   ★   ★

Florence stared around her. The evening air was full of strangely disparate sounds, sounds which somehow seemed to be coming together to make one long low note, a note that was determined to be sustained, perhaps until such time as darkness fell. From across the lawn came the murmur from a party of guests walking up towards the house from the car park; from the trees birds called to each other; and nearer to her, all of a sudden, came the short sharp military steps of the young waiters hurrying up from their staff quarters towards the kitchens.

She and Walter had adjoining suites on the ground floor of the hotel, with small tables and chairs set outside their French windows. They had agreed to meet in a few hours' time, for cocktails in Walter's suite. In the meantime Florence was enjoying the quiet of the evening, looking back on the changes that the last weeks had brought. Her house was sold, and a new cottage on Walter's estate was waiting for her. Nevertheless she had the feeling that her life was changing almost too quickly, which was why she had refused to move into the Manor House.

'We know nothing about each other's little ways . . . '

'We know we are in love, and as I understand it, love makes you tolerant.'

Walter managed to look both boyish and hurt at the same time, but Florence still resisted.

'Perhaps,' she conceded, trying to ignore both the hurt and the look of pleading. 'But we have yet to face what I call the toothpaste challenge.'

'Which is? You have to tell me, so I can make sure I don't fail.'

'You know, how do you squeeze your toothpaste, and all that kind of thing? Some people squeeze it in the middle, which I understand can be very irritating.'

'We will have separate bathrooms.'

Florence decided to ignore this, as there was no answer to it.

'And then there is the breakfast challenge,' she continued blithely. 'Breakfast with someone else can turn into a battleground. The rustle of the newspaper, the orange juice being quaffed too loudly, the incorrect timing of the boiled egg — it can all be a source of terrible tribulation, not to mention strife.'

'But Mrs Byers will do all that egg-boiling stuff — you won't ever have to boil an egg in my house, unless you want to, of course.'

'I might not like Mrs Byers.'

'You will love her, and she will love you.'

'Nothing will change my mind, Walter.'

'Love changes everyone's minds.'

But Florence had stuck to her point of view. She did not want everything to be spoilt early on.

'There is a way of going on, and this is mine,' she said firmly.

Walter had sighed, shrugged his shoulders and given in, but only in the sure and certain hope that Florence too would soon give in. Perhaps because of this he had returned to the emotional fray with renewed vigour.

'Marry me anyway.'

'No, not until we know each other better.'

'In that case we must get to know each other better quickly,' Walter told her, and promptly booked them into the Manoir for two nights, 'one for each of us'.

He now interrupted her reverie, standing in front of her small table looking elegant, sophisticated, and shy.

'You look so pretty,' he told her, and having kissed her he held her away from him.

'And you look so handsome.'

'Mutual admiration is so satisfying. Cocktails at my place?'

She followed him through the adjoining garden and into his suite, where he rang for a waiter to bring them two dry martinis.

'Now,' he said, sitting down opposite her. 'How do you want this evening to go?'

Florence gave him a deliberately innocent look, because they both knew what he meant.

'Well, I thought dinner followed by a walk around the garden might be a good idea?'

'Excellent. And then?'

'And then a good night's sleep?'

'Good. And then?'

'Then we will see. After all, what will be will be, will it not? I always think the morning can be very good, for all sorts of things.'

Walter sighed with satisfaction. 'You are a woman in ten million.'

Florence put her hands up to his face and kissed him lightly.

'I know, and I promise I shall love you for the rest of my life, for better and better. That is why I have to make quite sure I don't get on your nerves, you know?'

'You will never get on my nerves.'

'I could easily, everyone can. We have both been so unhappy we have to make quite sure that nothing spoils our happiness. It's the best way.'

'I understand.' Walter went to the door to let

the waiter in. 'We could do the first toothpaste test tomorrow morning though, couldn't we?' he asked hopefully, after the waiter had gone.

'We could.'

'We could, or we shall?'

'We'll see.'

They did, and happily both found that they passed most satisfactorily.

★　★　★

Jamie had been offered a job with a rival company. It meant moving out of Swinton to Westham, some fifty miles away. It also meant that Dylan would have to start at a new school, and her mother would not be near, which on paper would seem nothing but an asset, since it would mean that the ritual humiliation of their fortnightly lunch would be impossible. On the other hand, judging from Dylan's face when she broke it to him, it would mean that he would lose practically everything he was used to, including his grandmother.

Rosa and Jamie had not been in communication since she had walked out of lunch, so it was astonishing for Jamie to pick up her mobile and see that it was her mother ringing.

'I hear you have been offered a new position in Westham?'

Jamie stared at the screen for a second as if she could see her mother's face in it, and then pressed the phone back to her ear.

'How did you hear?'

397

'Dylan told me. He telephoned me the other night.'

Jamie stood still in the street, her mobile clasped ever tighter to her ear. People were passing by, cars were moving, everything was the same, except nothing was the same.

'Dylan called you?'

'Yes, he told me he misses me, and now that you are moving to Westham he will miss me even more.'

Jamie frowned, turning back on her route, moving restlessly up and down the pavement, as the knowledge that her son had been deceiving her started to make the pain of her own mother's words far worse than she could ever have imagined.

'I have no alternative. I have to go where there is work, Mother.'

She felt she could see her mother's complacent smile, and braced herself to hear her say something sarcastic.

'Yes, of course, I do understand that, Jamie.'

At that Jamie took the telephone away from her ear and stared at it. Her mother *never* called her Jamie. She always called her Lucinda.

'*What* do you understand?' Jamie said, sounding impatient and off-hand even to her own ears.

'I understand that you have to go where the work is, I understand perfectly. I have a proposition to make, however.'

Jamie's heart sank. For some reason her mother's plans were always unnecessarily complicated and if you accepted them and then did not do exactly as she wished, you found yourself not just in hot water, but laden with guilt for the next heaven only knew how long.

Oh please please help her to make a proposition that I can find impossible and will have to turn down. Please, please, please, she thought.

'What I am proposing, Jamie — '

Why did her mother calling her Jamie sound so peculiar?

'What I am proposing is that I should sell my house and buy a small cottage near Westham. That way I can help look after Dylan — I have promised him that I will not make him eat jelly, by the way — and with what is left over I can help you buy a flat in Westham. We could be near each other but not on top of each other, and Dylan will have a grandma and I will have a grandson, and you will have a mum whenever you want one, but not when you don't. I promise I shan't interfere with your life, however it goes.'

Of course Jamie wanted to ask her mother what had brought on the sudden change in her, but she didn't dare. Instead she just gazed around the street, at the boy bicycling in and out of the traffic, at the old woman shuffling along from the bakery, at the man trying to park his Rover in too small a space. What could she say? Her mother sensed her hesitation.

'Think it over, Jamie. It could be a good solution. My little house will fetch a great deal of money because it is so near to the station and the shops. I can get enough for it to set us both up in and near Westham.'

399

'I don't need to think it over — it's a great offer, but I have to ask Dylan first.'

'It was *Dylan's* idea, Jamie.' Her mother laughed suddenly. 'He rang up and said you were moving and would I come too?'

'Well, I'll still need to talk to Dylan, Mum.'

Jamie shut her phone suddenly and abruptly, and hurried home to Dylan, who was busy playing Snap with a far from interested Mrs Tippett.

'Did you phone Grandma, Dylan?' Jamie demanded, after the home help had left. Dylan, still seated in front of his cards, looked sideways, not meeting his mother's eyes.

'Have a game with me, Mum?'

Jamie sat down on the carpet opposite him, determined to confront the matter of his telephoning his grandmother behind her back.

'I asked you something, Dylan — did you phone Grandma?'

Dylan shook his head. 'She phoned first. Have a game, Mum? Please?'

'I — oh, all right.'

Jamie took up the cards and they started to play, shouting Snap louder and louder, which was an in-thing with them, until Jamie, having been topped by Dylan, gave in.

'You win.' She started to tidy up the cards. 'So Grandma phoned you, and then? Then what happened?'

'Sometimes — sometimes I ask Mrs Tippett sometimes to phone her, and we talk.'

'Don't you think you should have told me?'

Dylan's eyes once more shifted sideways. 'I like Grandma.'

'Well, I know, but I still think you should tell me if you're phoning her — '

Even before she had finished speaking Jamie knew that what she had just said sounded stupid. Why should Dylan tell her if he was talking to his grandmother on the phone? He was hardly calling out a fire engine on false pretences.

'I just would like to know, that's all. I like to hear what you've been doing. Didn't you think to tell me?'

Dylan fell silent.

'Didn't you want to tell me?'

Dylan shook his head. 'Mum's too busy, Mrs Tippett said.'

'I'm not too busy for you, Dylan.'

Dylan stood up abruptly and walked off, leaving his mother to stare after him and wonder whether it was true. Was she always too busy? The answer had to be yes. She was always too busy, and she had always been too busy, especially lately when she had been not just out at interviews but doing temporary work, trying to bring home the bacon.

'So . . . you would like Grandma to come and live near us, would you?'

'I love Grandma,' a small voice stated, floating back across the wood-block floor to where Jamie was still seated on her cushion feeling strangely lonely, and a little absurd. It was as if she was floating above her life, looking down at herself over the last weeks, rushing about trying to find a job, always worried about Dylan, never knowing whether or not something would turn up for which she might be suitable. Now she had been offered the kind of work she wanted, and to have her mother living nearby might mean less rushing about. It might mean they could finally really be a family.

'Why do you love Grandma, Dylan?'

'Because she is nice, and she's promised not to make me eat jelly ever again.'

'Oh well, two very good reasons, I suppose.'

Jamie sighed, staring ahead of her, imagining a life without Mrs Tippett or Psemisis. Perhaps not just one weight but many weights were about to be lifted from her shoulders. She picked up the telephone to call her mother.

'Mum?'

'Jamie?'

'Great idea. Come over, and we can talk.'

'I will fly — as flies the swan.'

Jamie replaced the telephone. Her mother's voice even sounded different, lighter, almost girlish.

She had just picked up Josh's photograph, which was still on the coffee table, and started to walk off towards her bedroom when the telephone rang again. It was Rob.

'What do you want?'

'To apologise profoundly to you, for taking your photograph, for not telling you that I was going to take your photograph, for upsetting Dylan, for everything really.'

Jamie sighed, and her own voice suddenly lightened.

'What *is* it about today?' she asked no one in particular. 'Everyone is being nice to me today. Life is being nice to me today. Any more good news and I think I will have to go back to bed and start over just to make sure it's really happening.'

'Oh, so this is too good a time?'

'You could say that, and some.'

'For any particular reason, besides my apologising for my heinous crime?'

'For the reason that I am moving from Swinton, I have a new job, my mother is selling her house, and buying me a flat and herself a cottage. Dylan is going to a new school, and my mother will be nearby to help with him whenever I wish.'

'So much good news is too much to take, I suppose.'

'Much too much. And it all happened within the last five minutes.'

Jamie never cried, but if she did she would now. Everything might be going to work out all right after all, which was almost too much for her to take.

'I want to make it up to you about the photograph, Jamie. Amy and I want to make it up to you about taking the photograph. It was our joint decision — '

'It's not important, really. It's back, that's all that matters.'

'I have to explain: the reason we took it was because we thought we had seen someone just like Josh.'

Jamie's heart seemed to have stopped. 'You what?'

'Well, we took it because Amadea and I thought we had seen someone just like Josh.'

'Josh went to Africa, Rob. He went to Africa. He was a summer romance, that was all.'

'I know, and Amy — Amadea — and I realised that, but seeing that he is Dylan's dad, we just thought it might be, you know, just might be, a fraction of a chance . . . that he might be back, from Africa that is.'

Rob was stalling, and Jamie knew it. He was stalling because he wanted Jamie to absorb the news that he and Amadea were now an item, hence his repetition of her name.

'It's very good of you and Amadea,' Jamie said, at length. 'And really, there's no need to apologise, but I just don't know why you never said. I would have willingly lent you the photograph.'

'We didn't want you to be disappointed, Jamie, you know how it is. We didn't want to set up your hopes.'

Jamie sat down suddenly. Everyone was turning out to be a great deal nicer than she had thought, which made her realise that she was a great deal less nice than she had imagined. It was a sobering feeling. It seemed she had not loved her mother enough to understand her, she had not thought enough about Dylan to see that he wanted to be part of a family, she had not loved her friends enough to realise that they had her best interests at heart, even when they did something which she found incomprehensible.

'This is like something in *A Christmas Carol*, Rob,' she confessed suddenly. 'I feel like I have been somehow reprieved. I imagine I'm feeling just like Scrooge must have felt — as if I've been let out of school, given a second chance.'

'We've all been through the mill, Jamie,' Rob said, after a pause. 'We all feel as if we have been let out of school. Good things do happen, even if we never seem to see them on the ten o'clock news.'

'So it seems — so what should happen next, do you think?'

Rob knew at once that this was the moment to tread especially carefully.

'What's next? Well, as you may have gathered, Amadea and I — Amy and I — we have realised that — '

'Yes, yes, of course — '

'That we love each other, more than as friends, considerably more than as friends, in fact if this is friendship it should be illegal.'

'At last — '

'Certainly at last.' Rob laughed. 'You guessed?'

'No, I always knew.' Jamie sounded rueful. 'Don't worry, Rob, I could never have been more than a very loving friend to you.'

'Which you will still be.'

'Sure, and some.' Jamie paused. 'I really must stop saying 'and some'. Sometimes I think I must stop saying everything, and just *be*.'

'Cool.'

'And that is one thing I sure am not. I'm not cool, Rob.'

'Speaking of which,' Rob continued, hoping against hope that he could segue into the main reason for his call. 'Speaking of which, Amy and I and some of the oldies too, would you believe, are all going to Glastonbury. Would you like to come?'

Glastonbury? The reason that Dylan had been born.

'Glastonbury? You're all going to Glastonbury?'

'Sure. It's very changed. Gone respectable, but could be fun, even if it pours with rain, which it most likely will.'

'I — well — I don't know, really. Would you want me to come? I'd have to bring Dylan.'

'Sure, everyone's welcome.'

'Well, good. Thank you.' A second or two, and then, 'I met Dylan's father, you know, at Glastonbury.'

'Yes, I remember you telling me,' Rob said, after only a second's pause.

'My mother always says I should have called him Glastonbury.'

'So, you'll come. We have a tent. It'll be great.'

★ ★ ★

Florence was walking around her small lake, trying to imagine someone else sitting on its banks, other children fishing in it, other friends picnicking beside it. She would soon be saying goodbye not just to the lake and the wildlife on it, but to the trees that she and Henry had planted, to the boat that David had used to dive from, to the fields beyond the garden that had become so much part of her that she could hardly imagine what it would be like to wake up and not see them, and yet she also knew that the

406

new life she was embracing was the right one. She would have her own cottage, her own independence, her work, and love. It was almost too much.

She stopped and, seeing Dottie pegging out her washing, she waved gaily to her.

'Come on over, do,' Dottie called. 'I'm just about to pour some ambrosial liquid into two long-stemmed glasses.'

Florence strolled through the adjoining gates and sat down in one of Dottie's comfortable chairs with their much-worn cushions. Dottie immediately joined her, followed by her clutch of elderly pugs.

'It is too much, Flo dear, much too much, to hear that not only are you nicely placed now, your house sold and a beau in your life, but Amadea too. It is all too much for this old body to take in. My cup floweth over, and so too did that nearly,' she joked as she handed Florence a glass of her best home-made elderflower champagne. 'Cheerio, ducks, what a wonderful time this is. We must all be so grateful for the good times, don't you think?'

'Oh yes, Dottie, we must,' Florence agreed with sudden emotion. 'I can hardly believe what has happened in these last few weeks. So much it is almost too much.'

'I do love a happy ending.'

'Happy endings are not fashionable — I read some lady novelist only the other day who poured scorn on them.'

'Humph.' Dottie frowned. 'Well, be that as it may,' she said, after considering the matter, 'as I understand it, far too many lady novelists are snobs — slaves to fashion. There is nothing whatsoever wrong with a happy ending, or, as I like to call it, a happy *pause*. We all know that life cannot be for ever, and if it was it would lose its delicious point. But it can be happy while it lasts. I know. I have been happy, and, what is more,' she ended, a note of triumph creeping into her voice, 'I have lasted. I'm still here, and I give thanks for that.'

'Yes, you are still here, Dottie, and thank heavens for it.' They sipped their elderflower champagne. Finally, Florence summoned up her courage. 'Dottie, do you mind if I ask you something?'

'Not at all, ducks. Ask away.'

Florence cleared her throat. 'Do you think — do you think I should marry again, Dottie?'

Dottie looked momentarily caught off guard.

'Well, now you really have stumped me, Flo.'

It was the champagne, drinking before midday, the sunshine, everything so warm and happy. It had all led Florence to ask Dottie the question that she had been asking herself for some days now.

'I am stumped too,' she confessed to her old friend. 'You see, Walter wants to marry me, but I'm not sure that I want to marry again. To me there is only one husband, and one wife. Henry the husband, and me his wife.'

'In that case, don't marry.'

'But Walter might be hurt if I don't marry him.'

'Not if you've gone to live in one of his

408

cottages and you see each other every day. I wouldn't have thought that was in the least bit hurtful.'

'No, perhaps not. We passed the toothpaste test, you know.'

Since they were old friends, Dottie knew of Florence's theory about the toothpaste test.

'Well, that bodes very well, love, very well indeed.' Dottie thought for a minute. 'Tell you what, why not let me ask the bees, see what they say?'

Florence smiled. 'Good idea, you ask the bees.'

'So now you must put the matter out of your mind, or it will start to become a beastly nuisance and give you headaches, as things do, if you think too much.'

'It seems Amadea is to marry quite soon. Rob is in a tearing hurry to marry her before she changes her mind.'

'She won't change her mind.'

'I think they might be going to be very happy.'

'As long as everyone lets them, they will be,' Dottie replied, suddenly looking at her most enigmatic. 'It's my belief that the worst thing that can happen to a marriage is other people. A marriage should always be left well alone, until such time as the watershed is passed. Let them fight their fights, love each other, and make their own way. Quite apart from anything else, that way they will have no one else to blame but each other.'

Florence thought for a moment. 'You're right, Dottie. Henry and I never had anyone but each other. Both our families disapproved of us in their own ways, so we ran away to the country and led our own lives, and we were very happy.'

'Not just happy, but all the better for it. I swear it. I've seen it in the village so many times, domineering mothers, interfering fathers, jealous in-laws. It leads to nothing but trouble. Now, tell me what is to happen about this Edward Green business?'

'Josh?'

'Yes, him. Can't get used to his name, but what is happening about all that?'

'What is happening is Glastonbury. All the young are going to Glastonbury, not to mention some of the old . . . ' Dottie stared at her. 'Dick and Theo are going. Walter can't, and I don't know whether I will if he can't. Besides, we have the fête champêtre soon. That is quite enough for me.' She paused. 'Do you want to go, Dottie? They have a tent.'

Dottie paused. 'As a matter of fact I think I might,' she said. 'I hear one of my favourite groups is going, the Silly Sisters. Oh, and Blue Eyed Boys. Love them.'

Florence stared at her old friend and started to laugh, knowing that Dottie knew as much about pop as Florence knew about bees. Dottie too laughed, but for a different reason. She laughed because Florence's reluctance to go to the festival without Walter must mean something.

★ ★ ★

410

Amadea was sitting with Josh, trying to bring back his memories of life before Africa. Africa had to be put on hold for the moment, as did Harlington Hall, although Amadea did not say as much to Josh, because, to say the least, she knew it would be dangerous ground. What she was trying to fathom was how much he could remember of his early life.

'So you remember training with Countries Without Barriers, and then?'

Josh frowned. He knew he had been ill, he knew he had lost his memory and that he must do his best to find it again, but try as hard as he might, he could remember only vague images. Dark faces, doctors in white coats, foreign languages, everything muddled and distorted.

'Not much. Landing in Africa, I remember that. The feel of it, the whole rhythm of it, the other volunteers, but not their names or anything, none of that stuff,' he confessed, sounding and feeling impatient, because although he liked Amadea and Florence, and Rob and all the rest of them, a great part of him wanted them to leave him alone to find a new life without them. 'I really can't remember much that was important. Certainly not when I became ill, and all that. Can't remember a thing about that.' He turned to Amadea. 'It's a bit like childhood, you know? My grandmother was always saying, 'You must remember going to Brittany?' or 'You must remember Mr Bertram, the gardener at Honeysuckle Cottage?' And I was always having to pretend that I did, but the truth was that I didn't. And quite frankly, I don't want to have to pretend with you. I don't see the point. I can't remember anything after I was ill, when I was found, where I went, and that is all there is to it.'

He folded his arms across his chest and stared ahead at Florence's herbaceous border, wondering if he was ever going to be allowed to leave the Old Rectory and live a life of his own. At the moment he felt as if he was being imprisoned, and he had no idea why.

Amadea must have guessed his feelings because she got up from the old steamer chair she had been sitting on and went inside to make them both a coffee. She would have liked to phone Rob and grumble about how difficult and ungrateful blasted Josh was being, but she couldn't because he was too busy, and a call to him at this time would have been about as popular with Rob as she was currently with Josh.

'Right.' She set the coffee on a tray between them. 'Right, now here we go.' She breathed in, and sat down. She was fed up. She was determined to get the whole thing over with as soon as possible. She would go for the jugular. 'Right, Josh, you can remember your grandmother, you can remember school, you can remember all that stuff, so what about Glastonbury?'

'What *about* Glastonbury?'

'You went to Glastonbury before you went to Africa.'

'How do you know?'

'I don't. I guessed,' Amadea lied, crossing her fingers.

'Sure, I went to Glastonbury, so?'

'Do you remember meeting anyone there?'

'Yes, I do, as a matter of fact.' He stopped, his face changing. 'I met a beautiful girl, and we fell madly in love, but then — then I had to leave, to go to Africa.' He shrugged his shoulders. 'And the rest, as they say, is history.'

Amadea wanted to stand up and shout 'Eureka!' Instead, full of excitement, she carefully put down her cup of coffee. Bingo! They had lift-off.

'Do you remember the name of the girl?'

'Yes, of course, I will never forget her.'

'And it was?'

'Lucy.'

'Lucy?'

'Yes, Lucy.'

Amadea's cup was carefully lowered on to its saucer, and now it was her turn to stare ahead of her. Terrific. Really terrific. That was all they needed.

★ ★ ★

So now it was Rob's turn to stare at Amadea. It was raining, and they were standing in the smoking hut outside the hospital. Rob was in his white coat, and badly in need of good news. It had not been a good day on the wards.

'Lucy.'

'That's what he says.'

Rob groaned. 'I can't believe what I'm hearing. We get this guy back from the dead — well, we didn't, but you know what I mean. We get him back from wherever he had gone and we're just about to face him with the love of his life, the mother of his child, and he turns out to be in love with someone else.'

'It's heartbreaking.'

'It's more than heartbreaking, it's — ' Rob thought for a minute. 'It's what my stepmum calls 'deeply irritating'.'

'To make matters worse, we both know that Jamie has never forgotten him or she would not have kept his photograph by her bed all this time. But he, it seems, has completely forgotten her, or worse, never remembered her.'

'So no go Glastonbury, no go the merry reunion?'

'No fun without a happy ending, Rob.'

'Oh to hell, let's go. Don't want to disappoint Dylan.'

'Or his grandma.'

'*Grandma's* coming?'

'You bet your sweet potatoes she is, and apparently bringing with her the largest hamper you have ever seen, not to mention her gardener to carry it.'

'Fine. So we just carry on as normal.'

'Do you want me to bring Josh?'

'If he wants to come.'

'That's a big 'if'. He's not at his most sociable at the moment,' Amadea explained. 'I think he feels we are keeping him against his will.'

'Which we are. But now you can tell him that, as of next weekend, he will be as free as a bird.'

★ ★ ★

That evening, as they set off with their hampers, and their somewhat optimistic plans to meet up outside the tent that Rob had promised he would have set up for them all, Florence could not help feeling glad that she had been persuaded to go along. It was not the music that finally drew her to the festival, but the promise of seeing so many people enjoying themselves. And to make matters better, if not perfect, it was sunny, and the sky was streaked with the kind of pink that old-fashioned organdie blouses used to be made of, and the underskirts of bridesmaids' dresses, and the edges of soft woollen blankets.

Rosa and Florence met up as arranged and made instant eye contact, as older people on an outing with the young so often do, and knew at once that they were on the same side.

'So good of Mr Harbison to volunteer to carry the hamper, don't you think?'

Rob and Amadea had gone ahead with Josh, much earlier in the day, to set up the tent and make it comfortable.

'It certainly is good of him,' Florence agreed.

'Come along, Dylan,' Rosa called, 'or we will miss out on your favourites.' She turned back to Florence, and dropping her voice she confided, 'My darling Lucy was always a dawdler.'

Florence stared at her. 'You have another daughter?'

'No. No, Jamie's my only daughter, but she's only Jamie for work and suchlike. She was actually Lucinda, or Lucy, until she went to work for that dreadful Psemisis and they made her change her name to something less what they call 'Sloane pony'. I mean to say ... ' She shrugged her shoulders happily. 'Really, imagine being that class-conscious, but there you are, that's nowadays for you.'

Florence stopped walking, and then, after a few seconds, she started to run ahead of Rosa and Mr Harbison, not to mention Jamie and Dylan and Dottie.

'I'm so sorry, I'm really sorry,' she called back to the startled Rosa, 'but I must go ahead and warn the advance party.'

'Warn them of what?' Rosa called after her, alarmed.

Florence turned back to her. 'I must warn them they're about to witness a happy ending.'

Epilogue

Summer is all about enjoyment. When summer is here it seems that winter will never come, just as when a wedding comes, it seems that nothing else will follow.

Amadea and Rob were to be married in the little church that had been built on the estate of Harlington Hall so many centuries before. The day that dawned was so warm, and so delightfully filled with everything that spoke of summer — roses and green meadows, grazing animals lazily moving through fields, soft-coloured roofs patterned with a patchwork of green moss and yellow algae, doves flying high, swallows watching their young take their first flights, swans resting under willows — which means that when Amadea's wedding car refused to start, it did not seem to matter in the least.

'We will walk up through the fields instead,' she determined to Dick, who had only just finished mopping his eyes, so beautiful did she look in a dress of slipper satin with matching shrug, her dark hair pulled back into a knot around which was twisted pale pink roses to match the pale pink roses in her bouquet.

Dick was about to agree and then he thought of the wedding party, made up of Florence and the bridesmaids, Dottie, Walter, the Colonel and Mrs Willoughby, not to mention Dylan dressed as a page boy from long ago, all of them waiting patiently at the church for the arrival of the bride.

'Oh, I don't think we should,' he said. 'We'll take my car.'

As they chugged serenely up the hill towards the church and Amadea's future life, it seemed to Dick that everything had come full circle. He had been at her parents' wedding, he had been at her christening, and now he was giving her away. Yet again he removed his silk handkerchief from his pocket and blew his nose a little too loudly.

Inside the church, as the congregation fanned themselves with their programmes, and the vicar looked anxiously towards the organist, and the organist looked anxiously towards the church door, Jamie and Josh sat together holding hands. They knew, and everyone knew, that no wedding, however joyous, could match the reunion that had been brought about by their friends. No love affair could have had a happier ending, no little boy could have been made happier than Dylan at the sight of his parents reunited. Indeed, as everyone had agreed, if a statue had come to life, as in Shakespeare's *A Winter's Tale*, no one would have been at all surprised; such had been the joy.

As Amadea had said to Florence and Rob many times in the ensuing days, 'No one will *ever* forget Dylan's shout of 'Dad!' as he ran into Josh's arms, and that's for sure.' Adding a few seconds later, 'I must stop saying that!'

Now she was to take Rob for better or for worse. Somehow, judging from both their smiles as they came back down the aisle, everyone knew that there would be very much more of the first than the second — and that *is* for sure.

We do hope that you have enjoyed reading this large print book.

Did you know that all of our titles are available for purchase?

We publish a wide range of high quality large print books including:

Romances, Mysteries, Classics
General Fiction
Non Fiction and Westerns

Special interest titles available in large print are:

The Little Oxford Dictionary
Music Book
Song Book
Hymn Book
Service Book

Also available from us courtesy of Oxford University Press:

Young Readers' Dictionary
(large print edition)
Young Readers' Thesaurus
(large print edition)

For further information or a free brochure, please contact us at:

Ulverscroft Large Print Books Ltd.,
The Green, Bradgate Road, Anstey,
Leicester, LE7 7FU, England.
Tel: (00 44) 0116 236 4325
Fax: (00 44) 0116 234 0205

Other titles published by
The House of Ulverscroft:

FRIDAY'S GIRL

Charlotte Bingham

When the famous portrait artist Napier
Todd stumbles across Edith Hanson
scrubbing floors, he is immediately struck
by her beauty. Within weeks Napier and
Edith are married. However, the marriage
is troubled and Edith falls seriously ill.
Napier takes her to Newbourne in
Cornwall to convalesce and Edith meets
Celandine . . . Celandine Benyon is a
struggling artist who fell in love with
another painter, Sheridan Montague
Robertson, and together they set up home
in Newbourne . . . Celandine tries to help
Edith with her troubled marriage, but her
advice causes tragic repercussions. And with
the dangerously attractive Alfred Talisman
waiting in the wings, will Edith ever find
happiness?

DISTANT MUSIC

Charlotte Bingham

Life was tough in England after the Second World War — at least it was for those who were not fabulously wealthy or part of the tiny coterie of British film and theatre stars. Little wonder then that Elsie Lancaster, the granddaughter of a theatrical landlady, thinks only of trying to become one of that shining constellation. Surprising, therefore, that Oliver Plunkett shares the same ambition, for his is the pampered background of old money. For his best friend, the kooky Coco Hampton, theatre is all about costume. That they all become involved with Portly Cosgrove — sometime manager, and soon-to-be agent — is part of the inevitable flow of theatrical life, as is the fact that they become emotionally entangled with one another.

THE SEASON

Charlotte Bingham

Portia and Emily meet to launch their daughters on an unsuspecting Society for the London Season of 1913. Both are determined that their offspring, Phyllis and Edith, will catch the eye of their friend May's son, a future Duke. Portia is recently widowed and Emily is away from her husband, so life is bound to get interesting. Meanwhile, their arch-enemy Daisy Lanford's protegee, Sarah Hartley Lambert, is not the wild success Daisy had hoped she would be. This is largely because of the machinations of Phyllis, who, having formed an unholy alliance with Edith, is intent on spoiling the American girl's chances.

THE LOVE KNOT

Charlotte Bingham

Unbeknown to three young women, their paths are about to cross. Beautiful Leonie receives a surprise visit from her wealthy godmother and is sent to work at Lady Angela Bentick's private nursing home near Buckingham Palace; Dorinda sails from France without her wastrel husband and becomes a celebrated member of London's demi-monde; and Mercy is saved from social ignominy by an older man with whom she falls passionately in love. That all three determine on making their own way at a time when to be independent was to risk social ostracism, or even tragedy, is partly due to the influence each comes to have on the others' lives.

THE BLUE NOTE

Charlotte Bingham

It is wartime and Miranda, little cockney orphan Ted and Roberta have been evacuated to an old-fashioned household in the country. Despite the war, the children's time spent with two unmarried sisters is idyllic and turns their underprivileged lives into something very near heaven. But the local Committee for Evacuation objects to the spinsters' attempt to adopt the children, and before long they are parted — seemingly forever. After the war, the three are reunited, purely by chance, and as intriguing complications arise, hearts are destined to be broken . . .

THE KISSING GARDEN

Charlotte Bingham

As children, George Dashwood and Amelia Dennison loved to roam the Sussex Downs and, just as their two very different families were friends, so too were they, until they are caught in a thunderstorm. Sheltering from the elements, the now mature George realizes that the way he feels about Amelia has changed. But it is 1914 and the declaration of war cuts across any romantic plans that the two might have. George is away at the front for four years, but when the miracle happens and he returns home safely, Amelia finds that the boy she loved has gone . . .

Mrs Collins
1/5/13
Mrs Shepherd
10/7/2013
mrs. Wells
7-8-13
Mrs May
5.2.14
mrs Collins 2/4/14

Mrs Cousins
28/5/14